ACCLAIM FOR *NOT OUR KIND*

"[An] enthralling portrait of a woman daring to defy convention in the face of rigid social confines. Lively period details of the bustling city breathe life into *Not Our Kind*, a story capturing issues of discrimination, the marginalization of women, and class disparities. Often veering in unexpected directions, the novel is filled with thought-provoking turns that explore timely subjects in a gripping light. . . . The book's greatest strength is exploring how the building of relationships can help dissolve ignorance. . . . Its themes linger long after the final page is read."   —*USA Today*

"A richly layered assimilation story set in post–World War II Manhattan. . . . Chapters that alternate between Patricia's and Eleanor's point of view enable these coprotagonists to be defined by more than their stance on a Jewish question that's both urgent and on the wane in the post–World War II era. . . . An historical novel that resonates in contemporary Trumpian America. . . . [A] very good novel."
      —*Washington Independent Review of Books*

"Drenched in rich and colorful prose, Zeldis portrays interpersonal relationships in a time and place framed in prejudice. *Not Our Kind* speaks to everyone, no matter what 'kind' you are."
      —*The Jewish Voice* (Philadelphia)

"Masterfully transports readers to 1947 New York to depict the relationships that develop between a young Jewish woman and a Protestant family. . . . Lively descriptions of 1940s clothing and culture complement the realistic characters. This is a vivid, winning novel."
—*Publishers Weekly*

"A young Jewish teacher and a WASPy married woman find an unexpected connection in post–World War II New York. . . . A compelling tale of friendship, class, prejudice, and love."
—*Kirkus Reviews*

"Zeldis uses the rich details of postwar New York—the music, the clothes, the cocktails—to tell the story of two women looking for fulfillment."
—*Booklist*

"Let the glorious period details wash all over you—the clothes, the glamour, the excitement of New York, circa 1947. But the most remarkable achievement in *Not Our Kind* is the complex relationship between women from two different worlds that Kitty Zeldis expertly explores. The questions and prejudices that each woman has to confront are issues we are still exploring today, which makes this novel timely as well as entertaining."
—Melanie Benjamin, *New York Times* bestselling author of *The Swans of Fifth Avenue* and *The Girls in the Picture*

"Kitty Zeldis has a gift for making even the smallest details of the past shine with vivid color. The story she tells in *Not Our Kind*—of two women in post–World War II New York trying to forge lives of integrity and purpose—resonates with the struggles of women today. Compelling, frank, and all too real, *Not Our Kind* kept me reading long into the night."

—Lauren Belfer, National Jewish Book Award–winning author of *And After the Fire*

"*Not Our Kind* transports the reader back to 1947, to the heart of New York's WASP-y Upper East Side. Zeldis has written a powerful and page-turning account of what happens when Eleanor—smart, beautiful, and Jewish—is employed as a tutor by the troubled Bellamy family, and finds herself out of place in their world. Can the fox and the hound ever truly be friends? This engaging novel succeeds in putting a fresh, feminine spin on that question."

—Suzanne Rindell, author of *The Other Typist* and *Eagle & Crane*

"Kitty Zeldis is one of those rare writers who doesn't just weave a story, she creates a world. In this case, 1947 New York—vivid, dazzling, challenging—where a young Jewish woman dares to cross the line into the land of WASP privilege, with unexpected results. With deeply human characters and resonant themes, *Not Our Kind* kept me reading well into the night."

—Jennie Fields, author of *Lily Beach*, *Crossing Brooklyn Ferry*, and *The Age of Desire*

"Rich, evocative, and atmospheric, *Not Our Kind* by Kitty Zeldis is the story of two very different women whose chance meeting changes both their lives in late 1940s New York. Zeldis weaves a beautifully written story not only about class and women's roles, but also about love, friendship, motherhood, and coming of age. I was absolutely captivated by this stunning historical novel."

—Jillian Cantor, author of *Margot* and *The Lost Letter*

"Kitty Zeldis shakes open a map of postwar New York City and draws the reader right down onto its streets and into the lives of the women who walk them. Her characters button up their coats and march their way through that decade's particular disasters— the polio epidemic, religious prejudice, class divisions, generalized misogyny—determined to locate power and happiness for themselves and the ones they love. *Not Our Kind* is a beautiful and compelling read."

—Adrienne Sharp, author of *The Magnificent Esme Wells*

NOT OUR KIND

NOT OUR KIND

A Novel

KITTY ZELDIS

HARPER

NEW YORK • LONDON • TORONTO • SYDNEY

HARPER

A hardcover edition of this book was published in 2018 by HarperCollins Publishers.

P.S.™ is a trademark of HarperCollins Publishers.

HarperCollins books may be purchased for educational, business, or sales promotional use. For information, please email the Special Markets Department at SPsales@harpercollins.com.

FIRST HARPER PAPERBACKS EDITION PUBLISHED 2019.

Designed by Bonni Leon-Berman

Library of Congress Cataloging-in-Publication Data has been applied for.

ISBN 978-0-06-284424-8 (pbk.)

19 20 21 22 23   LSC   10 9 8 7 6 5 4 3 2 1

For Paul—now and always

NOT OUR KIND

ONE

The yellow-and-black Checker cab nosed its way down Second Avenue in the rain. A newsboy in a sodden cap wove in and out through the slow-moving cars, hawking copies of the *New York Sun*; a man in a Plymouth exchanged coins for a newspaper as the drivers behind him honked.

Eleanor Moskowitz, perched on the edge of the backseat, didn't bother looking at her watch because she had just looked at her watch. It had been 9:29 then. It would be 9:30 now. In fifteen minutes, Eleanor had a job interview at the Markham School on Seventy-First and West End Avenue, thirteen city blocks down plus the width of Central Park away. It was unlikely that she was going to be on time. "Why is there so much traffic?" she asked the driver.

"Water-main break somewhere near here. And President Truman is in town," the driver said. "I'll bet you dollars to doughnuts that traffic's backed up all over the East Side."

Eleanor slid over toward the window and rolled it down, letting a fine mist into the cab. To her left, directly alongside the cab, there was a horse hitched to a dark red wagon. She was almost parallel to the animal and could see the sag of his belly, the matte black of his coat. He shook his head and snorted, as if in sympathetic frustration at the delay.

"Hey, do you mind closing the window?" said the driver, his irritation apparent. "It's getting all wet back there."

"Sorry." Eleanor rolled the window up again. She stared at the back of the driver's thick neck. His graying hair had been shorn by a razor, like all the soldiers demobilized from the army a couple of years back. The war was a memory now but certain images, like all those gawky boys with their fresh-cropped heads, stuck.

Sweat started to pool under Eleanor's arms and she took off the jacket of her navy crepe suit and laid it carefully across her lap so it would not crease. Her pocketbook and her umbrella—black silk with a bone handle—sat beside her. A navy hat made, like all her hats, by her mother, fit snugly on her head. Although it was fashioned from finely woven straw, the hat was still making her perspire, but she wouldn't take it off for fear it might get crushed.

She had been so nervous about today's interview that she'd been unable to sleep the night before. Around five she finally drifted off, and then sat up with a horrified start when she realized she'd slept right through the alarm and it was almost eight thirty. Her mother had had an early morning appointment and so no one had been there to rouse her. She dressed in a rush, cursed the rain that splattered against the apartment's windows, and once she was out in the street, decided to splurge on a taxi. Amazingly, the Checker cab had pulled up right to the corner of Second Avenue and Eighty-Fourth Street just as she stepped out of her building. She sprinted up to claim it and hurriedly climbed in.

But now the cab was barely moving. Eleanor looked down and discreetly straightened the seams of her new nylons. Not that the driver was paying attention; he was hunkered down over the wheel, muttering about the traffic. She sighed. It was not like Eleanor to be late, especially not for something as important as a job interview. And not when she needed a job so badly. She'd turned in her resignation at the Brandon-Wythe School just two days ago, feeling her hand had been forced by the Lucinda Meriwether incident.

Lucinda had been an excellent student, one of the very best Eleanor had encountered. Yet Eleanor didn't like her. Her insights were delivered in a slightly mocking tone, as if the class—and Eleanor—were somehow beneath her. She had also been the ringleader of a small group that had ganged up on Mary Watson, a shy, plump girl with a painful stutter, until Eleanor had stepped in. So when Eleanor discovered Lucinda had plagiarized a paper on Emily Dickinson she hadn't been entirely surprised. The girl was intellectually gifted but morally suspect. Eleanor had taken the whole matter to Mrs. Holcombe, the headmistress of the school, confident of her support. She had been wrong. And so she'd had no choice but to resign and scramble to find another job.

Odious as the whole business with Lucinda Meriwether was, its outcome had a silver lining—it gave Eleanor a reason to leave her job, a reason she could admit to in public. That she had another compelling reason to go, well, that she didn't have to tell anyone. Ever.

Starting back in the fall, she had allowed Ira Greenfeld, who taught physics, to slip his hands not only under the cups of her cotton brassiere, causing her small, startled nipples to jump to attention at the unfamiliar caress, but also under the scalloped hem of her slip, beyond the tops of her stockings, the metal clasps of her garter belt, and right inside her underpants. The gentle pressure of his thumb against that strange, nameless bit of flesh at her very core had been so intoxicating and addictive that she allowed these liberties to continue, despite the fact that they took place without the reassuring benefit of a ring—gold, or even one capped with the merest chip of a diamond—on her finger.

For the next few months Ira had brought her bouquets of tea roses, escorted her to dinners, movies, and the occasional concert or play, all as an elaborate prelude to the other, the thing which they both craved but did not discuss. Then, quite abruptly, Ira stopped calling or coming by. He also began to avoid her looks—at first wondering, then wounded—as they passed in the hallways at school. Soon the reason had become clear. Ira had turned his attention to the new young teacher in the science department, the effervescent and diminutive Miss Kligerman, whose dense blond curls looked like an electrified halo around her head, and whose breasts were so enormous Eleanor wondered that she didn't topple over from the sheer heft of them.

Of course everyone knew she'd been jilted. Brandon-Wythe was a small community. When Eleanor saw the way her colleagues looked at her—like a castoff, spurned for another—the shame she felt was like an actual substance coating her skin, something slick, oily, and vile. This had been in early March. The term did not end until the beginning of June. She had endured the humiliation, the pity, as well as her own resentment, stoically, and did not confide in her mother, who said, quite pointedly, "I haven't seen Ira lately. How is he?"

"He's been busy," Eleanor said. *Please don't ask me any more*, she thought. She and her mother had always been close but Eleanor could not reveal the extent of her intimacy with Ira; to do so would mortify them both.

"He must be *very* busy," said Irina.

Oh, Eleanor had wanted to tell her about Ira's dropping her, but was afraid that once she began her confession, she would feel compelled to reveal everything. As much as Eleanor longed to leave her job immediately, she did not have that luxury. She needed the income, and even if she were to forfeit it, she needed the recommendation from her employer, a recommendation that might not be forthcoming if she were impetuous enough to leave in the middle of the term. Then Lucinda had turned in her paper on Dickinson and between its cadged lines—*Despite her reticent nature and near-pathological reclusiveness, the belle of Amherst was, in her poetry, direct, confrontational, and even radical*—Eleanor had found a way out.

The taxi had been stalled for several minutes and a chorus of horns blared behind it. It was now 9:35 and they had gotten as far as Seventy-Ninth Street and Lexington Avenue, but still had a good distance to go. Finally there was an opening and the driver was able to move ahead. Eleanor used her fist to rub the surface of the window. A diaper-service truck was slightly ahead of them, its pink-and-white siding enlivened by a large painting of a baby blue stork. "Why did the president have to pick today to come into town?" she said to herself, but the driver caught her eye in the rearview mirror.

"You have a beef with him?" he asked.

"No," she said. Eleanor had nothing against Truman, though she'd never felt for him the fervent admiration that she had for FDR. She remembered accompanying her mother on election night, proud to cast her very first vote for him. "It's just that I'm going to be late for an appointment."

She checked her watch again and tapped lightly on the crystal, as if in so doing, she could halt the passage of the seconds. They reached Park Avenue, and through the window, Eleanor regarded the solid, stately apartment buildings, one set down squarely next to another, like a row of grand old dowagers at the opera. In front of one doorway stood a pair of massive urns densely filled with flowers, bright bursts of color in a gray day. A uniformed maid held two black standard poodles on a leash beneath an awning, presumably waiting for a lull in the rain.

As the cab crept along, Eleanor thought of the last conversation she'd had with the Brandon-Wythe headmistress. "This incident with Lucinda is certainly unfortunate," Mrs. Holcombe had said. She was an imposing woman who stood nearly six feet tall, and even seated she seemed to command the small, tasteful office with its polished mahogany desk, grandfather clock, and glass-fronted bookshelves.

"Unfortunate?" Eleanor said, flaring. "I'd call it reprehensible."

"We're talking about a girl of seventeen. That's strong language."

"It may be strong," said Eleanor. "It's also accurate."

"We don't have to parse the semantics any further," said Mrs. Holcombe. "Because the incident is not going beyond this office."

"Mrs. Holcombe, you do understand that she lifted whole sentences from Olive Thompson's *Voices in American Poetry*? Maybe even a paragraph. There's just no excuse for what she did. I've given the paper an F. She gave me no choice."

To Eleanor's surprise, Mrs. Holcombe leaned back in her chair, a tolerant and wry expression on her face. "Eleanor, you are a fine, principled young woman. And an excellent teacher. But when it comes to how the world works, I'm afraid you're as innocent as one of our girls."

"I'm not sure I understand," said Eleanor. She was angry but did not want to antagonize Mrs. Holcombe. As one of the three Jewish teachers on staff—Ira and the despised Miss Kligerman were the others—Eleanor knew her position was not rock solid.

"Lucinda's mother and aunt were students here. The Meriwethers donate a substantial amount of money to the school and Lucinda's father is on the board. And as surprising as it may seem to you, we need their support. Lucinda has applied to Radcliffe, Smith, Wellesley, and Bryn Mawr, and it's likely she'll be accepted by all of them. We don't want to do anything that would . . . endanger her chances because you see, Eleanor, we can't *afford* to."

Eleanor was quiet. Could this really be the case? To her, the school had seemed replete with privilege, with resources. Still, Lucinda's behavior was wrong and Eleanor had to say so. "But what she did——"

"Is a regrettable lapse. If it would help, I would allow you to speak to her privately. I'll call her into my office and you can join us. We'll explain that you are aware of what she's done and though you're not going to do anything about it this time, others may not be so lenient in the future. We could think of this as a kind of warning."

"With all due respect, Mrs. Holcombe, that makes us as culpable as she is."

Again there was that tolerant, almost bemused smile. "As impractical and unworldly as your position is, I respect it, I really do. And I respect you. But that's not the way it's going to be, Eleanor. Do you understand?"

She looked down at her lap and then up at Mrs. Holcombe. "I don't know where it leaves me though."

"You'll have to work that out for yourself. I've spelled out my position. If you can't accept it, then I'm afraid . . ."

"That I'll have to resign." The words were out before Eleanor knew it, a challenge between them.

"Why not sleep on it and let me know in the morning. You could talk it over with your family——"

"No!" said Eleanor, a little too loudly. She simply could not discuss this with her mother. "It's just that, I mean . . ."

"As you wish," said Mrs. Holcombe. "Of course I'll accept whatever decision you make. But I'd hate to lose you, Eleanor."

"And I'd be sorry to go." That was true; there was so much about the job that Eleanor loved. Then she thought of Lucinda's smug, supercilious expression; she doubted that the girl would be the least bit abashed by the meeting Mrs. Holcombe was proposing. And she thought too of Ira, turning away when they passed in the hallways or on the stairs. Out of courtesy, she would not tell Mrs. Holcombe what she realized she had just decided; she would pretend to think it over for a night. But in her heart she knew: it was time to go.

And so here she was, in this yellow whale of a taxi laboriously making its way toward the Markham School on the West Side. Eleanor had resigned, and begged off from a farewell party. In tacit exchange for her silence about Lucinda, Mrs. Holcombe had given her a month's severance and a glowing letter of reference, a letter that Eleanor had to refrain from reading too many times lest it become ragged and soiled from constant handling.

It was late in the year to be applying for the Markham job and she had only gotten the interview because her college friend Annabelle Wertheimer—the only other Jew in her dorm at Vassar—taught there and had managed to arrange it at the last minute. "The headmistress owes me a favor," Annabelle had said.

Eleanor knew her chances of landing this position were slim. But she had to try because she so badly needed a job. She could have gone to work in her mother's hat shop on Second Avenue, just downstairs from their third-floor walk-up tenement apartment. As a little girl she had loved being in the shop, with its gold-painted script spelling out HATS BY IRINA in a graceful arc across the window, loved the ribbons and bows, the veils, the bunches of silk flowers and faux fruit that made up the raw materials of her mother's craft. But her mother had adamantly refused her daughter's offer to join her. "Hats are good," her mother had said. "Teaching is better." This might have been the eleventh commandment as far as she was concerned. Irina had been nine when she came from Russia with her mother and two younger brothers; her father had been killed and her mother was fleeing pogroms and the revolution. She'd never gone to school past the fifth grade, and was determined to see her daughter surpass her. And Eleanor had. She'd gone to the prestigious Hunter College High School for Intellectually Gifted Young Ladies where she had been the editor in chief of the literary magazine and the class valedictorian. After high school she had attended Vassar on a scholarship. The job at Brandon-Wythe had been her first, and now it too was part of her past.

She'd been in this taxi for over thirty minutes, minutes during which she sat rigidly, watching the meter tick and the fare rise; it was now more than two dollars and the taxi had again hit a vexing snarl of stalled cars, unable to move at all. "Maybe you could try going down Fifth," she ventured.

"That might be even worse," the driver said. He continued on Park Avenue for a few feet then stopped—again!—for yet another red light. Eleanor was awash in a helpless rage.

When the light changed to green, she turned again toward the window and leaned back just the slightest bit, allowing some of her tension to dissipate. But as the driver was about to make a turn, there was a sudden jolt from behind. Instantly, she was thrust forward and her face was slammed against the unyielding surface of the driver's seat. Her hands flew to her lip, which the impact had split; she tasted blood. Then an ache radiated from her mouth outward until it seemed to engulf her whole body. She began to shake.

"He rammed right into me!" The driver opened his door. "Son of a bitch rammed right into me!"

Eleanor said nothing. She was trembling and kept her hands pressed over her mouth. The blood was dripping now, bright, round circles, onto her ivory silk blouse. *The interview*, she thought. *I've got to get to the interview.*

"Are you hurt?" the driver said, finally turning to Eleanor. "Hey, you're bleeding!"

"I'm all right," she said, removing a hand from her face to root around in her handbag for a handkerchief. "It's just my lip."

"Here, take this," he said, offering his own rumpled and rather grimy white square. Eleanor had no wish to offend him, but she didn't want to press the dirty cloth to her mouth either. She continued to hold her fingers against the wound. The driver's attention was elsewhere in any case, shouting at the other driver—also a cabbie—who had inflicted the damage. Eleanor cranked down the window.

"You hit me!" the driver of Eleanor's taxi said. "Just smacked right into me."

"You dumb jackass! You didn't signal you—"

"Didn't signal? What are you—blind? Or just a moron?"

Still trembling, Eleanor remained where she sat. Outside, a crowd had gathered. She heard someone say they were going to get a policeman from the station down the street. More shouting from the drivers, shouting that intensified when the police officer showed up several minutes later. The sight of him galvanized her; she clambered out of the cab, clutching her jacket, purse, and umbrella. Maybe *he* could help her, even drive her to the interview. She envisioned a wild ride through the wet streets, siren wailing and lights flashing.

"What's all the trouble?" The officer—young, with a round, pink face—looked back and forth between the two cabbies.

"This guy rammed—"

"He forgot to signal—"

"All right, all right," said the officer. He pulled out a thick notebook from his pocket; its edges were bent and its cover creased. "One at a time."

Eleanor stood there, the rain quickly wetting her thin—and now bloodstained—blouse, so that it adhered to her skin. She was still clutching her jacket and umbrella but was too stunned to put on the first or open the second. The officer was busy with the cabbies. She was not going to be *late* to the interview; she was going to miss it entirely. Her eyes anxiously scanned the streets, looking for a telephone booth. If she could call now, she might be able to explain what had happened.

"Officer, this woman has been hurt."

Eleanor turned to see that the passenger in the other cab had emerged. She looked to be in her thirties, and despite the rain, was flawless in her gray polished-cotton suit, with the kind of trim, fitted jacket and full, gathered skirt that Mr. Dior had introduced just months before.

"Are you okay, miss?" the officer said, looking away from the two cabbies. "Do you need an ambulance?"

"No ambulance," Eleanor said. "Just a telephone, please. I'm late for an appointment."

"I'll take you down to the station; you can use the phone there. But I have to finish up with these two guys first. And then I'll have to take your statement too."

Eleanor just nodded, her eyes beginning to fill. *The interview.*

"You're getting soaked," the woman said. Her gray mermaid hat, fitted close to her head and adorned with narrow white piping, was also a style endorsed by Mr. Dior. Eleanor's mother would have loved it. "Why don't you open that?"

Eleanor looked dumbly at the umbrella in her hand.

The woman regarded her indulgently. "Or, why don't you come and stand with me?" Her hand in its net glove gestured for Eleanor to join her under her umbrella.

Still clutching her own umbrella, Eleanor walked over and stood beside her as the two men continued to offer their conflicting versions of the story while the officer, who had clearly heard it all before, grunted softly, his pencil moving rapidly across the pad. Cars, backed up and idling, honked furiously at the delay.

"Are you sure you don't want an ambulance?" the woman said. "It couldn't hurt to have a doctor look you over." The hair that peeked out of the hat was blond, and her brows were unexpectedly dark, giving her a severe though admittedly dramatic look.

"I just want a telephone," Eleanor said.

"You're crying," the woman observed.

Was she? Eleanor touched her face as if it belonged to someone else; she had not even been aware of the tears. Her injured lip felt puffy and strange. "A telephone," she repeated. "Please!" So the woman went over to the officer; he nodded and the woman returned.

"There's a phone booth on the next corner," she said. "I told the officer you needed to make an urgent call and that we would be back as soon as you had finished."

And she took Eleanor's arm and propelled her along Park Avenue, where doormen stood like sentries, gold buttons gleaming on their dark jackets. Close up, the woman smelled of Chanel No. 5, a heady scent Eleanor could not afford to buy but had sniffed, often, when she and her mother "did" the ground floor at Lord & Taylor.

"I'll wait here," the woman said when they reached the phone booth. And she stood outside while Eleanor stepped in, dialed the number for the Markham School, and waited anxiously while the phone on the other end rang and rang. Finally someone picked up. No, the headmistress was not available now; she was in a meeting. Yes, the message would be delivered. The woman on the other end of the line seemed to doubt Eleanor's story. It was no wonder, since Eleanor knew she sounded slightly hysterical.

She hung up and looked at her watch. The crystal covering its brave little face was cracked and the hands were frozen in place. The watch had been a gift from her father, a year or so before he died. Its loss, heaped on top of the other losses of the day, seemed too much. She began to cry in earnest. And her lip started bleeding again. It hurt even more now, an awful, heat-laced throbbing. She pushed the door open, desperate for the air.

There stood the woman in the Dior suit. She had been waiting patiently all this time. "Oh you poor, dear girl," she said. "We'll finish up with the police and then you'll come straight home with me."

TWO

Sheltering the bedraggled young woman under her umbrella, Patricia Bellamy guided her the few short blocks to her apartment building. They had each given their statements to the officer and were now free to leave but Patricia had not wanted to let Eleanor go off by herself. Even though she had not been driving, she somehow felt responsible for the accident.

Patricia's own errand that morning—a trip to Bergdorf Goodman to pick up something for Margaux—could wait. Margaux didn't really care if her mother came home with another big orchid-colored box that held a cashmere sweater or a lavish party dress; the walking stick she was now forced to use had caused her to lose interest in new clothes and just about everything else.

As they entered the lobby, Patricia nodded to John, the doorman, and to Declan, the elevator operator. The girl, Eleanor, remained silently at her side. It was only when they reached the apartment and after Patricia had called out, "Henryka, can you get lunch started?" that she turned to her guest. "Did you want to use the telephone again?" she asked. Eleanor shook her head. "What about your interview?"

"I've missed it."

Eleanor seemed quite upset and Patricia thought she might begin to cry again. "How about freshening up a bit then? Wash your face and all that?" There was still a bit of blood on Eleanor's chin and her left cheek.

"Thank you," her guest said. "I'd appreciate it." She led Eleanor through the foyer, past the demilune table and the gilt-framed mirror, and the living room with its matched Louis XVI sofas and dove gray drapes, to the guest bathroom, where a stack of folded, monogrammed towels and a basket of shell-shaped bars of soap primly waited.

As the door closed quietly, Patricia realized that she had never entertained a Jew in her apartment before. At least not one that she had known about. She'd realized the girl was Jewish only after she'd already extended the invitation, when she'd heard her give her name to the police officer. The information came as a surprise. With her fine-boned face—her nose was narrow and small, her mouth delicate—Eleanor Moskowitz did not *look* Jewish. Of course there was the dark hair, but plenty of people of all backgrounds had dark hair. And, despite her understandable distress about missing her interview, she had a nice, even refined way of speaking. There was that suit, a cheap, skimpy thing, no doubt bought during the war when fabric—along with just about everything else—had been rationed. But it was a subdued color, and the cut wasn't all that bad. And the girl's hat was a little marvel—simple, but lovely. All these things added up to someone Patricia could not neatly categorize or pin down. This inability to precisely place Eleanor fell somewhere between unsettling and exciting; she was not sure which. Patricia wondered whether she would have invited the girl home if she'd known that she was a Jew. But once the invitation had been given, there was simply no way she could have rescinded it.

Patricia walked into the kitchen. "Henryka, what can you bring out for lunch?" she asked her cook. "Isn't there some ham?" Yesterday she'd hosted a luncheon and knew there were leftovers though she was vaguely aware that ham was a food a Jew might not eat. Should she ask, or would that be rude?

"There's ham. Sliced cheese too." Henryka swiped at the counter with a rag. A stout Polish woman in her sixties with thick gray-blond braids pinned up on her head, she had worked for Patricia's mother years ago. When Patricia married, Henryka had come to work for her. She was taciturn, and often sulky, but for Patricia, she was family.

As Henryka moved around the kitchen, Patricia ticked off the menu in her mind. She knew there was a fresh loaf of bread, a shredded carrot salad left over from the luncheon, and some petits fours one of the guests had brought.

"Do we have lemons?" Patricia asked. "If we do, you could make lemonade."

"Two left," said Henryka, her thick fingers wrapped around the chrome handle of the refrigerator.

"Two should be enough," Patricia said. "Can you squeeze them and prepare three glasses?"

"Miss Margaux eat too?" Henryka asked.

"I hope so," said Patricia, the words coming out sounding more tart than she'd meant. "Henryka, would you please ask her? I think she'd rather it came from you."

"All right. She like my lemonade." Henryka took the lemons out and put them on the counter. "Where I should set table, missus?" Even after decades in the United States, her English still suffered from many gaps.

Patricia paused. Usually they had informal meals in the breakfast room, off the kitchen. But Henryka had just that morning embarked on the task of reorganizing the pantry, and the table was covered with bags of flour, oatmeal, sugar, and salt. "I guess we'll eat in the dining room," she said. "But we'll only use one end of the table and place mats will be fine. Don't bother with a cloth."

Patricia and Eleanor were already seated when Margaux lurched into the room. At least she had put on a clean dress and her hair was brushed, Patricia thought. She introduced her daughter and exhaled silently when Margaux had crossed the room with no mishaps—there was simply no way she could move with anything approaching grace—and took her place across from their guest.

Eleanor helped herself to small portions of ham and carrots. "What are you studying in school?" she asked Margaux.

Margaux was busy spearing a piece of ham with a fork and did not answer. Once she had impaled the ham, she gnawed on it briefly and then left it sitting, rejected, at the rim of her plate.

"Miss Moskowitz asked you a question, Margaux," Patricia said, trying not to show her displeasure. Ever since the polio, a horrid changeling had supplanted Patricia's formerly charming daughter. The Margaux Patricia raised had lovely manners and could talk with considerable composure about school, summer vacations, and Clover, the strawberry roan they boarded at a barn near their country house in Connecticut.

"I'm not in school now," Margaux said sullenly.

Patricia could see the mild surprise register on Eleanor's face. "Since her illness, Margaux has had a tutor," Patricia explained. "She didn't feel comfortable—"

"Would *you*?" Margaux said angrily.

"Her father and I didn't insist. So we hired Mr. Cobb." She did not add that Margaux tormented the poor man; Patricia didn't know how he summoned the will to keep returning. Of course when he didn't come, Margaux was bored silly and spent her time navigating the apartment on her walking stick, bumping and knocking into things as she went. It was almost as if she did it on *purpose*.

This cheerless train of thought was interrupted by the appearance of the petits fours on a Limoges plate. The tiny squares, iced in white, were decorated with whimsical touches: pink candy bows on one, blue flowers on another, minuscule yellow dots on a third. "Please help yourself," she said to Eleanor, and when her guest seemed to have difficulty in choosing, Patricia urged her to take a second.

"Thank you," Eleanor said, passing the plate to Margaux, who ignored the silver serving knife and used her fingers to take the remaining four cakes.

"That's too many," Patricia admonished. Not that she wanted one; she actually found their sweetness cloying, but what if their guest wanted another? Patricia recalled one of her mother's many and oft-repeated lessons. "It's not just your job to make your guests feel at home," she had said, "it's your obligation."

"I'm hungry," Margaux said. There was a whine in her voice that would have been annoying in a child of five; in a girl of thirteen it was nearly intolerable. But Patricia ignored it, pouring herself a cup of coffee from the pot Henryka had brought in, and then passing the pot to Eleanor.

Patricia had been sick with worry when Margaux contracted polio and she had devoted herself to finding the very best hospitals, the very finest doctors. The iron lung, which had helped Margaux to breathe and had saved her life, was excruciating to see; the big metal cylinder with its tangle of hanging tubes looked like a coffin and appeared regularly in Patricia's dreams, even long after the need for it had ended.

But all that was over, thank God. Margaux had recovered. She did have that awful leg though, now thin and useless, that mocked her still healthy, still shapely other limb. Thanks to the immediate treatment she'd received, her foot hadn't curled under in the way that so many other victims' feet had, and the affliction was only in one leg, not both. Look at President Roosevelt: though the press tried to downplay it, he'd been stricken too, and there were rumors that he had had to spend his days in a wheelchair, a situation far worse than Margaux's. But was Margaux grateful? No, she slammed doors, uttered filthy words, and flung a crystal paperweight across the room. "Margaux, why don't you tell Miss Moskowitz about what you've been reading with Mr. Cobb?"

"What's wrong with your lip?" asked Margaux, ignoring her mother's prompting and looking up from her plate, where two of the petits fours had been mashed into a disgusting pink and white paste.

"I was in an accident this morning. In a cab. I hit my face."

"There's blood on your blouse. Did you have to go to the hospital?" Eleanor shook her head.

"I was in the hospital for months," Margaux continued. "I had polio."

"That must have been hard."

"I felt like I was breathing through a straw," Margaux said, holding her hands around her throat to demonstrate. "It was horrible. So they put me in the iron lung. And I couldn't eat because I was afraid I would choke; the nurses had to slather my food with mayonnaise to make it go down." She stared at Eleanor. "I despise mayonnaise; I'll never, *ever* eat it again."

"I can understand why you wouldn't want to," said Eleanor.

"I was lucky. I survived. But my leg atrophied when I was sick. It will never heal." Margaux gestured to the wooden walking stick that stood propped against the table.

"You seem to get around pretty well with that," Eleanor said. "I think you have a lot of pluck."

Patricia stared at her. No one had ever posited Margaux's situation in this light before and it was a revelation to hear it described that way.

"Pluck," Margaux repeated, as if she were weighing the word in her mind. "Do you really think so?" With the hand not holding the fork, she reached for lemonade; ice cubes rattled against the glass. She took a loud slurp before putting it down, something Patricia had asked her repeatedly not to do, but with supreme effort, Patricia remained silent.

"I do," Eleanor said. "I really do."

Margaux seemed to like this, because she actually smiled. Just for a second, but still. As the smile faded, she studied their guest carefully, and then asked, "Are you from Moscow?"

"No, but I suppose one of my ancestors might have been," said Eleanor.

Patricia thought she might have been a bit surprised by the question but noted that she still maintained a pleasant, even tone.

"Are you a Jew?" Margaux asked. The upraised fork in her hand could have been a small, spiked weapon.

"Margaux!" said Patricia, who felt her cheeks heat with embarrassment. "You're being rude."

"No I'm not," Margaux said. Now the fork was swiveled in Patricia's direction.

"I don't mind her asking," Eleanor said to Patricia. "Yes, I'm Jewish. Why do you ask?"

"I've never had lunch with a Jew before," Margaux said. She used the fork to pierce the single intact petit four that remained on her plate.

"Well, you're having lunch with one now," Eleanor said.

Margaux considered this for a moment, and as she did, Patricia noticed a glimmer of her daughter's former curiosity animating her face. Faint, to be sure. But it was there.

"My Sunday school teacher says Jews killed Christ. Is that really true?" Margaux finally said. "I mean, not you personally, but your people." She put the chocolate petit four, whole, into her mouth and chewed it thoughtfully.

Patricia was appalled. "Go to your room!" She stood up. "Right now."

"I hope you're not sending her away on my account," Eleanor said. "She really does want to know." She looked at Margaux. "Don't you?"

"Yes," said Margaux. "I do."

"The answer is, we didn't," Eleanor said.

"But Miss Clarke says you did. So does Henryka."

"Well, they're wrong and I'll tell you why. Jesus was a Jew, and so were his father and mother. He thought his fellow Jews had strayed too far from their faith, and all his preaching was an effort to get them to reform. So the Jewish leaders at the time wouldn't have killed him. They'd simply have excommunicated him."

"Excommunicated?"

"Expelled him from their church, only they called that church a synagogue," explained Eleanor. "As for the crucifixion, Jews never crucified anyone. That was a Roman punishment, and they did quite a lot of it in fact. The road to Rome was lined with crucifixes."

"If that's true, why does everyone say the Jews did it?"

"Although Jesus died, his following lived on. And those early Christians needed to appease the Romans, who were in power. They didn't want to antagonize the Romans by accusing them of killing Jesus. It was too dangerous. So instead, they said the Jews did it. Jews were the perfect scapegoats."

"That makes sense," Margaux said.

Patricia thought so too. The explanation was no less riveting for sounding rehearsed, as if Eleanor had delivered it before. The Christ-killer epithet was familiar; Patricia had heard it before and had never thought much about it one way or the other. Yet look at how deftly, and convincingly, Eleanor had dismantled it.

"Here's another thing I'll bet you don't know. Jesus's trial and crucifixion took place during the Jewish festival of Passover."

"What's Passover?"

"It comes around Easter and it's an important holiday. No Jewish courts would have convened. Instead, the Romans tried Jesus. And the Romans killed him. The Jews just got blamed for it."

"So Jews weren't powerful back then," Margaux said. "Or rich."

"No," said Eleanor. "They weren't."

"Oh. Well, I guess things are different now."

"I think we've had enough of this subject," Patricia said. The conversation was once again veering off into unpleasant territory. "More than enough, really."

"What do you mean?" Eleanor ignored Patricia and spoke directly to Margaux. It was as if she were addressing an equal, not a child.

"My father says all Jews have lots of money," Margaux said. "And that behind the scenes, they control just about everything." She looked at Eleanor, clearly assessing the modest suit, its lapels a bit shiny from wear, and added, "But I don't think you're rich."

There was a long, excruciating silence. This child had gone completely beyond the pale and Patricia could hardly bring herself to look at their guest, let alone apologize for her daughter.

Eleanor said nothing but sat still, hands splayed and pressed flat against the table. "Some Jews are rich. Some—in fact most—aren't. But in any case, you shouldn't be promoting those old stereotypes. It's hurtful. And rude."

Margaux, who had been lolling back in her seat in a most irritating way, sat up straight. Her abrupt movement jostled the table, tipping over her glass. The pale green linen place mat could not wick up the spilled lemonade quickly enough, and it began to drip down the side of the table, onto the carpeting.

"Now look what you've done!" Patricia, released from the acute mortification that seemed to render her speechless, finally spoke. "Henryka," she called sharply in the direction of the kitchen. "Henryka, could you come in here right now please?"

As Henryka cleaned up the mess, Patricia made a show of scolding Margaux. But secretly, she was grateful for the accident and the diversion it provided. Yes, Wynn sometimes said those kinds of things about Jews but never to anyone outside their circle. Never, for heaven's sake, in *front* of them. Margaux would have to learn this; Eleanor Moskowitz had just given her the first lesson.

After everything was cleaned up, Margaux reached for her walking stick so she could rise from the table. Patricia so badly wanted to help her but she knew the fury with which the gesture would be met, so she only watched as her child struggled until she finally gained purchase with the stick.

"It was interesting to meet you," Margaux said.

"It was interesting to meet you too." Eleanor stood. "I hope our conversation gives you something to think about." Despite her swollen lip and bloodstained blouse, she seemed poised and in control.

"Maybe it will." Margaux sounded surprised by her own admission.

At the door, Patricia tried to press a five-dollar bill into Eleanor's hand but Eleanor refused to take it. "Please," Patricia insisted. "So you can take a taxi home."

"Thank you, but I live only three blocks away," her guest said.

23

"I'd like to apologize for Margaux." Patricia folded the bill in half, and then in half again, fingers smoothing the creases as she did. "Ever since her illness she's become so rude. Unmanageable. I'm terribly sorry if anything she said hurt your feelings."

"She just said what a lot of people think. But wouldn't necessarily say." Despite the warmth of the day, her jacket was back on and buttoned, and her hat was firmly in place.

"As I said, it's the illness, it's kind of unmoored her."

"Maybe if you've been through something like that you become— unmoored. And it takes time to find your way back," Eleanor said. "Thank you for lunch."

Patricia waited until Declan appeared with the elevator, and watched as Eleanor stepped in and the doors closed behind her. It was only hours later that she noticed Eleanor's umbrella, still sitting in the brass umbrella stand. She could leave it with the doorman; Eleanor would no doubt remember where she'd left it and come back for it on her own. Or Patricia could contact her about it. Eleanor had mentioned that she lived on Eighty-Fourth Street, just a few short blocks east; it would be easy enough to track the girl down. Did she want to bother? She thought of the way Eleanor had handled herself during lunch. Quietly confident. Unapologetic. Altogether, an intriguing little person, Jewish or not. Yes, Patricia decided. She did.

THREE

Eleanor stood before the mirror in her bedroom, unsuccessfully trying to camouflage her wounded lip. Even though the swelling had subsided in the past three days, the tear in her skin had not fully healed and there was a dark scab that face powder and lipstick did not fully cover. In the mirror's reflective surface, she saw her mother behind her in the doorway, holding a pink silk rose. "I thought this might look nice on your dress." Irina did not wait to be asked into the room. "There'll be a lot of other girls at that employment agency and you want to stand out."

"Pretty." Eleanor took the rose. She was well aware of the importance of making a good impression, but she didn't say this, and instead submitted to her mother's fussing about the placement of the flower.

"I don't understand why you left a perfectly good job without another one lined up," said Irina. Her English was excellent, with only a slight trace of her Russian roots; she had worked very hard to get it that way.

"Are you going to bring that up *again*?" Eleanor felt she could not stand any more of her mother's frequent and poorly disguised inquiries; she was worried enough about being unemployed. But the wounded look that instantly came over Irina's face made Eleanor contrite. "No one else will have such a beautiful rose," she said. "I'm glad you thought of it."

"I know," Irina said, mollified. "The color is perfect."

She wanted, Eleanor knew, to have her talents acknowledged and admired—such admiration was compensation both for what she'd lost and what she'd never had. She wasn't an educated woman and she wasn't a wealthy one, but she was an expert hatmaker. She no longer blocked, sized, or dyed the hats in her shop, though she had done all those things in the Danbury factory where she'd worked before she met Eleanor's father. "I was a good coner," she had told Eleanor. "They paid by the piece and I could make a hat in fifteen seconds. *Everyone* wanted to be paired with me." She sounded so proud.

"Were these roses from last season's hats?"

Irina shook her head. "Next season. You're getting what's new, not what's left over."

Eleanor unpinned the rose and set it carefully on her dresser. In addition to coning, Irina had been trained in sizing, which had required her to spend the day with her hands immersed in steaming water that sloshed all over her dress, her shoes, and the floor. But coning and sizing were preferable to dyeing, which left indigo, cinnabar, or charcoal stains that took months to fade. She'd also had a brief stint sewing in linings and attaching hatbands, until a freak accident caused a needle to become embedded in the skin of her wrist. There had been no money then for a doctor to take it out, and even years later, when she could have had it removed, Irina chose to leave it where it was, a silent, steely reminder of her factory days.

***

At Forty-Second Street and Grand Central Terminal, Eleanor was disgorged from the subway car by the press of people behind her and made her way out onto Lexington Avenue toward the Chrysler Building. The bright, glittering spire was a fantastic oddity amid the buildings that surrounded it. Crescent-shaped semicircles of chrome-plated steel went up the surface, giving it the look of a stylized sunburst. Underneath, steel gargoyles of eagles' heads stared down at the city below. Her father had brought her here in 1930, when the building first opened. Eleanor had told him the building looked like a freshly sharpened pencil; he'd laughed at that. Afterward, he had taken her to Schrafft's, where they had sat on high, chrome stools and shared a hot fudge sundae. She missed her father, a mild, gentle man who sold men's suiting fabric for a living; he seemed free of the incessant worry that animated her mother. Irina was the one who, in addition to making hats, cooked, cleaned, and made sure Eleanor got to school on time; her father was more a playmate, engaging her in rambling conversations about trivia he'd read in the newspaper or taking her for walks in Central Park.

The lobby of the Chrysler Building, three stories high, was altogether dazzling, with its burnt sienna floor, red marble walls, and decorations of onyx, blue marble, and still more steel. Eleanor darted to get into the crowded elevator before the doors—adorned with inlaid wood and enormous golden lilies—closed. By the fifteenth floor, the crowd had thinned and she was the first one out.

When she entered the employment office, every seat in the waiting room was filled with young women wearing summer suits or dresses, their handbags perched on their laps or set on the floor beside their feet. One read a paperback while she waited, another picked at the remnants of her nail polish, and a third was powdering her nose with the aid of a bright, gold-toned compact.

Eleanor approached the receptionist. "I'm here to see about a job," she said. "I have an appointment."

The woman gave her a cursory once-over before handing her a printed form attached to a clipboard. "Have a seat and fill this out," she said. "Pencils are on the table."

"But there aren't any seats," Eleanor said.

"There will be," the woman said. Eleanor took a pencil, and retreated to the far wall to fill out the form. The room was warm, and now that two of the young women waiting had lit cigarettes, it was also smoky. As Eleanor completed the form, the door behind the receptionist opened and a woman walked out; another went in and Eleanor claimed her seat. She waited for more than twenty minutes, watching as women continued to walk in and out. Some looked elated, others dejected. There was a stack of *Life* magazines on the table and Eleanor reached for one. On the cover, Jane Greer looked up at the camera with a fey expression; one eye was partially obscured by a soft lock of wavy hair. Finally, Eleanor heard her name called. She gave the clipboard to the receptionist, and walked through the door just like she had seen the others do. Beyond the door was another, open doorway and a seated woman motioned for Eleanor to come in and sit down. On one side of her desk was an ashtray and on the other a small sign that read Rita Burns. She was about forty, with faintly pitted skin, cranberry lipstick, and a tightly fitting white blouse whose buttons gaped as they strained to cover her ample chest. Eleanor was reminded of Ira's beloved Miss Kligerman, and felt a new surge of loss.

"You can give me the form," said Miss Burns. "So you're a college graduate." She reached for a box of cigarettes from a drawer. "And a pretty fancy college at that."

"It was a very fine education," Eleanor said. She didn't like the insinuation, as if Vassar were all surface and no substance.

"I'm sure it was." Miss Burns extended the package of cigarettes toward Eleanor, who just shook her head.

"It says here you studied Latin, along with English literature and typing."

"Not at the same time," Eleanor said. Rita Burns rewarded her with a smile. "My mother thought typing was a good skill for a woman to have," Eleanor continued. "She said it would help me get a job."

"She's right," said Miss Burns. "But it looks like you took a teaching job instead. You didn't need to type there." She inhaled on the cigarette and blew smoke rings in the air above her head.

"No," Eleanor said. "I didn't."

"Brandon-Wythe. That's pretty fancy too." One of the smoke rings drifted toward Eleanor and Miss Burns waved it away. "Why did you leave?"

"I wanted to go in a different direction. Professionally, that is."

"I see," said Miss Burns, looking skeptical, and Eleanor felt a tiny prick of panic; it seemed that Miss Burns did not believe her. "You taught English literature and composition. So maybe you'd be interested in something in publishing? Books or magazines?"

"Yes, I'd like that," she said eagerly.

"We might be able to place you in an entry-level position," said Miss Burns. "A degree from a good school, a background in literature. Recommendations, I presume?" She looked at Eleanor, who nodded. Mrs. Holcombe's letter was in her purse. "You'll have to take a typing test, of course."

"I'm a good typist," Eleanor said.

"Good typists are always in demand. How about steno?"

"Some," admitted Eleanor. "But not my strong suit. I might be able to improve the typing though. If I did, what kind of salary could I expect?"

Miss Burns looked her over very carefully; Eleanor did not like the scrutiny but did not shrink from it either. "That depends," Miss Burns said finally.

"On what?"

"I might be able to get you thirty-eight, maybe even forty a week," said Miss Burns. Eleanor sat up straighter. She had only earned thirty-five at Brandon-Wythe. "But there is one thing . . ." Eleanor waited. "The name *Moskowitz* is not going to open a lot of doors. At least not the ones you want." She pulled on the cigarette again. "You should consider changing it; Moss would be good. Or Morse. That's even less obvious."

Eleanor felt slapped. Should she agree? Argue? Leave?

"Don't take it the wrong way," Miss Burns was saying. "I know what I'm talking about—"

"I'm sure you do," Eleanor interrupted, not caring if the woman detected the edge in her voice.

"There's no need to get so huffy," Miss Burns said. "I'm only trying to help." She let the ash accumulate at the cigarette's tip as she spoke. "I've seen it before—bright girl like yourself, nice education, good references, presents herself well. And goes exactly nowhere. *The position has been filled*, they say. Or, *You're not quite what we're looking for.* But after an easy little name adjustment, presto, everything changes."

"Oh," Eleanor said. "I see." And she did. She didn't like what Rita Burns was telling her, but she knew it to be true.

"No, you don't," Miss Burns said. "Not yet. But you will." She stood. "Are you ready for that typing test now?" She led Eleanor into a room that had been divided into a dozen cubicles. Each contained a desk holding a large black Remington Rand and a kitchen timer. Some, though not all, of the cubicles were occupied by young women clattering away on the keys. Eleanor sat down, placed her bag near her feet, and awaited further instructions.

"The test is five minutes." Miss Burns handed her three handwritten sheets. Two were office memos and the third was the first page of a quarterly report. "You'll start when I set the timer, and stop when it rings." Eleanor nodded. "I deduct a word from your final score for each error. Are you ready?"

"Ready," said Eleanor, lifting her hands over the keyboard.

"Then go." Miss Burns set the timer.

Eleanor typed as quickly as she could, hitting the carriage return with smart, efficient smacks. When she had completed the test, the tips of her fingers were tingling, and she waited in Miss Burns's office while the results were evaluated.

"Seventy-seven words a minute," said Miss Burns when she returned. "That's excellent. And it's all the more reason to consider the name change—"

"You already mentioned it," Eleanor said huffily.

"Yes, but you still don't get it." Miss Burns got up and closed the door to her office. "This isn't something I say to many people. But I'm saying it to you. My name isn't Rita Burns. It's Rachel Bernstein."

So she was Jewish too. "I appreciate you telling me, but I'm not sure that changes anything for me. I don't like the idea."

"Do you think I did?" Miss Burns paused. "Just consider it, all right? I'm doing you a favor, even if you can't see it now."

On her way to the subway station, Eleanor thought about what it might mean to change her name. Hers was not an observant family, and the few rituals her parents had adhered to had fallen away after her father died. So it wasn't deep belief or daily practice she was being asked to hide. Yet there were the occasional Yiddish words that slipped from her mother's lips, the challah that she made once a year, on Rosh Hashanah; the yahrzeit candle that sat on the kitchen table on the anniversaries of the deaths of her grandparents and her father.

And there was something else too, something that emerged only after the war. The news of the camps, the tattoos, the gas chambers, the multitude of tortures tailored and perfected for Jews. Adolf Hitler had systematically tried to annihilate her people. He hadn't succeeded, but his murderous goal made her want to ally herself more closely with those who'd survived. *Moskowitz* was the shorthand for the connection she felt, the thing that announced who and what she was. By giving it up, she'd be giving up a part of herself too.

Or would she? She wouldn't change inside, no matter what she chose to call herself. *A rose by any other name*, and all that. And she needed to get a job, to leave Brandon-Wythe behind, and start moving in another direction. Eleanor Moss. Eleanor Morse. She said the names aloud, to see how they sounded.

The uptown train came quickly and she was able to get a seat. The job at the Markham School had already been promised to someone else; it turned out the interview had been a courtesy only, and there was nothing else available. When she got off the train at Eighty-Sixth Street, Eleanor turned west rather than east toward her home. Yesterday she'd received a phone call from Patricia Bellamy telling her she'd left her umbrella at the Park Avenue apartment and that she could stop by at her convenience to pick it up from the doorman.

Walking down Park Avenue, Eleanor had to step past a large puddle on the sidewalk; a doorman in a crimson jacket was hosing down the pavement, which, like everything else on this avenue, had a clean, assiduously attended look. Brass plates or sconces shone in the sun, awnings were taut, even the trees and flowers in the islands separating the north and southbound traffic had the manicured appearance that could only be maintained by constant care. Service entrances on the side streets or at some distance from the main entrances allowed the inner workings of the apartment houses—their garbage and their packages, their plumbers and their maids—to be kept discreetly out of sight.

Despite being only three blocks east of Park, Eleanor's home on Second Avenue might as well have been in another borough. Lined with four- and five-story brick tenements, Second Avenue was always animated, always bustling. During the day the butchers, grocers, bakers, tailors, cobblers, newsstands, pharmacies, and shops drew a steady stream of pedestrian traffic; at night, there were bars and restaurants to entice prospective patrons. On Second, there were few awnings, no flowers, and a phalanx of metal garbage cans lined up along the curb on trash night. Sometimes rats scurried in and out between those cans; Eleanor had seen them. And even though the El was a full avenue away on Third, the sounds of the trains—wheezing as they stopped, clacking as they started—were always in the background.

Mrs. Bellamy lived in a twelve-story apartment building on the southwest corner of Eighty-Third and Park. Eleanor was more attentive today to the six limestone medallions, each depicting a wreath of fruit and flowers, the four massive Greek columns, two on either side of the door, as well as the black lanterns that were attached to the facade. With its limestone and brick exterior, the building projected a permanence, and even moral rectitude, that made the buildings in her own neighborhood seem almost provisional in contrast. Eleanor imagined that living here would feel safe; the reassuring solidity of these structures would provide insulation and protection against life's daily abrasions.

"Mrs. Bellamy left something for me," she said to the doorman, who wore a navy suit and matching cap trimmed with gold braid. "She said it would be here."

"And your name is?" he asked.

She hesitated. "Eleanor," she said finally. Something prevented her from saying Moskowitz.

"See Billy over there," he said, so Eleanor repeated her request to the uniformed man seated at the desk inside the lobby.

"Just a moment," he said, and disappeared behind a door. Eleanor looked around at the lobby while she waited; above was a six-armed brass chandelier; below, a black-and-white marble floor whose large squares had been positioned on the diagonal, so they read instead as diamonds. Beyond an open pair of double doors, the black-and-white marble continued, only in this adjoining space it was cushioned by a thick Persian rug. A sofa sat at the far corner and a few massive wing chairs dotted the perimeter; it was in one of these that Margaux Bellamy sat, walking stick propped on the arm of the chair.

"Hello there," she called out. "How are you?"

Eleanor did not especially want to talk to Margaux but felt it would be rude to ignore the girl's greeting. The doorman had not returned yet, so she walked over to where Margaux sat; the thick rug beneath her feet muffled the sound of her footsteps.

"What are you doing here?" Eleanor asked.

"My mother and I are going out, only she forgot something and had to go back upstairs." Margaux tapped her fingers on the arms of the chair. "Did you come to see us again?"

"No," said Eleanor. "I came for my umbrella."

"Oh." Margaux seemed disappointed. "I suppose you think I'm a very rude girl." She was looking at Eleanor as if she expected, or wanted, to be contradicted.

"I think you're ignorant more than rude," Eleanor said.

"Ignorant?" Margaux repeated, clearly offended. "You mean—stupid?"

"Not at all," said Eleanor. "I think you were repeating what you'd heard rather than what you honestly believed or felt."

"That's right!" Margaux said. "It's not like I really meant those things. How could I? I hardly know any Jews."

"Exactly," Eleanor said.

Margaux stared at her lap, silent for a moment. Though the day was warm, she wore slacks, which Eleanor guessed was a choice made to cover her bad leg. "I wish you were coming to visit us," she said, still not looking at Eleanor.

"Why is that?" asked Eleanor, unexpectedly touched. She sat on an upholstered chair and sank into its soft cushion.

"Because you're different." She looked up when she said that. "I like talking to you."

"Thank you," Eleanor said. "I like talking to you too." And at that moment, it was true.

"Would you then?"

"Would I what?"

"Come to visit us?" Margaux said. "Come to visit *me*." Eleanor was silent and Margaux pressed on. "My mother told me you're a teacher."

"Was," Eleanor corrected. "I'm looking for a different sort of job now."

"What sort of job?"

"I might work for a book or magazine publisher."

"Is that what you want to do?" Margaux asked.

"Well, yes. I suppose it is."

"More than teaching? Don't you like teaching? You make it sound like the other job is second best. A consolation prize."

"It's too late for me to get another teaching job for the new school year."

"So you're going to take another job that maybe you won't like as much," said Margaux.

"I hadn't thought of it exactly like that," Eleanor admitted.

"What if you took a job as my tutor?"

"I thought you had a tutor." And since when did children, even rich, privileged children, go around offering people jobs? Although Eleanor had taught the daughters of some very wealthy people at Brandon-Wythe, this was altogether new in her experience.

"Not anymore."

"What happened to him?" asked Eleanor.

"I made him so unhappy that he quit," Margaux said. "I tortured him. But I wouldn't do that to you."

"Why not?" asked Eleanor. She was actually warming to this girl—her candor, her intensity, and yes, even her anger.

"I told you before: I like talking to you. I like *you*." Before Eleanor could answer, the uniformed man reappeared holding her umbrella and, at the same moment, the elevator doors parted and Patricia Bellamy stepped out. She wore a dress of wine-colored silk whose skirt swished softly as she approached; her hands were raised to adjust the wide, white straw hat on her head. "Hello, Miss Moskowitz."

"I was waiting here, just like you told me to," Margaux said to her mother. "And I saw Miss Moskowitz at the front door. She was getting her umbrella. Mother, why can't she be my tutor?"

Eleanor was silent. Did Margaux think that the simple articulation of a wish was all that was needed to fulfill it? She glanced at the girl and saw the hope so naked, so blatant in her expression. The look was so powerful that for a moment, Eleanor thought that she might actually take the job if it were offered. But only for a moment.

Tutoring this girl was the last thing she wanted to do. Confined to an apartment, even one on Park Avenue, being at the beck and call of Patricia Bellamy, and, presumably, her husband—no, this was not for her.

As she listened to them talk, she again considered changing her name, the way Miss Burns had recommended. She would also hone her typing skills. If she could get her speed up to eighty or even eighty-five words a minute, it might not matter what her name was. Yet she did not wish to hurt Margaux, and so would humor her by pretending to consider the position. It was unlikely that Mrs. Bellamy would actually hire her.

". . . well, I don't know," Mrs. Bellamy was saying. "We haven't discussed it."

"No, but we could discuss it now." Eleanor finally spoke up. "The position at the Markham School was filled."

"Holly Benson goes to the Markham School," Margaux said eagerly.

Eleanor had to smile at her enthusiasm. "I've been pursuing other options. But I am an experienced teacher and I do have references."

"You would be perfect, I know it!" Margaux burst out.

"Lower your voice please," Mrs. Bellamy said. "Nothing's been settled yet." She beckoned to the doorman. When the umbrella was safely back in Eleanor's hands, Mrs. Bellamy added, "I'd like to consider you for this position, Miss Moskowitz. Would you send me a copy of your résumé? And your references? At your convenience of course."

"Certainly," Eleanor said. "I can leave a packet with the doorman."

"Thank you," Mrs. Bellamy said. "I'll look forward to receiving it." She turned to Margaux. "Time to get going."

Despite what she'd just said, Eleanor had no intention of dropping her references off for Patricia Bellamy's consideration. And when

Patricia Bellamy did not receive them—well, who knew what she would think? It wouldn't matter in any case. Eleanor would never see her again. She clutched her umbrella and waited while, with some effort, Margaux hoisted herself to her feet.

"Good-bye, Miss Moskowitz," Margaux said. "I really hope Mother hires you and you come back."

Eleanor was about to respond with some meaningless palaver, but when she looked at Margaux, the girl's face was filled with such naked supplication that she could not look away. And in those few, charged seconds, Eleanor realized that to ignore Margaux's blatant need, her unabashed appeal, would be not only wrong but cruel. It was a cruelty Eleanor could not bear to inflict. She would drop off the résumé and the letter, just as she had said she would. And in that moment, Eleanor decided that if Patricia Bellamy offered her the job, she was going to take it.

FOUR

The receiving line for Audrey Miles's wedding reception snaked through the opulent interior of the Metropolitan Club as the guests, a mix of elegantly attired men in tuxes and women in gowns, waited patiently to congratulate the bride.

"Why did she invite so many people?" Wynn said to Patricia. "It's a second marriage after all."

"That's no reason not to celebrate," Patricia said. But she too was a bit surprised by the crowd, as many members of their set had pointedly snubbed Audrey when she left her first husband. Perhaps her new husband's money had smoothed over the social awkwardness created by the divorce.

The wedding itself, held in a private chapel at St. Bart's down on Fifty-First Street, had been small, attended only by members of the immediate families. But the bride had wanted—and gotten—this lavish reception at the Metropolitan. "And the line *is* moving."

"No it's not." He checked his watch. "It's a quarter past eight and we've been standing in the same spot for ten minutes."

"The food here is supposed to be excellent. Everyone says so," Patricia said in an effort to distract him.

"I still don't like the place."

"I don't see why not." Patricia fanned herself with a small hand fan she kept tucked in her evening purse. A night this hot was unusual for June.

"For one thing, it was founded by parvenus and thieves who couldn't get into any of the better clubs."

"Oh, like J. P. Morgan?"

"A bunch of pictures and old books don't compensate for his nasty past."

Patricia did not reply, but instead glanced around at the white marble walls, whose glossy sheen was delicately threaded with black, and above, at the ornately coffered ceiling. A grand double staircase, the converging lines of which formed a giant X, would not have been out of place at Versailles; a pair of multiglobed torchieres stood sentry at its landing. Lots of debs she knew had had their coming-out parties here; the bride had been one of them. "Anyway, I guess I should be glad the reception's not being held at the Century," Wynn was saying. "Because I can't stand all those intellectual or would-be intellectual types."

"Tom belongs to the Century," Patricia reminded him. Even if Wynn disdained intellectuals as a rule, he was very fond of her brother.

"Is Tom going to be here?" Wynn brightened.

"No, darling," she said patiently. "Tom doesn't know Audrey. She's an old friend from Smith, remember?"

"I remember that she's got round heels, all right."

"Because she got divorced? And is now getting married again?" His habit of typecasting or dismissing people could be so annoying.

"I'm just saying that she had a lot of company between husband number one and husband number two." Wynn touched the bow tie constricting his thick neck. "And why black tie when it's so damn hot, I'll never know!" He stood glaring at her as if the dress code had been up to her. But before she could answer, she heard her name being called.

"Patricia! Patricia, over here!" She turned to see Johanna Gilchrist and Tori LePage, two friends from Smith, not far ahead of them in line.

"It's so good to see you!" Patricia said, hugging them in turn.

"You'll never guess who's here," Tori said.

"Who?" Patricia demanded eagerly.

"Should we tell?" Tori smiled at Johanna.

"I'm not sure," said Johanna. Clearly they were enjoying drawing this out.

"It's Madeleine Kendricks," Tori announced.

"You're joking. Where is she?" Patricia asked. Madeleine had been the brightest star of their little group. She had looks and brains, and the self-possession to deploy both to her ultimate advantage. Like Patricia, she had majored in art history. But unlike Patricia, she'd gone off to do graduate work at the Courtauld in London, then married an earl with whom she traveled the globe before settling down at his ancestral country estate and starting a family.

Patricia had been envious. Madeleine had been a year ahead of her, and Patricia considered her a role model. She'd even considered following in Madeleine's footsteps. What if she too went off to London? Pursued an advanced degree, prepared for a career as a curator or a professor? She'd been one of the top students, both in her department and in her class; her seminar paper on the seventeenth-century French painter Georges de La Tour had received much praise. And her brother, Tom, had made friends with actual artists, moving in their circles, surrounding himself with their work. But in the end she was neither bold nor brave enough to buck convention; she had married Wynn at the age of twenty, only months after she graduated. Madeleine was already in London by then and they lost touch. The tiny flame of her nascent ambition had gone out, never to be reignited.

A discreet pressure on her elbow reminded her that Wynn had been standing there quietly all this time. "You remember my husband, don't you?" she said to Tori. Yes, of course Tori did, and Johanna too. They all chatted for a few minutes, and then the line started moving more quickly.

When they reached Audrey, Patricia leaned in to hug her. "I'm so happy for you," she said.

"Thanks, darling," Audrey said softly. "This time I finally got it *right*."

Patricia knew what she meant; it was rumored that Audrey's first husband was a brute—drinking too much, spending her money on other women, and on at least one particularly awful occasion, hitting her. "I hope you'll both be very happy."

Then she heard Wynn's tightly uttered, "Congratulations," to the groom, who, in addition to being several years older than Audrey, was also balding and, it had to be said, a bit potbellied. But Audrey's face was radiant when she looked at him. Patricia stepped out of the embrace and the bride turned to the next guest in the line. With Johanna on one side of her and Tori on the other, Patricia's bad temper dissipated, her irritation with Wynn subsumed by the general air of gaiety. She had not yet found Madeleine, but she'd run into several other friends, all of whom had kissed her, hugged her, and cooed over her new Jacques Fath peach dress, with its self-shawl neckline and rather daring corset-style laced back.

The crowd at the bar was three deep and waiters wove through them bearing silver trays of hors d'oeuvres. Patricia sampled the prawns, Swedish meatballs, and stuffed mushrooms, and found them all quite good.

Better still, Wynn had happened upon an old Yale buddy, and, gin and tonics in hand, the two seemed to be having a fine time reconnecting. Patricia was relieved. Wynn's mood, so easily soured, was especially important tonight because, after reviewing Eleanor Moskowitz's impressive credentials, Patricia had hired her. Eleanor would be starting work on Monday but Patricia had not told Wynn yet. If all went well, she would tell him later on. She hadn't made a plan about how to handle her daughter's education if it didn't.

While she chatted with her little knot of girlfriends, Patricia kept careful tabs on Wynn, and when she'd decided it was safe, went off in search of Madeleine Kendricks, whom she finally found in the powder room.

"Tricia!" she cried. "It's been . . . decades."

"Not decades," Patricia said. "We're not all that old."

"Aren't we?" Madeleine said. "I feel old. No, ancient."

They hugged and Patricia said, "Well, you don't look it." She looked at Maddy's dress, a simple but elegant blue thing whose collar was an explosion of white chiffon. "Can we go somewhere to talk?"

"Of course," Maddy said, linking arms with Patricia. "Lead the way."

After getting their drinks, they took the elevator up to the library, notable for its elaborately carved mantelpiece and long, polished table. Cherubs frolicked on the ceiling overhead, and the ornamental plasterwork just below it had been recently gilded. Patricia was relieved to find it empty, and once the two had settled into their green leather chairs, Maddy told Patricia about what it was like being the wife of an earl.

"It's all very sporty," she said. "Quaint. The rituals, you know. And satisfying in its way. I have my children, my horses. And Phillip, of course. He's my rock. And now that the war is finally over, I feel like I can breathe again."

"What we heard from London was . . . devastating. Being bombed—that must have been horrible." Patricia knew they were lucky here, but morale had been low, what with the reports from Europe more and more dismal every week, and the cheerless rationing of just about everything. And all the young, or even not so young, men who were lost; Patricia was grateful that neither her husband nor brother had been one of them.

"We're deep in the countryside, miles from London," Maddy said. "So thank God we were protected. But of course we were aware of what was happening in the city . . ." Above her the skylight revealed the streaky gold-and-pink clouds, last remnants of the June day.

"How old are your boys?" Patricia had heard that Maddy had two sons. Or was it three?

"Maxwell and Roger are twelve. They're twins. Charles is eight. We had another, Byron, but we lost him."

"Maddy! I didn't know." Patricia used her free hand to grasp her friend's.

"He was just four." Maddy took a deep sip of her cocktail. "A bacterial infection. He was fine one day, droopy the next, burning with fever the day after that. He was gone within the week."

"Oh God. I'm so, so sorry, Madeleine," Patricia said.

Maddy dabbed at her eyes with her napkin. "I'm all right," she said. "Having the others really got me through. God knows what I would have done without them." She finished the drink and set it down. "But let's not get all weepy. Not at a wedding."

"No, not at a wedding," Patricia agreed. "Especially not at this one. I'm so happy for Audrey. She hasn't had an easy time of it."

"So I hear," Maddy said. "I'm surprised she stayed with him as long as she did."

"It's hard to disentangle yourself," Patricia said. "Even from a bad marriage."

Maddy put a hand on her wrist. "Here I've been rambling on and not letting you get a word in edgewise. How have you been? And that brother of yours? The Wandering Wolf?"

"Tom is—well, Tom."

"You tell him I say hello, would you?" Maddy had been charmed by Tom. "Now tell me about your family. How old is your daughter?"

Patricia told her about the ordeal from which Margaux had emerged alive but not unscathed.

"But she's all right then?" Maddy asked. "Over it completely?"

"Except for the leg, yes."

"What about your husband? You haven't said much about him."

"He's an attorney," Patricia said, but didn't add, *who did not make partner and who has not stopped being bitter about it for one blessed minute.* "Estate law." He'd had to switch firms after the partnership debacle and oh, how his pride, his precious masculine pride, had suffered.

"Does he find the work . . . rewarding?"

Maddy had always been one to probe beneath the surface of things. That was part of her appeal. "I suppose so. We never really talk about it." In Patricia's view, Wynn's days at work consisted of long, unutterably dreary hours sorting through the minutiae of people's wills, the nuances of the ever-changing inheritance laws, and a parade of dissatisfied and dueling heirs. Fortunately, his salary was augmented by the ample money his father had left him. But even though Patricia had sympathized at first—Wynn's work did sound stultifying—this turned to frustration, and eventually annoyance. Wynn just wouldn't see where he'd gone wrong. He was certain that the reason he'd been passed over was pure spite, not because he went into work late and left early, or that he'd bungled a major account, causing the client to seek other counsel. It wasn't his being passed over that had unmanned him in her eyes. It was his stubborn refusal to accept any responsibility for it.

"Men find it hard to talk about things like that. I sometimes think that's our role."

"Our role?" Patricia said.

"I feel it's women's job to help them understand themselves. They seem so ill-equipped for it."

"Wynn's not introspective. And he's more interested in what he does outside the office—sailing, golf, things like that . . ." She found she did not have all that much to say about Wynn. Or rather, what she wanted to say, she couldn't. Though Maddy had always been a good listener, and not one to gossip. "It's just that—we've grown apart."

"What do you mean?"

"I hate golf only slightly less than sailing. And the only time he talks about work is to complain."

"So he's not happy in his job."

"No, he isn't. But he doesn't do anything to make it better. He seems to . . . luxuriate in self-pity."

"And what about your love life?" That was Maddy—probing again. Patricia waited a beat before answering. "Well, after so many years of marriage, what can you really expect . . ."

"Listen, Tricia. If things are all right in the bedroom, then you see all the other failings through a different lens. But if they're not all right in the bedroom, they're not all right anywhere."

Patricia knew her friend was right but couldn't bear hearing it. "Well, there's not much I can do about it, is there?" She was sorry she had allowed this conversation to take this turn and wished she had another drink to fortify herself.

"Darling," Maddy said, "that is where you're dead wrong." And she proceeded to give Patricia a detailed plan for all the things she might indeed do. Both fascinated and supremely embarrassed, Patricia nonetheless drank in every word. When Maddy finished, she stood and the two women embraced. "Come and see us, why don't you? It'd be like old times."

"I'd love that." Patricia indulged in a brief fantasy: She, Wynn, and Margaux, walking through the English countryside. Drops of dew clung to fat roses that draped over low stone walls; in the distance, cottages with thatched roofs and sheep dotted the fields. In this fantasy, Margaux was as nimble as a goat, no walking stick in sight.

"I've got a book in the works," Maddy continued. "You should come when it's out. We'll be having a party to celebrate, and I'll be conducting a little tour of the house."

"Book? Tour?" Had Patricia missed something?

"I didn't tell you?" Patricia shook her head. "There are a few very fine portraits in the house. Some of them go back to Elizabethan times. I started to do some research—just for fun, you understand—but then I found out a few interesting tidbits, so I wrote an article for a local journal that a publisher happened to see and the next thing you know, I had a book contract. It's nothing really but Phillip's so tickled. Feels it does the family name honor and all that."

"Maddy, that's wonderful!" Patricia was able to summon the requisite enthusiasm but inside, jealousy pelted her like hail. Maddy had her husband, her children, her horses—and look, she still found time to research and write a book, and then say it was "nothing really." In comparison, Patricia felt herself to be useless and idle.

"There you are!" Tori stood at the doorway. Patricia was so relieved to see her. "We've been looking everywhere for you two." Maddy took Tori's arm and Patricia followed behind. The discussion about Maddy's book was mercifully over.

The three women took the elevator down and walked into the dining room. This was the most elaborate of all, with crimson drapes, ornate plasterwork, and a ceiling's worth of frescoes that could have rivaled those in a Roman palazzo. The Metropolitan was, and had always been, unapologetic about its ostentation. Two hundred–odd guests took their seats at tables swathed in yards of white linen; crystal vases of flowers—white roses, white lilacs, gardenias—scented the air, and the lights from the wall sconces shone brightly. The guests ate, chattered, and smoked; blue-gray wisps hovered above their well-coiffed heads.

After the meal, the party moved to the front hall. As Tommy Dorsey and his band played "I'm Getting Sentimental Over You," Audrey's new husband led her in the first dance. When it was over, Patricia and Wynn joined the others on the floor. Despite his bulk—he had played football at Yale and his solid heft had only grown heftier—Wynn was an expert dancer and Patricia enjoyed the showy flourishes he added. In his arms, she became reacquainted with an old tenderness she used to feel; she had always loved dancing with him.

"We don't need a wedding," she whispered to Wynn when the song ended. "Let's go dancing for no reason at all. Sometime soon."

"You want to go dancing?" he asked, still holding her close. "I'll take you dancing. Just name the day. We can dance until your slippers are worn right through and you have to dance barefoot." He nuzzled her neck.

Patricia thought of her conversation with Maddy in the library. She wanted to recapture the feeling she'd had about Wynn when they were newlyweds. They'd gone dancing all the time then; he used to call her Silver Slippers.

The musicians took a break when it came time for the bride to cut the first slice of wedding cake, a white, multitiered affair sprinkled with bits of coconut and studded with candied violets, which she of course fed to her groom. Then the servers took over, and sent thin slices all around the room. Wynn insisted on feeding Patricia, and though she was not in the least bit hungry, she appreciated the romantic gesture and went along with him. Through it all, Maddy's advice was going through her mind. *Men are really little boys at heart*, she'd said. *They yearn for novelty. Or at least the illusion of it. You have to seduce your husband over and over again. Pretend each time is the first time.*

While Wynn waltzed the wife of the Yalie around the floor, Patricia went off in search of a glass of water; she felt parched from all that champagne and dancing.

"Is that—Patricia Harrison?"

Patricia turned to see Candace Cummings. Patricia and Candace had been friends at Smith, but unlike Maddy, with whom the rift had been geographically determined, the falling-out with Candace was abrupt, shaming, and painful.

"Hello, Candace," Patricia said. Suddenly, she was sober.

"Long time," Candace said. She stood there with her own drink, looking as voluptuous as she had at twenty. Her hair, an uncommon shade of auburn, had been styled into an omelet fold, parted at the back and crisscrossed into an intricate pattern. There were emeralds at her ears and throat, and her dress, a brilliant green figured satin, set off her fair skin. Patricia had heard that she'd married well.

"It has been," Patricia agreed. "At least fifteen years." She made no move to embrace Candace.

"I haven't seen you since graduation." Candace did not drink from the glass she held, but pressed it to her cheek. "How have you been?"

"Not too bad. My daughter, Margaux, was sick, you know, but she's better now, all better, and she's gotten so pretty . . . Wynn's been busy, terribly busy, at work. It seems like there are so many people dying these days! It's wills, wills, nothing but wills." She was babbling, idiotically, to cover her discomfort.

"And your brother, Tom—how is he?"

"Oh, Tom is just Tom." The question felt like an assault. "Maddy was asking about him too."

"Was she?" Candace's expression conveyed disdain but not surprise.

"Anyway, that's enough about me! How are you? I heard you left New York." Wouldn't anyone come to rescue her? She looked around, hoping her desperation was not visible.

"I'm fine. My husband is from Georgia, and we've been in Savannah for the last several years." She moved the glass away from her cheek to consider its amber contents but she still did not drink. "I have no children."

"Tricia, Maddy's leaving and she wants to say good night." Here was Tori, heaven-sent to save her. Filled with relief, Patricia turned. "Excuse me." She grabbed Tori's arm in a way she knew to be unseemly but she couldn't help herself. "It was good running into you." She turned away, so she could not see the lie register on Candace's face before she and Tori moved toward the door.

The summer after junior year, Patricia had invited Candace up to their summer place in Maine for the month of August. Although Tom was already romancing a girl—or two—in town, he had not been immune to Candace's shining hair and the sight of her lush white body poured into her modest black bathing suit. He dropped the other girls and the two of them had quickly become a couple. When September came, Candace let it be known that Tom would soon ask her to marry him.

But when October and then November brought no word, she'd grown sad and withdrawn. Soon it was apparent why: Candace was pregnant. When she confronted Tom with her news, he offered sympathy, the name of a reputable and discreet doctor, and money. He did not, however, offer her a ring. Patricia had been furious with her brother. "She's in love with you, Tommy," she said. "You're breaking her heart."

"If I end things now, she'll get over me," Tom said. "But if I marry her without loving her, then I'll turn her life—and mine—into a nightmare."

"You got her pregnant," Patricia had said.

"If you're thinking I seduced and then abandoned her, you're dead wrong," Tom said. "It happened only once. I knew it was a bad idea, but she—she was one determined girl. And like a fool, I went along with it. But one foolish night isn't worth a lifetime of misery."

The gossip at school said that over Thanksgiving break, Candace's mother whisked her off to that hush-hush doctor on Long Island to "take care" of her problem. She took a medical leave, and when she came back for the new term in January, she was a different girl, her buoyant shape deflated, her face wan. Even her wondrous hair seemed dull and lifeless. Before this, she'd been a chemistry major and talked of becoming a nurse or even a doctor. Then her grades slipped and she fell to the bottom of the class. One day in late spring of their senior year, she came up to Patricia on East Quad and said, "You should have warned me." Then she walked away and they had never spoken again. Patricia had been so mortified that she never told anyone—not Tom, and not even Wynn.

Patricia felt unsettled by her run-in with her former friend, and after she had said good night to Maddy, she went right up to the bar. "I'll have a vodka," she said. "Straight up." She downed the drink as if it were medicine, and by the time the evening was over, she'd reclaimed herself. What had happened between Tom and Candace was not her fault and she was not going to let this encounter ruin her plans. Candace was not the only one who'd been hurt by life; everyone had their own little plot of hell that they learned to navigate.

Wynn was in a fine mood on the taxi ride home. He'd made plans to meet his Yale pal for lunch and there had been the hint of some work being thrown his way. The meal—prime rib with *haricots verts amandine*, mashed potatoes, and gravy—had pleased him enormously and he had considered the champagne "first rate."

"See, the Metropolitan isn't so bad after all," Patricia said, snuggling closer in the backseat. She was going to match his mood, whatever it took. In lieu of an answer, he squeezed her hand.

The apartment was quiet and dark. Henryka and Margaux were asleep, though Henryka had thoughtfully left the new Emerson fan on in their room. Wynn had already started undressing—the detested bow tie was tossed carelessly to the floor—when Patricia slipped into the adjoining master bath with the words, "Wait up for me." Behind the closed door, she hurriedly got out of her dress and undergarments, taking the time to appraise herself in the mirror. She was still attractive; her breasts did not show evidence—or at least not much—of that perilous descent so common to women after thirty. Her waist and hips were trim, her skin soft.

She undid her hair, shaking it out and running her fingers through it to give it more volume. A few sprays of perfume at certain strategic spots. Then she slipped her gold evening sandals back on, and added a heavy gold chain she rarely wore; it had been a gift from her mother and she'd always thought it overpowering and even a tad vulgar. But right now it seemed just the thing. What would her excruciatingly reserved mother have said if she'd known how it was going to be used tonight? Patricia smiled at the thought.

Naked except for her evening shoes and necklace, she stepped back into the bedroom. Wynn, stripped down to his boxer shorts, was stretched out on his side of the bed. She felt a rush of tenderness—he loved her, he was her husband and the father of her child. Into her mind floated a story he'd told her about the first—and only—time he'd gone hunting with his father, and how he blubbered like a baby when he picked up the bloodied carcass of the duck he'd shot. After that, he would go fishing but refused to pick up a gun ever again.

Right now, Wynn's eyes were closed but she did not think he was sleeping because when she approached, he opened them right away.

"Tricia," he said, clearly surprised. "What's all this?"

"Do you like my outfit?" she said coyly. She felt silly; she felt excited. She'd been taught never to initiate, but to let her husband take the lead. Now here she was, breaking all the rules.

"I like it very much." He ran his hands lightly up and down her thighs. To her surprise, she actually felt a thrum of the old thrill she had felt so often during their courtship but seldom during their marriage.

"I'm glad," she said. She stood while he caressed her for a few minutes but when he tried to pull her down beside him on the bed, she held back. "What's the rush? We have plenty of time."

"What's gotten into you anyway?" he said. But he was smiling and he allowed her to prolong things, even getting into the spirit of her game. Then he truly surprised her by shifting their bodies so that she was on top of him.

"I want to look at you," he said. "I want to touch you." And as he thrust inside her, he stroked her until she was convulsed by a wave of pleasure unlike any she could remember.

When it was over, he let one hand lazily caress her back while the other held a lit cigarette. Patricia was practically purring. But her work was not done; this triumph had conveniently paved the way for the next phase of her campaign. She just had to choose her words carefully.

Wynn stubbed out the cigarette and closed his eyes. *Not yet*, she thought. *Don't go to sleep yet.* "Darling, I wanted to talk to you about something . . ." Instinctively, she reached for her nightdress.

"Anything," he said. "Anything at all." But his eyes remained closed.

"It's important. You need to be awake."

Wynn sighed, opened his eyes, and positioned his hands behind his head.

"I've hired a tutor for Margaux." There, she had said it.

"Please, tell me he's an improvement over Mr. Cobb." His eyelids fluttered. "That man was such a boob."

"It's not a he. It's a she," said Patricia. "And don't go to sleep."

"I'm not going to sleep."

"Your eyes are closed."

"I can hear you with closed eyes."

"The tutor I hired is Eleanor Moskowitz, the girl I told you about. The one whose taxicab I hit."

"Eleanor Moskowitz?" Wynn's eyes opened and he sat up. "Really?"

"Yes, really." She knew what he was thinking. It was the name Moskowitz and everything that went with it. Patricia knew he'd wonder about how their friends might view their choice. It was one thing to hire a Jewish upholsterer or piano tuner, but a Jewish tutor, coming in and out of their home every day . . . "Did you know that she took four years of Latin in high school? And four more while she was at Vassar?"

"She went to Vassar?" Wynn said. "Lord, they're everywhere now, aren't they?"

"Yes, she went to Vassar. On scholarship. And she excelled in everything she undertook."

"I'm sure she's very bright. They usually are. But is hiring her a good idea?"

"Why wouldn't it be? Margaux likes her so much already and——"

"You have a kind heart, my darling," he said. "So kind that you forget how cruel the world can be."

"I don't understand what this has to do with——"

"Doesn't Margaux have enough strikes against her? Does she need a tutor who's going to cause people to talk? We want to make things easier for her, Tricia. Not harder."

"I don't care about all that!" Patricia burst out. It wasn't true. She did care and she had even had the same thought. But what Margaux wanted was more important, and Margaux wanted Eleanor Moskowitz. Since their last meeting Margaux had asked several times if she could see Eleanor again. Perhaps Eleanor would be the magic key, the one who unlocked Margaux from her prison of self-loathing and despair; Patricia could not, would not let Wynn stand in the way. Overwrought, she began to sob.

"Tricia, don't." Wynn moved closer; the mattress springs heaved slightly. Patricia continued to cry and he put his arm around her. "Is it that important to you?"

"Yes! But it's even more important to Margaux, don't you see?" He was always undone by her tears, and so she made herself cry even harder.

Wynn touched the gold necklace that she had not yet taken off.

"All right then," he said. "Hire her. Just try not to broadcast her background."

Patricia said nothing, choosing to conceal her jubilation. Yes, the lovemaking with Wynn, and her reaction to his unfamiliar caresses, had been an unexpected and lovely surprise. But even more important was her ability to fight for—and win—a precious bit of her daughter's happiness.

In the morning, Wynn was in an especially good mood, and actually spun Patricia around the kitchen as he hummed Perry Como's "Surrender" in her ear. Patricia was uneasy; would this display, enjoyable as it was, remind Margaux of her own inability to dance? But Margaux watched them with delight, clapping her hands when they were through. "Daddy, you're such a good dancer!" she said. "You and Mother look so glamorous!"

"Why thank you." Wynn swooped down to kiss her cheek. "Your mother is indeed a very glamorous woman. The most glamorous woman I know. And you're growing up to be just like her."

"I'm not," Margaux said, but she looked pleased.

"Yes you are. Just wait and see." Then he sighed theatrically. "But unfortunately, I have to head into the unglamorous office. No more dancing—at least not now."

"There'll be other times," Patricia said. And she followed him to the door, where they kissed, for longer, and more ardently, than usual. When he was gone, she stood alone in the foyer for several seconds. Maybe it was possible to rekindle her passion for Wynn— she had felt it once. And the way he treated Margaux—not all fathers were so tender with their daughters, or took such an interest in their lives.

When Margaux was born, Patricia's mother had been quick to suggest a number of family names: Elizabeth was one. Also Charlotte and Anne. Patricia thought those names were nice enough, but they seemed too expected. Too ordinary.

"Actually, Mother, we want to call her Margaux. And we're going to spell it M-a-r-g-a-u-x." This wasn't exactly true because she hadn't consulted Wynn yet.

"Margaux?" her mother said. "Isn't that the name of a wine?"

"It is, but it's also a French name. It means Pearl."

"No one in our family is French," her mother said.

"I'm not naming her for a family member," said Patricia.

Her mother looked at her, clearly trying to decide whether this was a battle worth fighting. "It's your decision," she said finally. "Though I would have expected Wynn to be more sensible. And of course everyone will misspell it."

Patricia didn't care. And later, when she shared the idea with Wynn, she told him something she had deliberately kept from her mother. "We were drinking Château Margaux that night when you first kissed me," she said. "I remember you ordering it at a restaurant and I thought you were so sophisticated—all the boys I knew ordered beer."

"Are you sure?" he asked. "It's a bit different."

"Isn't she?" Patricia led him over to the bassinet, where the as-yet-unnamed baby lay asleep on her back. Her hair was a dusting of gold, her mouth a tiny rosebud. Above her flickering eyelids, her faint brows arched delicately.

"Our Margaux." Wynn pulled Patricia close and murmured into her ear, "She's perfect."

And that was how he continued to regard her—the prettiest, the smartest, the best. Wynn was the one who'd taught her to ride a bicycle, to swim, and to sail. He would take her out to a restaurant and order her a Shirley Temple. Patricia couldn't even imagine going to dinner alone with her father; what would they have talked about? Like Patricia, Wynn had been devastated by Margaux's illness and they had been united in their grief and fear. It was only when she was over the worst of it that the gulf between them began to widen again. But last night, they had taken a step toward bridging it. Maddy, it seemed, had been right all along.

FIVE

On the Sunday night before she was to start working for the Bellamys, Eleanor stood in front of the mirror in her modest, peach-colored slip, running her fingers through her hair to fluff it out; the hot weather had made it go limp. Behind her, on the bed, lay her outfit for tomorrow: her best, black-and-white-plaid summer dress, a black straw hat adorned by a narrow white band, and a black patent leather pocketbook. She had dropped off her résumé, and she'd received a phone call from Patricia Bellamy the very next day.

"I'd like to offer you a position as Margaux's tutor," Patricia had said. "Five days a week, five hours a day, at least through the end of June. In July, we go up to the country, and we'd like you to come with us. Do you happen to drive?"

"I have a license but I'm not very comfortable doing it," Eleanor said. It was her father who had insisted that she learn, using a car borrowed from a cousin.

"Oh, that's all right. I was just curious. Anyway, we don't expect Margaux to be doing schoolwork all day long while we're there, but she's fallen behind and it would be good for her to keep up with her studies. If things work out, you can stay on into the fall." Patricia paused, and it sounded like she took a drag on a cigarette. "And oh—we can give you forty-five dollars a week."

Forty-five dollars a week! That was ten dollars more than she'd been making. Eleanor couldn't wait to tell her mother; maybe Irina's misgivings would abate. But she didn't want to let on to her new employer how much she needed the money. "That would be fine," she said.

"How soon can you start?" asked Mrs. Bellamy. "Margaux's been asking for you."

Mrs. Bellamy went on to fill her in a bit more on Margaux's bout with polio. "She was sick for seven months. Three weeks of that time, she was paralyzed from the neck down. And she had to remain in isolation too. We weren't even allowed in the room. When *that* agony ended, there were months of recovery and therapy, and learning to walk again with that stick. One therapist had her pick up marbles with her toes."

"That must have been hard for her. And for you."

"Hard doesn't even begin to describe it. And ever since, she's been so angry. Since we brought her home, she hasn't even looked anyone in the eye in months. But you—you touched something in her. I could see it. Feel it."

Finally satisfied with her hair, Eleanor clipped it to one side with a barrette. The vestiges of her own girlhood were still evident in this room: the rose-sprigged wallpaper her mother had hung herself, the white iron bed with its chenille bedspread, the bride doll her father had brought her back from a business trip to Florida when she was ten years old. Eleanor suddenly felt stifled by the confined, girlish space. At Vassar, she'd been part of a small but tightly knit group, mostly Jewish, and senior year, she'd shared a suite in Main with three of those girls. She missed that easy camaraderie now, the late nights spent talking, the intimate rituals of doing each other's nails or hair.

Picking up the doll, Eleanor blew on the top of her veil-covered head to dislodge a tiny puff of dust. Back then, she had loved the long satin dress, the white shoes that peeped out from beneath its hem, the cloud of netting that surrounded the doll's honey-colored tresses. Now the doll's bland, uninflected beauty taunted her, and Eleanor suppressed an urge to fling her out the open window. Instead, she went over to the wardrobe and stuffed the doll on the top shelf, behind a scratchy sweater she never wore.

The telephone in the kitchen rang and from the sound of Irina's replies, Eleanor knew it was her friend Ruth Feingold on the phone. She'd promised to meet Ruth to head over to a social at Congregation Orach Chaim on Lexington Avenue. But now that the appointed night was here, she was reluctant to go.

Irina appeared at the door. "Can I come in?"

"Is it Ruth?" Irina nodded. "Would you mind telling her I'm not feeling well?"

Irina gave her a look. "She already hung up. She said she'll be waiting at the Rexall on the corner. I told her you'd be there in a few minutes."

"Will you call her back and tell her I can't make it?" Eleanor knew Ruth was counting on her, but she suddenly couldn't bear to go.

"Why not? I thought you were looking forward to that social."

"I was," Eleanor said. "But now I'm not."

"It might be a good idea. Ever since you stopped keeping company with Ira—"

"Who said I stopped keeping company with him? I told you: he's been busy."

"Ellie, please. I never interfered but I could see how you were walking around for months, dragging that broken heart of yours wherever you went. And I know that Ira was behind your decision to quit your job at the school."

"Who told you that?" Despite the fact that she was wearing only her slip, Eleanor walked over to the window.

"No one had to tell me," Irina said. When Eleanor didn't reply, she added, "Rabbi Schechter's wife came in for a new hat; she asked if you would be at the social and I said yes."

"There will be plenty of people there. No one will miss me."

"Why don't you go with Ruth?" Irina said gently. "You might meet someone. Someone who will take your mind off Ira."

Eleanor turned away so her mother would not see her tears. But Irina knew anyway and got up to give Eleanor a hug.

"I guess I shouldn't keep Ruth waiting," Eleanor said.

Ruth chattered all the way up to the synagogue on Ninety-Fourth Street. Life behind the counter of her parents' delicatessen, where she was working for the summer, her older sister's new beau, the relative merits of getting a permanent—these were the topics that carried them along the avenue and across the busy streets.

The shops on Second Avenue were closed, but many of the bars and restaurants of Yorkville were open. They passed the white facade of the Heidelberg Restaurant, done up with timber beams to look like a German cottage, and the window of Schaller & Weber, with its multitude of glazed beer steins.

"You're very quiet tonight," Ruth said at last. "Are you all right?"

"I'm fine," Eleanor said. "Just thinking about tomorrow, that's all."

"And you're not thinking about the social tonight?" She pointed to the synagogue, which they had now reached. The brick facade, which was in need of repair, took up almost the entire block, and the three stone steps that led to the double doors were chipped and gouged.

"That too," Eleanor said.

"Ira was a fool," Ruth said, linking arms with Eleanor. "But some guy in there is going to thank his lucky stars because of that."

Eleanor smiled. "Let's go in." Orach Chaim was familiar ground. Her father had come here every week for years, and her mother had grudgingly accompanied him on the High Holidays. Eleanor went with them, listening to her mother's complaints the entire way. Yet when Eleanor's father died, Irina had arranged for the funeral to be held here and she still attended the occasional service. "I do it for him," she explained.

In the lobby, Eleanor could hear the din of voices and the strains of Ted Weems singing "Heartaches" from below. She and Ruth followed the music downstairs, and when they got there, the room was full. "Would you look at that!" Ruth said. "All these guys. Where do you suppose Rabbi Schechter found them? They're not all from this congregation, are they?"

Eleanor shrugged. There were indeed a lot of men in the room. All were wearing yarmulkes, many of them plain black, plucked from the box that the rabbi kept on a table, just inside the doors. They were dressed in lightweight summer suits or sport coats and slacks; a few wore army uniforms. The women's clothes were more festive and even sensuous: taffeta, brocade, chiffon, and a satin or two.

"I'm thirsty," Ruth said. "Let's get something to drink." Eleanor watched her go but hung back, not wanting to force herself into that crush of people.

"Can I offer you some punch?"

Eleanor turned to see a short young man in a tan sport coat holding two cut-glass punch cups. "Thank you," she said. "How did you happen to have two?"

"It took me such a long time to get to the punch bowl, I figured I might as well take an extra. But I haven't touched either of them."

In lieu of an answer, Eleanor sipped her punch. It had a vaguely cherry flavor and was very sweet, unlike the victory lemonade they all drank during the war. "There's rugelach too," her new companion said, gesturing to a table placed at the side of the room. It was covered with a lacy cloth that pooled on the faded linoleum floor and held several large plates of the fruit-filled pastries.

"Maybe later."

"I'm Harry," he said, extending his hand. "Harry Cohen."

"Eleanor Moskowitz," she said, taking his hand, which was small and moist.

They talked for a little while, and he told Eleanor that he worked in an accountant's office downtown and lived with his parents on Seventy-Seventh Street, just off Second Avenue. When he learned where she lived, he said, "We're neighbors," in a way that suggested he thought there was some significance in that fact. He also told her that he loved playing Ping-Pong, hated jazz, and dreamed of going out to Hollywood one day.

"You want to be in the movies?" asked Eleanor.

"Not be in them. Write them. You know—screenplays."

"Really?" Eleanor was surprised.

"Yeah, that's the exciting part of movies. At least to me."

Eleanor was intrigued. Writing for the movies sounded like an interesting job. Harry was earnest and just a little bit nervous, which she actually liked. But he had a high voice and talked very quickly; it was the sort of thing that soon became annoying. Also, he blinked so often she thought it might be a tic of some kind, and he kept fiddling with his necktie in a very distracting way. She would never want to kiss him, she decided, but then felt slightly shocked at her reaction.

Was that *all* she thought about? Kissing—and everything that went with it?

"There's my friend," Eleanor said, finally spotting Ruth. "I should go. She's been looking for me."

"Oh," said Harry, clearly disappointed.

"It was nice talking to you."

"Maybe I'll see you in the neighborhood sometime," he said.

She smiled and turned away before he had a chance to ask for her phone number. "There you are!" she called to Ruth. This time she was not shy about elbowing her way into the crowd. "I thought I'd lost you." She managed to get close enough to the punch table to set down her cup, where it was gathered up by the rabbi's wife.

"I saw you talking to someone," Ruth said. "Did he ask for your telephone number?"

"I escaped before he had the chance." Eleanor looked at Ruth, and Ruth looked back. Then they both burst out laughing.

"So he's not the fella who's going to help you get over Ira," Ruth said.

"No." Eleanor was suddenly serious again. "But look, Ruthie, look at all the other fish—or *fellas*—in the sea." And with that, she moved deeper into the crowd, headed in the direction of the rugelach.

The next morning, Eleanor got up early and had coffee with her mother. The single window in their kitchen faced the back of the building, and looked out onto a collage of other tenements, fire escapes, and clotheslines. Striped boxer shorts hung side by side with cotton housedresses, aprons, and tiny socks. She thought of the Bellamys' dining room: two windows on one wall, a third on another. The view from that apartment was, she knew, quite different: no clotheslines, no tenements.

It was a short walk to Park Avenue and Eleanor had started out so early that she had plenty of time to window-shop along the way. In a store on Lexington Avenue, she saw a lovely raw silk summer dress with a full gathered skirt. As she continued down the street, she entertained a fantasy of buying the dress with her new salary. She'd wear it with her hair up, and her pearl and cameo choker, though the pearls were fake. But then she tried to imagine who would be escorting her in this lovely outfit, and the fantasy collapsed, like a soufflé when the oven door banged.

At the synagogue mixer, after high-voiced Harry, she had talked to a stocky fellow with frizzy blond curls and another taller young man with wavy dark hair and the most adorable dimples. The stocky fellow did not do much for her but the one with the dimples did; unfortunately, he did not reciprocate her interest and had quickly moved on. Eleanor drank another cup of punch and sampled the rugelach—they were stale—before finding Ruth again, this time deep in conversation with a bearlike young man who had gentle brown eyes and a nice smile. Ruth seemed effervescent in his presence and talked about him all the way home. Eleanor just nodded, all the while wishing she had met someone who made her feel that way.

"Listen to me going on and on!" Ruth said when they had reached Eleanor's corner. "Next time it'll be your turn to get lucky."

As she reached Patricia Bellamy's apartment building, Eleanor hesitated for a moment before going inside. When Mrs. Bellamy had offered her the job, she told her to give her name as Moss, and not Moskowitz. "I hope you don't mind," Mrs. Bellamy had said. "It's just that the building is—"

"Restricted," Eleanor supplied.

"Yes, well, I know it's awkward, and of course I don't feel that way, but I'd just rather not ruffle any feathers, if you know what I mean."

"I know exactly what you mean." Ironically, Moss was one of the names Rita Burns had suggested. Eleanor had been less open to the idea when Miss Burns had floated it but now here she was, willingly walking into a situation where the subterfuge was not just expedient, but essential.

"She's expecting you," the doorman said, and directed her toward the elevator. Did she detect a slight sneer, as if he didn't believe her? Or was she imagining it? The lobby seemed even more intimidating than it had on the prior occasions she had seen it. And she was nervous about working with Margaux—the girl was unpredictable and touchy. Why had Eleanor thought she would be able to handle her? Perhaps she'd been rash in accepting this offer.

When Eleanor reached the ninth floor, Mrs. Bellamy was at the door of the apartment. She wore a belted china blue dress with a square neckline framed by a wide ivory collar. The collar was trimmed with miniature magenta roses and the pockets were adorned by those same roses. Eleanor had never seen such a pretty dress; it made the one she'd admired in the shop window seem quite ordinary by comparison.

"Good morning," Mrs. Bellamy said brightly. "Margaux's been waiting for you."

"I hope I'm not late," Eleanor said. Reflexively, she looked at her wrist. The watch was not there; since the accident she hadn't had time to have the crystal replaced.

"No, not at all," Mrs. Bellamy said, stepping aside. "She's just very eager. Let's go into the study."

Eleanor followed Mrs. Bellamy down a short hallway lined with finely rendered botanical prints in thin gold frames. Eager was good, she thought. Eager meant that whatever fragile rapport she thought she had established with Margaux was not just in her mind. Mrs. Bellamy stopped at an open doorway. Unlike what Eleanor had seen of the rest of the apartment——the dining room with its long, highly polished table and graceful chairs covered in a gold silk brocade, the soigné lines of the furnishings in the living room——the décor here, though clearly expensive, was in execrable taste. Dark, stifling drapes. Leather-covered sofa and chairs. A massive desk facing a full wall of shelves lined with matched sets of leather-covered, gold-embossed volumes that looked like they were seldom——if ever—— read. Over the mantel——a hulking thing in ponderous black-veined marble——hung an intricately worked antique gun; on the opposite wall, a large mounted fish with a flat black eye.

"Here's Margaux," Mrs. Bellamy said. Clearly, Margaux's demeanor was not affected by the cheerless and oppressive nature of her surroundings; she looked animated and alert. Her dark blond hair was held back by a black velvet headband and she wore a pair of slacks and a blouse with a small rounded collar. Unlike so many polio victims whose spines had been irreparably twisted by the disease, her posture was good; were it not for the walking stick, propped to her left, no one would guess that there was anything wrong. A carved library table in front of her held several books, all neatly lined up, as well as a few notebooks, a pad, and some pencils.

"I've been asking Mother when you'd get here." Margaux moved over so her tutor could sit down. Her eyes——a dark, intense blue—— sought out Eleanor's.

"I'm going to leave you two now," Mrs. Bellamy said. "Let me know if you need anything." She closed the door behind her.

"So tell me what you were working on with Mr. Cobb." Mrs. Bellamy had actually filled her in, but Eleanor thought it would be good to hear it directly from Margaux.

"Mr. Cobb was the most boring man in the world," said Margaux. "Does it really matter what we talked about?"

Margaux was right. Did Eleanor really care what the crushingly dull Mr. Cobb had said? She did not. Feeling a surge of confidence, she examined the pile of books on the table. A copy of *Romeo and Juliet*, an anthology of British poetry, *Jane Eyre*. Beneath these, several textbooks: algebra, American history, and biology. She picked up the copy of *Romeo and Juliet*. She'd found that, with its youthful protagonists, it was a play that often appealed to her students. She was a good teacher, she reminded herself; she could reach this girl. "So," she said, opening the book to the first page. "Let's begin."

Three hours later, there was a knock at the door and then Mrs. Bellamy's elegantly coiffed head appeared. "Ready for some lunch?"

"Is it lunchtime already?" Margaux asked.

"Yes, darling, it is," Mrs. Bellamy said. But her eyes were on Eleanor and her look clearly said, *Whatever you're doing here, would you please keep doing it?*

Lunch was lively, with Margaux an active, if not dominant, participant in the conversation. "Did you know that the first fourteen lines Romeo and Juliet say to each other form a sonnet?" she asked her mother. "And that Juliet is only fourteen when the play starts."

"And you'll be fourteen next year," her mother said with pleasure. "It seems like you're really enjoying Shakespeare."

"Miss Moskowitz makes it so much fun. We've been reading some of the scenes out loud—it's like we're actors onstage." Margaux took a large bite of her egg sandwich—made especially by Henryka without mayonnaise—for emphasis.

Eleanor could feel Mrs. Bellamy beaming in her direction, but she did not let her gaze meet her employer's; she did not want Margaux to feel patronized by their reaction to her enthusiasm. So instead she took a smaller and more decorous bite of her own sandwich, and nodded when asked if she wanted more lemonade. She looked forward to finishing the meal and returning to the study for an afternoon session with Margaux. They were going to tackle the algebra lesson and then biology. Tomorrow they would continue with Shakespeare and move on to history as well. And she'd promised to bring along her own Latin textbook; Margaux had been asking her about Latin and expressed an interest in studying it.

"Why not feed her interest?" Eleanor had said to Mrs. Bellamy.

"Why not?" Mrs. Bellamy had replied, eyes shining.

So after the tea and cookies were served, Eleanor and Margaux once again returned to the study and closed the door. "I used to fall asleep when he would try to explain this to me," Margaux said, settling into the sofa and fiddling with the brass rivets studding its edge. "But I have a feeling that I'll understand it better with you."

At three o' clock, when Mrs. Bellamy once again poked her head into the room, Margaux was aglow with her newfound understanding of the five basic concepts of biology; she insisted on enumerating them for her bemused mother: "Cell theory, gene theory, evolution, homeostasis, and the laws of thermodynamics." She turned to Eleanor. "Is that right?"

"It's perfect," said Eleanor. She herself had needed to brush up on the topic before she had taught it to Margaux and was pleased with how quickly the girl caught on.

Margaux's tremulous smile was its own sweet reward and when she asked, "You'll come back tomorrow, right?" Eleanor could answer with assurance, "Yes, I'll see you then."

Eleanor walked slowly home, welcoming the chance to be outside before returning to the apartment. She and her mother took turns making supper; it was something Eleanor had first initiated and then insisted upon. "But you work all day," her mother had said.

"So do you," Eleanor had replied. "And besides, my workday is shorter."

And so the pattern was set. Tonight was one of Eleanor's nights, and she headed uptown and east, toward the cluster of stores under the perforated shadow of the Third Avenue El, where they did the bulk of their shopping. She bought a cut-up chicken, which she would panfry and serve with rice. A greengrocer on the same block yielded a head of lettuce and two ripe tomatoes, along with three pounds of sweet peas for ten cents, and three of yams, for fourteen. She decided to splurge on a box of lace cookies from their favorite bakery on Eighty-Second. With their thin filling of dark chocolate sandwiched by the fretwork of pastry, they were her mother's favorites, yet she seldom bought them because of the expense. Still, tonight was a celebration of sorts—Eleanor's first day on her new job.

Her mother was already in the kitchen, taking the dishes out of the cabinet.

"I could have done that, Mother," Eleanor said, hurriedly putting down her bundles and taking off her hat.

"I can set the table," her mother said. "It's enough that you're making dinner."

"How was your day?" Eleanor asked as she washed her hands in the kitchen sink and put on an apron.

"Busy," her mother said as she laid out the everyday cutlery with its amber-colored Bakelite handles. "I had a bride."

"Really?" Eleanor put the rice up and began rinsing the chicken parts. Her mother's shop did not generally cater to the bridal trade.

"A second marriage," Irina explained. "She's going to be wearing a suit, and so I'm doing a little ivory toque, with silk orange blossoms and a half veil."

"Swell," Eleanor said. She patted the chicken dry gently, wondering if she would ever be a bride, even once.

"She had two bridesmaids with her," her mother continued. "They need hats too. We're doing those in periwinkle. But no veils or flowers; only a small crystal button on each."

"Sounds elegant." Eleanor began to prepare the salad. As she sliced the tomatoes, her mother had finished setting the table and discovered the bakery box. Cutting the red-and-white string to open it, Irina said, "Lace cookies. My favorite." Then she looked at her daughter. "You haven't told me about your day. Did it go well?"

"Yes," said Eleanor. "I really like the girl. Margaux."

"Well, that's a good start," her mother said. "But what about the future? Even if this does work out, what will happen when she gets older? You'll have no security."

"I told you: I can always apply for a teaching job in a school next spring. Or the fall after that. And I'm still in touch with that Miss Burns from the employment agency. Don't worry so much."

"Well, at least you're thinking ahead," Irina said. "Women have to think ahead. Especially women who don't have rich fathers or husbands to support them." She took down a blue glass dish from the cupboard and began to arrange the cookies on it.

Eleanor had heard all this before and even though she knew her mother was right, it irritated her. What if she didn't want to think ahead for once? What if she just wanted to see where life took her? She poured oil into a pan to heat. While waiting, she dusted the chicken parts with a mixture of flour, salt, pepper, and celery seed. When the oil started sputtering, she began laying the chicken in the pan. She thought of the day's small indignities: the slightly surly housekeeper, the cool look of the doorman when she'd given him the false name—and decided that the time spent with Margaux outweighed them all. This job was going to work, she told herself. She was going to *make* it work.

"Do you remember that dark green felt hat you made?" Eleanor asked when they were seated at the table. "It had a velvet ribbon and that one perfect faux jewel?"

"Yes!" Irina used a heel of bread to sop up juice from the chicken. "The woman who wanted to buy it asked if I could add another jewel, and another and another?"

"And you said, 'Madam, if I add one more ornament to this hat, people are going to think it's a Christmas tree!'" This was an old joke, but they both enjoyed the punch line as much as they had the first time Irina had repeated it.

"And she never came back!" Eleanor said.

"Never!" said Irina. "And you know what? I didn't care! Sometimes you just have to do what you think is right, even if it's *not* the practical thing."

"I'm glad you said that to her." Eleanor felt a flash of pride for her mother. "She didn't deserve that hat."

Eleanor put the kettle on and Irina fetched the new issue of *Vogue*, which they looked at together while they had their tea and cookies.

"Patricia Bellamy has a dress that color." Eleanor pointed to a lovely pink dress with a full skirt and bow at the neckline.

"You said she dresses well," Irina said.

"Very."

"What kind of woman is she?"

"She seems kind. Compassionate. When she saw how upset I was, she brought me to her apartment to get cleaned up. She gave me lunch."

"She was probably worried you would sue her."

"Sue her? That's ridiculous. She wasn't even driving."

"You don't know what she was really thinking. They're sneaky."

Eleanor didn't need to ask who "they" were—she was all too familiar with her mother's distrust of the Gentile world. When Eleanor had been accepted at Vassar, Irina's pride had been mingled with that same distrust. "They'll snub you. Mock you," she had said. "You'll just have to show them that you're as good as they are."

Her mother had not been entirely wrong about Vassar. On Eleanor's very first day, a girl with a flaxen pageboy had stopped her in the hallway of Main Building. "There's still time to switch rooms," the girl had said.

"What do you mean?" Eleanor asked.

"You haven't actually moved in yet, have you?" The girl gestured to Eleanor's suitcase and pair of hatboxes.

"No, but I'm about to."

"That's what I'm saying. I'm trying to warn you."

"Warn me?"

"It's your roommate. Her name is Eleanor Moskowitz. You can ask for a different roommate before she gets here."

"*I'm* Eleanor Moskowitz."

There had been a brief, mortifying silence during which the girl's hands flew to her mouth, as if to cram the offending words back in. Then she'd fled.

It had not ended there. Eleanor recalled the slights, the omissions. Invitations extended to an entire group—except her. Looks that passed back and forth between some of the girls as she walked by or took her seat in class. Certain coded words she had come to recognize: *ambitious* for *pushy*, *self-confident* for *arrogant*, *principled* for *stubborn*. But those same girls also taught her things that were valuable, things she wanted to know. They knew how to talk, to comport themselves, and to dress, even the ones without much money. She admired their manners, their confidence, their restraint. They didn't make her want to change who she was. But they made her want to be the best version of herself.

And then there was the intellectual awakening that had been invigorating, if not thrilling. The symmetrical beauty of a line of Latin verse. A lecture hall where an impassioned professor had held forth about *Pride and Prejudice* and *Vanity Fair*. A drama department production of *The Cherry Orchard* in which she'd played the role of Anya. Three-hundred-level seminars in Shakespeare, astronomy field trips that brought the night sky dazzlingly into view. Vassar had been all those things too.

The telephone rang, giving Eleanor a small reprieve. It seemed that she and her mother were never going to be in accord on this subject. Shaped by her past, Irina would always harbor a certain fear of those she considered other. But Eleanor was more curious than fearful; she wanted to find out more about Patricia, Margaux, and the world they came from. Maybe, just maybe, there would be a place for her in it.

SIX

Patricia sat at the breakfast table, sipping her coffee. Eleanor was due to arrive any minute for her second day on the job, and Margaux was already impatient. "It's after nine," she said. "She should be coming soon, shouldn't she?" she asked again.

"I'm sure she'll be here any minute," her mother said. She was nervous too, about Eleanor's arrival, but for an entirely different reason—Eleanor had not yet met Wynn. Yesterday he'd gone into the office early but today he was still in the apartment, taking what seemed to Patricia an unusually long time getting ready. What was he doing in there?

He finally sailed into the dining room, cheerful and magnanimous, pausing to kiss the top of Margaux's head before sitting down at the table, where he complimented Henryka lavishly on the shirred eggs. Then the doorman rang to say Eleanor Moss was coming up and when Patricia saw Wynn's eyebrows go up, ever so slightly, she felt a rope of fear tighten inside.

"I've heard good things about you," he said when Patricia introduced them.

"That would be from me," Margaux said. "I've told Daddy everything." She patted an empty chair beside her. "Sit with me and have some breakfast? Henryka's made eggs and they're so good."

"Thanks, I've already eaten," said Eleanor who nevertheless sat down beside Margaux. "But some coffee would be nice."

Henryka brought the coffee and set it down a little too hard on the table. A few drops flew up and landed in the saucer. Now what? Patricia could sense Henryka was cross, but didn't know why. Was it because of Eleanor? Patricia had anticipated a problem with Wynn, but not Henryka, who'd been with her forever, and knew every ripple and eddy in their household. Well, clearly she'd need to have a talk with her, though now was not the time.

"I noticed your hat as soon as you came in, Miss Moss," said Wynn. "It's very becoming."

"It is," Patricia agreed. Eleanor's hats were far nicer—and more expensive looking—than her clothes. "Where did you get it?"

"My mother made it," Eleanor said. "Maybe you know her shop? It's on Second Avenue and Eighty-Fourth Street—"

"You know, I think I *may* have heard of it," Patricia said. "But I've never been there." She was only being polite. She had not in fact heard of the shop; she rarely strayed so far east. But she was intrigued. Refined, Latin-reading Eleanor had a mother who was a milliner. How had a hatmaker's daughter ended up at Vassar, anyway? Eleanor continued to surprise her.

"Second Avenue," mused Wynn. "I never get over there. Do you think I should, Miss Moss? Is there a lot to see?"

"It depends on what you're looking for." Eleanor seemed slightly uncomfortable and Patricia felt like she was ingesting that discomfort along with her eggs.

"Nothing in particular," Wynn said. "I just like to . . . look."

"I doubt you'd be looking for a ladies' hat shop, Daddy," said Margaux as she buttered her toast.

"That's true," said Wynn. "I leave the hat buying to your mother. I just pay the bills." He took a forkful of his eggs and looked over at Eleanor again. "My wife tells me that you were at Brandon-Wythe."

"I was," said Eleanor.

"Good school. One of the best. What made you leave?"

The table seemed to go very quiet and Patricia watched as Eleanor set down her coffee cup. "Well, I just wanted to go in a different direction and—" Before she could finish, both the bell and the phone rang almost in unison. The bell turned out to be a delivery and the phone was Wynn's office and by the time he'd finished the call, Eleanor and Margaux had left the table and gone into the study to work.

"Just stop that!" Patricia hissed when she and her husband were alone.

"Stop what?" He gave her a wide-eyed look—the big phony.

"Stop grilling her."

"Well, aren't you the least bit curious about why she left? It can't have been easy for her to get that job. So why would she leave? Maybe she was fired."

"I doubt it. She had a perfectly marvelous letter from the headmistress."

"That still doesn't answer the question about why she left."

"Well, maybe it was about money. We're paying her more than she was making there."

"And how do you happen to know that?" he asked.

Henryka appeared with more coffee and Patricia waited until she'd gone before replying. "I asked around before I settled on a salary."

"Clever you." He patted his mouth with a damask napkin and stood.

"As for Miss Moss's decision to seek out *greener* pastures, I suppose that makes sense. Looking for a financial edge."

"Aren't we all?" Patricia was annoyed by her husband's dig about Eleanor's background. But Wynn had already left the room and seconds later, the apartment. It was only then that she felt she could finally exhale. At least the first meeting between her husband and her daughter's new tutor was over. Patricia would try to make sure all subsequent encounters went more smoothly; she didn't want Wynn to scare Eleanor off.

Walking down the hallway, Patricia stopped before the closed door behind which Eleanor was cloistered with Margaux. She used to do this when Mr. Cobb came too, and so remembered the various tones of voice—pleading, exasperated, resigned—that he'd used to deal with Margaux's seemingly intractable hostility. Today, though, she heard Eleanor's measured, quiet voice intercut with Margaux's higher, more insistent one. And then she heard something she had not heard in months: the sound of Margaux's laughter. Patricia's own face bloomed into a wide smile at the sound. What a sweet, pure delight. How long had it been since Margaux had laughed? Patricia couldn't recall. But here she was, laughing with Eleanor Moskowitz. Patricia did not care a jot why Eleanor had left her old job; nothing would turn her against the person who had wrought this little miracle.

She turned and went back down the hall. She did not need to insert herself into whatever was happening behind that closed door; she did not want to break the spell. She felt almost giddy with relief, and decided to get out, get away from the apartment that had felt oppressive and constricting all morning. Stepping into her bedroom, she fetched her gloves, handbag, and hat—thinking again of that straw number Eleanor had worn—and then went into the kitchen.

"Henryka, I'm going out for a bit. Do you think you can start on the packing without me? Miss Moss is working with Margaux, so you won't be disturbed." They were going off to the country soon and the preparations really did need to get under way.

"Yes, ma'am." Henryka was polishing a silver pitcher that had belonged to some long-dead relative of Wynn's. She kept her back to Patricia as she spoke, a silent but clear indication that she was still miffed about something.

"You don't have to bother with the silver today if it's too much," Patricia said.

"I can do," Henryka said. She turned around. "You go out now. You stay in too much. Fresh air do you good."

"Yes, I think it will."

"You be home for lunch?" Henryka clutched the rag, black with tarnish, in both plump hands.

"Probably not," Patricia said. When she saw Henryka's wounded look she added, "But I'll be looking forward to whatever dinner you're serving for tonight. What do you have planned?" She had to be careful with Henryka, who was visibly hurt if Patricia declined, for any reason, to eat; this was a pattern established years ago, and the intervening decades had not altered it one bit.

"Goulash, noodles, and creamed spinach. And coconut cake."

"You know I'm mad for your goulash," Patricia said. "And no one can resist your coconut cake."

"My coconut cake very good," Henryka said, somewhat mollified.

"You can serve lunch to Margaux and Miss Moss at around twelve thirty."

"She will eat here every day now?"

"Would that bother you?" Henryka said nothing, so Patricia pressed on. "It seems you don't like her."

"She nice girl," Henryka said. "For a *zhid*."

Patricia recognized the slur—Polish for *Yid* and just as insulting. So that was it. "Well, Jewish or not, Margaux likes her very much."

"She do." Henryka's subtle defiance had softened; she cared for Margaux and had suffered along with Patricia during her illness.

"So it's important that we make her feel comfortable here. Welcomed."

"Mr. Bellamy—he make her feel welcome?"

"He will," Patricia said firmly. "He'll get to know her better, and when he does, he'll come to like her as much as Margaux does."

"Oh, I think he like her right now. I think he like her just fine." She turned away and resumed her polishing.

Patricia stared for a moment at Henryka's back. What in the world did she mean by that? She waited a few seconds, but clearly Henryka wasn't going to elaborate. Fine. She'd had enough of this for one morning. She slipped on her gloves, but before she headed out, she saw that there was a stain on the front of her dress, so she quickly changed into the blue dress she'd worn yesterday. It was one of her favorites and she always felt so pretty in it.

It was a magnificent day. The previous night's heat had lifted and there was the most delightful breeze that swooped up random bits of paper from the sidewalk and raised them festively in the air, like confetti. Patricia took a big breath and, though she had no clear destination in mind, stepped up her pace.

It had been a day like this, just a little over two years ago, when the announcement came that the war in Europe was finally over. Hitler, that insanely evil, raving man—he spat when he spoke, Patricia had seen it clearly in one of the newsreels—had shot himself in April and by early May, the so-called thousand-year Reich had toppled.

Wynn had been about to go to his office on West Forty-Fourth

Street when they got the news, and on impulse, Margaux and Patricia had gone along with him. They couldn't find a cab, so they decided to walk down Fifth Avenue before heading west, to Times Square. The closer they got to their destination, the more crowded and jubilant the streets became. Cars honked and people cheered; some held up copies of the newspapers, whose headlines proclaimed "The War in Europe Ends! Surrender Unconditional" and "Nazis Give Up." Sailors in their dazzling white uniforms swarmed the area, pumping the hands of strangers, kissing girls. People were laughing, embracing, wiping tears of joy from their eyes. Policemen with bullhorns barked out instructions from Mayor La Guardia, telling everyone to behave.

Wynn had been spared from actual combat by the loss of hearing in one ear and had a desk job stateside for the duration, but Tom had been sent to France almost immediately and Patricia had been plagued with nightmares in which he'd been shot, blown up, or simply swallowed by the great maw of battle, never to be heard from again. Now she could put down the burden of that worry. The pinch of rationing would be over too. The country—and the world—would be at peace. That this monstrous dictator had been taken down, that the forces of justice and democracy had, at least for the moment, prevailed made her feel buoyant and hopeful about so many things. Maybe Wynn would make partner—he wanted it so very much—and maybe, even after all the years of disappointment, she'd have another child.

But the euphoric feeling didn't last. There was still fighting in the Pacific, and August brought the incomprehensible news that atomic bombs had been dropped not once but twice, first in Hiroshima and then in Nagasaki; thousands of people were instantly incinerated. The reports started trickling, then pouring in, about the so-called work camps where people, Jews mostly, but others too, had been warehoused and turned into virtual slaves. That is, if they had not been gassed or shot to death first. The pictures, when Patricia could bring herself to look at them, made her feel like she was witnessing the end of the world. Wynn did not make partner, and began drinking more heavily. Their marital relations turned into a chore rather than a delight. Patricia's hopes for another baby ended, as they always did, in a clench of pain and a puddle of blood. Then Margaux contracted polio and Patricia had embarked on the frantic, desperate quest—the specialists, the hot packs, and the dreaded iron lung—to save her life.

Still, on this glorious June day, hope made a tentative return. Margaux had laughed this morning. Laughed out loud, and Patricia had been there to hear it. Margaux was animated for the first time in months. She wanted to study Latin. The sun was streaming down on the sidewalks, and on the elegant facades of Park Avenue. Instead of heading down toward Fifty-Seventh Street, or west toward Madison or Fifth as she usually did, Patricia turned east, toward Second Avenue. She had a sudden yen to see Hats by Irina. So, swinging her bag by one hand, she set out to do exactly that. But the going was slow; the ground floors of the tightly packed brick tenements contained so many quaint and unfamiliar shops to tempt her. German and Hungarian delicatessens where whole roasted fowl gleamed in the windows, and a dozen different kinds of sausage hung on hooks from the ceiling. Strange cheeses in wedges, in wheels, in bars, and in blocks. Groceries that sold loose spices, sharp or sweet mustards, stores that offered gauzy white blouses thick with embroidery and hand-painted wooden eggs. Patricia stopped at a pastry shop for a cup of tea and despite the promise of coconut cake that evening, ate a piece of apple strudel, light and delicious, its still warm filling oozing onto the plate. Had she not feared offending Henryka, Patricia would have brought one home.

Fortified by the sweet, she kept going, only to be sidetracked by an appealingly jumbled antiques shop where her perseverance was rewarded by a crystal paperweight for Wynn—a replacement for one Margaux had broken—and a small gold ring with an oval-shaped moonstone at its center for Margaux. Then it was a secondhand bookstore that detained her. There, amid the crammed shelves and perfumed dust of the past, was a linen-bound edition of Shakespeare's sonnets illustrated with hand-tinted plates that seemed as if had been created for the sole purpose of delighting Eleanor Moskowitz. Not that Patricia had a specific reason to buy the girl a gift. On the other hand, she had every reason in the world, she thought as the shopkeeper wrote out the receipt.

It was past two o'clock by the time she reached Eighty-Fourth Street, and there it was, Hats by Irina. Eleanor had told her that she and her mother lived in the apartment above the shop. Patricia studied the window. There was a hat very much like the one Eleanor had worn today, a pale straw cloche with a small cluster of cherries on one side. There were others too, like the wide-brimmed black straw and the tipped tricorne made entirely of feathers. All looked very well made and stylish. They would not have been out of place in the millinery department at Bergdorf Goodman, and yet here they were, in this unprepossessing little shop far north of fashion's familiar center. She would have no trouble picking out a hat, that was clear.

Patricia peered inside, beyond the display. No customers were in the shop but there was a lone woman behind the counter. Not young, but possessed of good posture. Short gray hair, marcelled in a style popular at least fifteen years ago. Dark dress with a white lace collar. Silver brooch pinned at the center of the dress, between the collar's two points. So this was Irina Moskowitz, Eleanor's mother. The resemblance was there—the dark eyes, the delicate mouth—easy enough to see. Patricia went in and a small bell tinkled, noting her entrance.

"May I help you?" said Irina. She had just the slightest accent and her tone was pleasant, not pushy.

"Do you mind if I browse?" Patricia asked, eyes roaming around the shop. Should she reveal her identity as Eleanor's employer? She wasn't sure, but the indecision, and the feeling that she was somehow deceiving the woman by not revealing this fact, caused her heart to accelerate just a bit. "I've never been in here before; you have such lovely things."

"Thank you," Irina said.

"Do you make them yourself?"

"Yes. I do." The quiet pride in that statement was evident.

"So you're Irina." Patricia gestured to the window, where the gold letters spelling out the shop's name appeared backward. She knew the answer of course, but thought she was doing a good job pretending this was new to her.

"I am. And please let me know if you'd like to try anything." Patricia nodded as she surveyed the shop. Two small oval mirrors on stands stood on either end of the glass-topped counter, and in the corner was one large cheval glass. She approved; sometimes it was essential to see how the hat looked with the entire ensemble. Inside the glass-topped case lay hair ornaments, combs and clasps made of tortoiseshell, ivory, and mother-of-pearl. Patricia admired one of the latter; she thought it would look very smart on her own blond coif. But really, it was a hat she wanted.

"Actually, there's something I'd like to try," she said to Irina. "That one, over there." Patricia pointed to a tightly fitting paisley cap shaped like a broken eggshell, with jagged points extending down and framing the face on both sides.

"You have excellent taste," Irina said approvingly. "This is one of the most original hats in the store." She removed it from the black lacquer stand and handed it to Patricia. "The material is a textured silk, made in Italy. Can you feel the weave? Not every woman would have the confidence to carry it off."

Patricia took off her own hat and slipped on the cap, which fit perfectly. She walked over to the cheval glass. The hat gave her face an unfamiliar, even startling look. But it was also very chic and modern looking, with colors—deep fuchsia, scarlet, indigo, and a surprising bit of marigold—that were at once exotic and radical. She could see this hat with a dark suit, a dinner dress, or even her mink coat. It was a gem, a small, startling explosion that broke open the strictures of convention and predictability. Which, at that moment, seemed exactly what Patricia wanted.

"I'll take it," she said.

"You'll be the only woman wearing this hat," said Irina, looking pleased. Her smile made her look younger and Patricia had the realization that she wasn't old so much as careworn; hers had not been an easy life. "I just made one, and I won't make another." She took the hat back from Patricia and began to wrap it in black tissue paper that she pulled out from a drawer behind her.

"Really?" asked Patricia, feeling even more pleased with her decision.

"Yes. I felt that this hat should go to someone special and that there shouldn't be another." She climbed onto a stepladder and reached up, toward the shelf that ran the length of the store. On it was a row of round black hatboxes, each with a band of white bisecting its center. It was only when Irina had taken one down and packed the new purchase in it that Patricia saw the top: a series of black and white concentric circles, like a target. And in the black center, the same elegant gold script that adorned the window: HATS BY IRINA.

Patricia thought of the trademark boxes from stores all over the city. Henri Bendel had its signature brown and white stripes; Bonwit Teller, sprigs of violets. There was Schiaparelli's shocking pink box, and the black-gloved hand holding a single rose at Lord & Taylor. This pared down black-and-white box could hold its own with any of them.

Thanking Irina for her help, Patricia paid six dollars in cash for the hat, which would have cost three or even four times that at Bergdorf's or Bonwit Teller. She stepped out into the still glorious day. It was almost five o'clock so she hailed a cab. As she leaned back against the seat, her packages tucked safely beside her, she looked again at the hatbox and put her hands on it possessively.

She felt the thrill of the hunt that shopping often gave her and today there was the added frisson of having snared something that none of her friends would have. But there was more to it than that. This hat, and its maker, were two more pieces in the puzzle that was Eleanor.

The taxi dropped her off in front of her building and the doorman hurried out as she was handing the driver a bill. She took the elevator up to her apartment, and let herself in quietly. She was not sure if Eleanor was still here, but she took the precaution of going straight to her bedroom and stowing the hatbox out of sight. She'd disperse the gifts she bought at some later time. Today's outing was her secret, and it was not the only one. She had not revealed herself to Eleanor's mother, and because she hadn't, she realized that she couldn't tell Eleanor about the visit either. Why did this make her so agitated, as if she had committed some petty crime?

"Patricia?" That was Wynn's voice coming from the foyer; he must have just gotten home. "Coming," she called back. And closing the bedroom door behind her, she went out to greet him.

SEVEN

On the fifth of July, Eleanor met Ruth at B. Altman, where together they scoured the sale racks. It was a successful mission: Eleanor found a lightweight dress, two skirts, a pair of summer trousers—not unlike those worn by Katharine Hepburn, one of her favorite movie stars—and a navy blue Cole of California bathing suit with white polka dots and a halter neck. In the May issue, *Harper's Bazaar* had shown a very daring photo of a young woman in a two-piece swimsuit called a bikini; Eleanor could not imagine ever wearing such a thing and thought the one-piece was revealing enough. After they finished shopping, they stopped at Mary Elizabeth's Tea Room for lunch.

"I'll miss you this summer." Ruth drew deeply on her straw and the iced tea in her glass subsided in response.

"I'll miss you too," said Eleanor. "But I'll write." Her new employers had already left town for Connecticut; there hadn't been enough room in the car for all of them, so Eleanor was taking the train up tomorrow. She was glad to be spared the ride with Henryka, who she was certain disliked her, and Mr. Bellamy, who, while never anything but polite, still made her uneasy. His was the kind of civility that radiated insincerity and she did not trust it—or him. He'd only be up on weekends, and since the house had a guest cottage—where Eleanor would be lodged—she hoped she would not have to see all that much of him.

"Do you know what the house looks like?"

"White, with dark shutters," Eleanor said, taking a bite of her sandwich. "Patricia says there have been additions made over the years, like a third story and a sunporch out back. And there are at least two gardens. The pictures I saw showed a lot of flowers."

"Imagine having all that *and* a swanky apartment on Park Avenue."

"There's a guest cottage too; that's where I'll be staying. Two whole rooms, all to myself." There were two overlapping pickle slices on the side of the heavy blue plate; Eleanor speared one and popped it neatly into her mouth.

"I'll bet it's really posh," Ruth said. "Do they have a pool?"

"No, but there's one at their club."

"A club sounds dreamy." Ruth took a large bite of her own sandwich. "I'll bet they have dances and parties too. Maybe you'll even meet someone." Another bite and half the sandwich was gone.

"None of those clubs will admit Jews," Eleanor pointed out. "I use the name Moss when I'm with the Bellamys."

"Really? What does your mother have to say about that?"

"I haven't told her," Eleanor said. "And I'm not going to either, so don't you bring it up in front of her."

"I won't, don't worry," said Ruth. "But do you really have to do it, Ellie? What if you said no?"

"Not possible," said Eleanor. "Not if I want this job. And I do. Working with Margaux, helping her break through that shell—I can't tell you how satisfying that's been, even in the short time I've been doing it. And there's something about Mrs. Bellamy too. I can't imagine being her friend exactly but I wish I could get to know her better. So if I have to pretend about my name, it feels like a small price to pay." She finished her own sandwich. "Would you do it? If you were in my place?"

"I'm not sure," Ruth said. Unlike Eleanor, she'd stayed in the city after graduating from high school, and gone to City College for two years before she left to start working. "I can't really imagine myself with people like that."

The waiter appeared with dessert menus.

"I shouldn't order anything." Ruth was always struggling to lose a few pounds. "But I'll have the lemon pound cake if you'll share with me."

When the waiter had gone, Ruth reconsidered the question. "No, I don't think I would change my name," she said. "But, Ellie, that doesn't mean you shouldn't. You've always wanted something different. That's part of why you went to Vassar, isn't it? To get out of the neighborhood, meet new people?"

"It's true," Eleanor said. "But at Vassar, I was still Eleanor Moskowitz. I didn't have to pretend to be someone else."

"You'll always be Eleanor Moskowitz," said Ruth, who looked enchanted by the slice of cake that was set before her. "No matter what you call yourself."

And that, Eleanor realized, was true.

When she got home, Eleanor laid out all her new purchases on her bed; she'd show her mother when she came upstairs. Irina was working late, putting the finishing touches on the hats for the bridal party. Eleanor had picked up an inexpensive skirt steak on the way home; she'd broil it and fry onions to go on top; scalloped potatoes would be the side dish. For dessert, she'd slice some strawberries and sprinkle them with sugar. Dinner was pleasant, even festive. Irina took out a bottle of sweet wine she'd stowed away and they each had a glass along with their strawberries. After the dishes were done, Eleanor took her mother into her room to see the day's purchases. Irina approved of the dress, which was made of light blue eyelet. "It'll look fresh even on a hot day." She fingered the material in a professional sort of way. "I'd like to make you a new hat before you go."

"I have plenty of hats, Mother," Eleanor said. "You work too hard as it is."

"I want to," Irina insisted. "The right hat can make any outfit."

"So you've said." Eleanor smiled. "More than once."

Irina moved the clothes aside so she could sit down on the bed. "It's not just your clothes I'm thinking about. It's everything. I'm worried. You hardly know these people after all."

"That's not true. I feel like I know them quite well. At least Mrs. Bellamy and Margaux. And I don't have to deal with the husband very much."

"But you'll be stuck up there, not knowing anyone else. No one of your own kind."

"Really, Mother, do you think that matters anymore?" Eleanor was not being truthful; she knew it mattered quite a lot. Hadn't she admitted as much to Ruth?

"Anyway, I'll miss you."

Ruth had said that too. But hearing it from her mother was harder. When Eleanor had gone off to Vassar, her father had been alive. Now Irina would be alone. "It's not for that long," she told her mother. "And you could always come to visit," she offered, though she could not imagine how *that* was going to work.

"No, *tochter*, I don't think so." Irina only reached for Yiddish in moments of stress or sorrow. "You go hobnob with the goyim. I'll stay here."

Eleanor began folding her new clothes. "Maybe it would be nice to have a new hat after all," she said. "Something summery."

"I can start it tomorrow." Irina brightened. "First thing, before I open. The hats for the bride and her friends are done."

"All right," Eleanor said. "And even if no one else notices, Mrs. Bellamy will appreciate it."

"Does she wear nice hats?" Irina asked.

"Very nice. She shops at Bergdorf's and Bonwit's. Saks too. But I still think your hats are more original than theirs. That little egg-shaped one you made? From the gorgeous Italian paisley? I can see it in the pages of *Vogue* or *Harper's Bazaar*." With the folding completed, she turned to the valise—leather, somewhat battered—that waited on the floor.

"Did I tell you I sold it?" Irina said. "To a very elegant woman. I'd never seen her before. She wasn't one of my regulars." The valise, which Eleanor had put on the bed, was now open, and Irina began putting the new clothes inside.

"No, you didn't tell me," Eleanor said.

"Sometimes these rich ladies come back. And when they do, they bring their rich friends with them."

"Did you get her name?"

"No. I'd recognize her right away if she came in again though. She was a little taller than you. A little older too. Blond hair in a twist. Pearl earrings. And such a beautiful dress—blue, with little satin roses on the collar and pockets."

"What color were the roses?" Eleanor stopped, a white shell sweater and matching cardigan draped over one arm.

"Magenta, I think. With dark green leaves. Why do you ask?"

"Patricia Bellamy has a dress just like that. What kind of hat was she wearing?"

Irina described it and Eleanor said, "That was her. Patricia Bellamy. She came to your store, but she didn't tell you who she was?" She laid the sweater set on the bed before sitting down.

"Maybe she didn't realize I was your mother."

"That's not possible," Eleanor said, puzzled. "I've mentioned the shop—where it was, the name—to her. She must have known."

"If she knew who I was, why didn't she introduce herself?"

"I have no idea," Eleanor said. And she didn't. Why would Mrs. Bellamy conceal her identity from Irina? It made no sense. But it did suggest that Mrs. Bellamy was as curious about Eleanor's family as Eleanor was about hers.

EIGHT

The snug guest cottage just behind the Bellamys' house in Argyle was ready; Opal, the girl from the village who did the heavy work, had swept the brick path that ran across the lawn and between the two houses, as well as scrubbed, dusted, and aired out the entire place. Then she had changed the sheets and put a stack of fresh towels next to the claw-footed tub in the bathroom. Patricia had set a white ironstone pitcher filled with wildflowers on the table, flowers that Margaux had insisted on gathering herself. The sight of her daughter, on her knees in the grass, dragging her damaged leg behind her, made Patricia want to bury her face in her hands and sob. But then she thought of Eleanor, who would no doubt have a different way of viewing the scene, Eleanor who had called Margaux plucky. How they needed Eleanor—all of them. Patricia was as glad as Margaux that Eleanor was arriving tonight, on the 5:57 from Grand Central; she'd be here before dark.

Patricia was on the sunporch when Glow, a large ginger cat, jumped up to sit beside her on the wicker settee. Glow was their summer-only cat; in the off-season, she lived with Opal and her family. Stroking the smooth orange fur, Patricia checked her watch; it was only a little before 5:00, which gave her plenty of time to change and get to the station. She'd told Henryka to hold dinner until their guests arrived. Wynn would not be coming up until tomorrow, which was a good thing—she wanted to let Eleanor settle in before she had to deal with him. But even that didn't seem like it was going to be a problem. "Margaux seems . . . better. More like her old self," he'd said just a couple of days ago. "I have to admit that this girl you picked up has had a very good effect on her."

The other person she was expecting tonight was her brother, Tom, who was driving down from Maine. She wasn't sure when he'd get here though; Tom was virtually impossible to pin down about anything. A free spirit, he held no real job, able to live on the generous inheritance their father had left him. In fact, Tom had been left a disproportionately large share of their parents' money, but he'd chosen to give a portion to Patricia so that it was evenly divided.

With the money—quite ample—that was left over, he dabbled, buying paintings from his downtown artist buddies, which he collected, almost warehouse style. He tried his own hand at painting too, as well as poetry, pottery, and writing plays. Wynn called him a dilettante and said he was just waiting for him to grow up. "You'll have to wait a long time, old man," Tom had said. "A very long time."

But Wynn was charmed by Tom, as was everyone else. Tom mocked everything and everyone, most of all himself. His upbringing on Sutton Place, his years at boarding school and then at Princeton—he shrugged it all off, like an overcoat on the first warm day of spring. He adamantly refused to live anywhere respectable and instead inhabited a puzzling warren of rooms that he called an apartment, on Jane Street in Greenwich Village. For the last few months, he'd been in Paris, consorting and, for all she knew, living with an older, divorced woman he'd met when he was over there during the war. He'd fought, valiantly it would seem, inasmuch as he'd come home with a special commendation. But he never spoke of his experiences, no matter how much or how often Patricia badgered him.

"Can I go with you?" Patricia looked up to see Margaux standing in the doorway leaning on her walking stick. Her white dotted-Swiss dress was stained with grass and her braids were loose. "To the station?"

"If you change your dress and comb your hair, yes."

"All right." Margaux turned to go back inside. She had been relocated to a room on the first floor; she could take the stairs one at a time by holding on to the railing and using her good leg, but for what? To prove she could?

Patricia was debating whether to pour herself a gin and tonic— she did not like to drink alone, but she was really in the mood for one—when the front door slammed and a deep male voice called out, "Hello, hello, hello!" Tom! She stood, and the cat, whose nap had been disturbed, gave her a reproachful look before jumping down and darting away. "Trish?" he called. "Are you home?"

"It's Uncle Tommy!" Margaux cried. Tom strode into the room, almost colliding with her.

"Margaux, my kumquat! Let me look at you!" Tom scooped her up and spun her around; the walking stick clattered to the floor.

"Uncle Tommy!" Margaux squealed, her arms still encircling his neck.

Finally he set her down, using his arm to steady her while he reached for the walking stick and handed it to her. Then he turned to Patricia. "Your turn." And although he did not lift her off her feet, he spun her around in a tight, dizzying embrace. "How the hell are you?" he said and then added, "Sorry," when he saw the slight frown about his language crossing her face. He wore a linen shirt, very wrinkled, and khaki trousers. No jacket, no tie, no hat. Wynn would have teased him about his "bohemian" pretensions.

"I'm fine," she said, her momentary irritation dissolving. And now that he was here, she was. It was just so good to see him.

"Where were you, Uncle Tommy? And how long are you staying?"

"Damariscotta, and I'll stay as long as your mother will have me."

"You know you have an open invitation," Patricia said. "Do you want to get your things from the car so Henryka can take them upstairs?"

"Oh, that's right. I've been exiled from my cottage by another, more important guest. A usurper, it would seem."

"She's not a usurper—whatever that means," said Margaux. "Her name is Eleanor and she's wonderful. You'll love her; we all do. She's so smart and interesting and pretty. Even Mother thinks so. And she wears the best little hats in the world because her mother is a hatmaker."

"Well, I can't wait to meet this paragon, this tutor-with-the-best-little-hats-in-the-world," Tom said.

"You'll have your chance," Patricia said. "She'll be here soon." And then added, "Is it time for a drink?"

"Is it ever!" Tom said. "I'll just get my things and then we can settle in."

"We'll have to make it quick; I need to change before heading over to the station," Patricia explained. "Margaux, you still need to put on a clean dress if you're coming with me."

Patricia linked her arm through Tom's as her daughter went off to her room. "It's not what you think," she said softly to her brother when they were outside.

"And what is it that I think?" Tom asked. Always teasing her. But with such affection that she didn't mind; she never had. It was just his way.

"That she's some ordinary little drudge. But she's not. She's really quite special. And she's worked wonders with Margaux."

"I can see that," Tom said. He pulled one valise from the backseat, and another from the trunk. "In any case, she's bound to be prettier than Mr. Cobb. The man was a gargoyle."

"Tom." Patricia swatted his arm. "You're terrible." As they began walking back to the house, she added, "Eleanor *is* pretty. But you just keep your hands to yourself."

"Why, Patricia, are you implying that I'm not a gentleman? You wound me, yes you do."

"She's a Jew," Patricia said, and stopped walking. "Eleanor Moskowitz. But I'm introducing her as Eleanor Moss. So please don't cause any trouble and don't give me away, Tom. I'm counting on you."

"The plot thickens," said Tom. "Does Wynn know? He must. But your tony neighbors and pals—that's a different story, isn't it? I detect a hint of deception in the air. Yes . . . What fun."

"Tom. I'm being serious. Eleanor Moss—"

"You mean Moskowitz," he interrupted.

"*Moss,*" she continued, "is the first real ray of hope we've had since the doctors told us Margaux would live. If you say or do anything, and I mean *anything,* to jeopardize that—" Her eyes pooled.

"Trish," Tom said. He let his bags drop softly to the lawn and grabbed her by the shoulders. "I'm an incorrigible tease. But I would never do anything to hurt you. Or Margaux. You know that, don't you?"

"I do," she said. Back when they were children, Tom had been her ally, her protector, and her occasional coconspirator. He often interceded with their mother on her behalf—Tom was her clear favorite—like the time Patricia longed to take a trip to Bermuda with a group of girls and her mother forbade it, saying she was too young. He, and not their father, had taught her to drive, and he was her most faithful correspondent, sending her twice-weekly letters at summer camp and later at Smith. Those early letters were especially precious, for they contained installments of his hand-drawn comic strip, *Petunia in Wonderland*, which featured a little blond girl who embarked upon the kind of adventures that Patricia could only dream of having.

She tipped her head so that it touched his chest. "It's been hard though."

"Well, it's about to get easier," he said. He released her and picked up his bags. "Tommy is here, and he's here to stay."

Back on the sunporch, Tom decided against gin and tonics; he wanted to make sweet Manhattans instead. He was a stickler about their preparation, inspecting the vermouth bottle to make sure it was not dusty and insisting that the drinks be stirred and not shaken. "Shaking makes bubbles," he said. "And bubbles change *everything*." Patricia didn't think she could have detected the difference but was willing to concede that the stirred Manhattans, with their slightly caramel flavor and hint of cherry juice, were delicious.

"Can I have a sip, Mother? Please?" Margaux asked. She was seated on one of the wicker chairs, her walking stick on the floor nearby. Patricia hesitated. Had Wynn been there, she would have said no. But he wasn't, and so she gave her daughter a taste.

"It's so good!" Margaux said, wiping her mouth crudely with the back of her hand. Really, since her illness, the girl's manners had gone straight to hell. "Like drinking silk." Patricia was mollified by the description. Margaux had her own distinctive way of looking at things, and there were moments when an observation of hers filled

Patricia with a rush of pride. This was one of them. By the time they needed to leave for the train station, Patricia was in a very fine mood indeed.

"Come with us?" Margaux asked her uncle. She had changed into a long navy blue skirt and white blouse. Her freshly brushed hair was held in place by a headband.

"I'm going to take a shower before dinner," Tom said. "Shake off the road dust. I'll be all fresh and ready to meet your new tutor when you get back. Do you think she'll make me a hat?"

"Silly!" Margaux said as he hugged her. "It's her mother who makes the hats." Margaux returned the hug. Patricia's eyes met Tom's over her daughter's head. *Don't worry*, he seemed to be communicating. *She'll be all right*. Everything *will be all right*. With Tom around, Patricia could almost believe this was true.

As soon as Eleanor had arrived and settled in, they all sat down to a dinner of boiled lobsters, corn on the cob, and tomatoes from a farm stand down the road. Henryka passed around a stack of white dish towels, each bordered by a stripe of a different color.

"It's a bib," Tom said, seeing Eleanor's confusion. "Tuck it into your collar."

Eleanor nodded, but Patricia could see that she was even more daunted by the flushed and steaming crustacean set before her. "There's a claw cracker right by your fork," she began.

"Lobster's a down-and-dirty meal," said Tom. "You're supposed to get messy eating it. Let me show you."

He got up, and leaning over her shoulder, picked up the claw. The shell was soft enough to crack with his bare hands. Liquid squirted out and landed squarely on the bib. "Oh!" exclaimed Eleanor, clearly surprised. Tom handed her a napkin and she dabbed at the spot. "Good thing we protected you," he said, using the lobster fork to extract the succulent meat from the broken shell. Tom dipped the morsel in butter and offered her back the fork. She chewed slowly. "Delicious," she said.

"Good girl!" he said. "That's the spirit." Eleanor lifted her fork to her mouth for another piece. "Have you ever had steamers? Or oysters?" Tom was working on the other claw now. She shook her head. "Henryka, did you hear that?" he called out. "Miss Moss has never had oysters. We have to remedy that. Can we add your incomparable oyster stew to the menu anytime soon?"

"I make for you, Mr. Tom," Henryka said, coming in from the kitchen with a basket full of dinner rolls. "I know you like." She placed the rolls on the table right in front of him.

"Not *like*, Henryka, my love. I crave your oyster stew. It's my all-time, flat-out number one favorite. Do you know that I was raving about your oyster stew when I was in Paris?"

"Oh, go on now," Henryka said, but she was all smiles and her cheeks had turned pink. "You teasing me."

"I'm not teasing," Tom said. "Every last word is true." He stopped his dissection of Eleanor's lobster long enough to seize Henryka's hand and kiss it. Henryka giggled, an unexpectedly girlish sound.

Patricia watched as Henryka—widowed, in her sixties, the mother of three grown daughters—basked in the warm pool of Tom's attention. And she was equally aware of how Eleanor, her lobster meat temporarily forgotten, was looking up at him with a similarly besotted expression. That was Tom, all right. Always enjoyed chatting up the ladies, young and old. Couldn't help himself. He had started with their mother and widened his circle to include Patricia, all the female teachers he'd ever had, the mothers and sisters of his school chums, Margaux and her friends, both past and present. And then of course there were the women he actually dated. Lord help them all.

But Tom was, in his own words, a gentleman. True, there had been Candace, but that was a long time ago. And there was that woman in Paris, though according to Tom she had been the one to end their liaison. Besides, all that happened on another continent; Tom's French affair was not likely to be known or talked about here. Argyle was different though, and she'd have to trust Tom to remember that. As she looked at Eleanor's face, the slightly parted lips and shining eyes, she realized that she'd have to make doubly sure that he did.

NINE

Eleanor and Margaux quickly settled into a pleasant summer routine: three mornings a week they worked on English, history, and the rudiments of Latin; the two other mornings were devoted to math, science, and French, the latter subject aided and abetted by Tom, who had lived in France and was fluent. After lunch, they engaged in some nonacademic pursuit, like drawing, which Margaux enjoyed. Or Tom would drive them to nearby Lavender Lake, where Margaux would swim, an activity at which she still excelled. She refused to swim at the club, despite its attractive, glittering pool; to do so would mean to expose her leg to the pity and curiosity of the other members.

By contrast, the lake was deserted and quite lovely. Cattails and marsh grass ringed its perimeter; the water was still and clear. Sitting on one of Patricia's old blankets in her polka-dot swimsuit, Eleanor saw geese, ducks, and on one memorable occasion, a regal pair of swans skimming the tranquil surface. The next day, Tom brought along binoculars. While Margaux played by the water's edge, they looked for birds or sat and talked. Tom had been so many places, seen so many things; Eleanor felt quite provincial in comparison. But it was also not entirely clear to her what he *did*, at least apart from meeting fascinating people in a variety of exotic settings. Curiosity finally won out over discretion, and she asked him flat out.

"What do you mean by *do?*" he said, tilting his head as if he'd gotten water in his ear.

"You know——for a living," she said.

"Ah, that . . ." His head resumed its ordinary angle and he smiled. "Well, the fact is, I don't have to earn a living. So I'm free to do what I want."

"Which is?"

"I meet with people——artists mostly. I look at their work and talk to them about it. I give them advice——only when they ask, of course. But plenty of them do. People seem to think I have an eye. They trust me. And I help them sell their work. Or at least I try to."

"So you're a dealer of sorts."

"Not exactly," he said. "But does it matter? Do I have to be any one thing or another? Why put a label on it? Why not just live?"

"Because you do need to put a name to whatever it is that you're doing," Eleanor said earnestly. "By naming it, you're laying claim to something. To yourself."

"I never thought of it that way," he said. He seemed to be regarding her in a fresh light.

"If you really were a dealer, what would you do?"

"I suppose I might rent a space and show some of the older work I've collected. And the newer work I champion."

"That sounds intriguing. Exciting even."

"It would be, wouldn't it? I'd love to have a space where I could show the work . . ." He was musing now. "My apartment is so . . .

crowded. If I had an uncluttered, well-lit space, the work would be seen to greater advantage. That would help the artists too."

"Absolutely."

"You," Tom said, "are an enthusiast. Are you always such an ardent cheerleader?"

"When I like someone, yes," she said.

"I'll consider that a compliment," he said, eyes steady on her now.

"It was meant as one." Her own look did not falter, but stayed locked on his. He had dark brows, like his sister, and his cheeks were sun kissed and pink. Eleanor yearned to reach out and touch him—

"Eleanor, Uncle Tom, look what I found!" Margaux came lumbering up from the edge of the water, one hand on her walking stick, the other clutched around something that turned out to be a butterfly she'd captured. The mood was broken, but only temporarily. Something had shifted between them.

And the next day, seated on an old blanket near the water's edge, the glassy surface of the lake reflecting back the sky and clouds above, Tom returned to the conversation as if they had only paused a few minutes earlier.

"You take things seriously, don't you?" he said, reaching for her hand. "Very seriously, it seems to me." He began to tap out a quick rhythm on the inside of her wrist.

"Yes, I do." The touch of his fingers against her skin was tantalizing and hypnotic; she didn't want it to stop.

"There are already a bunch of galleries on East Tenth Street. It might be a good idea to rent a place there. And I can think of at least four artists whose work I'd want to show." Tom looked at her. "I'd need someone to help out though. A person to sit at the front desk and to handle some of the office work. What about you, Eleanor? Are you up for another job?"

"You're teasing, right?"

"Not exactly, no."

"I have a job, remember?"

"But it won't be forever. Margaux should go back to school at some point."

Eleanor knew that was true. Still, working in a gallery? "I don't know much about art," she said.

"You'd learn. You'd be a natural, I can tell."

Eleanor studied his face; he seemed sincere. And he was right: she could learn if she chose to—about color and line, brushstroke and technique. Hadn't she always been a good student, one of the best in fact? If she set her mind to it, she would learn about painting the way she'd learned calculus and Latin, the puzzling variables and cumbersome declensions resolving themselves into perfectly balanced equations and graceful tropes and similes. Of course, that was assuming she wanted such a job, which she was not at all sure she did. Teaching was more than a job for her; teaching felt like a calling. But she liked that Tom wanted to share his world with her; he was inviting her in.

They stayed later than usual that day, neither one wanting to pull away and leave. When they finally did, Eleanor felt as if she were cocooned in a soft glow, even as she was helping Margaux into the backseat of the car and then climbing in to sit beside her.

"I think you should come to live with us when we get back to New York City," Margaux said, jolting Eleanor from her thoughts. The girl rested her head—the blond hair dark and saturated with lake water—lightly on Eleanor's shoulder.

"Live with you?" Eleanor said, straining for a neutral tone. But the remark alarmed her.

"I'd really like that," Margaux said. She withdrew her head to study Eleanor. "Wouldn't you?"

"Of course I would," Eleanor said. "But I don't think it would be the best thing for you."

"Why not?" Margaux asked. "I'm doing really well with my work, aren't I?"

"You're doing beautifully," Eleanor said. The car window was open and warm air rushed in. "It's not about that at all."

"Then what?"

"I think you need to go back to school," Eleanor said. "Maybe not right away. But soon."

"I don't want to go back," Margaux said.

"Why not, pumpkin?" Tom, who had been quiet until now, spoke without turning around. "If Eleanor says you're ready, I'm sure she's got a good reason for saying it."

"I'll be a cripple. Everybody will make fun of me. I can't stand it."

"Margaux, don't ever use that word about yourself," Eleanor said.

"Why not? Other people do. Even Daddy called me that once." Her hair, now dry, was blowing around her face; she gathered it in her hand and formed it into a loose knot at the nape of her neck.

"He did?" Eleanor's eyes sought out Tom's in the rearview mirror.

"Yes, when he and Mother were having an argument."

"I doubt he meant it," Tom said.

"Oh, yes he did," Margaux said.

"Well, I'm with Eleanor on this one," said Tom. "It's an ugly word. If your father used it, he must have been upset. But you shouldn't use it about yourself. And as for going to school—"

"I told you: I won't go back there."

"What about a different school?"

"You mean one for cripples?"

"Margaux!" Eleanor said. "Your uncle is right. You need friends."

"I have you," said Margaux, taking Eleanor's hand and squeezing it.

"Friends your own age," Eleanor said. She returned the gesture, and kept Margaux's hand—tanned from the sun, nails bitten painfully short—in her lap.

"I'll think about it," Margaux said in a way that clearly indicated she would do nothing of the sort. They had reached the house. She yanked open the car door and, putting her walking stick on the pebbled ground first, got out. Then she moved with impressive alacrity toward the door. Eleanor stepped out and watched her go. Tom followed and came to stand by Eleanor. He said nothing, only placed his hand on her shoulder. Eleanor did not acknowledge the gesture in any way. But his fingers against her bare skin were so pleasurable that she remained where she was, not ready for the sensation to end.

Two nights later, Eleanor sat alone in her room in the guest cottage, fountain pen poised over the letter she was writing to Ruth. *I think I'm in love with Tom Harrison*, she wrote in her clear, firm hand. *I love him with all my heart*. There, she'd admitted it to herself, and now to Ruth too. Then she read the words over again. What a clichéd and foolish pair of sentences. She wadded up the sheet of paper and dropped it in the wastebasket.

She did want to tell Ruth about Tom though. She could describe him: his height, the fine shock of blond hair that spilled over his forehead, the skin that burned so easily. And she could tell her friend how she loved the impish, mocking look in his eyes, the sound of his laughter. Also, about their idyllic trips to the lake, the perfect cocktails he mixed, the small offerings—a bit of sea glass from the beach in Maine, jagged edges worn smooth and color muted by the water's erosion—with which he surprised Margaux, the amusing anecdotes he culled and read aloud from the local paper, the way he regaled them with stories of Paris, which he said was dirty and dilapidated but also beautiful and alluring, if in a tragic, ruined sort of way. Eleanor could tell Ruth all that.

Was that love though? Wasn't it just a great big schoolgirl crush, even if she was a little too old for such a thing? Eleanor thought of Ira. Had she loved him? They had avoided the word, as if by tacit consent. She'd liked Ira, and had thought he'd make a good husband: serious, practical, kind. What she had loved—and she admitted this only to herself—was what he did, with his hands and his lips, to her body. Was that the same as loving him? She didn't know and had no one to ask. Her mother had met her father when she was eighteen; he was two years older and her brother's best friend. They were married within three months—Irina's mother wouldn't allow him to spend time with her daughter unless he had serious intentions.

"Did you love Papa?" Eleanor had asked Irina.

"I learned to love him," Irina said. "That's even better."

Eleanor looked at the sheet of paper, still blank. It was almost midnight and she was alone in the cottage; Tom and the Bellamys had gone off to the club for drinks and dancing, Henryka was in her third-floor room, and Margaux had gone to bed about an hour ago.

"Are you sure you wouldn't like to join us, Eleanor?" Patricia had asked before they left; just last week she had asked Eleanor to use her first name and Patricia had stopped using Miss Moss except when introducing her to someone new. Her employer had looked especially pretty in a silver voile dress and a cluster of black and crystal beads knotted at her throat, covered with a shawl made of the same material as the dress. "There's plenty of room in the car, isn't there, Wynn?" Wynn had hesitated just a beat too long before saying, "Of course there is. The more the merrier."

Even if Wynn hadn't waited that telling second, Eleanor would have declined. She'd had enough of the club to last her an entire summer. A lifetime, in fact. She had gone, twice, with Patricia; once for lunch, and another time for cards. Both times she had felt extremely self-conscious, and all too aware of the other patrons— well, the women anyway—sizing her up, asking her questions, angling to find out who she was and where she had been raised. The name Moss was a poor shield against their pointed interest. "You say you live on Second Avenue? But aren't there only *shops* on Second?" one had said. "What year did you graduate from Vassar?" asked another. "You look about the same age as my sister. She lived in Jewett. Maybe you knew her?"

She was too restless to write or read, too restless, surely, to sleep. A light shone from upstairs in the main house across the way. Henryka. She had not warmed toward Eleanor one bit, even though Eleanor had steadily tried to win her over. Knowing how proud Henryka was of her cooking—especially her desserts—Eleanor had made a campaign of compliments, all sincere. It was to no avail. But oh, how that woman could bake! There had been a pie at dinner tonight, a luscious mixed-berry pie with a flaky crust and a sweet, dark filling. Eleanor was seized with a sudden hunger for a second slice. She walked out of the cottage and along the brick path that led to the house. The night was hazy; no stars were visible. Still, the air smelled sweet and the pale fluttering moths seemed somehow benign, and even, quite possibly, magical.

The kitchen door was unlocked, and Eleanor stepped inside, flipping the switch to illuminate the empty room. There was the pie, sitting on the counter under a glass dome. Maybe Henryka had left it out for the Bellamys, in case they wanted a piece when they came home. Well, she'd take just a tiny bit for herself so there would be plenty left for everyone else.

When she went to the cupboard for a plate, she heard music; it seemed to be coming from the next room. The light was off though; maybe Patricia had left the radio on? Or it could have been Henryka or even Margaux, who quite enjoyed listening to her "stories" at night. Thinking it would be best to turn it off, Eleanor opened the door and patted the wall for the switch. When the light came on she gasped softly—there, as if conjured up by her imaginings, sat Tom, his lanky frame resting against the back of the wing chair, his feet resting on an ottoman. In one hand he held a drink, and the other propped up his chin. Even from where she stood, she could see that his sunburned cheeks had begun to peel.

"Well, hello," he said. "Another night owl." He smiled and raised his glass to her.

"What are you doing here?"

"Enjoying the music." "It Had to Be You" was playing on the radio. "And the dark." He smiled.

"I thought you went to the club."

"I did. But I got bored. What a dreary crowd. Not an interesting or original thought among them." Eleanor loved him for saying that. "The Talbots were leaving early so I got a lift with them. What are *you* doing here?"

"Having another slice of Henryka's pie."

"Ah, Henryka and her pies," Tom said. "Let's drink to that. Except you don't have a drink. Well, that's easy enough to fix." He stood and ambled over to the liquor cabinet. "What can I get you?"

"What are you drinking?" He held a dark, ruby-colored glass in his hand; she could not tell what was in it.

"Scotch on the rocks. But that's not a drink for you. Let me make you something else. What about a sweet Manhattan? Patricia loves them. Margaux too."

"Patricia is letting Margaux have a drink with you?"

"Only a taste, and only when Wynn isn't around."

"She must love that." Eleanor enjoyed trying to picture it.

"How's she doing anyway? With her schoolwork and all?"

"Really well. She's a bright girl. I wouldn't be surprised if she turned out to be a writer."

"Our Margaux? You think?"

"I do," Eleanor said. "You just wait."

"You sound very sure of that." Tom handed her the drink.

"She's already shown a lot of promise." Eleanor sipped her drink. It was *so* good. Or did she feel that way because Tom had made it? "Some of her compositions are first-rate. As good as any student I've ever taught. Better in fact."

"Oh, that's right. Trish said you used to be at Brandon-Wythe." Eleanor nodded, hoping to discourage further questions. "An excellent school. Or at least that's what I hear. Why'd you leave?"

Mr. Bellamy—she couldn't call him Wynn—had asked her the same question. "It was time to move on." Eleanor hoped her voice remained light, and did not betray her. The song ended and Nat King Cole's "Sentimental Reasons" came on next; she jumped on the distraction, swaying her head and humming along to the music.

Tom took another sip of his drink, set it down, and grinned at her. "Shall we dance?" he said. Clearly, her ploy had worked. Pie forgotten, Eleanor set her own drink down and moved easily into his open arms. They danced without speaking for a few minutes, but the silence brimmed with sensation. Tom felt so different from Ira—tall, sinewy, with an expansive, easy way of moving.

The song ended and an announcer's unctuous voice came on, extolling the many and considerable virtues of the latest-model Chrysler. Tom let his arms remain around Eleanor and she did not move away. They stood listening as the sounds of the commercial—which had now shifted to an engine revving up—filled the room. When it was over, Tom tilted her chin up toward him and kissed her. She closed her eyes—yes, kissing really was better that way—and felt his tongue bloom inside her mouth. The kiss was long, slow, and gentle. When it finally ended, she was desperate for it to happen again.

"I've been wanting to do that since I cracked your lobster," he said. "But Trish won't like it." He traced her lips with a finger.

"Does she have to know?"

"Trish makes it her business to know everything," said Tom. "Haven't you figured that out by now?"

Eleanor thought about the visit Patricia had made to her mother's shop, the visit she had never mentioned. "We'll be careful," Eleanor said. She wanted him to kiss her again.

"You're such an optimistic girl," he said, his arms still around her. "That's what I like about you."

"Is that all?" Eleanor knew she was fishing for a compliment but she didn't care, she wanted him to flatter her wildly, shamelessly, extravagantly.

"No," he said, "it's not." And then he leaned down, finally, to kiss her again. But as much as she'd wanted the kiss and reveled in it when it came, she was the one to pull away first. Tom was the brother of her employer; she knew she was treading on dangerous ground. She'd already walked away from one job because of a man. She could not afford to walk away—or get fired—from another. Tom seemed to understand her reticence, and did not press further. "Come on," he said. "I'll walk you back."

He took her elbow as they crossed the meadow separating the house from the cottage, and when she'd stepped inside, he did not kiss her again, but cupped her face in his hands. "Good night, lovely Miss Moskowitz," he said.

"Miss Moss, if you please."

"Moskowitz is just fine with me," he said. Then he turned, and she watched until he had walked across the grass and disappeared into the house.

TEN

Two days after the party at the club, Patricia was driving toward the outskirts of town, to the farm where Margaux's horse, Clover, was boarded. Next to her in the passenger's seat sat Margaux, glumly staring out the window and kicking the floor in front of her with her good leg.

"Would you please stop that?" Patricia said, trying to keep her voice even. "It's quite annoying." Margaux gave her a look that said she thought Patricia was annoying. The kicking continued. Patricia fought the impulse to snap at her daughter, but it was difficult. This was the post-polio, pre-Eleanor Margaux, the one who sulked, stormed, and generally made everyone around her miserable.

They drove in silence for a few more minutes. Patricia had been looking forward to this ride all week and she was not going to let Margaux spoil it. She had always loved horses and had been quite an accomplished rider as a girl. Even when she was at Smith, she'd driven the little sports car her father had bought her out to a local stable on the weekends. She'd placed first in a couple of local shows, and her father had offered to buy her a horse as a graduation gift. Patricia was tempted by the offer, but said no. She had developed a crush on Wilhelm Lustenader, a senior at Amherst who boarded his horse at the same stable. Instead of the horse, she asked for a white fur capelet that set off her blond hair and hugged her shoulders in such a flattering way. Willie—that's what she had called him—told her she looked like an angel. Then she'd met Wynn at a dance and she forgot about Willie. Would she have been any happier as Mrs. Lustenader?

But this was a pointless way of thinking. She had been so happy when she first married Wynn. So happy and so much in love. All the little pet names he had for her—not just Silver Slippers, but also Princess Patricia, Blond Venus, and when she was riding, Galloping Gal. He'd leave her notes under the pillow and in her books, chocolate-covered cherries—her favorite—on her dressing table, a heart-shaped gold locket in her coffee cup. Where was that locket now? And where was the man—not yet drinking so much, not yet so bitter—who'd put it there?

Patricia glanced over at Margaux. The kicking had stopped, only to be replaced by a series of sighs—loud, exasperated, and clearly for her benefit. She decided to ignore them as she slowed the car and guided it down the long dirt driveway. Then she turned off the engine and faced her daughter. "Don't you want to see Clover?"

"I told you before: no!" Margaux leaned back in the seat. "I'm only here because you made me come."

Patricia said nothing. She had thought that once they got here, Margaux would change her mind. "Are you sure?" she asked finally.

"Why would I want to see her when I can't ride her?"

"Can't or won't?" Patricia said quietly. The doctor had said Margaux could ride, albeit in a carefully monitored setting. He thought it would be good for her, and might even build up some muscle in her weakened thigh.

"Can't! Can't!" Margaux was shouting now.

"Lower your voice," Patricia said.

"You can't make me! I'll be loud if I want!"

Margaux was right. Patricia couldn't make her. She got out of the car. "Suit yourself. You can wait for me here." She opened the back door and reached for her black velvet riding hat.

"Where are you going?" Margaux's defiance had suddenly evaporated.

"Riding of course. You know that's what we planned to do." Patricia gestured down at her lightweight khaki jodhpurs, white cotton shirt, black boots, and the riding hat, now tucked under her arm.

"Without me?"

"I *told* you I wanted you to go with me," Patricia said. "I *begged* you."

"I can't." These were the same words Margaux had used only a few minutes ago, only now they were a lament.

"Yes, you can," Patricia said, thinking of how Eleanor treated Margaux—as someone who could do things, not as someone who could not. Instead of answering, Margaux began to cry silently, the tears sliding down her face and dripping off her chin into her lap.

"Baby," crooned Patricia, opening the door so she could slide in and embrace her daughter. "Darling girl." She held her while she wept, smoothing the hair away from her face and offering her the monogrammed handkerchief she kept tucked in the glove compartment of the car.

"I'm afraid," Margaux said finally. "And I'm afraid Clover will know I'm afraid."

"The doctor said you could try to ride," Patricia reminded Margaux. "He said it would be good for you."

"I know but . . ."

"But what?" Patricia prompted.

"I wish Eleanor had come, that's all. I might have been able to do it if she'd been here."

"She needed some time to herself today," Patricia said evenly, unwilling to let Margaux know just how much this remark had hurt her.

"I guess . . ." Margaux blew her nose loudly. "How about if I don't ride today, but just say hello to Clover? And then I can watch you ride."

"All right," Patricia said, eager to accept the compromise. Just getting Margaux to make any contact with the horse was good. As for Eleanor, well, maybe she *would* come next time. Margaux had asked her along today, but Eleanor had demurred, saying she was afraid of horses. Odd. It was not like Eleanor to be afraid of much, and certainly not a horse she would not even be riding. Still, Patricia did not press. Eleanor had devoted herself to Margaux utterly these past weeks; if she wanted a little time on her own, Patricia was not going to begrudge her a few hours. Yet she suspected that the reason Eleanor had said no was that she hoped to spend time—alone—with Tom. Patricia had not been keen to leave them together; on their various outings to the lake—a forlorn little spot whose appeal utterly eluded her—and elsewhere, Margaux had been their unwitting chaperone. The only reason she'd felt at all comfortable driving over here today was that Tom had gone to Greenwich and she knew that he would be gone for hours—a long lunch with potential art buyers at the club, maybe swimming or tennis after that, cocktails or even dinner before he drove back to the house. Patricia would be home well before he would.

Geraldine Morris, the owner of the stable, was there to greet them when they walked out to the barn. "It's good to see you again, Margaux," she said. "Would you like to visit Clover?" Margaux nodded, and Geraldine led the way. The horse—who had clearly been well tended in their absence—seemed to recognize Margaux; she came right up to the edge of the stall and nudged her. Patricia felt a flash of fear: What if the horse knocked her down? But Margaux gripped her walking stick tightly and remained steady. "She wants an apple," she said.

"I brought one," Patricia said. She rummaged through her bag to find it and handed it to Margaux, who in turn offered it to the horse. Clover peeled back her lips to reveal large, stained teeth. The apple disappeared between them, and in a crunch it was gone. She nuzzled Margaux again, as if asking for more.

"You're so greedy!" Margaux said. She balanced on the walking stick so she could rub the velvety spot between the animal's wide, quivering nostrils. "That's enough!"

"She's glad to see you," Geraldine said. "Will you be riding her?"

"Not today . . . ," Margaux said, looking down. "I'm not ready. But I can stay with her, right? While Mother rides?"

"Of course," Geraldine said. "She's yours after all." Then she turned to Patricia. "Do you want me to saddle her up?"

Patricia patted the muscled column of the horse's neck. "She's too small for me. I'll feel like I'm riding a hobbyhorse."

"I've got Sparky and Midnight available," said Geraldine.

Midnight was a large horse, maybe seventeen hands, but he was gentle, a big baby. Sparky was smaller, yet as his name suggested, more spirited. "I think I'll go with Midnight," said Patricia. Geraldine tacked him up and walked him out into the ring so Patricia could mount.

"Do you want to take the trail through the woods?" Geraldine asked. Patricia glanced over at Margaux, whose eyes clearly communicated *No, don't.* It was as if she had regressed several years since their arrival and could not stand to have her mother out of her sight.

"No, not today," Patricia said. "I'll do a little warm-up in the ring and then take the bridle path around the barn." Geraldine nodded, and Patricia gave Midnight the command to move. So there would not be a long trail ride through the woods today; that was all right, she was a bit out of practice. She hadn't been riding all year, and even this summer, whenever she'd planned on going, something had always seemed to prevent it. But perhaps most inhibiting of all was the *situation*—what looked to be a budding romance between her daughter's tutor and her own brother. Tom had turned his charm, full force, on Eleanor, and the naive girl—she was a virgin, Patricia was certain of it—had succumbed so very easily. Their behavior was so obvious, so transparent—the glances that passed between them, the hectic flush on Eleanor's face whenever Tom was around—how could they think she didn't know? Honestly, in other circumstances, it would have been funny, in a drawing-room-comedy sort of way, except that these were not *other circumstances*, this was Tom, amusing himself with the young woman she had found to save Margaux from being engulfed by despair. There was nothing even remotely funny about it.

Midnight stalled and she gave him a prod to get him going again. "That's a good boy," she said when he began to move. The next time she came out here to ride, she'd be sure Eleanor accompanied them. Maybe in her presence, Margaux would get on Clover and she and Patricia would ride together; they used to do that, and it had been such fun. One year there had been a mother-daughter horse show in Argyle and they had taken first place. Patricia remembered how straight and proud Margaux had been on the horse, and the way her thick blond braid had gleamed in the sun. Patricia looked over at

Margaux, who was standing by the fence and watching her; Margaux waved.

Midnight was fidgety; he could sense she was not fully in command. She tightened her grip on the reins and rode him toward the gate, which was unlatched. Just a short ride around the perimeter and then back again. She had to make it clear to him that she was in charge. Then they would be fine. But just as Midnight reached the gate, he abruptly reared and bucked violently. Patricia was not expecting this and let the reins slide from her hand; in a moment, she had been pitched forward and tumbled to the ground.

"Mother!" Margaux came hobbling over as quickly as she could. "Mrs. Morris!" she called out. "You have to come! Midnight threw her!"

Patricia struggled to sit up in the dirt. She was damp with sweat, panting, and streaked with dust, but she knew she was more stunned than hurt. Midnight pranced away and was heading out of the gate when Geraldine came hurrying up. She grabbed the reins and gave them a sharp tug before securing the horse to a hitching post. Then she turned to Patricia.

"Are you all right?" she asked.

"I think so." Patricia got to her feet.

"You didn't hit your head, did you?"

"No, I broke the fall with my hands." Patricia extended them now; they were grimy with dirt.

"He's never done that before," said Geraldine. "But there's been a lot of construction on one of the houses nearby; he doesn't like the noise, and he's been edgy lately." She had Patricia loop her arm around her neck as they walked slowly back to the house; Margaux hovered anxiously alongside, touching Patricia's shoulder and reaching for her hand. Inside, Patricia went into the bathroom to wash up. Despite Geraldine's concern, she did not feel she needed to see a doctor. Her wrists hurt, but not excruciatingly so; she could bend them and nothing seemed swollen or distended. But to appease Geraldine she agreed to stay for lunch.

It was almost four o'clock when they got back in the car. The day had grown appreciably hotter and Patricia felt sticky in her riding clothes. She was looking forward to a long, cool shower and a drink. Wynn would not be here for dinner; he was in town and not due back up until tomorrow night. And she did not think Tom would be back either. Just as well; they could have a little hen party, maybe play checkers, which Margaux liked, or even a hand of cards.

"You were right," Margaux said as they drove along the quiet country road. When Patricia gave her a puzzled look, she added, "About Clover. I *did* miss her and I'm glad I saw her."

"I had a feeling you would be," Patricia said. "Sometimes a mother knows." She would have reached over to touch her but she couldn't take her hands from the wheel.

"It was scary seeing you get thrown," Margaux continued. "But you're all right now. It was just a tumble."

"Just a tumble," Patricia repeated. Margaux seemed to be talking more to herself than to her mother. Patricia was quiet, waiting to hear what she would say next. A bee flew in through the open window, buzzed for a few seconds, and then flew out.

"So many bad things *could* have happened," Margaux said. "But they didn't."

For some reason, Margaux's remark made Patricia want to weep; she turned her face away. "Daddy said he'd take you sailing this weekend," she said. "How would you like that?"

"I'd love it," Margaux said. "We haven't been since——"

"You got sick," Patricia said. "But that's all over now. Daddy says if

Henryka packs lunch, you two can stay out on the boat all day." How dear of Wynn to have suggested it.

"Can Eleanor go with us?" Margaux asked.

"We'll see," Patricia said, knowing that this would be a terrible plan. The sailboats were rented through the club, a place where it was clear Eleanor was uncomfortable. And Wynn had continued to grumble sporadically about having *one of them* under their roof for so long. "She wants something from you, can't you see that?" he'd said.

"That's ridiculous," Patricia had said. But that was before she'd realized the extent of Eleanor's infatuation with Tom. And though it pained her to consider the situation in this light, now she had to wonder if Wynn had been right after all. Maybe Eleanor did have designs on Tom, though what exactly those designs were Patricia could not say. Surely she couldn't be thinking he'd *marry* her. Or could she? Suddenly, she was in a hurry to get back to the house and she pressed down on the gas pedal.

But now the road was clogged with cars; the traffic slowed, and then stopped. "What's wrong?" Margaux asked. Patricia couldn't answer until a policeman came along to explain; there was emergency roadwork up ahead and traffic was being diverted through Nottingham.

"That's way out of our way," Margaux said.

"I know," said Patricia. "But it seems we have no choice."

By the time they pulled into their own driveway, it was almost seven o'clock. Patricia's wrists had begun to throb. God, but that first drink would taste good. The second one too; this was definitely a two-drink evening.

"Eleanor!" Margaux called, getting out of the car and hobbling down the path on her walking stick. "Eleanor, where are you? We've had such an adventure!"

Patricia got out as well and stretched her sore limbs, her aching wrists. The relief she felt at being home turned brittle when she saw that Tom's car was already in the driveway. She could bet, then, that wherever Tom was, Eleanor was sure to be with him. She got out of the car and walked toward the house so quickly that she overtook Margaux, who said, "Wait for me!" But Patricia kept on going.

The screen door was unlocked and she moved from room to room, in search of them. Not in the dining room, living room, sunporch, or kitchen. Surely they weren't upstairs in Tom's *bedroom.* "Where are they?" Her voice was sharp when she spoke to Henryka, who was at the table, rolling out dough for biscuits.

"Mr. Tom and Miss Eleanor?" As if she didn't know who Patricia meant.

"Yes."

"They in cottage."

Of course. Patricia started walking out the kitchen door just as Margaux walked in.

"Mother, where did you go? You rushed off so quickly," she said accusingly.

"I'm sorry, darling. I was looking for Tom and Eleanor." Her wrists continued to throb, her white blouse, now smudged and stained, was sticking to her skin, her boots squeezed her swollen feet, and she really wanted a drink. But it was imperative that she find them immediately.

"I'll come with you," Margaux said.

When they reached the cottage door, Patricia knocked and then opened it before she had a reply. There, as she suspected, sat her brother and her daughter's tutor, side by side on the love seat, drinks in hand. Their positions were chaste enough, but Patricia's shrewd gaze caught the fact that fastidious Eleanor's blouse was not buttoned properly. Was that because she'd taken it off and had to button it back up in a hurry?

"Hello, you two beauties," said ever unflappable Tom. "How was your ride?"

"I didn't go but Mother did and Midnight threw her—she could have been hurt!"

"Oh no!" cried Eleanor with real concern. "Are you all right?"

"I'm fine," said Patricia. "Just a little shaken and in desperate need of a shower."

"And a drink," said Tom. "I'll go back to the house and make you one right now."

"Don't let me break up your little—party," Patricia said. "I can make my own drink."

"Maybe so. But why should you?" Tom stood and so did Eleanor. Patricia noticed that she looked flustered. Not Tom though.

As the sun dipped gracefully behind the trees, the four of them walked back across the lush and sweet-smelling grass. The trees were lush too, and some of the boughs dipped low, almost to the ground. Everything seemed to be in full bloom, bursting urgently with life. Why, Patricia wondered, did she find this quite so unsettling?

ELEVEN

A few nights later, Margaux came into the living room proffering Patricia's crystal atomizer filled with Chanel No. 5. "Want me to spray you?" Eleanor wavered; she did love the scent, which Margaux had already applied to herself quite liberally. But Eleanor was afraid that Patricia would think she had helped herself without asking. She shook her head. "Why not? It smells so good," Margaux said.

"Your dress is enchanting," Eleanor said, changing the subject.

Margaux looked down at her high-waisted organdy frock. "Do you really think so? It's not too babyish?"

"Not at all," Eleanor said. "It's perfect."

Margaux beamed. "Well, if you're sure about the perfume . . ."

"I'm sure," Eleanor told her. "Now I should get dressed too. It's almost eight."

Eleanor left Margaux in her room and hurried back to the guest cottage. It was Friday night and the Bellamys were having a party; they'd asked Eleanor to join them. She really would have preferred not to, but Margaux had been quite insistent and it was for Margaux's sake that Eleanor had agreed.

The guest list included the Talbots, John and Dottie, from across the road; they didn't seem so bad, but some of the others—the Maitlands, for instance, and the Olsens—she had met either in town or at the club and their response had been discernibly frosty. What was it they perceived about her that made them so hostile? Was she so different, so alien?

But Tom would be there, and that would make everything better. Since that first kiss, they had not been able to find many opportunities to be alone. But they had shared two more such moments, including one two days ago, before Patricia had barged into the cottage. Each kiss had been more intoxicating than the last. Maybe there would be an opportunity for another tonight.

It was this thought that buoyed her as she quickly stepped into her black taffeta skirt and pale pink silk blouse. The skirt was a bit faded and, because she had bought it during the war, short and skimpy and therefore out of style; the blouse was slightly limp from frequent wearing. But she'd worn her new summer dress several times already and wanted to choose something different. And she did have a darling silk fascinator her mother had made, pink with black trim along the crown and a saucy black tassel at the back. It would, she knew, revitalize her rather wan outfit.

In the bathroom, she reached for the round box of Djer-Kiss to powder her nose and thought longingly of the Chanel. One day soon she would buy a bottle for herself. Then she carefully applied her new lipstick: Dorothy Gray's Portrait Pink. She seldom wore lipstick but the color was subtle and pretty; she hoped Tom would like it.

When Eleanor went back over to the house, several of the guests had already arrived. Tom was not among them though. She stood stiffly near the window, wishing he would hurry and get here. Mr. Bellamy was busy pouring drinks; Patricia was dispensing hugs to the Maitlands. "What can I get you, Miss Moss?" asked Mr. Bellamy. It seemed that he was mocking her slightly, but then, she always felt he was mocking her.

"A glass of ginger ale, please," she said.

"Ginger ale? I've seen you drink before. With Tom. Have you gone on the wagon?" He took a long sip of his own drink; Eleanor was quite sure it was not the first of the evening.

"No," she said. "I like to pace myself, that's all."

But when he returned with the ginger ale, he seemed more affable. "I added a cherry," he said. "To pep it up. It's summer, and you're young. You have to enjoy yourself. Gather ye rosebuds and all that."

Eleanor reached for the glass but at the last second, he pulled it away, moving his hand here and there, always managing to stay just ahead of her reach. She began to get frustrated and was ready to walk away without the drink when he suddenly stopped and gave it to her.

"I was just teasing," he said. "No hard feelings?"

"Of course not." The cherry bobbed on the fizzy drink, and she pulled it out and popped it in her mouth.

"Now the cherry's gone," he said, lowering his voice suggestively. "And it will never come back." He was practically leering. "No more cherry for Eleanor."

His crude insinuation was clear and she didn't answer; why should she? Instead, she turned away, and as she did, she felt his hand glance off her backside, a light, insolent smack. She was instantly furious and whirled back around. Over the rim of his glass, his expression was both predatory and challenging. *What are you going to do?* his eyes seemed to say. But then her fury was replaced by something equally primal—fear. She wanted to get away from him, as quickly as she could. And suddenly there was Tom, tall and rangy in his seersucker jacket and bow tie. Just in time. Not caring how it might look, she rushed right over.

"Hello, Eleanor," was all he said. But to Eleanor, it sounded like music. She had to restrain herself from reaching out to stroke the smooth polished cotton of his shirtfront. Then that odious Olsen woman—she was the one who'd been incredulous to learn that anyone actually *lived* on Second Avenue—pounced on him and Eleanor moved away. She turned to look for Margaux instead and when she caught sight of her, sitting by herself with a drink on the sunporch, she walked right over to join her.

"It's a Shirley Temple," Margaux said when she saw Eleanor eyeing it. "But Uncle Tommy promised me a taste of his Manhattan later. You can't tell Daddy though!"

"I promise." The memory of his hand on her body made her feel slightly sick and she sat down on the chintz-covered wicker sofa next to Margaux. "Are you having a good time?" An overstuffed, fringed pillow prevented her from leaning back; it felt like the pillow wanted to push her from her seat. She reached behind and moved it out of her way.

"All right, I guess," Margaux said. "I don't like how people try to look at my leg though. Spying almost. They look because they can't help themselves; they really do want to see it. Then they look away. Because they're ashamed. Or worse—because they don't want me to see how relieved they are."

"Relieved?"

"That it's my leg that's withered. Not theirs."

Eleanor thought, as she often did, of how precocious Margaux could be. Was it because of her illness, or would she have been that way even if she hadn't been stricken? She looked up to see Patricia standing in front of them; she wore a wine-colored dress of watered silk and a tight, manufactured smile.

"Margaux, darling, why don't you play something for our guests?" she said, gesturing toward the walnut upright that stood in a far corner of the living room.

"I don't want to," Margaux said. She reached over toward a silver bowl filled with nuts and took a large handful. A few nuts slipped from her fingers and into her lap. She did not appear to notice, though Eleanor was sure her mother did.

"Why not, darling? You play so well." Patricia stood there, expectantly, hands clasped tightly in front of her. In actuality, Margaux was an indifferent music student possessed of only a moderately accomplished technique.

"I just don't." Margaux crunched loudly on the nuts. Eleanor knew how this behavior irritated Patricia. She also knew that Patricia was determined to prove to her friends that despite Margaux's illness, the girl was still intact, still capable of performing parlor tricks and taking her rightful place in her mother's world. Eleanor knew Patricia genuinely loved her daughter; why would she put the approval of her guests before Margaux's feelings?

"Eleanor, would you ask her? She seems to be in your thrall," Patricia said.

There was an edge to the remark and Eleanor felt it immediately. What to do? She hated being drawn into this contest of wills, but there was no graceful way to refuse her employer's request. "Margaux," she began, "I'd like to hear you play something too. Would you please play for me?"

"If you'll sit with me while I play," Margaux answered, and when Eleanor nodded, Margaux hoisted herself onto her walking stick, scattering nuts to the floor. Eleanor followed her out of the sunporch, into the living room and toward the piano. Patricia clapped her hands to get everyone's attention. "We're going to be treated to a little concert tonight," she said. "Margaux asked if she could play something for all of you."

Eleanor looked down at the ivory-and-black keys. She did not like hearing Patricia lie; she thought it demeaned her. But Margaux did not protest. She slid onto the bench, Eleanor beside her, where she proceeded to play a serviceable—if dull—rendition of "Für Elise." Polite applause followed the performance and then, mercifully, Patricia turned to one of the other guests.

"What about you, Freddy? Isn't it your turn?" He must have had a following among the company because everyone began to urge him to play. Freddy—thinning hair; wide, flat face; bright blue eyes—seemed happy to oblige. He made a great show of flexing his fingers and cracking his knuckles before bursting into a rousing, syncopated version of "The Whiffenpoof Song."

Margaux used her walking stick to go back to the sunporch, and Eleanor followed. "Why does she do that?" Margaux asked when they were safely out of earshot.

Eleanor didn't pretend not to understand. "She worries about you. She thinks you're too isolated. She wants you to feel comfortable with people." Eleanor sat down on the wicker sofa again, but not before placing the offending pillow on the floor. Margaux flopped down next to her; the little sofa quivered in response.

"She can't know what it feels like to be me," Margaux said. "And she can't know what it feels like to have *this*." She looked down.

"Say, what are the two prettiest gals in the room doing way over here by themselves?" Tom strode up and yanked over a footstool so he could sit.

"We're having a little talk," Eleanor said.

"It looks very serious. Too serious, if you ask me." He turned to Margaux. "Have you seen this one before?" His long, aristocratic fingers made a few graceful gestures near the side of his head and voilà! he'd pulled a quarter from his ear and presented it with a flourish to Margaux.

"Uncle Tommy, you're so corny," she said, taking the quarter and holding it tightly. But she was smiling, her gloomy mood of a moment ago seemingly dispelled by his sunny presence.

"Corny? For producing money out of thin air? Today it's a quarter, but tomorrow it could be a silver dollar. Or a gold doubloon. Nothing silly about that. No, ma'am."

Freddy was still regaling the other guests with his piano playing; he had moved on to "I Get a Kick Out of You." Several people began to dance to the music and Tom, after glancing over in their direction, turned to Eleanor. "May I have the honor?" he said. And to Margaux, "Can I borrow her for a little while? I promise to give her back."

Eleanor got up and handed Margaux her evening purse. "My new lipstick is in there, along with a mirror. Try it if you want."

"Really?" Margaux asked as she undid the clasp and extracted the small gold cylinder. "What would my mother say?"

"You leave her to me," Eleanor said as she moved into Tom's arms. "I'm sure when I explain it to her, she'll think it's just fine." She was aware of the slight pressure of Tom's hand on the small of her back.

"Very nicely done," he said. Eleanor could see how Margaux had painted her lips and was experimenting with various expressions—a moue, a smile—in front of the tiny mirror.

"I just don't want her to feel she's been left out of everything," she said.

"Lovely, kind, compassionate Eleanor," Tom said, spinning her adroitly. "How lucky we all are that Patricia's taxicab rammed into yours on that rainy day. And I do mean all."

She pressed her face against his shoulder, too filled with happiness to reply.

It was after two when the party broke up. Margaux had fallen asleep on the wicker sofa; Tom and Wynn carried her to her bed. Eleanor said good night to the few remaining guests and to her employers. There had been no opportunity for a proper kiss tonight, but the time she and Tom had spent in each other's arms, dancing as Freddy played one tune after another, had been gift enough. At one point, he'd been daring enough to let his lips graze the top of her ear; the spot where they had touched felt electrified.

Feet slightly sore, Eleanor slipped off her shoes and hooked them onto two fingers as she walked back across the lawn to the cottage. The dew-drenched grass felt good on her bare skin, and she intentionally avoided the brick path. Once inside the cottage Eleanor felt too keyed up and restless to sleep. She went to the window to look over at the house. It was dark, except for a single lighted window. Henryka still up? No, Henryka's room was on the third floor. The light was coming from the second-floor bedroom, the one that had been Margaux's but where Tom now slept. She knew just where it was because Margaux had told her.

Just knowing that Tom was awake excited her. What was he doing? Was he thinking of her? She continued to stare at the window, where the light was beckoning her. She wouldn't go, of course. It would be foolish. Dangerous even. She could lose her job. Besides, Tom might not like her showing up at his door—he'd think she was too forward.

But earlier, at midnight, Wynn had started to uncork the champagne bottles, and she'd had two bubbly, lovely glasses. And before that, one of Tom's expertly mixed Manhattans—*It's our drink*, he'd murmured as he handed it to her. So now she was pleasantly, mildly inebriated. The alcohol was weakening her resolve, and fueling her desire, both at the same moment. And so, without bothering to put on her shoes, she set off back toward the house.

The darkened living room was a mess, glasses and plates everywhere, an ashtray overturned on the rug. Eleanor resisted the urge to straighten up. Tom. She had to find Tom. Treading very carefully, she ascended the stairs. Her bare feet made no noise. Or at least not very much. But all the adults up here were drunk; no one was apt to hear her.

Once she got to the dark upstairs hallway, she waited until she had oriented herself. There, at the far end, was a thin line of light under a door. Tom's door. She moved toward it, and when she reached it, she put her hand on the knob and turned it. "Eleanor?" he said simply. He'd been reading and an open book was splayed across his bare chest. The blades of the electric fan that sat on the bedside table made a subtle clicking sound as they spun and she could make out his long form under the sheet. She ought to leave. Now.

"I was kind of hoping you would come."

"You were?"

"Okay, maybe not hoping. But wishing. Fantasizing."

She said nothing, but felt a pleasurable heat rising up, spreading across her face.

Tom was still looking at her. "Would you come and sit by me?"

"Where?"

"On the bed." He shifted to make room and patted the space beside him.

She hesitated. "You're . . . naked under that sheet, aren't you?"

"Yes. But don't be afraid."

"I'm not afraid," she said. "Not at all. It just means I have to be naked too." Had she really said that, or just thought it? Oh, she really was drunk. Drunk and had taken leave of her senses. Tom had said nothing. What if he were repulsed by her boldness? Thought she was a girl with no morals, a slut? There had been a night, more than a year ago, when she had permitted Ira to remove her bra entirely and place first his palms and then his lips on each of her naked breasts. She had not, however, allowed him to remove her panties, though he himself had slid down his striped boxer shorts and stepped out of them. He had pressed himself against her closed thighs, trying to cajole her into stripping off the last little scrap of material—pale blue rayon, ribbon edged—that separated them. She had said no. How many times since then had she replayed that scene in her mind, wishing it had ended differently, wishing she had said yes, that she had not deprived herself of the fulfillment of her desire. Now she was glad, no, not glad, jubilant that she had waited. For this. For Tom, who stirred both her body and her soul.

Carefully, she stepped out of her skirt and undid the buttons on her blouse. Next came her brassiere, her slip, and finally, her underpants. It was only when everything else was off that she realized she was still wearing the fascinator; she reached up, removed it from her head, and placed it on the neat pile she'd made of her clothes. She was aware of him watching the entire time. When she too was completely naked, she stood there, feeling his gaze take in every visible bit of her.

"Won't you sit down?" Tom finally said, sounding oddly formal. "I promise I won't touch you unless you say it's all right."

"It's all right," she said, and gently let her weight down onto the mattress beside him. She did not say any more; she could not, she was too busy listening to the rush and roar of her own blood in her ears. It sounded so loud to her; could he hear it too? She reached out to put a hand on his chest; his skin was so warm. And he was so long and lean; not a bit of extra flesh on him. He caught her hand and brought it to his lips. Then he pulled her to him, so that her naked breasts were pressed against him, no space between the two of them at all. They kissed slowly, tentatively, for a moment before he disengaged himself and leaned back against the pillows.

"What is it?" she said, disappointed. "Did I do something wrong?"

"You're a virgin," he said as if that were the logical answer to her question.

"Does it make a difference?"

"It does to you," he said. "I can tell." He smoothed the hair away from her face, but it was the gesture of a father or a brother. Not a lover. "Don't you want to save yourself? For your husband?"

"I did save myself," she said. "For you." She didn't like the way he was touching her now; it made her feel trivial. Undesirable. She pushed his hand away.

"But I can't be your husband," he said. "Even though I want to."

"I don't care," she replied, trying to tamp down the joy she felt at hearing these last words. *He wanted to be her husband! He wanted her!* "I can be your mistress instead."

He laughed, and then became serious. "No," he said. "You can't. I won't let you."

"What do you mean you won't let me? It's not your decision. It's mine."

"Wouldn't you say that it's a decision that needs to be mutual?" When she said nothing, he added, "And if I don't agree . . ." Eleanor looked away. She would not beg him, she would *not*.

"I'm not leaving," she said finally.

"Who said anything about leaving? I never asked you to leave."

"But you said . . ."

"I said I would not deflower you. Not because I don't want to; I want to very much." The smile returned to her face and she did not care if he saw it. "But I think I would end up hurting you, and I don't want to hurt you. I hurt a girl once, a long time ago. She was a friend of Tricia's. I would never want to hurt you that way."

"So then if you won't, I mean, you know . . ."

"There are other things we can do," he said, and he pushed her back gently on the bed. "Plenty of other things. Let me show you." He slid down her body, nudging her thighs open with his hands. He began to kiss her lightly—her stomach, the bones of each hip, the flesh inside her thighs and then—

"Tom, what are you *doing*?" she said, alarmed, intoxicated by the pleasure of having his mouth there, *there* of all places! "Shh," he said when she began to moan. "If Trish finds you in here, all hell will break loose."

TWELVE

When Patricia woke the following morning, she felt as if bits of broken glass had been scraped over her corneas. Horrible. She closed her eyes again.

She'd had too much to drink at the party and then she'd had to deal with Wynn and his *urges*, as he called them, when she got to bed. Their one night of mutual passion, ignited after Audrey's wedding, had never been repeated. But their relations had not quite reverted to their predictable and stale routine since then either. Wynn had changed over these last few months. Some nights he was rough with her, treating her body as something to use, rather than arouse or delight. As bad as this was, even worse were the nights that he became abject and pleading. It was then that he seemed pitiable to her, and she didn't know how to respond. If only she could have confided in Maddy again—maybe Maddy would have had an answer. Fortunately, last night he had been quite drunk and by the time she emerged from the bathroom, he'd passed out on their bed. At some point during the night he'd woken and reached for her, but she'd been able to evade him and he'd gone back to sleep.

A bird squawked rudely in a nearby tree and she opened her eyes once more. She could just imagine the god-awful mess out there; she supposed she'd better go and oversee the cleanup. She put on her silk robe and marabou-tipped slippers, and thus garbed, shuffled out to the living room, vowing to go a little easier on the drinking for a while.

To her astonishment, the room was immaculate, with no sign of last night's excesses in evidence. Glasses and plates were gone, surfaces wiped and waxed. The overturned ashtray she'd spotted had been cleaned up too; Patricia could see the marks from the carpet sweeper crisscrossing the rug. The kitchen too, was tidy, and she found a vase filled with early yellow mums—their color so insistent that she almost needed to close her eyes again—and a pot of coffee on the stove. Had Henryka done all this? It seemed unlikely; she must have had help. But who? Patricia considered this and then her eyes settled on the note:

Darling, Tom and I took Margaux sailing at the club. Wanted to let you sleep in. If the weather holds, we'll be out all day. Margaux was very eager to be on the boat again. It did me a world of good to see her enthusiasm.

Love,
Wynn

Her irritation with last night's inept fumbling was replaced by a rush of affection. Yes, Wynn had been oafish lately, especially in bed. But he was good to their daughter. He'd taught Margaux to love sailing, and she would come home from their outings, hair blown wildly around her face, eager to tell Patricia how far they'd gone, or show her a new knot Wynn had taught her to tie.

After a cup of black coffee and a hot shower, she felt significantly improved. When she came back downstairs, wearing a cotton piqué dress in a flattering shade of apricot, she decided that she wanted to spend the day out of the house. Maybe drive to Dudley for lunch; she could ask Eleanor to go with her. That might be a good thing, she reflected. She'd wanted some time alone with Eleanor; this would give her the perfect opportunity.

She stepped out of the front door, into the sunshine. There, across the road, was Dottie Talbot. "Hello!" she called to her neighbor. Dottie turned and waved. Patricia crossed the road. "Was your head as bad as mine when you got up?"

"Was it ever!" Dottie said. She had her hair wrapped in a printed turban and wore linen slacks, a halter top, and a very large pair of sunglasses.

"But it was fun, wasn't it? Isn't Freddy something else?"

"Everyone loves Freddy," Patricia agreed.

"And your Miss Moss! At one point she was reciting poetry out on the sunporch—Shakespeare, John Keats, or was it John Donne? I can't remember; I don't care much for poetry. But I was in the minority, let me assure you. She drew quite a crowd."

"Eleanor was reciting poetry last night? I had no idea," said Patricia. Certain parts of the evening were a blur.

"Oh yes, and with great feeling. Where in the world did you find her?"

"It was really quite a fortuitous accident. Literally. My taxi rammed into hers on Park Avenue one day in June. Margaux adores her."

"I can see why." Dottie lowered her voice. "Tell me—is she a Jew?"

"What makes you ask that?" Patricia said. Whatever fragile sense of well-being she'd felt about her prospects for the day were rapidly crumbling.

"It's just a feeling I had. She was rather evasive when I asked where she lived back in town. I've never seen her in church with you. And then there's that name; it could have been shortened from something else."

"Dottie, please don't mention it to anyone," Patricia said. "It really could be quite awkward, if you know what I mean. Margaux's very fond of her and she'd be devastated if she were to leave." She couldn't believe she was even talking this way, but she guessed these were Dottie's thoughts, and she needed to address them head-on.

"Oh, I won't say a word," Dottie said. "It's entirely your business whom you want to hire. But there is one more thing . . ."

"What's that?" Patricia had thought that she could handle this—the need for secrecy, even the illicit thrill it gave her. Now she was not sure at all. "No one else knows, do they?"

"I couldn't say. But it seemed to me that she was very chummy with Tom last night . . . maybe a little too chummy, if you get my meaning. People noticed. And they started to ask questions. About her."

"You know what a flirt Tom is," Patricia said, now desperate to grab hold of this conversation and turn it in another direction. "Such a ladies' man. He's always been that way, even when he was a boy."

"I know all about Tom. So does everyone else. But do they know he would take up with a girl like that? It could hurt his reputation—and yours."

"I'm sure it's nothing serious," Patricia said, struggling to sound casual. "But all the same, it can't hurt to mention it to him."

"Might save you some heartache," said Dottie. She took off the sunglasses and without them, her eyes were still a bit bloodshot.

"Of course, of course," Patricia said, and turned to look across the road. She knew Tom was off sailing, but where was Eleanor?

"Will you be at the club at all this week?" Dottie's glasses were now back in place, masking her expression.

"Yes, I think so. Well, I suppose I should be getting back now." She waited for what she thought was an appropriate beat. "About that other thing . . . you will keep it to yourself, won't you?"

"You can count on me," Dottie told her, squeezing Patricia's hand. Her nails, freshly lacquered, were bright red, a shade Patricia often selected for herself. So why today did they make her think of blood?

Back in her own kitchen, Patricia was surprised to find Eleanor and Henryka together. Henryka had baked a batch of her beloved sticky buns and was pouring coffee. "Good morning, missus," she said. "You want coffee? Bun?"

The sight of the glazed pastry made Patricia's still unsettled stomach clench, but she wanted to be part of whatever this was, so she sat down and accepted both a sticky bun and a second cup of coffee. "Thank you for doing such a good job cleaning up," Patricia said to Henryka. "You got everything done so quickly."

"Mr. Wynn—he help." Henryka added a generous amount of cream and several teaspoons of sugar to her own coffee.

"He did?" Patricia was surprised.

"Oh yes. He insist."

"Well, isn't that . . . thoughtful." Patricia was puzzled. When had Wynn ever shown any interest in, much less *insisted* on, helping with housework? As she picked at the pastry, she reflected on her husband's dual nature: he could be such a boor, but then he'd surprise her, like he had this morning.

"Now I go change sheets," said Henryka. Opal was sick and Henryka was picking up the slack. After she'd gone, Eleanor remained quiet and kept her gaze down. Why was she so subdued this morning? The conversation with Dottie replayed in Patricia's mind, and her anxiety began to spike. "How would you like to drive over to Dudley with me today?" She pushed the bun away, reminding herself that she'd have to get rid of it without Henryka's knowledge; if it was discovered that she had not finished it, there would, inevitably, be sulking. "There's a little place in town where we could go for lunch. And we might do a bit of window-shopping too; they have a couple of nice stores."

"All right," Eleanor said. She was eating her sticky bun with a knife and fork, and taking small, discreet sips of her coffee. Patricia had to allow that she had exceptionally fine table manners; she wished they would rub off on her daughter.

"Finish your coffee first," Patricia said. "I'll tell Henryka we're going to be gone for lunch." Then she went into Tom's room to retrieve his keys from inside a large tarnished golf trophy that had belonged to Wynn's grandfather. Since Wynn had taken their car to the club, she would use Tom's; she knew he wouldn't mind. The room was not too untidy though the bed had not been made, which was hardly a surprise given Tom's casual attitude toward housekeeping. She saw the trophy, located the keys, and was about to leave when something on the pillow caught her eye. Something pink. Putting down the keys, she went over to inspect. There was a streak, small, of what appeared to be lipstick on the pillowcase; she rubbed it and it smeared in just the way lipstick would smear. The way *Eleanor's* new pink lipstick—she'd even let Margaux try it, for God's sake!—would have smeared, had she been in this room, in this bed, last night.

Patricia walked over to the window. The hydrangeas were particularly vivid this year, a deep, even lurid, pink that seemed almost to glow against the green of the grass. Pink, pink, pink. That shaming streak of pink lipstick. Hadn't Dottie said that Eleanor was reciting Shakespeare and that everyone was lapping it up? Did everyone include Tom?

Closing the door quietly, Patricia left the room. In her pocket were the car keys; in her hand was the offending pillowcase. She did not want Henryka, Opal, or anyone else to see it.

Patricia took the coastal road to Dudley, thinking the glimpses of dunes, beach, and ocean would calm her down a little. She was wrong. The distant waves crashing to the shore only echoed and intensified her anger. How prim the girl next to her seemed. Prim and oh so proper. But she had been in Tom's room! How could she? How dare she? The car felt stifling. Patricia rolled down the window. "Is that all right?"

"It's fine. Delightful, in fact," said Eleanor. "What a gorgeous day. Perfect for sailing."

Patricia had no interest in the weather, only in what she planned to say to Eleanor when they got to Dudley.

"I detest sailing." Patricia had never actually said this aloud. "Wynn and Margaux love it. Tom too—he used to sail with our father." She quickly looked over to see if Tom's name brought on any reaction—a blush, a smile perhaps. It did not. "But I never took to it. It always made me seasick, and my father had no patience with anyone who got seasick. He thought it was a moral failing of some kind."

"I'd hardly call seasickness a moral failing," Eleanor said. "It's not something you have any control over at all."

Despite her simmering anger, Patricia was interested in Eleanor's point of view. "But that was my father. No babying, no coddling. I'm sure he'd think I was indulging Margaux terribly if he were here to see it."

"I don't think compassion should be confused with coddling," said Eleanor. "She's had a very hard time and you're responding to that with love and acceptance."

The waves seemed less violent now, their ebb and flow more soothing. This was one of Eleanor's rare gifts—her ability to alter the way you had always thought about something, to turn your assumptions upside down, so you felt changed, released even. Patricia had absorbed so many of her father's attitudes, and even though he was no longer alive, she often felt herself engaged in a silent struggle with him, a struggle in which he always won. Now here was Eleanor, who with a few words could completely subvert the terms of their relationship.

"How does Margaux seem to you these days? Do you think she's doing better?" Patricia couldn't help asking. Concern about her daughter trumped her indignation over Eleanor's compromising interest in Tom—at least for the moment.

"As far as her schoolwork?" asked Eleanor. "There's no problem there, none at all. You must have been told already how bright she is, how intellectually gifted. She has an amazing grasp of literature. Her insights are so mature and astute. They astonish me sometimes."

"Well, yes, we knew she was bright, but after her illness and all that misery with Mr. Cobb . . ."

"Mr. Cobb was not the right teacher for her, that's all." Eleanor shifted in her seat so she was facing Patricia. "But academics aren't everything. There's still the social aspect to her development. Which is why I think she should be going back to school. She's ready, you know."

"She flat out refuses to go," Patricia said. She and Wynn had had this conversation—well, argument, actually—with their daughter many times, and whenever they did Margaux seemed more firmly entrenched in her position.

"It's because of her leg. She doesn't want to be made fun of or ostracized. Or pitied—she'd hate that most of all. But I've heard about a boarding school called Oakwood where the entire student body is in the same situation."

"You mean . . . ?" A school filled with polio victims. The thought made Patricia unutterably sad. But also—curious.

"Yes, every single one of the students has had polio. The headmaster's son had it, and he wouldn't go back to school either. So the father—he'd been headmaster at a very fine school in Albany—decided to start a school for other children who'd been similarly afflicted. It's kind of new—maybe three years old—but what I've heard has been excellent."

"But do we really want to put her in a school for—cripples?"

"Don't think of it that way. Think of it as a school for survivors. Because that's who Margaux is—a survivor."

They had reached Dudley and Patricia pulled into a space in the town center, which was a grassy square with a bandstand at its center and several handsome old oak trees at the perimeter. She turned off the ignition and shifted to face Eleanor. "If we did consider such a place, and actually sent her there, you do know it would mean you'd be out of a job."

"I'd be sorry about that," Eleanor said. "But it's Margaux I'm thinking about. The more isolated she is now, the harder it will be for her to lose that sense of isolation in the future. She needs to be in school with her peers. And if her peers have suffered the way she has, all the more opportunity for her to find companionship and build real friendships. I wrote asking for an application. I can show it to you as soon as it comes."

Patricia was stunned. Here she'd been preparing to lambaste the girl for what she'd been doing behind Patricia's back and it turned out that one of those things was researching a school for Margaux and requesting an application to it. "Thank you," Patricia said awkwardly, as she tried to navigate the abrupt shift in her own feelings. "Thank you very much." Yet the business with Tom—she had to say something. But she would wait until lunch.

They got out of the car and began to walk along Old Post Road, the town's main street. When Wynn had suggested sending Margaux away, Patricia had balked, but that was because he had made it sound like a punishment. What Eleanor was proposing was quite different. A school where Margaux could be herself, yet have friends her own age . . . What could be more ideal?

Her righteous indignation had evaporated, leaving Patricia pensive and unsure of what to say. Accusing Eleanor of being promiscuous, a gold digger, or both seemed wrong, even beside the point now. And yet she was still worried about the girl's connection to Tom; she knew it would result in nothing but disappointment. The fact that Eleanor was Jewish would make it difficult, if not impossible, for her to fit into Tom's world. Didn't he know that? Didn't she?

Besides, Tom was thirty-eight; he'd never even been engaged, let alone married. He was just an incorrigible flirt, toying with Eleanor the way he'd toyed with so many before. When their mother used to lament that she'd never see him walk down the aisle, he'd say, "I'm waiting for the one who's half as wonderful as you are, Mother darling," which always got her to smile. And to end the discussion. Their mother had died, of cancer, five years ago, and their father of a heart attack shortly after that; Patricia clung to Tom even more closely in the wake of their deaths. But that didn't mean she was always happy with his behavior—and she certainly wasn't happy with it now.

As she and Eleanor walked along the tree-lined main street, they passed a florist, a jeweler, and a sporting goods store, where they paused to look at the window. Mannequins cavorted in tennis whites and a large sign offered 70 percent off on all ski equipment.

"Margaux used to ski," Patricia said. It went without saying that she'd never be able to do it again. "She was good too."

"That's too bad. I'd love to have gone with her sometime."

"Do you ski?" Patricia hoped her surprise was not audible.

"Ever since I was a little girl. My uncle Oscar owned a ski shop on Long Island. I used to go upstate with our cousins a few times every winter. Of course I haven't done it in a long while. My cousin Sylvia is married with children now."

"Were you close to your cousin?" Patricia asked. Now Eleanor was the one who sounded regretful.

"Back then, yes. But our lives are so different. The boys take up so much of her time. They're just darling."

"You'd like to have children, wouldn't you?" Patricia said.

"Well, yes," Eleanor said. She sounded guarded. "When the time is right."

"Is there a special young man in your life?" asked Patricia.

"There was," Eleanor said. They had moved beyond the sporting goods store and had come to a dress shop.

"But no more?"

"He decided he preferred the company of someone else, only he didn't have the courtesy to tell me. He let me . . . figure it out for myself."

"I'm sorry."

"Don't be," Eleanor said with quiet dignity. "If he was the sort of person to do that, then he wouldn't have been the sort of person I'd have wanted as a husband. Or the father of my children." She smiled then, a small, and to Patricia's eye, brave smile. *Tom*, Patricia thought, *do not break the heart of this one. Please.*

Eleanor had turned away and was looking at a dress displayed in the window. It had an allover pattern of pansies—yellow, several shades of purple, dark green—as well as a full, gathered skirt and becoming scooped neckline. Eleanor's own dress was made of blue eyelet. Patricia had seen it several times already this summer; she guessed it was Eleanor's best and pressed into service often. Her hat, a fine straw with a matching blue grosgrain ribbon fastened to the underside of the brim, must have been made by her mother to go with the dress. It was far nicer than any of the hats in the window.

"Lovely dress," Patricia said, and when Eleanor agreed she added, "Do you want to go in and try it on? We're in no hurry to get back." But Eleanor shook her head and they kept walking. *She must be concerned about the price*, Patricia thought. A pity, because the cut of the dress would suit Eleanor's delicate figure and the bright print would offset her dark hair and eyes. It really was too bad, wasn't it, that the girl had to worry about every penny she spent.

Patricia stopped when they reached a cheerful apple-green-and-white-striped awning. Beneath the awning was a familiar sign:

TRACY TOLLAND, LUNCH AND TEA

"Here we are," she said, pushing open the door.

Tracy Tolland's restaurant had been serving the ladies of the area for decades; Patricia could even remember coming here once with her own mother, both of them in matching summer dresses and identical pairs of short white gloves. The round tables were still laid with white napkins and green cloths; a bud vase holding a single white rose stood at the center of each. In the wide picture window was the same brass birdcage, though, presumably, not the same pair of canaries that flitted from perch to perch, occasionally bursting into a chorus of song.

The hostess, whom Patricia recognized from more recent visits, took them to a window seat, where a waiter held out two green-and-white-striped chairs.

"This is so charming," Eleanor said, looking around.

"It's where we've always come," Patricia said, trying to see it through Eleanor's fresh eyes. The waiter came to fill their glasses with ice water and Eleanor drank hers down quickly. *Thirsty girl*, Patricia thought. Why did this bother her?

The waiter returned to take their orders: Lobster Newburg, endive salad, and the house beverage, raspberry limeade.

"I'll talk to Wynn about the school," Patricia said when he'd gone. Eleanor was silent. Patricia could guess the reason. Henryka may have thawed toward Eleanor but Wynn had not. "I don't trust her," he'd said to Patricia when they were alone. "Never did, never will."

"Why not? What has she ever done to make you say that?"

"Nothing. Yet. You wait though. You just wait." And, unwilling to elaborate, he'd gone back to the newspaper.

At the time, Patricia had dismissed his comment. But after this morning's conversation with Dottie—coupled with that telltale smear of lipstick on the pillowcase—she was once again thrown into doubt. Yes, the concern and initiative Eleanor showed about the school revealed the best of her character. But her behavior with Tom—did that reveal the worst? Was she conniving, as Wynn had said so often, and looking to Tom for a way to advance her place in the world? Or was she just an innocent, about to get her heart not just broken, but shattered?

The waiter appeared with a basket of rolls. Patricia took one and summoned her nerve. *Now,* she told herself, *say something to her now.*

"Eleanor," she began. "There's something I want to discuss with you. It's about Tom." There, she had started it; her stomach felt as if she had just taken a swooping dive off a precipice.

"What about him?" Eleanor did not look away.

"It seems to me that you two have become very friendly."

Eleanor looked uncomfortable. "Well, yes . . ."

"Eleanor, I know Tom's effect on women," Patricia said. "All women. He even charms Henryka."

"Is that . . . a problem?" Eleanor reached for a roll.

"It would be a problem only if you read too much into his behavior. If you thought that it meant more than it does."

"I don't think you're in a position to know what his behavior means." Eleanor put down the roll.

The effrontery of that reply forced Patricia to look away. The gall of her. The waiter came back, bearing their food, and so they were spared having to make conversation while it was placed on the table.

"Be careful," the waiter said. "Those plates are hot." When he'd gone, Patricia looked over at Eleanor again.

"I'm sorry if I offended you," Eleanor said. "But I think I can judge for myself whether Tom is being . . . sincere in his attentions."

"I don't think that you can," Patricia insisted. "That's the point. He's darling, he's lovable, and everyone adores him, including me. Especially me. But he's not to be trusted, Eleanor. He's just not." She took a bite of her food.

"How can you say those things?" Eleanor was visibly upset. "He's your brother." Her Lobster Newburg remained untouched.

"That's exactly why I can say them," Patricia said. She was twisting the napkin in her lap, winding it into a tight, angry coil. "Because I know him so well. I've watched him do the same thing over and over. Someone's heart always gets broken. I don't want it to be yours."

"My heart's already been broken," Eleanor said. "I'm not as innocent as I seem."

"Evidently not," Patricia said, unable to curb the sarcasm, and yes, cruelty in her voice.

"What do you mean?" Now Eleanor looked alarmed. She still had not touched her lunch.

"I was in Tom's room this morning," Patricia said. "I needed the car keys and knew he kept them in that golfing trophy. While I was in there, I couldn't help noticing that there was a smear of lipstick on his pillowcase."

"What does Tom's dirty linen have to do with me?" But color seeped into her cheeks; Patricia saw that she had struck a nerve.

"It was pink. The exact shade of pink lipstick that you were wearing at the party."

"Are you saying it was mine? That I was in Tom's room? In his bed?"

"It certainly seems that way," Patricia said. When Eleanor did not respond, she went on. "*Were* you in Tom's room last night?" More silence. "I can't prove anything. But it certainly has the look of impropriety, and given that you are acting as teacher, companion, and role model for my daughter, it poses a problem." She stopped twisting the napkin and forced her hands to remain still.

"You know how much I care for your daughter." Eleanor seemed to be choosing her words carefully. "And how much I've helped her. Still, if you feel I'm 'not a good influence,' you're free to let me go. I'll be very sorry if you do. And I think Margaux will be too." Eleanor was fighting for self-composure; Patricia could see the struggle playing out on her face. "But I'm a grown woman and I can make my own choices. I won't let you, or the *appearance of impropriety*, make those choices for me."

Patricia felt smacked. Had she *ever* been spoken to in this way by someone in her employ before? She was certain she had not. She could fire Eleanor on the spot. But beyond the momentary satisfaction this would give her, what good would it do? She, and most significantly, Margaux, would feel the loss of Eleanor's presence far more than Eleanor would feel the loss of theirs. Eleanor may have been the employee, but right now, she had the upper hand. Did she know it?

"Is everything all right, ladies?" Patricia looked up to see the waiter fairly bouncing on his toes in anticipation of fulfilling their next wish. "Can I get you anything else? More rolls? A refill on your drinks?"

"Everything's fine," Patricia said. "And no, we don't need anything just now." Would he ever go away? The waiter, looking crestfallen, retreated. Eleanor picked up her fork and probed the lobster; Patricia picked listlessly at her own. The birds in their brass cage trilled and chirped. Neither woman was interested in dessert and when the waiter asked if they wanted to take home the mostly uneaten meal, Patricia shook her head and asked for the check. This entire enterprise had been a failure, and she could not wait to get home. They turned and walked back along the main street, toward the car. When they reached it, Patricia said, "Can you wait for me here? There's something I need to do. I'll just be a few minutes."

"All right." Eleanor got into the car.

Patricia returned a few minutes later, stowed something in the trunk, and then joined Eleanor in the front seat. During the ride back, they both seemed intent on keeping the conversation light and inconsequential. Patricia skipped the coastal road in favor of the highway and they arrived home very quickly. Wynn's car was in the driveway, so she knew that Margaux—and Tom—were back.

"Thank you for lunch," Eleanor said as she got out of the car.

"My pleasure," Patricia said, mouthing the expected, rote phrase that was of course an utter lie. She waited until Eleanor had crossed the lawn, gone into the cottage, and closed the door before she got out of the car. Only then did she exhale, and she went into the house, in search of a drink.

THIRTEEN

―――――――――――――

Tom did not appear at dinner. After her conversation with Patricia, Eleanor certainly wasn't going to be the one to ask where he was, but Margaux volunteered that he'd met some old friends while at the club and decided, impromptu, to go off to Saratoga Springs with them.

"He didn't even come back for a change of clothes or a toothbrush," added Wynn, waving his tumbler of whiskey in the air as he spoke. "But that's Tom for you. Soul of a gypsy."

"Did he say when he'd be back?" Patricia patted her mouth with her napkin.

"Nope," said Wynn. "Not a word about it." He took a drink and set down the glass. "Henryka, this fish chowder breaks all records; is there any more in your magic pot?"

Henryka came in from the kitchen to refill his bowl. "More for you?" She turned to Eleanor. "You too? I can make hot."

"No, thank you, Henryka." Eleanor was not hungry but felt touched just the same.

Wynn launched into an account of the day's sail and Margaux

eagerly joined in. Eleanor tried to appear interested, especially when Margaux had something to say. But she was preoccupied by Tom's sudden departure. Of course he'd had no reason not to go; it wasn't as if he'd made any promises. Still, after the night they had shared, well, she would have thought he'd have found some way to contact her, some way to let her know his intentions. She hadn't seen him since just before dawn, when she'd left his room, gone quietly down the stairs, and across the lawn.

As the conversation eddied around her, she tried to observe Patricia without being too obvious. Her employer seemed animated enough, asking her husband questions, offering praise, and clearly pandering to his monumental ego. Eleanor remembered his crude remark, and the way he had touched her, as if she were a part of the house and he owned her too. How she disliked him. But then he made no secret of his dislike for her either, his phony manners and pretend goodwill aside. She wondered how such a man had produced a daughter like Margaux. Or what Patricia had ever seen in him.

When dinner was over, she joined Margaux on the sunporch for checkers. Eleanor won once and Margaux twice before they decided to put the game away. "You're not letting me win, are you?" Margaux asked.

"I respect your intelligence too much for that," said Eleanor.

"Uncle Tommy said he would teach me to play chess." Margaux dumped the red and black wooden pieces back in their box.

"Now there's a game of strategy," Eleanor said. She folded the checkerboard and handed it to Margaux. "I think you'd be good at it."

"Do you play chess?" Eleanor shook her head. "Maybe Uncle Tommy will teach you too," she said. "Do you want to learn? It would be fun to play together."

"It would. We'll ask him when he gets back."

"*If* he gets back," said Margaux. She put the board on top of the pieces and covered the box.

"Don't you think he will?" Eleanor felt the sudden weight of disappointment, like a stone, press down on her at the thought that he might not.

"You heard what Daddy said: he's a gypsy."

"Well, I think he'll be back," Eleanor said, getting up.

"You like him, don't you?" Margaux asked.

"Of course I do." Eleanor tried to keep her tone light, but it was not easy.

"I mean like a boyfriend. *That* kind of like."

"We hardly know each other," Eleanor said. She was blushing, she was sure of it.

"Not true! You've been here over a month. And anyway, in the movies, people fall in love right away. They just look at each other"— she demonstrated a soulful look for Eleanor's benefit—"they kiss, and presto! They're in love."

"That's in the movies," Eleanor said. "And you're old enough, and smart enough, to know that what goes on in the movies has very little to do with real life."

"Mother said she fell in love with Daddy right away." Margaux sounded like she was an expert on the subject. "They met at a Smith-Yale mixer. He was wearing a white dinner jacket and as soon as he saw her, he went over and asked her to dance. She said by the time the dance had finished, she knew."

"Is that so?" Eleanor said. She had gone to those mixers too, taking the bus from Poughkeepsie to New Haven, though she'd never found love, or anything even faintly resembling it. "How romantic." She stretched and yawned, signaling that this conversation was over.

"Maybe Tom will fall in love with you," Margaux said. She awkwardly got to her feet, gripping her walking stick. Eleanor knew better than to offer any help. "Then you could get married and be a part of our family. You'd be my aunt!"

"What an imagination you have," Eleanor said. How had Margaux divined her wishes, seen right into her secret heart? "You'll have to start writing your ideas down. I predict you're going to be a writer someday."

"Maybe I will," said Margaux, suddenly losing her dreamy look and becoming serious. "If you're a writer, no one has to know you have a withered leg or use a stupid old walking stick."

"That's true," Eleanor said. "When you write, you can be—anyone."

Back in the guest cottage, Eleanor found a large pink shopping bag on the table. She recognized it as the bag she'd seen Patricia carrying; it came from the dress shop in Dudley. She extracted a box from the bag, untied the ribbon, and pushed away the tissue to find the pansy-printed dress she'd admired in the window.

Patricia. She'd bought it, and left it here—her way of apologizing. When they sat down to lunch, Patricia believed herself to have the upper hand. And at first, Eleanor had felt the familiar pinch of fear: her reputation, her job. But as they talked, she realized Patricia was not about to fire her, and once Eleanor understood that, she stopped being afraid. As a Jew in a Gentile world, she'd learned it was best to remain on the margins, and had become accustomed to the deferential role. Today had been different—she was in charge and oh, how good it had felt.

She took off the dress she'd been wearing and slipped into the new one. There was a mirror on the closet door in the bedroom and she took a turn in front of it; the pansies on the skirt fluttered before settling down around her calves. A perfect fit. Should she keep it? Or wrap it back up and leave it without any word, as Patricia had left it here? She spun around in the other direction, and once again, the full skirt billowed and then settled. It was a lovely dress, an enchanting dress, and she was going to keep it—she'd earned it somehow.

Eleanor unzipped and then stepped out of the dress. She had been truthful today when she talked about Margaux, and although she had not used these exact words, she really did love the girl. She also loved the challenge of teaching a girl with the problems Margaux faced. At Brandon-Wythe, the curriculum and the methodology were all pre-ordained; she had a bit of flexibility in her classroom but only a bit; mostly she followed a plan conceived of and established by others. Whereas now, she was on her own, inventing the plan herself. And she was good at it. Other people saw this as well. One of them was Millard Hightower, the headmaster of the special school in upstate New York, with whom she'd had a lengthy telephone conversation. He was enormously interested in her observations about Margaux. "I'm always looking for teachers of a special caliber," he'd said. "If you'd ever like to come up for a formal interview, I'd be happy to reimburse your expenses. I feel confident that we could offer you something." So in the unlikely event that Patricia did fire her, she had options.

Eleanor smoothed the full skirt before hanging the dress in her closet. She would have to thank Patricia—tomorrow. But she didn't want to leave the cottage again tonight; she was worn out from both the lack of sleep last night and the drama of the day. A bath in the claw-footed tub was what she needed, and after that, one of the big white towels from the stack Opal always provided.

Immersed in the hot water, Eleanor leaned her head back and closed her eyes. Her thoughts turned to Tom. Would he like her new dress? Remembering what they had done last night made her long to do it all over again. How bold she'd been, taking off her clothes and getting into bed with him. Maybe he thought she was a tramp, and that's why he'd gone off to Saratoga Springs without telling her. But Eleanor did not believe it. And she did not believe the things Patricia had said about him either. Tom *did* feel something special for her, she was sure of it.

Eleanor stepped out of the tub and pulled the plug; the water made a loud gurgle as it began to disappear down the drain. Swathed in one of the big, soft towels, she took out the package from her mother that had arrived earlier in the week. It contained a set of cream-colored rayon pajamas with cropped pants and a Chinese-style top. The pajamas were covered in a pattern of red, blue, and green pagodas. She slipped them on and because the evening had gotten cool, added the matching wrapper. The material had a slippery feel, and she thought of Tom touching it, and then her bare skin underneath. After combing out her hair, she settled into the love seat to read a little from *Great Expectations*, which she had just started working on with Margaux. But she was more tired than she realized. Her eyes closed and she let her head sink to the cushion as the book slipped unnoticed from her hand.

A loud knock woke her. Perhaps Tom had come back and was here to see her. She hurried to greet him, but no, it was Wynn Bellamy. The sleeves of his white shirt were rolled up to the elbow and the shirt itself was untucked and partially unbuttoned so she could see the ribbed undershirt he wore beneath it. His feet were bare. She'd never seen him so unkempt. And he'd been drinking too; she could smell it.

"Well, hello," he said. "Aren't you going to invite me in?"

"At this hour?"

"If you don't mind." He leaned heavily against the door frame.

"It's kind of late and I was going to . . ." She didn't want to say the words *go to bed* in front of him.

"Just for a little while," he said. "I promise I won't stay too long." And then, without waiting for a reply, he pushed past her and strode into the cottage, his sense of ownership clear. When he sat down on the love seat, she remained standing.

"That's a nice outfit you have on. Very nice." He let his knees flop open so that even if she'd wanted to sit, there wouldn't have been any room. "Does it come with a matching hat?"

"It's not an outfit. I'm wearing *pajamas*." Eleanor instinctively tightened the wrapper's sash around her waist.

"Pajamas. Of course." He looked her up and down appraisingly. "I was just teasing you about the hat. Because you wear such nice hats. My wife is always saying so."

"Thank you." How she wished she were fully dressed. Or that he would just leave.

"Say, would you like a drink?" And he produced a silver flask from his pocket. "It might help you to relax. Loosen up a little, you know?"

"No, thank you," she said. "I'm relaxed enough."

"You're not," he said. "You're anything but relaxed. You're a bundle of nerves. And you want me out of here. I can see it all over your face."

She felt the heat pricking her cheeks. "Well, I was just getting ready to go to—"

"Bed," he said. Why did that word sound so fraught? He unscrewed the top of the flask. "You don't mind if I do? Even though you're not joining me?"

She shook her head, but she did mind. He'd had enough. What was he doing here anyway? He'd never come to visit her at the cottage before.

Mr. Bellamy took a drink and then leaned back. "Can I ask you something, Eleanor? Because it is all right to call you that, isn't it? Something of a rather personal nature?"

"You can ask anything you like," she said. "But I might not answer."

"Clever." He took another sip. "Very clever. Everyone's always saying how clever you are. But then your people are clever——" He stopped himself.

Eleanor was becoming quietly frantic. If she was going to get him to leave, it had to be his idea. "Are you planning to go fishing tomorrow?" Fishing meant getting up early—a reason for him to leave the cottage now.

"Fishing? I hadn't thought about it actually." He raised the flask to his lips—again. "Back to my question though. The one you said you might not answer. Here it is. I want to know why you don't like me."

"Who said I don't like you?"

"Come on now." He smiled. "We don't have to pretend, do we? You haven't liked me from the start."

What could she say? "Maybe I've felt that it was you who didn't like me, Mr. Bellamy."

"Wynn," he said. "Surely we're on a first-name basis by now."

"All right . . . Wynn." She had never actually said his first name aloud.

"Now we're getting somewhere!" He took another drink and when he saw she was watching he asked, "Are you sure you wouldn't like to have a sip?"

"Quite sure," she said.

"I wish you did like me," he said, gazing into the shining surface of the flask as if it were a mirror. "You seem to like everyone else around here—my daughter, my wife, my housekeeper. And my brother-in-law. *Especially* my brother-in-law. And they all like you!

So much. It's always, *Eleanor says this* and *Eleanor does that*. I feel left out, excluded in my own home. It's not a good feeling, Eleanor." He took a big swig from the flask. "So I propose that we start again. Fresh. You and I. Do you think we can do that?"

Eleanor did not know what to say, but her panic receded just the slightest bit. He was drunk, that was obvious, but maybe, just maybe, he really did want to make amends. And if that was the case, shouldn't she accept the olive branch he was offering? "All right," she said finally. "A fresh start."

"Splendid!" He jumped up from the love seat, surprisingly graceful for such a bulky man, and turned, as if looking for something. "Is there a radio in here?"

"Yes, but why do you—"

"I think we need to inaugurate our newfound understanding. Celebrate it even. And since you won't drink with me, you can at least dance with me. I'm a good dancer, you know. Anyone will tell you that."

"I'm not going to dance with you." Her voice was quiet but firm.

"Why not?" He spied the radio and turned it on. "Smoke Gets in Your Eyes" was playing. "Just one little dance. How can it hurt? Pretend we're at a party. A party for two."

"I said no."

He stood facing her, his chest heaving slightly, and she felt the challenge implicit in his stance. She had to get away—now. But in the few seconds of her hesitation, he'd crossed the room and grabbed both of her arms tightly. His face was close to hers now, much too close. And he was angry. Maybe she ought to dance with him— give him what he wanted, and then he would leave her alone. "One dance," he pleaded.

"All right," she said. "One."

Immediately his grip relaxed and he let one arm slide down so it was resting lightly on her waist. "There," he said. "Isn't that better?"

Eleanor didn't answer, but concentrated on keeping her body as far from his as she possibly could. She acknowledged that he was a good dancer and that had he been someone—anyone—else, she might even have been enjoying herself. The song ended and she stopped but he did not release her. "You said one dance," she said.

"The song was practically over when we started," said Wynn.

"This is the last one," she said. "Really."

He said nothing but tried to draw her body nearer to his. "That's not dancing when you're so far away," he said.

She moved toward him, acutely aware that her breasts, naked under the thin fabric of her pajamas and robe, would be pressing against him if she stepped any closer. As it was, the hand at her waist was rhythmically kneading her flesh and—

"Kiss me," he said softly. "Please."

Again, Eleanor stopped moving. "Mr. Bellamy, I'm not—"

"Wynn, it's Wynn—"

"Mr. Bellamy," she repeated. "You have to leave now." Panic was banging in her chest, her head. Why had she agreed to dance with him? She was a fool, an idiot— He brought his mouth close to hers but she turned her face away. "No, I won't, you can't force me—"

"Why not? What do you have against me? I'm trying to be nice. I'm trying very hard."

"You've had too much to drink, Mr. Bellamy." They were no longer dancing, but he hadn't let her go. "Please go back to the house now."

"I'll bet you kiss other men," he said. "You kiss my wastrel brother-in-law. I've seen you. And I'll bet you two do more than kiss. Everyone knows about your people—they're hot blooded."

"Let me go," she said. "Let me go right now!" She could scream, but then Patricia would hear—and Margaux. Unthinkable. So instead of screaming, Eleanor gave a sudden, violent twist away from him; she was unable to break free but she'd succeeded in unbalancing him. The two of them staggered together briefly and then went crashing down, her head smacking the floor with a sound like a bowling ball hitting a strike. The pain was instant and enveloping.

And even worse, she was now pinned under him, his chest a crushing weight, his alcohol-laced breath foul in her face. "Come on," he said. "A kiss, just one measly little kiss." With one hand, he held her face and tried to press his mouth against hers and with the other, he reached inside the robe for the opening to her pajama top and yanked until the buttons gave way. Her panic gave her strength and she managed to rake her nails along his forearms, drawing blood in their wake.

"What the—" He pulled away to run his fingers over the wounds and she used the opportunity to scramble to her feet. But oh, her head hurt. It hurt so much. Her eyes couldn't focus and instead of one Wynn Bellamy, she saw two. Yet she still was able to grab the ironstone pitcher from its spot on the side table. "If you come any closer, I'll throw it." He hesitated and then he was across the room and out of the cottage, door banging behind him.

She remained where she was, head throbbing, eyes still not able to focus. Mr. Bellamy—she would never, ever think of him as Wynn—had grabbed and imprisoned her in his meaty arms. Danced with her. Tried to kiss her. Tore her pajamas. And then, thank God, left. She touched the back of her head, where a lump was forming; there was a soft but menacing ringing in her ears. She began moving clumsily toward the bathroom and the tub. She wanted to wash his touch from her skin, the water as hot as she could bear. Then she vomited, a pale, foamy pool of liquid on the wooden floor.

Forget the shower. She had to get to a doctor. Where? How? Across the lawn, Tom's window was still dark but the light in Henryka's window glowed. She was still up. And she knew how to drive. Eleanor's own driving skills were too rusty to pull out now. She needed help. But would Henryka be the one to offer it?

She went to the closet. Somewhere inside was her raincoat, and she pawed through the rack of clothes until her trembling hand seized it. She put it on, slid into her shoes, and picked up her purse. She was shaking, but a desperate energy propelled her through the dark, toward the house. When she got to the door, she stopped. There was a good chance Mr. Bellamy was inside. The shaking intensified. Her only hope was in that house too. She would have to take the risk.

Once inside, she removed her shoes and found the stairs. A soft thudding noise made her freeze, and she waited, immobile, until she realized it was just the cat. Her chest released in a long exhale. She continued upstairs and down the hall until she reached Tom's room, still empty. Here were the car keys nestled at the bottom of the trophy, just where Patricia had said they would be. Deep into her coat pocket they went. Then she climbed the staircase that led to the third floor—and to Henryka's room.

"Henryka," she called softly. "Henryka, are you up? It's me, Eleanor." Henryka opened the door and gasped. No wonder—Eleanor could just imagine what she must have looked like. "I'm sorry if I scared you. But I saw your light. I need help. Please help me."

"What happen you?"

"I don't want to talk here. Won't you let me in?"

Henryka stepped back. She wore a faded robe and her hair was down around her shoulders; she was obviously getting ready for bed.

"Henryka, I have to see a doctor. Now. Can you drive me?" She pulled the keys from her coat pocket and held them up.

"It very late."

Eleanor could see that she was weighing the situation, trying to determine what had happened, where her allegiance belonged, what she should do. "Please, Henryka," she begged. "My head hurts so much and there's no one else I can ask."

All at once, Henryka's expression softened. "You wait." She stepped behind a fabric-covered folding screen. As she dressed, her head was still visible. "Sit down," she instructed. Eleanor sank gratefully into a chair. Henryka stepped back out from behind the screen clad in a skirt and blouse. "Dr. Parker. He close by," she said. "Give me keys. I take you."

As they drove along the dark, quiet road, Eleanor waited for Henryka to ask her what had happened to her but it was only when they had reached the doctor's house that she spoke. "Mr. Wynn—he do this to you." It was a statement, not a question.

Eleanor looked at her with astonishment. "How did you know?" Henryka didn't offer anything more, but the answer was suddenly so clear. "It's because he did it to you, isn't it?"

"Long time ago," said Henryka. "At Christmas party. He drunk and follow me into kitchen."

"He was drunk when he showed up at the cottage tonight. He wanted me to have a drink with him. I said no."

Henryka nodded, as if familiar with the script.

"Then he wanted to dance with me. To kiss me. But I wouldn't, I didn't . . ." Eleanor hadn't cried when Mr. Bellamy was in the cottage and she hadn't cried since. Now the tears let loose—a flood, a torrent.

"It be all right." Henryka leaned over and patted her back. "You see."

Eleanor's tears slowed. "Did you tell Patricia? Threaten to leave?"

"What I say?" Henryka asked. "Where I go?"

Eleanor could easily fill in the blanks. She knew that Henryka had been widowed young and left with three girls to raise on her own. Her parents were still in Poland, and all this must have happened during the Depression, when jobs were scarce. So naturally she had stayed on at the Bellamys'. How far had it gone? Had it happened only that one time? Or had Mr. Bellamy made a habit of it? But when she looked at Henryka, stoic and even serene in the muted light of the dashboard, she realized that the older woman wasn't going to tell her any more. And she wasn't going to ask.

FOURTEEN

On Sunday, Patricia slept until noon, although she'd kept her vow and had nothing at all to drink the night before. It was the pill she had taken for her headache, she realized as she surfaced, reluctantly, from the insistent swirl of her dreams. It had never affected her like this before though; she felt like she was emerging from a state of dark enchantment.

Downstairs, the house was eerily quiet. There was no sign of Wynn, Margaux, or even Henryka. Only Glow, curled up on the rug and fixing her with her green-gold gaze. Then the back door opened and Henryka stepped inside. In one hand, she held a bunch of phlox, taken from the cutting garden behind the house; in the other, a pair of shears.

"Where is everyone?" Patricia asked.

"Mr. Wynn at club," Henryka said, averting her eyes. "Miss Margaux sleeping."

At this hour? That was strange. Patricia sank into a chair; the strange, befuddled feeling was still enveloping her. "How about Eleanor?" she asked. "Have you seen her yet today?"

"No," said Henryka. She seemed to be deliberately avoiding Patricia's gaze. What was wrong with her?

"Well, I guess she's sleeping late too," she said with forced cheer. "Is there any coffee on the stove? I'd love a cup."

"Of course." Henryka filled a vase with water and placed the flowers in it before turning her attention to the coffee.

"Have you baked anything?" Patricia asked. There were no enticing smells emanating from the oven, no pans or trays in evidence.

"No," Henryka said. "You want I should bake now?"

"That's all right, Henryka," Patricia said, moving toward the door to go check on Margaux. "Just the coffee; we'll eat when everyone is up."

Henryka nodded and finally let her gaze meet Patricia's. In her cool green eyes, Patricia saw an unfamiliar expression she could not quite identify.

Margaux was asleep, curled on her side, the covers peeled back, her bad leg exposed, snoring lightly. Patricia stood staring at the leg for a moment; she rarely saw it anymore since Margaux was so careful about keeping it covered. But now she could look all she wanted at the thin, malformed limb, its ankle as shrunken as a toddler's. She forced herself to look elsewhere, at her daughter's face. When had the girl ever slept so late? She closed the door quietly and went into the kitchen where the coffee waited. Then she picked up the black telephone and asked the operator to put her through to the club. Mr. Hennessy, the day manager, picked up on the first ring.

"Good afternoon, Mrs. Bellamy," he said once she identified herself. "How can I help you?"

"I'm looking for my husband," she said. "I'd like to speak to him, please."

"Mr. Bellamy hasn't been here today," said Mr. Hennessy. In the background, there were short bursts of laughter. The club on a Sunday afternoon in the summer was a lively place.

"Are you sure?" Patricia asked. "Perhaps he's gone sailing?"

"I'm quite sure, Mrs. Bellamy," Mr. Hennessy was saying. "All guests have to sign in. That's the rule."

"I must have been mistaken then," she said. "Thank you just the same, Mr. Hennessy."

If Wynn was not at the club, where was he? And why had he told Henryka that was where he was going? Glow, who had wandered into the kitchen, wound herself around Patricia's ankles. When Patricia reached down to stroke her fur, the animal unsheathed its claws to slash the back of Patricia's hand. "Ouch!" She looked down at the bright red streaks; Glow twitched her tail and walked off. Patricia went to the sink to wash away the blood. The cat had never done that before. As Patricia dried her hand, Eleanor came in. "Good morning," Patricia said. "Or rather, good afternoon."

Eleanor did not reply. Patricia thought she looked dreadful: gray smudges under her eyes, her skin pale and waxy. "Are you feeling all right?" she asked. Maybe she had a hangover? But Tom had not returned last night and Patricia doubted she would drink alone.

"I'm fine," Eleanor said though it hardly seemed true. "I didn't sleep very well, that's all."

"And I slept too well. I had a headache last night and I took something for it. I forgot just how strong it was. I didn't get up until noon. And now it's like the whole house is under a spell. Margaux's still asleep. Tom's gone and who knows where Wynn is."

At the mention of Wynn's name, a shudder of almost palpable revulsion seemed to pass over Eleanor's face. Did she really dislike him that much?

"Would you like me to check on her?" Eleanor offered. "Maybe I should wake her if she's still asleep."

"Yes, why don't you?" Patricia said. She went up to her room to get dressed and when she returned to the kitchen, Henryka was making French toast and Margaux was sitting at the table with Eleanor. "How are you this morning, darling?" she asked.

"I slept and slept," said Margaux. "I've never slept so late in my life."

"You certainly did. Are you sure you're not sick?"

"I'm fine, Mother. Truly."

After they were all seated, Patricia began to feel as if things were returning to normal. Margaux gobbled down three slices and drank two glasses of milk. Patricia allowed herself a second slice, or at least a few bites of one. Eleanor, however, had hardly touched the slice she had been served. "Aren't you hungry?" Patricia asked.

Eleanor jumped perceptibly, as if she'd been prodded. "Not really," she said. "Do you think I could have a cup of tea?" she said to Henryka.

Patricia's sense that everything was all right quickly dissipated. The looks passing between those two; what could they mean? She got up from the table. "I'm going down to the club," she said. This idea had just come to her. Even if Wynn was not there, perhaps someone might know where he was. Besides, she could not sit around this house all day. Everything felt decidedly off-kilter, verging on bizarre. She needed a change of scene, that was all. The keys to Tom's car would be in his room; he had left with his friends and not returned for it. So Patricia would borrow his decrepit Oldsmobile—he could afford a better car; why did he drive that jalopy?—to see if she could find Wynn.

The club, as she had anticipated, was bustling. There were several card games in progress and the dining room was full. The chaise longues out by the pool would all be taken. Through the open doors, she could see the sailboats bobbing merrily on the shining surface of the water. Inside, a nautical theme prevailed: anchors, coils of rope, and buoys were used as décor, and a series of pastel seascapes adorned the walls. Patricia spotted Dottie Talbot, who was seated alone at a table by a window, and headed over.

"What are you drinking?" she asked Dottie when she sat down.

"A martini. Won't you have one with me?" Dottie motioned the waiter over and he brought Patricia a martini as well. It was cold, dry, and delicious. One martini easily led to another. Soon it was almost five o'clock. Dottie said she was going to have an early dinner at the club; would Patricia like to join her?

"Where's John tonight?" Patricia asked. The second drink had calmed her nerves and she felt better, almost, if not quite, herself.

"Oh, I don't know and I'm not sure I care," said Dottie, lighting a cigarette. "Husbands can be such a bother sometimes, don't you think?" Patricia said nothing and Dottie asked, "Speaking of husbands, where's Wynn?"

That's what Patricia wanted to know. "I was hoping he was here."

"I haven't seen him." Dottie blew elegant smoke rings up into the air. "Who needs husbands anyway? We can have dinner alone."

Patricia hesitated. She had no desire to go home, but felt guilty leaving Margaux. "Let me call the house." She stood and made her way a little unsteadily through the club and to the bank of telephone booths, just off the powder room.

"How is everything?" she asked Henryka.

"Everything be fine."

So why didn't Patricia believe her? "Let me talk to Margaux."

Margaux said the same thing, and Patricia returned to the table, where a glass of wine awaited her. "I ordered for you," Dottie said, raising her own glass. "Cheers." They each drank another with dinner, and their conversation grew quite animated, if somewhat rambling. By the time Patricia drove home—very slowly, the car weaving back and forth across the nearly empty road—she had succeeded in distancing herself from the strange and troubling day.

At the house, there was no sign of Margaux or Eleanor, though she had seen a light on in the guest cottage when she got out of the car, and another light on in Henryka's window. She paused in front of Margaux's door and knocked softly.

"I'm still up," Margaux called. "You can come in."

Her daughter was sitting up in bed, dark blond hair spread out across her white cotton nightgown. Seen this way, her daughter looked perfect—you would never know that anything was wrong. "What are you doing?" Patricia asked, trying to mask her sudden rush of emotion.

"Just reading." She held up her book—*Great Expectations*—for Patricia to see.

"Fine choice," Patricia said.

"Eleanor suggested it," Margaux said. She placed the open book down beside her.

"Eleanor makes good suggestions," Patricia said. "How is Eleanor today?" she asked. "She didn't look well."

"She wasn't." Margaux gestured for her mother to sit down. "Do you know what she told me?"

Patricia shook her head.

"She's homesick! I didn't think grown-ups got homesick."

"Anyone can get homesick," Patricia said. Was that really all that was wrong with Eleanor?

"She wants to go home," Margaux said. "I told her to ask you. You'll let her, Mother, won't you?"

"Won't you miss her?"

"So much. But I don't want her to be sad. She could go for a week-end and then come back to us."

"She certainly could," Patricia said, smoothing the quilt that covered Margaux's ruined leg. "And it's very kind of you to consider her feelings."

"Then you say yes?"

"I'll talk to her about it tomorrow." Patricia got up. "You're probably not very sleepy."

"No, I'm not," Margaux said.

"Well, you can stay up and read until you're tired."

Though she had had a lot to drink, Patricia wasn't tired either, and after getting undressed, she sat up reading in bed. Wynn finally came in sometime around midnight. He looked a fright too, with his hair uncombed and his clothes all wrinkled. "Where were you?" She hadn't meant to start out this way, but honestly, what did he mean by disappearing all day and then coming home in such a state?

"I was out."

"I didn't see you all day."

"I told Henryka: I was at the club and then later I met up with John Talbot."

"You may have been with John Talbot, but it wasn't at the club. I called and Clarence Hennessy said you hadn't been there. And then I stopped by myself, later. I would have seen you."

"What is all this about, anyway? Am I on trial?"

"Should you be?"

He glared at her.

"You've been gone all day. Eleanor's been acting strangely, and Margaux slept past noon. I'm just wondering what's going on."

"Margaux stays up too late. And no wonder, seeing how she's con-tinually *stimulated* by that so-called tutor you had to hire."

"What are you implying?" she said.

"Just that she's a little tramp, that's all. Hardly the sort of person to set a good example for Margaux."

"A tramp?" But she knew where this was heading. Knew, and could do nothing about it because from all appearances, it was true.

"Haven't you seen the way she and Tom are mooning at each other? Or has she got you hoodwinked so completely that you're oblivious to what's going on right under your nose?" He removed his pants and laid them over a chair.

"Nothing is going on under my nose."

"Oh Christ, Tricia, will you grow up? That brother of yours is canoodling with our daughter's tutor. Everyone can see it but you."

"Tom is a hopeless flirt," she said. Wynn was right of course. Dottie had seen it. Eleanor wasn't even denying it. And then there was the lipstick smear on the pillowcase. "You're blowing this way out of proportion."

"Oh? Just wait and see what happens when he knocks her up. She's angling to get money from you—that's all they ever care about. Money." He finished undressing and got into bed beside her.

There was a silence, tense and angry. Patricia closed her eyes and tried to sleep. But Wynn moved closer, and nudged her nightgown up. She moved away and he moved with her; if this continued they would both fall off the bed. He continued his exploration until she put a hand on his wrist to stop him.

"Why not?" he asked.

"I just don't feel like it."

"But why?"

"I don't know," she said peevishly. "Isn't it enough to say no?"

"You always say no." He rolled away from her. "Always." His voice had lost its petulant edge and just sounded sad.

She felt sorry for him then, but that did nothing to arouse her desire. Instead, she turned toward him and began to stroke his hair, almost as if he were her child, not her husband. His breathing slowed and became more regular; soon he was asleep.

On Monday morning, she woke to find him packing. "Are you going somewhere?" He had planned to stay at the house this week—or so he had told her.

"I've got some business in Boston. I'll be gone for a couple of days." He would not look at her.

"You never mentioned it."

"It's a case involving a Boston firm. Nothing that important."

"It's important enough for you to be going there. And staying overnight." She stared at him but he still would not look back.

"Why are you asking me all these questions? Don't you trust me?" He finally met her gaze.

Patricia got out of bed. "I just don't understand why you won't give me a straight answer."

"I'll telephone you from Boston," he said, tossing balled-up pairs of socks into the open suitcase. "You'll be fine. And I'm not leaving yet. I'll have breakfast here."

"All right," she said, "I just wish that—" The telephone's ring cut her short and she went down to answer it. It was Tom, calling from Saratoga Springs.

"Where are you holed up?" she asked. "And when are you coming back? Margaux's been asking about you."

"I'm staying with Jasper Collins. He's bought this great old mansion. Eight bedrooms. Bathrooms galore. And a conservatory and a ballroom. Who has a ballroom these days?"

"It certainly sounds . . . ostentatious," she said. Patricia knew Jasper Collins. He was a very wealthy, very flamboyant character prone to waistcoats, top hats, and brilliantly colored silk ascots. She remembered seeing him at a New Year's Eve party where she could have sworn he was wearing lipstick.

"You sound so disapproving, Trish. What have you got against Jasper? He's a great host, a real gas—dinner parties, lawn parties, pool parties, and of course, days at the races. You and Wynn should drive up. Jasper's always asking after you."

"The feeling might not be mutual," she said. She could hear the floorboards creak upstairs; Wynn was still moving around in their bedroom.

"Why not?"

"You know why not," she said. It was well known in their circle that Jasper preferred the company of men to women, including—no, *especially*—in the bedroom. Despite his money, he was not exactly the sort of person with whom she wanted to socialize. And she would never have spent the night in his home.

"Oh, that." Tom was dismissive. "Who cares? He's great company, you know. You should hear him talk about opera—the man's a walking musical encyclopedia. He's promised to take me when we're back in town. He's had season tickets at the Met for years."

"You should care, Tom," she said. "People will talk if you stay up there too long."

"People will talk no matter what. I'm not going to live my life differently because they do. And neither should you."

Before she could reply, Henryka came into the kitchen. Patricia put a hand over the mouthpiece and said, "Could you excuse me for a moment?" Henryka left the room.

"Was that Henryka, my sweetheart, my darling? You tell her that even Jasper's fancy chef can't compete with her cooking. Will you tell her that for me?"

"You can tell her yourself, if and when you ever come back. I'm not your go-between, you know."

"What's wrong with you today? You've done nothing but scold me. Why?"

"Eleanor," she said quietly. "Or should I say, Eleanor and you."

"Ah," said Tom. "So you know?"

"Know what? Is there something I *should* know? Though she is in my employ, after all. Living in my home." When Tom said nothing she added, "I found her lipstick on your pillowcase, Tom. I don't need to tell you how that looks. I didn't tell Wynn, but he's already predicting that you're going to get her pregnant."

"Wynn believes the worst about people," Tom said. "But you don't, Trish. You never have. So I don't want you to judge her harshly. She's not what Wynn thinks she is."

"And what would that be?"

"Cheap. Common."

"Well, it certainly looks that way, doesn't it?"

"Forget the way it looks. Eleanor has the purest heart of anyone I've ever met."

"So why are you in Saratoga, instead of here, with Lady Pure Heart?"

"To tell you the truth, she scares me."

"Scares you?"

"It's that purity of hers. It's fierce. There's no dissembling. She says what she thinks. What she feels. I've never known anyone quite like her. And her effect on me is a little . . . unsettling."

"What are you saying?"

"I feel like I'm falling in love with her. That's why I left. I don't want to be in love. Not with her, not with anyone."

"In love?" Alarm ignited inside her like a fire. It was one thing for

Tom to flirt with and even seduce Eleanor. Love was another thing entirely. "I thought you wanted to be free. Free as a bird."

"I do. I always have been. And I've liked it that way."

"Well, it's been an illusion. No one is free, Tom." He didn't answer, so she went on. "What you're doing is dangerous and even cruel. Someone is going to get hurt."

"I've never wanted to hurt anyone," Tom said. "You know that much about me, don't you, Trish?"

"Don't be an idiot. What makes you think your wanting has anything to do with it?" She heard footsteps on the stairs; Wynn would be down any moment and the conversation, like it or not, was over.

FIFTEEN

On Monday morning Eleanor lay in bed, reluctant to get up. The air was at first cool, and then warmed gradually. A brilliant, orange-and-black monarch butterfly went fluttering past the window, and somewhere in the distance, a dog began to bark. She shifted, but remained where she was. In her dreams, she'd stumbled through a menacing darkness, been assaulted by loud, percussive sounds. Although she could not actually see him, she knew that a large, hooded figure crouched behind a door. He was waiting—waiting for her.

It had been roughly thirty-six hours since Wynn Bellamy paid her his unannounced and unwelcome visit. Yesterday she had been over to the house but had quickly retreated to the cottage and not gone out since. Late in the afternoon she cautiously opened the door and was grateful to find a tray containing a thermos of soup and two slices of fresh bread wrapped in a kitchen towel. Henryka. Eleanor sipped the soup but had no interest in the bread, and instead balled it into crumbs, for the birds.

How had Henryka managed to face Wynn Bellamy in the weeks, months, and years since he'd done whatever it was he had done to her? And how had she faced Patricia? Eleanor had not seen Patricia or Margaux since Sunday morning. She knew she ought to contact Margaux and yet she couldn't—she felt paralyzed. There was no one to turn to, no one to ask. She was flooded with shame, guilt, but most of all, self-recrimination. Letting him in when she wasn't dressed. Agreeing to dance with him. And why hadn't she screamed? She thought she was protecting herself, but really she was protecting him. She was a fool, an idiot. She deserved what she had gotten—or at least that was what people would say if they knew. But they wouldn't know because she wasn't going to tell anyone—ever.

Eleanor forced herself to get up and to dress. She was going to go over to the house. The longer she postponed it, the worse it would be. Outside, the grass was wet. It must have rained during the night. When she reached the back door and let herself into the kitchen, she found Henryka at the stove, frying doughnuts. Oil sizzled as she set rings of dough into the pan. "You all right?"

"Yes, Henryka, I'm all right," Eleanor said. "Thank you for asking."

On Saturday night, Henryka had accompanied her to Dr. Parker's house. After the exam, Eleanor followed him out to the waiting room where Henryka was sitting. "She took a pretty bad knock on the head," he said. "She has a slight concussion, so someone will need to keep an eye on her." Henryka had nodded gravely, and she had insisted on seeing Eleanor back to the cottage. And although Eleanor said it wasn't necessary, Henryka spent the night with her, cramming herself into the love seat as best she could. "You can no be alone," she had said. "Doctor say so."

Now Henryka was looking at her anxiously. "Everyone in there," she said. "Mr., missus, and the girl." When Eleanor didn't reply, she added, "You need food. Go sit. I bring it."

Eleanor hesitated for a few seconds; she heard Patricia's voice, and Margaux's in reply. And then—Wynn Bellamy. She pushed open the door and there he was, freshly shaved and hair still wet from the shower. He'd been looking down as he spooned his oatmeal but he looked up when she came in. "Good morning, Eleanor. I heard you weren't feeling well. You're better, I hope?"

"I'm fine," she murmured and took a seat. Henryka hurried in with a bowl of oatmeal.

"That's good," he said. "We can't have you getting sick, now can we? Not on our watch."

Patricia and Margaux were quiet and their silence made Eleanor as uncomfortable as Wynn's joviality. Could either of them know what had happened to her? That was impossible though. Or maybe it *hadn't* happened—or at least not the way she was remembering. Wynn showed no sign of discomfort, no apparent remorse.

"Do you want another cup of coffee before I drive you to the station?" Patricia finally said. "Henryka's bringing out a fresh pot."

His mouth was full, so he nodded.

He was leaving. Mr. Bellamy was leaving. Eleanor's relief was so enormous she could have laughed out loud. But she didn't. Instead she paid careful attention to their conversation. Mr. Bellamy seemed his usual self, but Patricia was clearly on edge. And Margaux said nothing, which was not at all like her. Henryka appeared with the coffee and a platter of fresh doughnuts. Mr. Bellamy reached for one, and his sleeve rose up just the slightest bit. Peeking out from his crisp, white shirt cuff were a few small scratches, scabbed over and innocuous. But Eleanor stared as if they gushed fresh blood and she could not look at them a single second longer— "You'll have to excuse me." She rose so abruptly that she knocked her chair back and it hit the floor. "I'm not well, I'll just go back to the cottage and—"

"Eleanor, what's wrong—" Patricia got up and righted the chair.

Margaux cried, "Are you all right?" The only one who said nothing was Wynn Bellamy, who continued drinking his coffee.

"I'll be all right," she said, waving off Patricia's efforts to accompany her. "Please, just let me go and lie down."

Back in the cottage, she got into bed, burrowed under a blanket, and let the trembling overtake her. She couldn't stay here, she couldn't go. Then she remembered the conversation at the table—Mr. Bellamy was leaving, *he* would be gone. She wouldn't have to see him for a few days. Her decision could wait. The trembling subsided and she got up.

During her examination on Saturday night, Dr. Parker had asked if she'd been drinking. "No," she had said. "Why do you ask?" She was mortified that he thought she was a falling-down drunk.

"That bump on the back of your head. An injury like that suggests there was a strong impact, like you were pushed or fell down a flight of stairs. Do you want to tell me what happened?"

Eleanor looked at his thin, lined face, with its incongruously dapper pencil mustache above the upper lip. His dark-brown eyes seemed neither especially kind nor especially hostile; they were opaque, cutting off all access to his thoughts. She hadn't anticipated this conversation when she'd asked Henryka to bring her here. She only knew that her head hurt, badly, and she needed some kind of medical attention.

"No," she said. "I wouldn't."

He hadn't pressed.

Eleanor went to the window. Tom's car was still there, but the Bellamys' car was gone, which meant Patricia and Mr. Bellamy were gone too. What a relief. She could go back over to the house and call home. Yes, that was a very good idea. Since she'd been here, she'd been writing to Irina. But right now she needed to hear her mother's voice. It was a long-distance call, and she hadn't asked if she could make one. She could mention it later though. And offer to pay for the charges.

When Eleanor let herself in, the kitchen was empty and with shaking fingers, she dialed the number and clutched the phone tightly as it rang and rang. Strange. It was Monday, a time Irina ought to have been in the shop. But she was not. Eleanor put the phone back on the receiver and went out onto the sunporch, where Margaux was sprawled on the sofa, listening to the radio. When she saw Eleanor, she sat up and switched it off. "How are you?" she said. "Mother was worried. So was I."

What about your father? Was he worried too? "I'm fine now," said Eleanor. "You don't need to worry."

"I told Mother you were homesick," Margaux said.

"Why did you tell her that?" Eleanor sank into the sofa.

"Because it's true," Margaux said. Glow walked by, swishing her tail, and Margaux reached for her. The creature adroitly eluded her grasp and padded off. "I told her to let you go home for the weekend. To see your mother."

"What did she say?" Eleanor asked. This was it—the answer to her dilemma. She could go home for a few days and see Irina, maybe see Ruth or one of her college friends. It would be just what she needed. Then she could come back and all would be as it had been before.

"She said she'd talk to you." There was the sound of a car pulling up to the house. "That's her now. You can ask her."

Patricia came in adjusting her blouse, which had come untucked from her skirt. "Eleanor!" she said. "I was just going to check on you. Maybe we ought to take a drive over to see Dr. Parker."

"No!" Eleanor said.

"Well, all right." Patricia seemed a little surprised by her reaction. "If you're sure . . ."

"I'm sorry, I just don't want you to go to any trouble. I'm fine. Really."

"Ask her about going home," Margaux urged.

"Going home?" Patricia said.

"Yes. I wanted to visit my mother. It wouldn't be for long. I'd leave on Friday afternoon and be back on Sunday."

"You really miss her, don't you?" Patricia said.

"Yes," Eleanor said. "And she misses me too, though she won't come out and say so."

"That's sweet," Patricia said. "You must be very close. I'd like to meet her sometime."

"I think you did. She said you stopped by the store one day and bought a hat from her." Eleanor had not meant to bring this up but the words felt like they leaped from her mouth of their own accord.

"Oh, that's right." Patricia looked uncomfortable.

"You didn't introduce yourself," Eleanor said. Why was she going on about this? She knew she shouldn't.

"No? I thought I had," said Patricia.

Eleanor was angry that Patricia was lying about a visit that at this moment felt like an invasion. Yet another one. Then she regretted her tone. "Not, of course, that it matters. I'll just let her know I'm coming."

She followed Patricia into the kitchen and placed the call. "Your timing couldn't have been better," Irina said. "I need your help— there's been a flood."

"In the basement?" asked Eleanor. Her mother had a small storage area and it had flooded before.

"Where else?"

"Have you told the landlord?"

"Yes, but you know how he is about that . . ." Irina was the only one in the building who used the basement, so the landlord felt she ought to be the one to maintain it, especially since he was already giving her a break on the rent.

"Did you lose a lot of stock? Supplies?"

"There's at least six inches of water on the floor so I haven't been able to check," said Irina. "But I know I lost a whole box of silk flowers, another one of netting, and—"

"I'll be down on the next train." Eleanor could see her mother's familiar, worried expression, the crease between her brows, the nervous pursing of her lips. She'd be perched there on those rickety little steps, trying to calculate the severity of the damage, the extent of her loss. Of course Eleanor had to help her. She turned to see Patricia; she had forgotten she was in the room.

"I'm sorry, I heard everything; is there anything I can do?" Patricia said.

"There's been a flood at the shop. I've got to get down to New York today, actually."

"Of course," Patricia said. "I'll take you to the station myself. That's really too bad."

"I'll need to pack," Eleanor said. "It won't take me long." She left Patricia in the kitchen and walked out the door, in the direction of the cottage. Then she stopped. Why had Wynn Bellamy suffered no censure, no consequence? Instead, he got to eat doughnuts and drink coffee; his unsuspecting wife had driven him to the station where he boarded a train to Boston and conveniently left Eleanor—mortified, questioning, churning—behind. The injustice of this felt intolerable.

Eleanor walked out of the house and over to the pair of cars that were parked side by side. The Bellamys' car was new and sleek, a burnt orange Cadillac with a gleaming silver bird on the hood. Tom's car was a bit of a wreck, but it still ran. Where was Tom, anyway? Why hadn't he been in touch?

To her surprise, the keys were still in the Cadillac; Patricia must have forgotten them. Eleanor had a sudden urge to get in the car and drive off—but where? Somewhere far away from Wynn Bellamy. Those scratches on his arm—did he know or care that she had seen them? And why didn't he worry about what his wife or daughter would think? Because he wasn't afraid of her, that was why—he knew she wouldn't tell.

Eleanor opened the door on the driver's side and got in. Hit by the morning sun, the keys shone brightly. *You can do this*, they seemed to say. *You must.* She turned the ignition and jumped a little as the car came to life. Here was the gas pedal, there was the brake. Could she remember what to do? Yes, she thought, as she slowly guided the car down the gravel driveway and out toward the road. She could.

Going slow enough to elicit honks of annoyance from passing motorists, Eleanor made her way down one country road and then the next until she came to the road that led into the town. There was the newsstand, luncheonette, toy store, grocery. She continued on, past the library and municipal building. The police station was in there—Patricia had mentioned it once.

Eleanor slowed down and pulled over. Her heart throbbed as she imagined walking into the station, saying she wanted to report a crime. Because what he'd done was a crime, wasn't it? He'd attacked, no, molested her. Surely there was a law against such behavior and he'd violated it. But how to describe to the policemen what he'd said, what he'd done? Who would believe her?

She started the car and began driving again. The police would be of no help to her, even if she had told them what happened. The station receded from her vision and she let it go, becoming instead gripped by a strange, trancelike fascination with the particularities of the Cadillac: the easy glide of the wheel under her hands; the hum of the engine; the chrome dials; the sleek, toffee-colored leather of the seat. She was in this moment supremely grateful that her father had insisted on teaching her to drive; Irina had never wanted to learn. "A car is nothing but a big, hulking menace," she had said. But Eleanor's father prevailed. "Driving is a useful skill," he'd said. "You never know when it might come in handy."

She pressed the gas pedal and felt the Cadillac accelerate. The car she'd learned on was a Ford Model A; even then it was a relic. But this car was a sensitive instrument, almost animate in the way it responded. She felt her breathing relax and slow; driving was a drug, hypnotic and lulling. When she saw the sign for the highway, she impulsively merged with the outbound traffic. She could just keep driving—way up north, as far as Canada, or south, to the palm trees and turquoise waters of Florida. Mexico even. She took note, in a detached, impersonal way, as the needle of the speedometer moved past sixty, then seventy and—my God, she was speeding. What had possessed her anyway? And she shouldn't be out here at all—she had to get back to catch that train to the city, where her mother was waiting. She eased off the gas, found the next exit, and eventually circled back to the road she'd first taken from the house.

Eleanor parked the car—rather well she thought—and then returned to the cottage. She'd been gone longer than she'd meant to be and she had to hurry. Flinging open the door, she pulled her valise out from under the bed and began to toss things inside. In went clothes, shoes, a few books. The pansy-printed dress. The pajamas and robe she knew she would never wear again.

"There you are. I've been looking all over for you. Where have you been?" Eleanor glanced up and saw Patricia in the doorway. "I checked the schedule and there's a train to New York in a little less than an hour. If we leave now, you can make it."

Eleanor snapped the valise shut and grabbed the handle. "I'm ready. Let's go." She followed Patricia back to the Cadillac and got in, surreptitiously patting the seat. She felt like she and the car now shared a secret.

"Eleanor, did you take the car out today?" Patricia said.

"Why do you ask?" The question startled her, though it shouldn't have. But she hadn't given a moment's thought to how she would answer it or what explanation she would give for her actions.

"I noticed that it was gone and I thought it had been stolen. And then it was back again. It was all very strange."

When Eleanor didn't reply, she added, "Where did you go?"

"Go?"

"Yes, where did you go?" Patricia sounded exasperated.

"Oh, just for a little spin."

"You were in such a hurry to catch a train and you just decided to take the car—without asking me—for a little spin?"

"I know it sounds odd, but . . ."

"It's a little more than odd." Patricia paused, as if waiting for Eleanor to explain. But there was nothing Eleanor could say. "It certainly seems out of character—you're always so responsible—so I suppose I shouldn't get too upset. Only the next time you have a yen to take my car out for a *little spin*, will you please tell me first?"

"Of course." Eleanor looked away, relieved that it would go no further.

They drove the rest of the way to the station in silence and when they arrived, Patricia saw her off on the platform.

"I'll let you know when I'll be back," Eleanor said as she boarded.

"I hope everything's all right," Patricia said. "Margaux will miss you. We all will."

Your husband too? Eleanor thought with a shudder. She found her seat and settled in. There was a jolt—the train had started. It moved slowly at first, and then began to pick up speed as it left the Argyle station.

On the way to New York City, Eleanor tried—and failed—to sleep. Every time she tried to lean back on the seat, she was reminded of Wynn Bellamy's assault by the bump, still tender, at the back of her head. She'd been so woefully naive, thinking she could come up here and, with the flimsy protection of an assumed name, meld seamlessly into a pattern of life that was defined by its exclusion of people like her. And at first, it seemed like she had proved her mother and Ruth wrong. She loved Margaux and teaching her was a pleasure. She admired Patricia—her ease in the world, her polish, her graciousness—and strove to emulate her. She allowed herself to become smitten with Tom and it seemed her feelings were reciprocated. Then Wynn Bellamy barged into the cottage and everything had changed. Carefully, she touched the bump. *Not our kind*, her mother had said of the Bellamys. And as galling as it was to admit, even if only to herself, her mother had been right all along.

SIXTEEN

"I wish Eleanor hadn't left," complained Margaux. There was a heat wave in Argyle and the rising temperature, coupled with Eleanor's absence, had brought Margaux to breakfast in a snit.

"You encouraged her to go," Patricia pointed out.

"I know." Margaux sulked. "But I have nothing to do today and I'm *bored*." Overnight, Margaux seemed to have reverted to the irritable girl she'd been before Eleanor arrived. Patricia thought the sound of that whiny voice would drive her mad. She had to do something.

"Let's go swimming," she said, and when she saw her daughter's face, she hastened to add, "Not at the club."

"Then where?"

"The place you went to with Eleanor and your uncle," Patricia said.

"Lavender Lake?" asked Margaux.

"Yes." Patricia thought it a wretched little spot, but so what? It would be cooler and it would give them something to do. She needed the distraction as badly as Margaux did. During the short ride, Margaux grumbled and groused; it was only monumental self-control that kept Patricia from barking at the girl to just shut up.

They arrived at the lake to find the place deserted. Patricia lugged the umbrella she'd tucked in the trunk and did her best to jam the pointed end of the pole into the gritty sand behind a clump of bushes; then she spread out a blanket and slipped out of her sundress. Ordinarily she would not have gone into the water—despite the name, it was nothing more than a poky little pond—but the unrelenting heat and her own agitation made her set aside her aversion. Margaux was already immersed and beckoning her to come in. Patricia waded out to join her and when she was in deep enough, began the easy, confident crawl she'd honed as a child; swimming and diving were just two more things on which her father had insisted. She still remembered standing on a dock in Maine with him one summer day, when she was only about three or four. He didn't toss her off the end; that was not his style. He simply pushed her—a nonchalant, even elegant gesture—and when she shrieked and flailed in the cold water, he calmly instructed her to paddle.

Today, the water was not murky, as she had expected, but surprisingly clear and cool. "Doesn't it feel good?" asked Margaux.

"It does," Patricia agreed. She switched to a backstroke. They swam companionably for a while and then Patricia waded back to the shore. God, but it was a relief to cool off. She was seated on the blanket, wringing the water from her hair when she saw another family trooping along the pebble-strewn grass, toting their own umbrella and blanket.

Patricia's eyes quickly glanced to the water, where Margaux moved in a steady line, parallel to the shore. She was still a good swimmer, something the disease had not taken from her. She had not seen the other family yet; well, there was nothing to be done about it. This was a public beach after all.

"Over here," called the boy. "This is the perfect spot." Patricia watched them settle in. It was only when the boy had taken off his long-sleeved shirt—an odd choice in this heat—that she saw the shrunken arm dangling uselessly at his side. Polio. Like Margaux, this child had survived. The arm was his battle scar, his emblem, the unmistakable legacy of the disease. Concealed by the bushes, Patricia could stare openly; they could not see her.

The boy was younger than Margaux. Ten or perhaps eleven. Small, with a wiry, scrappy little body. Sandy hair, an alert manner. Since the polio had ravaged an arm, not a leg, he was more mobile than Margaux. And she could see he had learned to compensate for his infirmity. "I'm heading in," he called to his mother.

"Just stay where we can watch you," she said.

"You heard her, Larry," said the man. He was lighting a pipe. "Not too far out."

"I heard, Dad," the boy said, eager to be released. He scampered down to the water's edge just as Margaux was emerging. She'd left her walking stick on the shore, and was on both hands in the shin-deep lake, propelling herself along until she reached the stick and used it to hoist herself up. Patricia watched as the two children took the measure of each other. It was clear to her that this family had sought the privacy of this lakefront beach for the same reason she and Margaux had.

Patricia got up and dusted sand from the backs of her legs. She hurried over to where Margaux stood, staring uncertainly at the boy. He turned in her direction.

"Patricia Bellamy," she said. "And this is Margaux." The boy's parents had joined them and the father extended his hand. "Ray Sharp," he said, and gesturing to the woman added, "This is Pauline, and that's our boy, Larry."

"You had polio," Margaux said to Larry. Patricia's first instinct was to chastise her, but something told her to keep still.

"Yeah," Larry said, looking at Margaux's leg. "So did you."

"When?" Margaux asked.

"Three years ago. I was eight." He scratched his ear with his good hand. "How about you?"

"Over a year ago. It was like being in hell."

"Margaux!" Patricia couldn't contain herself any longer.

"That's all right," said Ray Sharp. "Don't worry about us."

"We understand," Pauline said. And lowering her voice she added, "It *was* like being in hell."

Patricia smiled in nervous relief.

"And we're the lucky ones. So many of the children on his ward didn't come home at all."

"Where was this?" Patricia asked.

"Outside of Boston. There was a special hospital there."

"Is that where you're from?"

"Norwalk," Ray told her, then puffed on his pipe.

"Mother, Larry and I are going in the water," Margaux said.

"As long as you stay where we can see you."

"That's just what I told him," Ray said with a smile. Pipe smoke wafted around his head.

Margaux set down her stick but instead of dropping to her knees, she took the arm Larry extended. Patricia had to make an effort not to show her surprise. It was rare that Margaux let anyone help her; she'd rather struggle, or even fail. For her to let someone she'd met only moments ago offer any kind of assistance was a radical departure.

"Will you join us?" Pauline said. "There's plenty of room where we're sitting."

"There's plenty of room everywhere," said Ray, looking around.

"That's why we came," Patricia said. "Margaux won't expose her leg in most public places. She doesn't care how hot it is."

"Larry's the same way about his arm," said Pauline.

Ray helped Patricia relocate her blanket and umbrella and the three of them chatted while Margaux and Larry frolicked in the water. She told them about Oakwood; Pauline said she had heard of the place and had been considering it for Larry as well. Despite the horrible tension she felt about Wynn, something in Patricia released as she watched the children play; how long had it been since Margaux had spent time with anyone even close to her in age? Wasn't that Eleanor's point?

She looked up to see Margaux, dripping water in a small dark puddle at her feet. Larry was standing right next to her, creating a puddle of his own. "We're hungry," she said. "Can we have lunch now?"

"We didn't bring any sandwiches," Patricia said. "Remember when Henryka asked, you said no, you wanted to drive into town for lunch?"

"Oh," said Margaux. "I forgot."

"We can all do that together," Patricia said. She looked at Ray and Pauline. "Would you like to join us? My treat."

She saw Ray and Pauline look nervously at each other. "No, that's all right," he said. "We were just going to have a picnic here." He gestured to a wooden basket sitting at the edge of the blanket.

"Can't we go with them instead?" Larry asked. "Please?"

"Not this time, honey," said Pauline gently.

Patricia wondered why they declined. Maybe they felt patronized and she ought not to have offered to pay.

". . . but if you'd like, you can join our picnic. Pauline always makes too much food, don't you?"

Pauline nodded. "Please do. I've got sandwiches and soda. And grapes."

"I'd love a sandwich," Margaux said.

Patricia looked at her sternly but Margaux ignored the look. How many times had she been told not to ask, but to wait to be offered?

"I've got peanut butter and jelly or cream cheese on date-nut bread," said Pauline, rummaging in the basket.

"Can I please have one cream cheese and one peanut butter?" asked Margaux.

"It's *may I*, not *can I*," said Patricia. But at least the girl had said please.

The Sharps were a welcome distraction from her own oppressive thoughts. Ray sold insurance in Hartford; Pauline had been a librarian. Like Patricia, she had wanted more children. "We tried and tried," she said. They had finished eating and Ray was down at the water with Margaux and Larry. "But it just never happened."

"The same with us," Patricia said. She found a package of cigarettes in her bag and lit one. She didn't feel as hot now and the smoke filling her lungs felt oddly cooling. "We wanted another but it wasn't meant to be . . ."

"And then when the one you do have takes ill——" Pauline did not have to finish.

"We didn't lose them though, did we?" Patricia extended the package of cigarettes to Pauline, who took one and lit it. The tip glowed, a small orange jewel against the blue of the day.

Ray, Margaux, and Larry returned to the blanket. "Mother, Larry's invited us back to his house for dinner. Mr. Sharp said it was all right with him but that we would have to ask you and Mrs. Sharp. Please will you say yes, Mother? Please?"

Patricia looked at Pauline. "We're having a cold supper. Because of the heat," said Pauline. "If you don't mind that, we'd like for you to share it with us."

"I've got a new rabbit," Larry said. "His name is Bucky. He won first place at the county fair and I wanted to show him to Margaux."

"Mrs. and Mr. Sharp say yes," said Margaux. "And I really do want to see Bucky."

The Sharps' house was a perfectly acceptable, if slightly shabby, colonial set behind a massive oak on the front lawn. When they got to the door, she noticed something small attached to its frame. It had Hebrew letters and so must have been one of those things—she didn't know what to call it—that Jewish people posted on their dwellings. So they were Jews.

Pauline was gracious; they both were, really. *Decent, hardworking, intelligent* were words to describe the Sharps. Not *brilliant*, not *scintillating*. But Margaux seemed so comfortable here, and was inexplicably smitten with Bucky, a docile gray creature with floppy ears and a ceaselessly twitching nose. When it was time to leave, she said, "Larry invited me to spend the night."

"We'd love to have her," Pauline said. "You see how much room we've got." She lowered her voice. "And it's such a pleasure to see them having a good time together."

Patricia had to admit that it was. "But what about your things?" she said to Margaux. "Maybe we'd better make it another time."

"I could follow you back to Argyle and pick up her bag," Ray offered.

"You see?" Margaux said. "It would be so easy, Mother. Everything's all worked out."

Patricia did not answer. Dinner with the Sharps was one thing; leaving Margaux here with them was quite another. Then she looked at Margaux, arms around the rabbit, face shining with hope. "All right then, if you're sure it's no trouble," Patricia said to Pauline. "I'll call Henryka and ask her to pack a bag."

"Oh, Mother, I love you!" Margaux cried. She kissed Bucky's furred gray head.

Was this all it took to make her so happy? A chance to spend some time in this dreary house with a little Jewish boy and his pet rabbit? Patricia got back in the car, this time as the leader, while Ray followed behind. At the house Henryka was there to meet them with Margaux's bag and a bundle of brownies wrapped in wax paper, which she handed to Ray through the open window.

"We'll take good care of her," said Ray from behind the wheel. "You don't have to worry." Patricia could see the curved pipe stem protruding from his breast pocket. "And I'll have her back safe and sound tomorrow."

The next day, the house felt too quiet, so Patricia went to the club, but she found the conversation—the extramarital affair of one member, the scorn-worthy new interior decorator hired by another—an unappealing mixture of spite, venom, and stupidity. Back home, she tried weeding but the heat was intolerable; she picked up a copy of the latest *New Yorker* but couldn't concentrate. Around noon, she set out to organize the three large boxes of photographs that had been sitting in an upstairs closet for years; she had even bought new albums with handsome tooled-leather covers. But sifting through the old pictures—Wynn standing on a sailboat, wind blowing his hair to one side, Margaux as a toddler, two sturdy legs planted on the ground, or pedaling her tricycle—made her unutterably sad, and she carted both albums and boxes back to the closet, where they would no doubt remain undisturbed for another decade.

She showered—again—and dressed in a flared skirt and blouse with a pattern of fruit all over it; the buttons were made of red plastic and shaped like cherries. She was strangely lethargic, even blue, but she still forced herself to dress and primp. Then she sat down to a small salad, which, despite Henryka's protests, was all she could tolerate for lunch. "You waste away," the housekeeper fumed. "No healthy." Patricia just nodded, eyes straying to the clock on the kitchen wall. Margaux would be home soon, she consoled herself.

There was a sound from the front of the house—a key turning in the lock—and Patricia looked at Henryka. "Maybe it's—"

Wynn came in through the kitchen door. Patricia put her fork down as Henryka hastily retreated.

"I'm back," he said pointlessly. "We finished early and I caught a ride down."

"How was your trip?"

"Fine." He put his bag down and looked around the room. "The house is so quiet. Where is everyone?"

"Tom's still in Saratoga. Eleanor went home for a few days. And Margaux's staying over at the house of a family we met at Lavender Lake."

"You were at Lavender Lake? Why go to that muck-filled pond when you could go to the club?"

"You know perfectly well Margaux won't go to the club." Patricia pushed her plate away.

"So this family—they're not anyone we know?"

"No."

"And you let her stay with them overnight?"

"Yes, I did. Is there a special reason you're making such a fuss? Margaux and the boy liked each other. You *know* how impossible she can be. I was just glad that she found some diversion."

"I see." He lifted his hands to loosen his tie. "I'm going to fix myself a drink. Can I make one for you?" He went to the cabinet to take out a bottle of vodka and then said, just a shade too casually, "That family Margaux's staying with? What's their name?"

"The Christiansons," she said without hesitation. "They live in Darien."

"They live in Darien and they go to the lake?"

"It's actually a lovely place," she said. "You should go with us some-time."

He said nothing as he mixed their drinks and when he'd finished his—very quickly, she noted—he said he was going up to lie down.

Patricia sipped her own drink slowly and let him go. When she'd finished, she felt a slight buzz, which was odd considering she'd had only one. But she hadn't finished even the light lunch Henryka had served her and the afternoon was even hotter than the day before. A rest sounded like a good idea and she went upstairs to join Wynn.

She found him stretched out and reading the newspaper on the bed, his shoes peeking out from under the dust ruffle and his shirt laid over a chair. "What happened to your arms?"

"Oh those," he said, looking at the scabbed-over marks. "Didn't I tell you? That damned cat—she went crazy and attacked me. I had to swat her away. Good thing she didn't get near my face."

"Good thing." Patricia remembered that Glow had clawed her too, for no apparent cause. They had found Glow in the woods, years ago, as a kitten. Maybe now she was in her dotage, and returning to some feral state. She had an urge to stroke the cat and went downstairs in search of her. "Glow," she called softly. "Here, kitty." But Glow was nowhere to be found.

SEVENTEEN

Eleanor spent the day helping her mother clean up the mess in the flooded basement. She'd lost some but not all of her inventory, and the two of them brought whatever was salvageable upstairs. Irina had closed the shop while they worked, and late in the afternoon, she turned her attention to finishing up a hat she had promised a customer. Eleanor watched as her mother regarded the red tricorne that was perched on a wooden form. "That color is very bold." Irina began to circle the hat so she could view it from all angles. "Very strong. It needs something to tone it down."

"Black?" suggested Eleanor, who had always loved to watch her mother "build" a hat.

"Possible," said Irina. "But navy might work too." She began her dance around the hat form, hands drawing possible designs in the air. "In any case, I like the shape. Mitch sent me a good batch."

Eleanor went to the cupboard, took out big spools of ribbon—black, navy, and a muted teal that she thought might go well together—and presented them to her mother. Irina unfurled the navy first and began to experiment with different options: wrapping a length of ribbon around the crown, creating streamers down the back, running ribbon first along and then under the brim. She'd gotten her first taste of trimming back at the Danbury factory and it had quickly become her métier. When she returned to New York, she had first worked in a hat shop on the Lower East Side that catered to observant Jewish ladies, and then at Gimbels in Herald Square. She developed such a devoted following that she'd eventually decided to open her own shop, relying on Mitch Neely, the old foreman from Danbury, to supply her with hat forms three or four times a year. Irina set down the lengths of ribbon. "Maybe not," she said. "Or not just ribbon. I think it needs some netting too." And she went to another cupboard in search of it.

The afternoon dwindled and it was soon dusk. Irina hadn't wanted to cook, so they ate cold cuts from Schaller & Weber on Second Avenue. Then Eleanor did the dishes and got her coat.

"Where are you going?" Irina asked.

"The movies. I'm meeting Ruth."

"Oh, she's not seeing her young man tonight?"

"No." She didn't want Irina to start in on why she didn't have a young man of her own. "Anyway, we won't be late."

In fact, Eleanor had no idea of what Ruth was doing tonight because she wasn't seeing her.

Instead, she headed downtown on the subway. When she emerged into the unfamiliar tangle of streets, she got lost not once, but twice, in search of the right one. Orchard, Allen, Rivington, Essex. She hadn't been down here in years, not since her father was alive and took them all to see the neighborhood where he'd first lived when he'd come from Russia as a child. Her mother hadn't wanted to go. "Why look back?" was what she had said. "We're here now—thank God." But in the end she agreed to the trip, gamely eating her blintzes with sour cream and applesauce at Ratner's. Afterward, they had visited both the tenement where her father had lived and the synagogue on Eldridge Street where he'd worshipped. "It's not what it once was," he said. "But you should have seen it when I was a boy. The streets were always packed, there was such life here, such energy. The shops, the restaurants, the vendors on the street. And the synagogue was at the center of it all. It shone like a queen." Eleanor had taken in the imposing Moorish-inspired facade and the enormous round window that stared out at her like a cyclops and could see that yes, it had once been very grand indeed. Irina, more practical than sentimental, was less interested in the synagogue than in the nearby button and bedding shops.

But today Eleanor hurried past the synagogue, which seemed even more derelict than it had on her last visit. These last few days, she had not been able to tolerate the sight of her own naked body. It filled her with a sense of shame she had never known before. Neither Ira's nor Tom's caresses had evoked this feeling; their touch had filled her with desire, made her feel more alive. But Wynn's touch elicited only disgust and she felt polluted by what he had done. She tried undressing and even bathing in the dark. She covered herself with a towel as soon as she stepped out of the tub, and did not look in the mirror until she was clothed. It didn't work. Even if she couldn't see herself, she imagined she could smell herself, something rank under her arms, between her legs, no matter how much soap she used. Maybe there was something wrong with her, something that had drawn Wynn Bellamy to her. She had to get rid of it.

That's when she got the idea of visiting the mikvah, the Jewish ritual bath. The thought began to preoccupy her, so much so that yesterday she had walked up to Congregation Orach Chaim in search of the rabbi's wife. Mrs. Schechter taught a Bible class; Eleanor found her in a room where posters of large Hebrew letters—red *aleph*, blue *gimmel*, green *hey*—decorated the peeling walls.

"You want to go to a mikvah?" Mrs. Schechter had clearly been surprised. "Are you sure?"

"Yes," Eleanor said. "I am."

"I've rarely gone myself," said Mrs. Schechter. "The women of our congregation don't usually do that. Does your mother?"

"No," said Eleanor, not willing to offer anything more. Her mother had said—defiantly, even proudly—that she would never go to a mikvah again. Irina associated such places with her doomed past and wanted nothing to do with them. She and Eleanor's father did not often argue, but when they did, it was usually over some aspect of ritual observance. Her father leaned toward the customs of his childhood and spoke fondly of the old country. Irina had scoffed at what she considered a foolish and sentimental attachment. "The country that burned down your family's business? Murdered your uncle? And my father? That's the country you love?"

"Well, I can tell you where to go." Mrs. Schechter studied her carefully and then added, "If there's ever anything you'd like to talk about, my door is always open." The pause lengthened uncomfortably until Mrs. Schechter had finally taken a scrap of paper and written down the address, 5 Allen Street, which Eleanor was now trying her best to find. But the streets were off the numbered grid and she wandered fruitlessly, getting more and more frustrated. She passed shops, mostly closed, displaying prayer shawls, Hebrew books, menorahs, and candlesticks in their windows. But the mikvah remained hidden.

Finally, she went up to a pair of women, both in the very obvious wigs that Orthodox women wore. "Excuse me," she said politely to the older of the two. "Can you tell me where this is?" The woman looked at the scrap of paper and up at Eleanor's face. It was obvious she did not understand why someone who looked as Eleanor did— clearly not observant—would be searching for a mikvah. But she led Eleanor down a short street, turned a corner, and indicated a brick building wedged between two taller structures.

Eleanor saw a sign in Hebrew, which she could not read, but when she went around the corner, she saw another that read RUSSIAN AND TURKISH BATHS. Mrs. Schechter had mentioned that, so Eleanor knew she was in the right place. Raising her fist, she knocked. There was no answer, but when she pushed the door gently, it opened. An old woman sat at a small table, her head bent over an embroidery hoop. Her hand moved gracefully, up and down, the silver needle piercing the cloth held tightly within the circle. Eleanor was so mesmerized by the birdlike motions of the embroiderer's rising and falling hand that she stood silently for a moment. Finally, the woman looked up. "Can I help you?"

"I'm here for the mikvah," she said.

The woman looked at her left hand. "You're married?" Eleanor shook her head. "Getting married?" Again, Eleanor shook her head.

The woman seemed to consider this. Finally she said, "Wait here." She then laid the embroidery hoop down on the table, shuffled through a doorway just to the left, and returned with another old woman who was carrying something folded and white. "Gittel will take care of you," she said. "Follow her." Eleanor thanked her and put a quarter in the empty jelly jar, as Mrs. Schechter had told her to do.

As they descended down a long flight of stairs, Eleanor saw beads of moisture on the wall, and detected a faint disinfectant smell. They passed several small, curtained chambers; in a couple of them, Eleanor saw wigs hanging suspended from hooks above the piles of folded clothing. Then Gittel showed her to an empty chamber; behind its limp curtain was a wooden seat, two hooks, and an ancient-looking showerhead poking out from the ceiling. "Are you clean?" she asked.

"Excuse me?"

"Your last time of the month. When was it?"

"About two weeks ago," Eleanor said.

"And you've had no relations since then?"

Eleanor felt herself coloring. "No," she said. "I haven't."

"Good. Then you can take off your clothes and leave them here," said Gittel. Eleanor looked at the hooks; hanging from one of them was a wooden body brush with coarse, splayed bristles. "Then, you wash. Everything, and everywhere. Face. Body. Hair. Don't forget the hidden places. Under your nails. Your *pupik*." Eleanor nodded. "You brought soap?" Eleanor nodded; Mrs. Schechter had told her to bring these things. "Toothbrush too?" Again, a nod. "Good. Go to work. When you're done, call me." She handed Eleanor the white bundle she'd been carrying; it turned out to be a simple cotton robe and a rough terry cloth towel.

The water was surprisingly hot, and Eleanor scrubbed herself vigorously under the spray. She had forgotten shampoo but managed to lather her hair with the bar of soap she'd brought, taking care not to press on the back of her head, which was still tender.

As Gittel had instructed, she washed everywhere—her breasts and belly, shoulders and thighs. She washed between her toes and behind her ears and hesitated only when she got to the place between her legs, the place that had engendered first so much pleasure and then recently so much disgust. But she didn't let herself think about the pleasure or the disgust now, she just lathered herself until the soap achieved a luxurious sheen, rising in plump, frothy clusters before succumbing to the rushing water and disappearing down the drain. When she was done, she dried herself, donned the robe, and combed out her hair. Only then did she call for Gittel.

"Let me see your hands," Gittel said and inspected Eleanor's nails closely. She gave a grunt of approval. "Now bend your head." She raked her fingers over Eleanor's scalp, parting her wet hair, and checked both behind and in her ears. Eleanor flinched a little when Gittel touched the sore place on her head. Gittel noticed. "I hurt you?"

"It's nothing," Eleanor said. "Just a little bump."

Gittel continued her probing. She even had her stick her tongue out. "You did a good job, especially for the first time," she said. "But first time, tenth time—it doesn't matter. The mikvah cures all ailments, and washes away all sins."

"All?" Eleanor asked.

Gittel looked at her appraisingly. "Yes. The mikvah will wash you clean—no matter what you've done."

"Or what was done to me?"

"Ah." Gittel took Eleanor's hand in hers. "It will be better, *tochter*—you'll see."

Wearing just the robe, Eleanor followed the older woman along a short hall until they came to an open doorway. Six white marble steps led down to a rectangular bathing pool around six or seven feet long and lined with tiles as white as snowdrops. The gleaming body of water looked as if it belonged somewhere else more exalted—a beautiful garden, a palace, not this dim subterranean space.

"I'll take that," Gittel said, indicating the robe. Eleanor loosened the belt and shrugged the thing off. It was momentarily terrifying, standing so exposed, but she quickly stepped down into the mikvah. Her feet touched the bottom of the pool; the water came up to her shoulders. Why had she come? What was she seeking—healing? Transformation? Or was it grace? She wasn't devout, yet here she was.

"Dunk," said Gittel. "Like this." She held her arms aloft, elbows bent. "The immersion must be complete."

Eleanor held her breath and complied, then lifted her head out of the water.

"Now the prayer," said Gittel. When Eleanor looked confused, she pointed to a sign on the wall. But the letters were in Hebrew. "Just repeat after me. *Baruch ata adonai eloheinu melech ha-olam asher kid-shanu b'mitzvo-tav v'tzi-vanu al ha-tevilah.*"

Some, though not all, of the words were familiar from the Passover seders she'd attended. But she intoned them fervently, and in them heard echoes of her father's voice. "Good girl," said Gittel. "Do it again."

By the third immersion, Eleanor had succumbed to the simple rhythm; dunk and bless, dunk and bless. She stayed under much longer the last time, eyes open under the water so she could see her hair floating around her, and the patterns made by the rippling surface above. She closed her eyes, pulled her knees close to her body, and wrapped her arms around them, floating. Her lungs began to tighten and burn. Then she untucked her limbs and spread her arms and fingers wide, as if to embrace the water. Maybe then she would be washed clean. Finally, she burst up, gasping for air in great, voracious gulps.

"Why did you stay under so long?" Gittel asked. But her voice was gentle, not admonishing. Eleanor had no answer. After the last blessing, she climbed out; the robe and towel were waiting.

The rhythmic swaying of the uptown subway car lulled Eleanor into a quiet and contemplative state. She actually dozed for a few minutes, riding right past her stop, and had to get off at Ninety-Sixth Street. Instead of catching the downtown train, she decided to walk the twelve blocks home; it would give her time to reflect on what had happened today, an interval between the sacred realm of the mikvah and the bustling, profane life of Yorkville. She did not feel cleansed so much as quieted, the clamor in her head subdued. But even that small change was a relief.

As she headed down Lexington Avenue, she realized her hair hadn't fully dried. Would her mother believe she'd been caught in a sudden shower even though it was only her hair, and not her clothes, that was wet? But when she climbed the stairs and let herself into the apartment, she found that her mother had gone to bed, saving her from telling yet another lie.

EIGHTEEN

——————— ▬ ———————

The heat had finally broken, so Patricia told Henryka they would be eating outside. Tom had returned that morning but Eleanor was still in New York. Margaux's friend Larry Sharp would be joining them too; his parents had dropped him off earlier in the day. Oh, she'd had to tap-dance her way around the lie she'd originally told Wynn about the family in Darien when she revealed the true identity of the boy Margaux had met at the lake. Wynn had blustered a bit when he found out. But after she engineered an unexpected afternoon detour to the bedroom, his grumbling subsided and turned into a mercifully brief lecture about the importance of Margaux having the right kinds of friends from the right kinds of families.

The table looked lovely—pale pink cloth, white napkins, some late-summer dahlias in a vase—but Patricia realized there were no dinner rolls for the meal. She went into the kitchen to ask Henryka if she could quickly bake a batch before they all sat down.

"No flour," said Henryka.

All right, so there wouldn't be any rolls tonight. "How about iced tea? Can you make a pitcher?"

"No tea."

"We're out of flour and tea?" Patricia couldn't figure it out. Henryka prided herself on running the household with nearly military precision, so running out of two items was somewhat surprising.

"I go to market."

"Thank you. And could you pick up some ice cream while you're out? Vanilla, and that rum raisin Margaux likes so much."

"Of course, missus."

After she had left, Tom wandered out into the yard, newspaper under his arm and drink in hand.

"Where were you all afternoon?" Patricia asked. She hadn't seen him all day.

"In the arms of Morpheus," he said. "Jasper threw a party last night and I didn't get to bed until dawn, and then drove down here on almost no sleep—I was exhausted."

"Well, I'm glad you had a chance to rest. I need you to keep the conversational ball rolling at dinner."

"Something wrong?" He settled himself on a chaise longue.

"Wynn's not enamored of our houseguest."

"That boy Margaux invited?"

"Larry Sharp. She met him at the lake. Wynn thinks he's not the sort of person she should be . . . cultivating."

Tom shook out the paper with a decisive snap of his wrists. "Wynn should leave the cultivating to the gardener." He looked at her with his disarming smile. "Don't worry. I'll make sure everyone has a good time."

"Thanks." Patricia felt something inside her uncoil slightly. She headed toward the kitchen. "I'll make myself a drink and come and join you."

"By the way, when is Eleanor coming back?"

Patricia turned. Tom's face was hidden by the paper. "I thought you said you were afraid of her."

"Actually, I'm afraid of *me*."

"Well, she was supposed to be back tonight but she called to say she needed another day or two in New York. She's helping her mother." When he didn't answer she added, "Are you relieved? Or disappointed?"

"Maybe a little of both." He set the paper down and gave her his most endearing, rueful smile.

When Henryka returned, she'd bought a five-pound bag of flour and two boxes of tea but no ice cream. "I sorry," she said as she began to assemble the ingredients for the rolls. "I forget."

"That's all right," Patricia said, though again, she was surprised and, quite honestly, exasperated. "Tom can pick it up, can't you, Tom?"

"Sure, I'll go now."

As Patricia went upstairs to change out of her slacks—Wynn preferred her in a dress at dinner, even here in the country—she had to acknowledge, if only to herself, that something really was amiss with Henryka. Did she need a raise? A vacation?

Dinner was a little later than usual, but by eight o'clock, the table had been set and Henryka was taking the rolls out of the oven. "Margaux," Patricia called, "why don't you and Larry wash your hands and then you can sit down?"

As they ate, Tom regaled them with stories of his dabbling in the art world. "And there's this guy I met, Jackson. Jackson Pollock. He doesn't even use a paintbrush. He just drips and flings the paint all over the place—a crazy, wonderful mess."

"I don't believe you," said Margaux. "Who would do that?"

"Scout's honor," said Tom as he passed the rolls. "I bought one of his paintings, and when you get home, I'll take you downtown to see it."

"Why not take her to the Metropolitan or someplace where she can see some real art and not something that sounds like any five-year-old could make it?" asked Wynn.

"There are lots of artists who weren't recognized in their own time," said Patricia.

"Like Vincent van Gogh," said Larry. It was the first time he'd spoken during the meal.

"Van Gogh was a sick man who sliced off his own ear," said Wynn. "I don't think he's much of an example."

Patricia shot her husband a look—did he really need to demolish a child, and their guest besides? "There's no doubt that van Gogh was a tormented soul," she said gently. "But that has nothing to do with his painting. In fact, I think he was his best self when he painted. Not his worst." She turned to Larry, saying, "And he's a perfect example. He couldn't sell a painting in his own lifetime but now his work is admired and revered."

"That's right, Daddy," said Margaux. "I saw that painting, *Starry Night*, at the Museum of Modern Art and I loved it."

Patricia loved that painting too, but during the short, tense silence that followed, she didn't want to say so. Then Tom said, "Look at the Impressionists. They weren't even allowed to show their paintings with the more established artists but had to create their own venue, the Salon des Refusés. Now they're part of the canon."

Patricia let out her breath. Tom was always a bridge over troubled waters. Larry looked less stricken and dug into his baked chicken. Despite his useless arm, he was surprisingly adept with both fork and knife. The charged moment passed, but Patricia couldn't forget the sharp edge in Wynn's voice when he'd gone after Larry.

Once the pie and ice cream had been served, the children asked to be excused so that they could play a board game, leaving Tom and Wynn at the table. Wynn lit a cigar, and even outdoors, the stench was offensive. "Did you play the ponies up in Saratoga?" asked Wynn.

"Not even once." Tom took out a pack of cigarettes. "Jasper kept me busy—he's a regular impresario. You wouldn't believe the guest lists at his parties—poets, painters, opera singers, a composer or two, and a whole gaggle of ballet dancers he'd invited up from New York. You could spot one from all the way across the room—perfect posture and necks like swans."

"Does he know anyone who actually makes any money?" Wynn puffed on the cigar.

"Making money isn't the only thing in life," Tom said.

"Maybe not, but it's the most important thing."

"Not to me." Tom usually got along with Wynn, but right now he seemed testy.

"Well, if you've never worked a day—"

Just then, Margaux reappeared. "Uncle Tom, come play with us!"

Tom stood and stubbed out his cigarette. "You'll excuse me," he said, all at once gracious again. "I'm being summoned."

When he'd gone, Patricia glared at Wynn, or rather at the glowing end of the cigar, since the dark now obscured his face. "What's gotten into you?"

"Why blame me? Did you hear him?"

"You started it. You know Tom. He lives to charm, not quarrel."

"Well, he's a little too charming if you ask me."

"What are you talking about?" But she knew.

"He's just waiting for her to return so they can start their little hanky-panky again."

"Eleanor?"

"No. Henryka."

"Very funny. But Tom and Eleanor are not news."

"Still, I don't like it."

"Neither do I." She sighed. "There's nothing we can do about it though."

"We can ask him to leave before she gets back."

"But Margaux will be sad. And besides, we're going to be in New York soon enough. They'll be able to see each other then if they want."

"It won't be under our roof. Do you want Margaux exposed to that sort of thing?"

"No, I suppose not." She had said pretty much the same at that lunch in Dudley, and she still burned a bit when she remembered how Eleanor had deftly but firmly put her in her place.

"Talk to him." Wynn rose from the table, taking his odious cigar to befoul some other part of the yard or house. "Or else I will."

Patricia remained where she was. She could hear laughter from the sunporch, and from the kitchen, Henryka, who was singing a Polish song as she cleaned. Her voice wasn't particularly good but the song had a tender, even mournful sound. Finally Patricia got up, but she didn't want to go back inside, so she began walking outside, around the house, toward the front door. Just as she had turned the corner she spied a woman sitting outside—the white dress made her visible. Dottie. Patricia called out to her and then crossed the road.

"Out for some night air?" she asked.

"I'm just so relieved there's been a break in the heat," said Dottie.

Patricia sat down beside her and they chatted briefly about Dottie's daughter, who would soon be a freshman at Bryn Mawr. Then Dottie put a hand with manicured, rosebud pink nails on Patricia's arm. "There's something I've wanted to tell you. I'm not sure if you know it already, and if you don't, maybe I'm speaking out of turn. But I know that if the situation were reversed, I'd want someone to tell me."

"Tell me what?" Patricia prayed this didn't have anything to do with Eleanor, or Larry Sharp; Larry's parents had seemed hesitant about letting him spend the night but Patricia had assured them it would be fine, perfectly fine. They had not expressed exactly what their concerns were but they didn't have to.

"It's about Henryka."

"Henryka!" said Patricia. "What about her?"

"Well, she told Colleen that she was looking for another position, and asked her to keep her ears open. Colleen was supposed to keep it a secret. But she told me anyway."

"I had no idea," Patricia said. "She hasn't mentioned wanting to leave."

"She's been with you a long time, hasn't she?"

"I've known her since I was a little girl." Patricia had been four or five when Henryka had come to work for her mother, and while Henryka had not been a warm presence, she'd been a constant one. Patricia remembered sitting in the kitchen of their Sutton Place apartment while Henryka baked, her plump arms covered in a blur of flour, the commingled smells of cinnamon, vanilla, and browning butter in the air. This was thirty or so years ago. Henryka's hair had not gone gray yet, and her braids were as yellow as the butter. Patricia was not even supposed to be there; her mother had not wanted her anywhere near the kitchen. But Patricia was drawn to the place, and to Henryka's dominion over it.

"Well, she ought to have told you first."

"Yes . . . I wonder why she didn't."

When the cookies or cake or pie or tart was done, Henryka would pour her a tall glass of milk and offer Patricia the first serving, still warm from the oven.

"Really, some of these people don't have a shred of loyalty. I'm sure you've been very good to her."

She was very good to me, Patricia wanted to say. When she had a cold, it was Henryka's dill-infused chicken soup that helped her mend; when she returned to Smith after a weekend at home, a tin of Henryka's pecan turtles went with her. Henryka had been with her and Wynn through the deaths of all their parents, and Margaux's birth and her illness. And now Henryka was planning to leave them. Leave, and wield her whisk and her rolling pin in some other woman's kitchen.

"Patricia, you're so quiet. Are you all right?"

"Of course I'm all right. Honestly, she's only a cook. I'll find someone else in no time."

"Absolutely. I can even ask Colleen if you'd like."

Patricia got up and brushed off the back of her dress. "Oh, that won't be necessary." And then she turned and walked back across the road before Dottie saw the tears that brimmed in her eyes, and then began rolling slowly down her face.

NINETEEN

———————

Two nights later, Patricia had just slipped out of her shoes and taken off her dress when Wynn walked into the room. She could barely look at him. All through dinner he had once again seemed intent on baiting her brother. Tom, to his credit, didn't take the challenge. But the strain of watching this, along with her bottled-up confusion and grief over Henryka's planned defection, had put Patricia in the worst of moods. Wynn, however, seemed quite cheerful. "I've just had a chat with my brother-in-law," he said.

"You certainly can't blame him if he felt attacked—"

"Nothing of the kind," Wynn said. "We understood each other perfectly. He'll be gone in the morning."

"Gone in the morning? What are you talking about?"

Wynn began to undress. "Tom's going back to New York. Trust me. This will be better for everyone."

"Everyone?" Patricia felt things were moving too quickly. "What about Margaux? What about me? I like having Tom here. So does she."

"Well, you have Eleanor to thank," said Wynn. "If she hadn't let your brother push up her skirt and—"

"Oh, would you stop! Would you please, please just stop such smutty talk——" She broke off when she saw his expression reflected in the mirror above the bureau. She wore only her brassiere and diaphanous half-slip and he was staring.

"Of course I can push up *your* skirt." He walked over to her. "I can do that because we're married, and it's my right." His hands were on her shoulders, nudging down the straps of her brassiere.

"Not if I say no, it isn't." She stepped forward, reaching for her robe. She'd finish undressing in the bathroom. But he moved along with her and this time he was more insistent, yanking the whole brassiere down so that her breasts were momentarily exposed before he grabbed them.

"Wynn, no."

"You don't mean that." He was kissing her neck and roughly kneading her flesh.

"Yes, I do." She tried to free herself, but he was too strong.

"I'm tired of your excuses. So many nights it's *Not now, I'm not in the mood* . . . Well, I'm in the mood."

He was being petulant, even ridiculous. She would have laughed, but there was something in the way he gripped her arm that was unfamiliar—and a little frightening. Fear took the defiance out of her and it just seemed easier to acquiesce. She let him lead her to the bed, and pull her down. And she lay still while he climbed on top of her and did what he always did. When he was done, he rolled away, still breathing heavily. Soon he began to snore. Patricia thought of that night last spring, when she'd taken the lead in a way that had been new for both of them. But the newness had not lasted, and the next time she'd tried it, he'd rebuffed her. "Once was fun," he said. "I'm not about to make a habit of it."

Tonight it had been different, though not in the way she used to hope for. She had seen something violent in him. Or maybe the violence had always been there, and she'd just willed herself not to look. In any case, that moment of fear had dissipated. Now she was just—disgusted. She slept fitfully and was up with the light, dressing quickly while Wynn slumbered on.

Early as it was, Henryka was already downstairs, engaged in the familiar ballet of rinsing, wiping, storing, stacking. Her braids were neatly pinned, her lace-trimmed apron fresh. Making lace was her hobby and her signature; Patricia remembered how as a child she'd sat transfixed as Henryka's nimble hands moved this way and that, spinning inches, feet, and yards of the snowy, lavish stuff.

"Why do you want to leave us?" Patricia burst out. Oh, that was all wrong, this wasn't what she wanted to say or the way she wanted to say it.

Henryka stopped what she was doing to look at Patricia. "I sorry," she said. "I no want to leave. But I no can work here anymore."

"Why on earth not? Do you need a raise? I'll give it to you gladly. More time off? You can have that too."

Henryka just shook her head.

"Then what? Have I said something? Done something?"

There was a pause during which Henryka took a pan to the sink to soak. "No you," she said finally. "Mr. Wynn."

Wynn! What had he done? "Can't you tell me what's happened? Please? We've known each other such a long time and—" She'd started to cry, and she used her napkin to blot the tears.

"Missus, I so sorry." Henryka came over and sat down across from her. "You husband—he no good. He hurt Miss Eleanor . . . I take her to doctor."

"He hurt Eleanor? I can't believe it. What did he do?"

"You ask. Maybe she tell you."

"But you don't even know if she was telling the truth."

"I know."

"How?" Patricia asked.

Henryka looked down at her hands. Even though she was long widowed, she still wore her wedding ring, the plain gold band cutting slightly into the flesh of her finger. "Long time ago, he hurt me too."

"What are you talking about?"

"At Christmas, he try kiss me. And when you were in hospital having Margaux . . ."

"What did he do while I was in the hospital?" Henryka was silent. "Please, you have to tell me, I need to know——"

"I no want say."

"But you never gave any indication . . . You should have *told* me."

"How I tell?" Henryka said. "Besides, my girls, they little then. I need job."

Yes, of course she did, Patricia thought. She knew about Henryka's fifth-floor walk-up above a butcher on First Avenue, the three daughters she'd raised alone. "Is there anything I can do to change your mind? Or at least persuade you to think it over for a little while?"

"No." Henryka placed her work-worn hand over Patricia's. "Time for me go, missus. I give notice today."

Patricia got up and went to her room. Fortunately, Wynn was in the shower so she didn't have to face him yet. Wynn had done something to Eleanor. And to Henryka. Was there anybody else? She remembered a secretary in Wynn's office who'd left very suddenly, with no explanation. Was it because of him? Things had been happening—serious, troubling things, and she'd known nothing. How could she have been so blind?

Looking around—four-poster bed, pair of wing chairs, footstool, bureau, wooden settee—it seemed that everything was suddenly strange. But it wasn't the furnishings that were unfamiliar—it was her entire life. What she thought she'd known turned out to be untrue, and what she hadn't known was a threat, even a danger. The water in the bathroom went off. Wynn was through showering.

"You're up early." He came in toweling off his hair, and when he untied the sash of his robe to dress, she looked away.

"I had some news this morning," she said.

"Bad news?"

"Yes, I would say so."

"What's happened?" He moved closer. Although he'd put on his boxers and pants, his chest was still bare.

"Henryka's decided to leave us."

"Oh." He stepped back, and sat in a chair to put on his socks. "That's not exactly *bad* news, is it? I mean, she is getting older. Maybe she wants to retire."

"No, she's not retiring. She started looking for another job behind my back. Dottie told me."

"Really? Now that seems kind of sneaky. Disloyal even. After all these years . . ." He tied his shoes and looked up. "I know you're attached to her, but we'll have no trouble finding someone else."

"Do you want to know why she's leaving?"

Wynn went to the bureau for an undershirt and she saw the faint traces of the scratches she'd noticed last week. They were practically gone. "Do I have a choice?"

"She said that she was leaving because of you. Because you did something to Eleanor. And—years ago—to her."

"What are you talking about?" His tone was truculent but his face began to get mottled—a sure sign he was upset.

"She wouldn't give me many details, so I'm going to ask Eleanor.

But I wanted to talk to you first. Did something happen between you? Something I should know about?" He was still seated and she took the other chair, facing him.

"Did she say something happened?"

"Not to me. But clearly something did and I want to hear your side."

"This isn't going to sound good," he began. "I shouldn't have gone over there but—"

"Where? To the cottage?"

"Yes."

"Why?"

"Because I was sick of how everyone worshipped Eleanor. Eleanor, Eleanor, Eleanor. She makes me feel like a second-class citizen—in my own home."

"You don't like her. You never have."

"It's true. But I was sorry and I went over to make amends."

"When?"

"One night in August—I don't remember the date. It was late," he said. "You were sleeping."

"So you went over to the cottage to offer an olive branch to Eleanor. Then what? She invited you in?"

"Yes, that's it," he said—too eagerly it seemed. "She asked me in and offered me a drink."

"A drink? Of what?"

"I don't know. Scotch, I think. Yes, that was it. Scotch."

"Eleanor kept a bottle of scotch in the cottage? I've never known her to drink scotch."

"Why are you interrogating me?"

"I'm not interrogating you. I'm just asking because Henryka accused you of something. And whatever it is, it's serious enough to make her leave us after nearly thirty years!" Tears filled her eyes, but this was no time to cry and she brushed them away. "So please, just tell me what happened."

"All right," he said. "All *right*. I went over there, I had a drink, and then another one. She was drinking too. The radio was on and she wanted to dance, so I obliged her. She wasn't really dressed . . ."

"What do you mean she wasn't dressed?"

"It was late. She was wearing some robe over her . . . pajamas, I guess. Anyway, we danced and she pressed very close to me. And I was . . . that is . . ."

"You got . . . aroused."

He looked at her imploringly. "I did, and I'm sorry. I knew it was wrong but the feel of her was just . . . I tried to kiss her."

"Kiss her!" Patricia may have lost her desire for Wynn but she didn't like the idea that he was kissing anyone else. Especially Eleanor.

"She pulled away. There was a struggle and we fell. I think she hit her head on the floor pretty hard. I got scared and I left."

"You didn't stay to make sure she was all right?"

"No, I was embarrassed. Ashamed. I just wanted to get out of there."

"And those scratches on your arms—Glow didn't make those. It was Eleanor." He nodded. Patricia was quiet, trying to take it all in. "How did Henryka come to know all this?"

"I don't know. Maybe Eleanor told her."

The thought of the help gossiping about them soaked her in shame. "And what about Henryka? Why did she say that about you?"

"One Christmas, forever ago, I may have tried to steal a kiss under the mistletoe. But it was a joke—as if I'd go after Henryka. She's practically old enough to be my mother. Obviously she's held it against me all these years."

"She also said there was something that happened a long time ago—when I was in the hospital, after Margaux was born."

"Are you really going to believe that?" He was indignant. "And what, exactly, is she accusing me of?"

"I don't know what to believe. She wouldn't say anything more."

"Well, then what does that tell you? How can I defend myself if she won't say what it was I did?"

"Wynn, why should you need to defend yourself at all?"

"This is an outrage. My wife, the cook who's been on my payroll for a decade, a tutor who came out of nowhere to infiltrate my home—all of you accusing me, condemning me——"

"All right," she said. "That's enough. You can stop now." He wasn't going to tell her about the other time. Neither was Henryka. But there was a chance Eleanor would tell her what had happened in the cottage—if she asked the right way.

Wynn went to the closet. "You'll forgive me, won't you?" he said. "What I did wasn't so terrible. No one was hurt, not really. I'm a man and a man has urges. Sometimes it's hard to . . . tame them."

"Like last night?" She hadn't meant to say that—it just came out. She moved toward the bedroom door.

He was by her side in an instant, but she stepped away and this time he didn't come after her. "I'm sorry," he said. "So sorry. But if you only knew what you looked like in that flimsy slip and bra . . . I needed to feel you were mine, Trish. All mine. And that was the way."

Once, a long time ago, those words would have meant everything to her. She'd loved Wynn then and had wanted nothing more than to be his. But she no longer felt the same way, and Henryka's decision to leave had torn away the protective curtain that had allowed Patricia to live her life with some equanimity. She didn't know what she would do now that it was gone.

Patricia left Wynn in the bedroom and went back downstairs. Propped up beside a bowl on the counter was a letter that had come for Eleanor; Henryka must have placed it there, ready to take over to the cottage. Eleanor. She'd returned from the city late the night before last, taken Margaux out for the entire day and begged off dinner, saying she was tired. Eleanor, who was faultless, blameless, and clearly the injured party. And yet Patricia found herself inexplicably angry with her—had she not become part of their household, Henryka wouldn't be leaving. The feeling passed, and in its wake came a bit of remorse for having it at all. Maybe things would be better when they returned to New York. Patricia could only hope so—she was more than ready for this strange, altogether unsettling summer to be over.

TWENTY

———————

Eleanor reveled in her return to the city. Yes, September in New York was still wretchedly hot, and the buses that lumbered up Third Avenue and down Second fouled the already fetid air with their clouds of black exhaust. Garbage was piled high by the curbs, or overflowing from cans, and the streets were thronged. But Eleanor felt protected by the noise, the dirt, and the heat. Even her prim little room above the hat shop was a safe haven and she was grateful for it. She had managed to get through the remainder of her time in Argyle—avoiding Wynn Bellamy, though just knowing she might have to encounter him kept her on the alert. Also, Tom had left quite abruptly and Henryka had given notice; Patricia seemed like a wire pulled taut and ready to snap. It was altogether a fraught atmosphere and one she was glad to leave behind.

Back in New York, Eleanor regained a measure of control, at least as far as Mr. Bellamy was concerned, and she took to arriving at the Park Avenue apartment after he left for the office and leaving before he returned. Of course living with her mother presented its own set of challenges and she had to navigate them as well as she could.

"School is starting," Irina would point out. "Do you think it might be possible to apply for a job as a substitute teacher? Isn't there always a demand for substitutes?" Eleanor tried to deflect or ignore her comments, but it was a strain. She thought wistfully of her sitting room, bedroom, and private bath in Argyle and wished there were some way to take the best of what it had offered and transplant it here.

One morning after Eleanor had been back for about a week, Patricia stopped her before she went into the study. "Would you be able to join me for a drink at the Carlyle when you've finished with Margaux today? Wynn is coming home early and he's taking her to the theater and I'd rather he didn't know about it."

Eleanor agreed, but for the rest of the morning, and the afternoon too, she wondered—and worried—about the purpose of this meeting. Was it about Tom? She had told him he could call her apartment during the day, while Irina was in the shop; the last time they had spoken was over a week ago.

"Everything's all mixed up," he'd said. "*I'm* all mixed up. I think I just need some time away."

"Away where?" She'd been angry. He was mixed up, but what about her? He was batting her back and forth like a Wiffle ball and she didn't like it.

"I haven't decided. I may go to Martha's Vineyard. Or even to Nova Scotia. September is the most beautiful month up there."

"I'm sure it is." As if she knew anything about it—she'd never been to Nova Scotia, in September or at any other time. And then he'd gone, without telling her where he'd ultimately decided on going. This new disappearance filled her with less longing than the first time and more bitterness. He'd been using her after all—maybe not intentionally, but in the end, it didn't matter what his intentions had been. He'd made her feel cheap and disposable.

***

Margaux chattered about the play—*The Importance of Being Earnest*, by Oscar Wilde—and Eleanor said they could read it. Finally, the day, which seemed to pass so very slowly, was over. Eleanor phoned her mother, to let her know she'd be late, and was able to escape from the apartment with no more than a brief nod to Mr. Bellamy.

The September evening was as warm as summer but the light was appreciably different, already fading as Eleanor walked from Park Avenue to Madison and turned south. The stores were just closing and she saw women exiting with delicate shopping bags whose handles were mere ribbons dangling from their wrists. What could such insubstantial bags hold? Silk stockings? Powder puffs? A woman in a fitted red suit walked a glossy dachshund; another held the hand of a small child in a pink-and-white pinafore. All these women—so protected, so cosseted—had homes and husbands, dogs and children. Eleanor felt like an exile in their midst. Would these things that seemed to come so easily to other women ever come to her? Ruth had just announced her engagement to Marty Tolchin, the boy she'd met at the synagogue mixer. Two other Vassar friends were also newly engaged, and a third had just gotten married in Philadelphia. Eleanor hadn't been able to attend the wedding but she'd gone in with some of the other girls for a set of crystal wineglasses and a matching decanter.

Eleanor was the first to arrive at the Carlyle Hotel, and was ushered to one of the chocolate brown leather banquettes. A waiter appeared with a menu and a glass of ice water that Eleanor sipped as she looked around at the nickel-trimmed black glass tabletops, the black granite bar, and the gold leaf that covered the ceiling. On the walls were whimsical scenes of Central Park—picnicking rabbits, ice-skating elephants, a giraffe slipping his neck between the bars of his cage. She had just glanced down at the menu—what prices on the drinks!—when Patricia appeared. "Thank you for meeting me," she said. "I just wanted a chance to talk to you—alone." Patricia flashed a smile as the waiter appeared and ordered a Green Dragon for each of them; Eleanor had no idea what was in it.

"Is it something with Margaux?" she asked.

"Margaux is just blossoming." Patricia sipped the vividly colored drink that had just arrived. "Thanks to you. So no, it's not about her. It's about Henryka."

"Henryka?" Eleanor took a sip of her drink. She tasted crème de menthe and something else too. Whatever it was, it was powerful—she had better go slowly.

"Did you know she'd given notice? She'll be gone by the end of the month."

"Yes, I know." Eleanor had been surprised when Henryka told her. Also sorry because she had come to depend on Henryka as an ally in the household. But why did this disclosure demand drinks at the Carlyle?

"Well, did you know the reason she gave for leaving?"

"No, she didn't mention—"

"She said it was because of you."

"Me? What do I have to do with it?"

"Do you remember the night she took you to the doctor in Argyle?" Patricia's elegant fingers seemed to be holding the stem of her glass very tightly.

"She told you about that?" Eleanor was sure her face was flaming. That Patricia had known but not said anything seemed beyond understanding.

"Only what she knew—that you'd been hurt and needed to see a doctor. And that the person who hurt you was—Wynn."

"He didn't hurt me, not exactly, it was just that we fell and I hit my head on the floor . . ." Eleanor couldn't finish.

"Why don't you tell me what happened?" Patricia's voice was surprisingly gentle. "From the beginning."

Eleanor did not think she could bring herself to tell the story, but found she was able to do it, all the while staring down at the luminous green liquid in her glass.

"Wynn admits that he came to see you," said Patricia. "But he said that you invited him in, offered him a drink, and asked him to dance."

"No." Eleanor finally raised her eyes to look at Patricia. "It wasn't like that. You know it wasn't. I would never . . . He was your husband. And my employer."

"I don't know what to think." Patricia finished her drink and signaled to the waiter to bring two more.

"I think you know that I'm telling the truth, but to believe me, you have to accept what kind of man your husband is. And that can't be easy."

"The kind of man my husband is . . . I knew that when I married him. Or I thought I did. But people change and you can't even see it because you're still stuck in the past."

Eleanor was flustered. She had never planned on sharing what had happened with Patricia and yet Patricia had found out anyway. "I wasn't going to tell you," she said. "I wasn't going to tell anyone, not even Tom. And I didn't even tell Henryka, but she guessed."

"So, what are we going to do?" All of Patricia's defenses seemed gone, and she was asking a question to which Eleanor did not have the answer.

"What do you want to do?"

"Well, I'm losing my cook, which grieves me more than I can say. I don't want to lose you too."

"You don't?" This was a surprise; Eleanor thought Patricia would have wanted her gone immediately.

"No," Patricia said.

"What if we never talk about it again? Pretend it didn't happen, and after a while, it will feel like it never did."

"Would you really agree to that? Tell no one? Not even Tom?"

"Of course. I'm the one who suggested it," said Eleanor. She never wanted to think about that night again. Now she wouldn't have to.

"Then I think we have a plan. Can we drink to it?" She touched the rim of her glass to Eleanor's, and when the Green Dragons were gone, signaled to the waiter for the check.

It was dark as Eleanor walked along East Seventy-Sixth Street toward home. Irina would want to know if she'd eaten, and if so, what and with whom. Just thinking about these questions felt oppressive; having to answer would be even worse. How much longer would she have to tolerate them? She thought of the women she'd seen earlier in the evening. Would she ever join their magic circle? Ira had jilted her and Tom had vanished—but even if he hadn't, she saw too many obstacles to imagine a life with him.

When she came to Second Avenue she turned and headed uptown. What if there were another way to live? Not with a husband, not with Irina, but—alone. The thought was terrifying. Also exhilarating. And once it had coalesced in her mind, it was followed by a rush of others. Where might she want to live? Not Yorkville, where, apart from her four years at Vassar, she'd spent her whole life. The West Side perhaps? Or downtown, in the Village, like Tom? She had some money in a savings account. What would her mother think? Her friends? But oh, imagine how it would feel to be answerable to no one other than herself.

Eleanor came to their building. The window of Hats by Irina was dark and the gate was down. She let herself in and went up the stairs. She'd just stepped inside the apartment when she saw her mother, seated in the lamplight with the evening newspaper spread across her lap. "Have you eaten?" Irina asked. Eleanor wanted to scream, *Yes! No! Please don't ask me that ever again!* But looking at her mother's worried, loving expression, she said only, "No, but don't get up. I'll fix something for myself."

In the weeks that followed, Eleanor harbored her plan in secret, adding money to her account faithfully every payday. Not that anyone would have been interested. Ruth was busy planning her wedding and wanted to talk of nothing else. Tom was still away and she'd received only a folded sheet of paper with the words, *Thinking of you*, penned in a bold, sloppy hand. The postmark was from neither Martha's Vineyard nor Nova Scotia, but Quebec. She looked at the note for a few minutes before ripping it in half.

By October, the weather had turned cooler, and Eleanor pulled out the black princess-style coat she'd had since college. She remembered how pretty she'd thought it was when she purchased it, but that had been several years ago. Now the coat seemed to droop on its hanger, and its cuffs and collar were starting to fray. A new coat would have been so nice, but her own apartment would be even nicer; she put the purchase on hold and hunted through Irina's trimmings for some black velvet ribbon with which she could conceal all the fraying. That, combined with black jet buttons, freshened the whole look.

"What a nice coat," Patricia said when Eleanor arrived wearing it for the first time. "The trimming just makes it."

"Thank you." Eleanor hung the coat in the hall closet and continued on to the study.

It was shortly after lunch that Eleanor heard the apartment's front door opening and then closing. "Good day to you, sir," said Bridget, the cook who'd been hired to replace Henryka. Her voice, with its strong Irish brogue, was loud enough to carry. Eleanor didn't hear the reply, but she didn't have to. She knew it came from Wynn Bellamy; he must have been home early from the office.

"Eleanor, I asked you a question. Didn't you hear me?" said Margaux.

"I'm sorry. I wasn't paying attention. What did you say?" Eleanor tried to blot out the knowledge that Mr. Bellamy was here. Since that evening at the Carlyle, she'd been doing what she promised Patricia: keeping mum and putting the incident in Argyle out of her mind. This had proved less difficult than she expected, especially when she made sure to time her arrivals and departures to avoid her employer. She hadn't seen him for weeks. Well, if she were careful, she wouldn't have to see him today either. Hearing him was quite enough.

Still, knowing he was in the apartment unnerved her and she had trouble keeping her mind on Margaux and their lesson. She managed to get through the rest of the afternoon, relieved when it was over. Margaux accompanied her to the foyer, where she retrieved her coat and pocketbook from the closet, anxious to leave as soon as possible. She wasn't yet out the door when Patricia, resplendent in a velvet opera cape, swept into the room.

"Mother, you look so beautiful," said Margaux.

"Thank you, darling." The cape was lined with ivory satin, visible as she moved, and her hair was gathered into a black, sequin-encrusted snood. "But I can't find my pearl drop earrings anywhere. Have you seen them?"

"No," said Margaux. "Not since the last time you wore them anyway."

"I just can't imagine where they could have gone. I always keep them in the jewelry box right on top of my bureau."

"I hope you find them." Eleanor's hand was on the doorknob. "And that you have a lovely evening."

"Where are you going?" Margaux asked.

"To a formal dinner." She checked her reflection in the mirror above the demilune table. "I suppose I could do without them. But I'd still like to know where they are."

"So would I," said Wynn Bellamy as he walked in adjusting his bow tie. He wore a tuxedo, a highly starched white shirt, and an expression of sorely tried patience. "They came from Harry Winston and were very expensive."

"Really, Wynn, no need to harp on about how much things cost—"

"Except when I'm the one who paid for them!"

Patricia said nothing, but Eleanor saw her lips compress into a thin, tight line.

"It's all right, I'll look for them when we get home."

"No, you should find them now."

"But I've looked everywhere."

"Maybe Bridget would know."

"She's been in the kitchen all day. I don't think she went into the bedroom once, and besides, she's gone now anyway."

"What about you, Miss Moss?"

"What about me?" Why was he bringing her into this?

"Have you seen my wife's earrings today?"

"Not today or any other day, for that matter. I don't even know what they look like."

"Are you sure?"

"Wynn, what's wrong with you? She said she hasn't seen them. Now really, let's go. It's getting late."

"Eleanor would tell us if she'd seen them," said Margaux.

"Of course I would," Eleanor said. This badgering was perverse, it was cruel, it was—

"Miss Moss, I'd like you to show me the contents of your purse—"

"Have you gone mad?" Patricia said. "She's not going to do any such thing. I don't understand why you're making such a scene—"

"It's all right," Eleanor said, though of course it wasn't. "I'd be more than willing to show you." She walked over to where he stood and snapped open the clasp of the black leather purse. She felt revolted as he pawed through its contents—worn leather wallet, comb, lipstick, compact, keys. "There," she said. "You see? No earrings."

"Daddy, I don't know why you're treating Eleanor like this. She'd never, ever take anything from Mother, not even a hairpin," Margaux pleaded.

But Mr. Bellamy just said, "Your pockets. Could you please turn them inside out?"

"No, Eleanor. Don't." Patricia walked swiftly to the door, causing the cape to ripple around her ankles. "Wynn, I am leaving right now, with or without you. I won't stand here while you insult Eleanor—"

"No, really, it's fine." Eleanor set her purse down on the console table under the mirror and reached into her pockets. "Here, you can see for yourself—" From the left pocket, she pulled out a subway token and a half-finished roll of Pep O Mint LifeSavers, and from the right, a glittering pair of pearl-and-diamond earrings.

TWENTY-ONE

Patricia spoke not one word to Wynn during the short walk to Audrey's apartment building on Fifth Avenue, and as soon as they were greeted at the door by her friend's roly-poly little husband, she took off, determined to ignore him for the rest of the evening as well. Fortunately, there were plenty of distractions to make that goal easier to attain: champagne, a glorious view of the Metropolitan Museum of Art from the oversize windows, and the dinner for twelve served in Audrey's spacious dining room. The room had been newly decorated—cabbage-rose chintz drapes, a shiny black ceiling, acid green woodwork, and a cherry red floor—by none other than Dorothy Draper, the most sought-after decorator in town.

Thankfully, Audrey never seated husbands and wives together, and Patricia found herself next to a translator on one side and a scholar whose specialty was Byzantine mosaics on the other; the translator, who spoke several languages, was quite entertaining, and the scholar, soft-spoken and serious, had the manner of a fourteenth-century monk. Audrey's dinner guests were always more interesting than the bankers, stockbrokers, and lawyers that Patricia was accustomed to; Tom would have enjoyed himself here. But she hadn't heard from him in weeks.

After the dessert—a pavlova piled high with berries and whipped cream—the men went into the library to smoke their vile cigars while the women went to the living room. Audrey found her way over to Patricia and sat down next to her. "Good to see you, darling. I'm so glad you could come." She squeezed Patricia's hand.

"It's good to see you too. Married life seems to agree with you— you're looking wonderful."

"It does. Second time was the charm for me. When I think of what I used to put up with . . ." Her smile vanished and then reappeared again, wider than before. "But why am I dwelling on the past? Harold is just a lamb. An angel. He's letting me hire Dorothy to do this room as well; don't you just love what she did with the dining room? I mean, a black ceiling?" And without waiting for a reply, she continued, "And we're renting a villa in the hills overlooking Florence next spring. It sleeps six very comfortably—maybe you and Wynn will come and stay."

"That sounds lovely." The thought of being in such a remote place with her husband made Patricia feel as if someone were pressing down on her windpipe, and when Audrey got up, she went in search of another drink.

It was past one a.m. when they left the party and began their walk home. Wynn seemed inebriated and was humming softly to himself, whereas despite the many drinks she'd consumed at the party, Patricia felt thoroughly and disappointingly sober. The anger she'd been able to fend off all evening sifted back down over her like ash.

"How much do you think he's got?"

"Excuse me?"

"Audrey's new husband—Howard, Hal—"

"It's Harold, and how would I know such a thing?" She was so tired of the unutterably crude way he went on about money.

"I thought you ladies talked. Isn't that what you do best? Get together and gab, gab, gab?"

"Honestly, you're being—"

"And in all that time you spend gabbing, the subject of Harry's money never came up—?"

"Why did you plant my earrings in Eleanor's pocket?"

"Excuse me?" He had the offended air of someone who'd stepped in dog excrement.

"Stop pretending. You put my earrings in Eleanor's pocket. Did you want to smear her entirely?"

"She doesn't need me for that—she can do it well enough on her own."

They came to a red light at the corner of Madison Avenue and she remained on the sidewalk. But Wynn walked on ahead.

"What are you doing?" As soon as she had the light, she hurried across, cape billowing around her.

"There weren't any cars," he said. "It was perfectly safe."

"You want to distract me," she said. "But it's not going to work."

"Fine." He stopped, a few feet from the awning to their building. Eamon, the night doorman, nodded in their direction. "I didn't plant them. She took them, plain and simple. I told you she was trouble—"

"That is the most preposterous thing I have ever heard." She swept past him and into their building. He followed her to the elevator and they rode up in silence. But once they were back in the apartment, she turned to him again. "I don't believe you."

"Oh, so you believe her—a girl you picked up in the street—"

"That's hardly what happened, and anyway, she's done wonders for Margaux, you *know* that, and yet you're doing your best to undermine her at every turn. First you go barging into the cottage—"

"The cottage, you should remember, is mine. Mine, and I'm free to visit it whenever I like—"

"Barging in, drunk no doubt, trying to make a pass at her and when you fail—and I find out—you decide you'll do anything you can to discredit her, even stooping to something as obvious as to put those earrings in her coat pocket. As if she'd have done that! My God, you're not only a liar and a bully, you're an idiot—"

He was across the foyer in seconds and his hand shot out, delivering a clean, smart slap to her face. "Never say that to me," he hissed. "Never, do you understand?"

Her own hand flew to her cheek, which was stinging and no doubt red. He'd hit her—he'd actually hit her. It hadn't been that hard, and so it wasn't the pain that made her recoil. It was the shame of it, the shame and the blatant disregard for the sanctity of her—what? Her being.

"Why are you shouting?"

Patricia turned to see Margaux, leaning heavily on her walking stick and regarding them in horror.

"Darling, why don't you—" Patricia started.

"Go back to bed," Wynn said sternly. "Now."

"But I want to know what's going on." Her pillow-mussed hair and flannel nightgown made her look so young. So vulnerable.

"Do as you're told."

Something in his voice made her obey. Watching her retreat, Patricia moved to follow. Then she realized she was still wearing her velvet cape, which felt like it belonged to another evening, another *life*; she hastily unfastened it and draped it over her arm.

"Come back here," said Wynn.

"I'm through talking to you tonight."

"Come back!"

From the darkness of the hall, she turned to look back at him; he stood there, bulky and massive, his feet planted on the parquet floor like some latter-day Henry VIII. "And if I don't? Are you going to hit me again?"

"Tricia, I'm sorry, I didn't mean . . . I never wanted . . . But you were goading me and—"

"I'm going in to see Margaux—God knows what she's thinking— and then I'll go into the guest room. Or you can. We can talk in the morning." And then she left him, standing alone in the light. Again, she felt that flash of anger at Eleanor, irrational as it was, for being the cause of yet another ugly quarrel.

The next morning, Patricia stoked the embers of last night's fury as she dressed. To think he had raised a hand to her, struck her . . . she would leave him, yes she would. She'd take Margaux and go to Argyle. Or they would go somewhere, *anywhere* else. She finished buttoning her dress and gave her chignon a final pat.

But when she walked into the kitchen, there was Wynn, freshly showered and smelling of bay rum. He wore a pale blue shirt that looked well with his ruddy skin and blond hair, even if the latter was thinning. Margaux was seated very close to him, the *Times* spread out between them, and they were doing the crossword puzzle. He didn't look up when she came in but Margaux did. "Good morning, Mother." She sounded surprisingly cheerful; did she remember the ugly scene from the night before? If so, it didn't show. "Do you want a cinnamon bun?" She indicated the plate where the glazed, raisin-studded buns were piled high.

"Where did those come from?" Patricia knew Bridget hadn't baked them.

"Daddy went out early and brought back a bagful. I've already had one and they're delicious."

"That was very nice of you," Patricia said uncertainly.

Wynn looked up at her then, an apology written all over his cleanly shaved face. "I know they're Margaux's favorite," he said. "And I just want to make my girl happy."

He was trying, Patricia realized. Trying very hard. But if Margaux seemed to have put the previous evening aside, Patricia was unable to shake off the unpleasant memory as easily. Then she looked at Wynn again, arm now draped casually over Margaux's shoulder. If he was making an effort, maybe she needed to make more of an effort too. "Let me try one of those buns," she said as she sat down. "They're my favorite too."

TWENTY-TWO

The next day Eleanor approached the Bellamys' apartment with dread. She waited long enough to be sure Mr. Bellamy would not be home, and gave her name to the doorman, aware that this was the last time she would need to use the false moniker. Margaux was at the door to greet her with a hug. "Eleanor, I'm so sorry about what Daddy said. Mother and I know you would never have taken those earrings." Eleanor had no reply. Of course there was no question of her continuing to work for the Bellamys after what had happened. She was just here to say good-bye to Margaux.

Last night, when she first saw the earrings, she was so startled that she dropped them. But in the few seconds it took her to kneel and retrieve them, indignation overpowered any fear or embarrassment.

"You put them in my pocket," she said to Mr. Bellamy.

"Me? I would never—"

"How else would you have known they were there?" She handed them to Patricia.

"Daddy, did you really do that?" Margaux looked horrified.

"Wynn, can you please tell me what this is all about—" Patricia interjected.

Eleanor wasn't going to listen to another minute of this. Maybe she was even a little relieved—her little minuet of avoidance would be over. "I'll be going now," Eleanor said. "Good night."

Now Eleanor was back in this apartment for what she imagined was the last time. Patricia came into the foyer. "Margaux, darling, Eleanor and I are going to need to talk—alone."

"Why can't I be there too? You're going to be talking about me."

Eleanor looked at Patricia. "She's right, you know. Can't she join us?"

"I don't think it would be suitable," said Patricia. "I'd like you to go to your room, Margaux. When we're done, I'll call you."

"No." Margaux planted her walking stick firmly in front of her. "I'm not going."

"Why don't you do what your mother asks? We'll have a chance to talk later," said Eleanor.

"Promise?" Margaux asked.

"Promise," said Eleanor, and after a brief hesitation, Margaux went to her room.

Eleanor followed Patricia into the study. She had never liked the room, but in these past months, she'd been so engaged by her work with Margaux that its offensiveness had receded. Today, however, it loomed large again: the monstrous black mantel, the hulking desk, the dead fish on the wall. She sat down on one of the leather chairs and Patricia took the other.

"I'm at a loss," Patricia said. "But I do want to apologize for Wynn's behavior last night. He was entirely out of line."

Was Eleanor supposed to say, *That's all right, I understand*? Because it wasn't and she didn't. "I don't know why he's so dead set against me." She chose her words carefully. "I only know that he is—and that I can't work here anymore."

"I understand," Patricia said. "It will be hard for Margaux though."

"For me too." Eleanor touched the chair's dark, hobnail-studded leather. "I'll miss working with her. I think you know how close we've become. But she's ready for the next step now."

"And if she won't agree to Oakwood?"

"If I'm not here, she will. It would be best for her. Really."

"I hope you're right."

"There's one more thing . . . I'd like to be able to stay in touch with Margaux. With your permission, of course."

"I don't see why that wouldn't be possible . . . eventually," Patricia said.

"Eventually?"

"Of course I want you two to be in touch. But right now it may be . . . problematic. I want to give Wynn a chance to settle down . . ."

"I see." What Eleanor saw was a roadblock; Patricia was going to control her access to Margaux and Eleanor would have to accept that. Was there anything left to say? She stood up.

Patricia got to her feet as well. "I'll write you a check," she said.

"You can prorate the amount."

"That won't be necessary." She went to fetch the checkbook. Margaux slipped into the study as soon as she'd gone.

"You didn't go to your room," Eleanor said.

"No," said Margaux. "I tried to listen at the door. But I couldn't hear anything. You're leaving us, right? You're leaving *me*."

"Don't think of it that way. I'll always care for you. Always. And we'll be able to be in touch again. Just not—now."

"What am I going to do without you?" Tears had formed in Margaux's eyes.

"I told your mother about a boarding school upstate."

"Boarding school? I won't go!"

"All the students have had polio. You won't feel out of place."

"I still don't want to go."

"Will you try it? For me?"

Patricia reentered the room holding a check in her hand. "Margaux, I thought you were in your room."

"We were talking about Oakwood," Eleanor said. "She's willing to give it a try. Isn't that right, Margaux?"

Margaux said nothing at first and then muttered, "Maybe. All right. If you want me to."

"I do," Eleanor said. "Because I think it's exactly the kind of place where you should be."

Margaux didn't answer, but clomped angrily out of the study.

After she had gone, Patricia said, "I'll telephone the school today." Then she handed Eleanor the check.

Eleanor looked at the sum Patricia had filled in. "This isn't right," she said. "You've given me too much money."

"Consider it severance," Patricia said.

Once she was back out in the chilly morning, Eleanor had to figure out what to do with her day. She felt exiled and furious—all because of Wynn Bellamy. After several minutes of indecision, she realized she was close to the Metropolitan Museum of Art, so she walked over and spent a tranquil hour looking at Etruscan statues and another with the ancient Greeks. But even then it was only a little past noon; she couldn't show up at home until late in the afternoon. She thought again about the luxury of having her own apartment, and the freedom it would grant her.

Maybe she could get in to see Rita Burns again. Yes, that was a good idea. She'd even save the nickel and walk downtown. By the time she reached Rita's office in the Chrysler Building, she was cold, and hungry too, but she didn't want to spend money on anything to eat. The office was as crowded as Eleanor remembered, but she took a seat in the waiting room and stayed until it emptied out. It was close to five o'clock, and the sky was already darkening, by the time she was face-to-face with Rita again.

"I remember you," Rita said. "But we didn't place you. What did you end up doing?"

"I found a position as a private tutor, but now it's ended."

"Can you get me a reference if I need it?"

Eleanor thought of Patricia. "Yes," she said. "I can."

"All right then. I'll be in touch if something comes up."

"There's just one thing—you won't be able to telephone me."

"No?" Rita seemed surprised. "Why not?"

"I'd rather not bore you with it," said Eleanor. "Can I phone you or stop by to check in?"

"I suppose that would be all right." Rita regarded her with some speculation but Eleanor just picked up her coat and left.

The next morning, she left the apartment as she always had, only she surreptitiously slipped an apple and a hard-boiled egg into her bag so she wouldn't have to spend money on lunch. Then she set off for the New York Public Library, where she could stay for hours. The subterfuge worked for a few days, but the following Monday it poured. Still, armed with an umbrella, she decided to walk downtown. She'd gotten as far as Seventieth Street when the umbrella blew inside out and was destroyed; she deposited its carcass in a nearby trash can. The rain had tapered off by then anyway, but just as she reached the pair of stone lions in front of the library, a bus tore through a curbside puddle, drenching her with cold, dirty water. She looked down at her stockings, which were splattered and wet, and knew her little charade had come to an end.

The next morning at breakfast, she told Irina she was no longer employed by the Bellamys.

"I thought you loved the job, or at least the girl. What happened?"

Eleanor was prepared. "They decided to send her to boarding school. She was ready."

"Just like that!" Irina exclaimed. "They didn't give you much notice, did they? I told you their kind were no good."

"She gave me a very generous severance payment," Eleanor said.

"That's the very least she could have done." Irina drained the last of her coffee and stood up. "But now what? You won't find another teaching job and I won't have you helping me in the store. You'd be wasting your talents."

"I'll find something," Eleanor said.

"I hope so." Irina turned to the sink to rinse out the cup. "But this is now the second time you've left a job without finding another first."

Eleanor didn't say anything, but she felt the weight of Irina's disapproval pressing down on her and she longed to rid herself of its yoke.

After that conversation, she preferred to spend her days away from the apartment. Sometimes she went to Rita's office, as well as the other employment agency with which she had registered. She put the word out to Ruth and her other friends, who promised to share any leads with her.

The days grew shorter and colder; she wore down the heels of first one pair of shoes, and then another. At dinner, she was ravenous, taking second and even third helpings of whatever her mother had prepared.

"You're wearing yourself to the bone," Irina commented. "You're eating plenty but you're thin as a rail."

Eleanor just slathered butter on another slice of pumpernickel and said nothing.

In early December, Ruth called to say her cousin's husband worked at Macy's in Herald Square, and there was a position in the small appliances department. "He'd hire you in a minute," Ruth said. "You'd bring some real class to the job." Eleanor said no. But after another week, one of traipsing around in the cold, feeling her mother's worry tighten around her every day, she decided that she would give the Hoover vacuum cleaners, Silex coffee makers, and shiny chrome Toastmasters a try. She was seated in a Horn & Hardart sipping coffee when she came to this conclusion, but decided that before she called Ruth, she would stop by Rita's office; it was only a few blocks from here.

Settling herself into the waiting area, Eleanor picked up a magazine. But her name was called almost immediately. "Are you sure?" she asked the receptionist. "I don't have an appointment and she usually sees me late in the day."

"She told me to tell her when you showed up," said the receptionist. "I'm supposed to send you right in."

Eleanor shifted her coat to one hand and smoothed her hair with the other. She was sorry she hadn't had time to reapply her lipstick.

"I've been waiting for you," Rita Burns said before she even sat down. "I think I found you the perfect job."

"I'm all ears," said Eleanor as she sank into the chair across from Rita.

The next morning, Eleanor put on her best sweater, a black, jewel-neck cashmere, and took the subway downtown to Greenwich

Village, another neighborhood with which she was almost entirely unfamiliar. Her breath made little white puffs as she walked past Italian butcher shops and bakeries as well as several intriguing little bars and cafes where she imagined poets and painters sipped wine and smoked Black Russian Sobranie cigarettes. It occurred to her that Tom lived somewhere down here. He knew this neighborhood, he'd probably walked these streets. A spike of pain went through her—best not to think of him now, but to focus on the interview.

After a bit of backtracking, she finally found her way to the office of Zephyr Press, on Carmine Street. Up two flights of stairs, she walked into an open loftlike space in which papers, books, and file folders covered all the available surfaces. Although she couldn't see anyone, she heard a voice call out, "Are you the girl Rita was raving about? Come on over and let's have a look at you."

Eleanor made her way through the towers of books that stood between her and the sound of the voice. When she extended her hand, a woman who looked to be in her thirties reached out to shake it. "Adriana Giacchino," she said. "And you're Eleanor Moss?"

"That's right." So Rita had used that name; well, she wasn't going to dispute it now.

"Sit down," Adriana instructed. "That is, if you can find a place. And if you can't, just go ahead and make one." She had severe black bangs and bright red harlequin glasses that matched her red lips.

Eleanor carefully moved some of the papers on the nearest chair to the floor.

"So tell me about yourself," Adriana instructed. "Rita says you went to Vassar. I did too—class of '37."

"I was class of '43," Eleanor said. "I majored in English."

"Did you have Professor Westinhall for Chaucer?" Adriana asked.

"I did," said Eleanor. "She was . . . ferocious."

251

"So she was!" said Adriana. "Ah, old Westie. I wonder if she's still there. Old professors never retire. Or die. They just haunt the stacks of the library, making sure that the book you need is never on the shelf."

The interview grew even less formal as it went on. In fact, Eleanor was having such a pleasant time comparing notes on other professors, dorms, and their favorite desserts at Alumnae House that she was almost surprised when Adriana stood up and said, "Well, Moss, Rita was right. You're hired. You can start right now if you like."

"I am?" said Eleanor. "I can?"

"Sure, why not? You can see I need help. It's been like a three-ring circus around here." And, as if to underscore what she'd said, not one but two phone lines rang simultaneously.

Eleanor reached to answer one of them as Adriana went for the other. "Good afternoon, Zephyr Press," she said. "Give me a moment and I'll check." She put her hand over the receiver and said softly, "Ian Marshall for you."

"Heaven forfend!" Adriana mouthed as the caller on her line talked into the phone. "Tell him I'm not here."

"I'm sorry, she's stepped out," Eleanor said smoothly. "May I take a message?"

At Zephyr, Eleanor typed, filed, opened mail, answered the telephone, and sifted through the unending stream of novels, stories, essays, and poems that poured in over the transom. She liked this part of the job best of all, and sometimes brought home manuscripts to read at night, when the workday was done. On the few occasions she did spot something of real merit in the avalanche of unsolicited manuscripts, she brought it to the attention of her new boss. "Good work, Moss," Adriana would say. "Keep it up."

The job was fulfilling and Eleanor was grateful to Rita Burns for leading her to it. She did miss teaching though. And she especially missed Margaux. But when she called Patricia to ask if she might write or call Margaux at Oakwood, Patricia said, "Let her get settled in. She needs time to adjust before she hears from you." Eleanor tried a second and then a third time, but Patricia always found a reason to say no. Finally Eleanor had to accept that Patricia just didn't want her to be in touch with Margaux. She was hurt, and tempted to write to Margaux anyway. But respect for Patricia's wishes kept her from doing it. Much as she loved the girl, she would not go where she clearly was not wanted.

Soon the streets of Greenwich Village became more familiar to her, and as she walked them—easily now, and with a growing sense of ownership and authority—she thought of Tom and wondered if she'd ever run into him down here. She knew the number of his apartment building, and she could have looked up his phone number in the telephone book or written to him. But she had her pride. He knew where he could find her.

It pained her to realize just how little she'd meant to any of them really; when she'd finished serving her function, they had no further use for her. She could have confided all this to her mother, who would have been quick to agree, and in the past, she would have. Yet she didn't. Though there was no longer any overt tension between them, Eleanor sensed a rift that was growing deeper and wider as the weeks passed. She was keeping more and more of herself hidden from view, saving her money, biding her time. And then, when the moment was right, she'd break away and walk freely into the new life she was only just beginning to devise for herself.

TWENTY-THREE

Christmas was a misery that year, though not from a lack of effort. Patricia had tried—oh, how *hard* she had tried!—to inject some meager joy into the season. After Eleanor had left them, Patricia contacted that upstate boarding school and was relieved to find they were willing to take Margaux on in the middle of the term. Despite what she'd said to Eleanor, Margaux grumbled about what she called a *prison sentence*, but when she learned that Larry Sharp had just started at Oakwood, she was somewhat mollified. Once Margaux was settled, Patricia took the train, alone, down to Florida, where Dottie kept a house in Palm Beach. Wynn offered not a word of protest.

But with the impending holiday, she returned to New York. Her marriage may have been in tatters but there were still appearances to keep up: presents to be bought and wrapped, cards to be written and mailed, the apartment to decorate. Wynn brought home a nine-foot tree—evidently he too was trying hard—and set it up in the living room once Patricia moved a chair and an end table to accommodate it.

Then Margaux got home. In less than an hour, it was clear she had completely reverted to the unhappy, aggravating girl she'd been in those awful months between her recovery and Eleanor's arrival. Margaux did not want to go to Rumpelmayer's on Fifty-Ninth Street for hot chocolate, and she spurned her mother's invitation to view the elaborately decorated store windows on Fifth Avenue, or the resplendent tree—an eighty-foot Norway spruce covered in multicolored lights—at Rockefeller Center. She even refused to help trim their own tree. While Patricia carefully lifted the glass balls from their boxes and positioned them on the fragrant branches, Margaux sat on the sofa with a book, ostentatiously ignoring her.

Christmas morning was the nadir. Margaux was only minimally responsive to Patricia's gifts: a sage green cashmere twinset—Margaux's first—and a satin-lined muff, but she was visibly upset by Wynn's gift of a handsome, and surely quite costly, leather saddle.

"What's this for?" Margaux asked, tears welling as she looked from the shiny cognac leather to her father's face.

"It's for your horse," said Wynn. He seemed truly surprised by her question. "Don't you think Clover will look splendid with *that* on her back?"

"But I haven't ridden her in the longest time," Margaux said, swiping at her eyes.

"The doctor says you should be riding," said Wynn. "And when you do, you'll have this brand-new saddle."

Margaux touched the leather and said nothing more.

He looked so genuinely unhappy that Patricia found herself feeling sorry for him. But unfortunately, his present to Patricia was equally off the mark. When she tore away the silver paper and took the lid off the glossy black box, she found a sumptuous fur stole. "It's chinchilla," Wynn said proudly as Patricia lifted the garment from its nest of tissue. "Go on, try it."

Reluctantly, Patricia stood up. She already owned two furs—a full-length mink and a short fox jacket—and had no desire for a third. The stole was obscenely soft and plushy under her fingers; it almost made her feel sick to handle it. She put it on anyway, though she could not seem to manufacture the requisite enthusiasm when she modeled it for him. Watching her, Wynn's expression once more changed from initial delight to disappointment, like a sky darkening from blue to gunmetal gray. "Everything I do is wrong," he said, kicking aside the torn paper and discarded ribbons. "Wrong, wrong, wrong." He strode off and, though it was only ten in the morning, Patricia could hear the clink of the ice in the glass as he fixed himself a drink.

Poor Wynn. Although he hadn't consulted her about the saddle, Patricia understood his intent. The very first time Margaux had gotten up on a horse he'd been so excited, so proud, that you'd have thought he was up there with her. He had made it a point to attend every show, every competition, and had been her biggest fan and supporter. Because of her own experience, Patricia always found herself correcting some aspect of her daughter's riding—her form, the way she'd handled a jump. Not so for Wynn, whose delight in Margaux's performance was uncomplicated and pure. When she won first place at a regional event, he'd ordered a floral arrangement in the shape of a horseshoe and handed it to her, beaming. His gift of the saddle was as much about their connection as anything else. And as for the stole, how could he have known that she would find the thing ostentatious and offensive? She'd always loved her furs; was it his fault that her taste for them had soured?

Somehow they managed to endure the few days between Christmas and New Year's, and early in January, Patricia drove Margaux back up to Oakwood. Much of the ride was spent in silence, or listening to whatever Margaux, who fiddled incessantly with the dial, found on the radio. But shortly before they arrived she asked, "Why haven't I heard from Eleanor? Doesn't she care about me anymore?"

Patricia kept her eyes on the road ahead where crescents of snow could be seen at the edges. "Yes, I think she does," she said finally. "But maybe it's best that you don't hear from her now."

"Why? Because Daddy doesn't like her?"

"That's not it." It was though, wasn't it?

"Well, whatever it is, it's not fair."

They were about to turn onto the drive that led to the school. "I'll see what I can do," said Patricia. Which was probably going to be absolutely nothing. She didn't tell Margaux that Eleanor had asked whether she could write or call; she didn't want to stir up those feelings again. Now that Eleanor was no longer their employee, Patricia had to recognize that she had no place in their lives anymore. Or rather, the place she had was problematic. Even the mention of her name in front of Wynn could cause an argument. And she wasn't exactly the sort of person they were used to socializing with. Tom may have cultivated his colorful assortment of creative types, but Patricia had not. Eleanor was, at this moment, quite frankly, a headache. What was even more annoying was that Eleanor kept pressing her— couldn't she read between the lines and just discreetly back away?

When Patricia arrived back in New York City, she sat down to dinner. Bridget was adept at stews and roasts—tonight it was lamb— and she baked delicious soda bread. But she didn't have Henryka's touch with desserts or make any of the dishes that Henryka had perfected. And unlike Henryka, who was a quiet and unobtrusive presence, Bridget announced herself in a dozen ways—all of them loud.

"How was the drive?" Wynn asked.

"Fine." She turned to Bridget, who was hovering, waiting to see if they needed anything else. "I think we have everything we need here."

"Very good, Mrs. Bellamy," Bridget boomed.

Patricia had to will herself not to flinch and was relieved when the woman stepped into the kitchen.

Wynn cleared his throat. "Margaux was all right? I know she wasn't keen on going back but I think the school's the best thing for her." When Patricia didn't reply, he asked, "Don't you?"

"Don't I what?" Bridget's roast was fine, but not hot enough.

"Think that the school is a good place for her."

"Yes." Patricia took a bite of the mashed potatoes. Not even tepid, but cold. Still, she didn't want to bring it to Bridget's attention because that meant calling her into the room and having to listen to her apologies; she would mention it later.

"I'm glad you agree." Wynn looked down at his plate, where the pyramid of carrots and peas appeared to fascinate him.

Patricia thought this conversation might drive her quietly mad. But ever since that night in October when he'd slapped her, Wynn had been nothing but meek and contrite. At first his ingratiating attitude had appeased her, but as it continued, she found it tiresome and even contemptible. He'd moved, by unspoken agreement, into the guest room, though he continued to take his meals with her. They spoke to each other with elaborate courtesy and formality, their conversations littered with phrases like "could I trouble you" and "would you please." Their apartment was a series of well-appointed rooms in hell.

When the dinner was over, she declined dessert. "I'm awfully tired," she said. "I'm going to bed."

"Good night." He looked at her with the abject expression of a dog just scolded for chewing the master's slippers. "I'll see you in the morning."

Patricia escaped to the privacy of the bedroom, where she undressed and slipped under the covers, and tried to focus on a rather tawdry novel that Dottie had loaned her. She was just about to turn out the light when she heard a light tapping on the door.

"Come in," she called, and Wynn stepped into the room. It was only when he was standing there that she noticed how much weight he'd lost recently; the robe seemed to billow around his body.

"May I sit down?" He walked toward the bed, their bed, but instead of sitting down on it, he chose the pale blue slipper chair nearby.

"Is anything the matter?" She tightened her robe more securely around her waist; she was glad she was wearing it.

"Yes," he said. "There is."

"Did something happen at work?"

"No. Work is—work. I meant things are wrong between us," he said. "I don't like the way we're living. Sleeping in separate rooms. Acting like acquaintances. I'm lonely, Tricia. I miss you. I miss *us*."

Despite everything, this admission touched her, yet she had no adequate response. The "us" Wynn spoke of seemed so far in the past, she couldn't see it, she couldn't touch it. Too much had gotten in the way.

"Is this how it's going to be from now on?"

Patricia had not been able to think very far ahead. Every time she did, a heavy curtain came down in her mind. Behind that curtain lay her future, but it was blocked, and she could not see it. "I don't know," she said. She gestured to the place beside her on the bed. "Come here. We can talk in the dark. It'll be easier that way." She switched off the light.

He sank into the space beside her. "It's her, you know. That girl. Everything was fine until she showed up."

"Everything was not fine." She ran her fingers over the folded-down hem of the sheet. The raised bumps she felt were an embroidered monogram, the *P* on one side, the *W* on the other, and the larger *B* in the middle, uniting them. "Our daughter was suffering. Eleanor helped her. Why did you want to drive her away?"

"I know she was good with Margaux," he said. "But hadn't her time with Margaux come to an end? Margaux couldn't stay holed up here forever. She had to start living again."

"You have a point." And it was one Eleanor had made as well. "But even so, why go about it like that? Putting those earrings in her pocket . . ."

He was silent for a moment and then he began to cry. "Don't," she said gently. "Please don't." Her arms went around him instinctively and he sought her throat, and then her breasts.

"No." She put her hands on his chest to stop him. "Not now." She couldn't let this happen; it was—unendurable.

"All right." He moved away. "Not now. But—when?" When she didn't answer he said, "You've got to give me some hope, Tricia. Some little scrap."

"Don't make so much of it," she said. "I'm just tired, that's all."

He put a hand to her cheek—the same cheek he'd slapped. "Do you think it's too late?"

"Too late for what?" She pitied him, and that pity frightened her; it might engulf and drown her.

"For us to start over. I want to leave New York," he said. "I hate my job. I've hated it for years." He took his hand away. Patricia was relieved; she did not want him to touch her again.

"I know you have."

"We don't really need the money either. Especially if we lived some-where else, somewhere less expensive. Remember Uncle Walter's house?"

"What does your uncle's house have to do with us?" Patricia had never been there but recalled that Wynn's uncle had left him a house and property upstate a few years ago. She'd always assumed they would sell it.

"It's lovely up there. And the house, Tricia, you'd love it. Big, spa-cious, well constructed. There's a garden too. I remember the lilacs covering the entire back fence. What a smell."

"Wynn, I don't want to live in Rochester," she said quietly. Roch-ester was so . . . provincial—no theater, ballet, or opera, and what-ever museums there were couldn't begin to rival the institutions to which she had access in New York City. And she knew no one up there, not a soul. Pity was receding now, driven away by her dread of such a scenario.

"We'd be closer to Margaux," he continued as if she had not spo-ken. "She could come home on weekends. We could go to visit her too. It could be wonderful. Leaving this slick, nasty town behind, finding a simpler way of life. I could devote myself to you, Trish. To you, and only you."

"Did you hear me?" she said. "I don't want to live upstate." Her tone was sharp and painful even to her. But she had to stay strong or else she'd succumb, and in so doing, lose herself for good.

"I just thought . . ."

"I know what you thought. And it can't be."

"What can't be?"

"Us," she said simply. "At least not the us we were—before." Pa-tricia got up. "I'm not asking you for a divorce." Divorce to her meant failure and unending shame. Divorce would stigmatize Margaux.

"But I won't share your bed ever again. Do you understand? Our private lives are going to be separate."

When he remained motionless, Patricia leaned over and touched his shoulder. "It's time for you to go back to your room." Because this room was hers, and hers alone.

TWENTY-FOUR

Early in February, Eleanor received another note from Tom, *Missing you*, two terse words orphaned in an expanse of white paper. She ripped it up and burst into tears. How, after all these months, could he think that was enough? But she hadn't ripped up the envelope, and later she checked the postmark. New York City. So he was here. She couldn't stop the swoop of her heart, though it made her angry that he still had that power over her. The cad.

The following Saturday, Eleanor went to the shop to help her mother and spent the morning attaching small red tickets to all the hats earmarked for Irina's big winter sale. When she'd finished, she took a break and went upstairs for a cup of tea. The phone rang and it was Tom. "Why are you calling me now?" she asked.

"Because I miss you. Really. I understand if you don't believe me though—I acted like a heel."

"I don't know what to believe." Despite her hurt and her anger, the words were a balm.

"Look, we should talk in person. Can I see you, Eleanor?" She thought about putting the phone down. Instead, she remained on the line, and the next night, she told her mother she was going to an engagement party for Ruth and that she'd be home late. Then she went downtown to meet him, walking along streets that had by now become familiar. She was even familiar with the place he'd suggested, Caffè Luigi, and when she came to it, she paused in front of the big picture window. The place was softly lit and cozy, with a blaze in the brick-lined fireplace and a convivial cluster of small round tables. And there, seated on a black bentwood chair, was Tom. He didn't see her, so she was free to gaze at the fine blond hair that had felt so smooth under her fingers and at the aquiline cast of his profile. He was drinking from a tiny white cup and still wore his coat, though his scarf was draped over the empty chair—the chair that would be hers as soon as she crossed the threshold to join him.

Only she didn't. She stood outside in the cold, watching as he glanced toward the door—she stepped back so he couldn't see her—looked at his watch, and called the waiter over to order another cup of whatever it was that he had been drinking. She was chilled all over but the longer she stood there, the more impossible it seemed for her to move. There was a hard, knotted piece of her heart that wanted to hurt him as she'd been hurt. *Let him see what it's like to wait and wonder. Let him suffer too.*

Finally, Tom took his scarf and got up, leaving some money next to the empty cups on the table. As he emerged from the cafe, she scurried back and hid in a doorway. He began to walk, his long strides making it hard for her to follow, but she felt pulled along in his wake. Now this was crazy. She didn't go in when he was waiting for her, and yet she was following him? She kept him in her line of sight, but stayed far enough back so he wouldn't be aware of her.

He walked quickly, hands in his pockets, until he came to Jane Street. His pace slowed and hers did too. Then all of a sudden he whirled around and with his long stride, doubled back so he was right in front of her. "Why are you following me—" He stopped. "Eleanor! I waited and waited—"

"I know," she said. After thinking about him so much and for so long, seeing him was jarring. "I was there. I saw you inside."

"So then why didn't you come in?"

"Because I didn't want to," she said.

"But you followed me." He stepped closer, as if to embrace her, but she stepped back. "It's good to see you," he said.

She nodded, but didn't know what her nod meant. That she thought yes, it was good to see her? Or that it was good to see him? Which, in fact, it was. He wore a camel chesterfield coat and plaid scarf but no hat; his dark blond hair, so like Patricia's, was pushed back carelessly from his forehead and the tip of his nose was pink from the cold. "I live here," he said. "Please come up. We can talk in my apartment."

Should she go up with him? His key was in his hand, the same hand that had fed her that first morsel of lobster, that had touched her so deftly in so many places. "All right," she said. He unlocked the front door—no doorman for him—and let her walk in first. There was no elevator either, and they took the stairs to the second floor. Then he was ushering her in, taking her coat and hat, inviting her to sit down. "I'll be right back." She sank into a worn though elegant sofa, covered in a plum-colored velvet that was balding around the arms. The rugs were beautifully patterned but fraying and worn too.

Tom disappeared into the kitchen to make drinks and Eleanor looked around. A carved wooden mantel but no actual fireplace. Several mismatched candlesticks—brass, silver, crystal—lined the top of it, their white tapers in various states of molten decay. A mirror with an ornate gilt frame hung above the candlesticks; flecks of gilt littered the mantel and the rug. The walls were covered with paintings, drawings, and even a few photographs. There was a still life in oil—blue-and-white vase, yellow flowers, patterned table-cloth. Portraits in pencil, in ink, and in charcoal. Another oil, this one no bigger than twelve inches, that depicted a bird's nest filled with three pale blue, faintly speckled eggs. More framed artwork was propped on the floor, around the perimeter of the room, some-times two and three deep.

Tom returned with two Manhattans and joined her on the sofa. "Our drink," he said, handing her a glass. "Remember?"

Eleanor took a tiny sip. *Our drink.* There was no *our* anything. "Why did you disappear?" she said.

"I guess you believe in getting right to the point." He lifted his glass and touched it lightly to hers. "Cheers." But he hardly sounded cheerful.

"Yes, that's exactly what I believe in."

"You think I behaved pretty badly," he said.

"No," she replied. "I think you behaved terribly."

"I deserved that."

"Tom, what was I supposed to think? After that night we spent—"

"A night I've thought about and relived a hundred times."

"Then why did you disappear? Not once, but twice."

"I just felt our being together was . . . too complicated."

"Well, maybe it is."

"But not because of Patricia or Wynn. It was you—you scared me, Eleanor."

"*I* scared *you*?" She sat up. "Why? Because I'm—Jewish?"

"No, that has nothing to do with it. It was because I felt like I was falling in love with you."

Falling in love with her! "Were you planning on telling me anytime soon?"

"I didn't know," he said. "I just knew I had to see you again. That's why I called you, asked you to meet me—"

"That is about the craziest thing I've ever heard," she said.

Instead of answering, he leaned over and kissed her.

Had she thought she was over him? Well, she was wrong. He continued to kiss her and she gave herself over to it. The drink she was holding but not paying any attention to spilled, wetting the front of her skirt.

"I've missed you too," she said, when he finally lifted his face from hers. "Even though I hated you sometimes."

"I deserve for you to hate me. Especially after what happened with Wynn."

"What are you talking about?" She moved away.

"I had a call from Margaux. She was at that school . . . what's the name of it?"

"Oakwood."

"Oakwood, right. She told me some wild story about Wynn's having planted a pair of earrings in your pocket."

"He did, and I left because of it." But she was relieved he didn't know about that night in the cottage. "I might have told you—if you'd been around."

"I was an idiot," he said. "Can you forgive me?"

"I don't know yet," she said.

He leaned over to put his arms around her, and she stiffened. That earlier kiss notwithstanding, she was still nursing the hurt she'd felt when he disappeared. And there was that night Wynn Bellamy barged into the cottage too. She'd thought that if she didn't talk about it, she could make herself believe it hadn't happened. Not true. He was here in this room with them, right here, right now.

Tom didn't press her. "It's all right," he said. "We don't have to do anything. We can just be here together. Would you like that?"

She nodded, grateful that he seemed to understand.

"I'll put on the radio, okay?" He got up to switch it on and then rejoined her on the couch. The moody, jazzy notes of a clarinet filled the room, pushing the memory of Wynn to its margins. Tom began to stroke her hair, a soothing, even hypnotizing caress. His hand moving from the crown of her head and down, over and over again. She closed her eyes, trying to relax. Then the music changed to something loud and percussive and she jumped. Tom stopped his stroking and got up to change the station. But the mood was spoiled. No, everything was spoiled. She had wanted to be with Tom. Wanted it so much. Then why did it feel so wrong?

"You're upset," he said.

She thought of the night in his room last summer, when she'd gone to him without fear, without shame, with her desire for him glowing like a candle cupped by her two willing hands. She wanted to be that girl again, but that girl no longer existed. The realization made her cry.

"Ah, Eleanor, no. Don't."

When she didn't stop, he asked, "Can't you tell me what's wrong?"

"Something happened last summer. Something I didn't want to tell you, ever. But it's no good—I have to tell." She blotted her face, blew her nose, and began to speak.

"That son of a bitch!" Tom exclaimed when she finished. "He didn't, I mean you weren't—"

"Raped?" she said. "No."

"Why did you wait so long to tell me?"

"He was your sister's husband. I knew you'd be loyal to her. And I was afraid you'd think I encouraged him in some way. That I deserved it."

"I would never think that," he said. "I know you too well." His face changed. "And I know *him*. Or I thought I did. He was always a little too free with his hands, but I never dreamed he'd cross the line. I'm going to have it out with him—"

"You're not going to hit him, are you?" There was something horrifying about the idea. Also thrilling.

"Hit him? No, I wouldn't stoop to his level. I just want him to know how contemptible I find him."

"I thought it was all behind me." She blew her nose. "I was wrong."

"I'm sorry," he said. "So sorry."

He began to stroke her hair again and she wanted to give in to the feeling it stirred. Yet before she could succumb, there was something else she had to say. "I'm still a virgin—at least in the literal sense. But Wynn took something from me that I can never have back. I don't feel the same anymore."

"He did. You are different now. I can sense it," he said.

"So you see it too?"

"I do and it makes me sad. That trusting quality you had—it's gone. I know it was bound to go for one reason or another. I'm just sorry it was because of my brother-in-law."

"I am less trusting. I don't even trust you." She had to look away then.

Tom put a finger under her chin to turn her face back to his. "Last summer when I told you I wouldn't let you become my mistress, it was because I knew that no matter what you said, deep down you wanted to save that part of yourself for a husband, Eleanor. It's what you were raised to believe was right, and you did believe it. I never met anyone who believed it more. To have slept with you then would have been selfish. Cruel even. I still want to sleep with you—I want that very much. But I'm not going to pressure you. I have to know that you want it as much as I do. And that you'll be able to wake up tomorrow with no regrets."

No regrets? How could she know that? Yet he was leaving it up to her—he respected her and would let her take the lead. As they continued to look at each other, she realized that she wanted to have this night with him. She leaned into him and this time, she initiated the kiss. She saw his eyes widen a little in surprise. Then they closed as he pulled her even more tightly to him.

Afterward, Eleanor lay next to Tom as he slept, eyes gradually adjusting to the dark. On the nightstand, next to a lamp, was the green-and-red tin of Romeos, the brand of rubbers Tom used. She had never seen one up close before.

Tom let out a single, clipped snore but didn't wake. She had done it, crossed the threshold, surrendered, or rather, put aside, her virginity. The act itself had hurt, but Tom had been gentle and reassuring; he said it would be better the next time. She nodded and went into the bathroom to wash away the coin-size smudges of blood on her inner thighs before returning to bed. She was sorry, but her regrets—and yes, she did have them—were not about what she'd done, but how she felt when she had done it. Again she traveled back to the time last summer when she'd gone up to Tom's room, and wished she could graft that night on to this one. It was like she'd told Tom—she'd already lost her innocence and she mourned that more than anything else.

Eleanor got up quietly, feeling around for the clothes that had been tossed to the floor. Tom stirred and rolled over on his side. "Do you have to go?" he said.

"I do. My mother expects me."

"You'll come back? Soon?"

"Very soon."

"Will you be all right getting home?"

"I'll be fine. It's not even that late."

"Let me at least come downstairs." He reached for his clothes.

They were very quiet on the stairway and Eleanor turned away quickly, before he could kiss her. Then she waited on the curb while he hailed the taxi, and without looking at him, took the bill he pressed into her hand. "I'll call you," he said.

Settled in the backseat, Eleanor looked out at the city as the Checker cab made its way uptown. The somnolent streets of the Village gave way to the liveliness of Times Square, where people were streaming out of theaters and movie houses, and the lights from the marquees illuminated the throngs on the sidewalks. She wondered whether her mother would still be up and began to come up with some details about the party. The need to lie to Irina was about to end though. She was going to get a place of her own. What had been a wish, a dream, a speculation became in this moment a certainty. She couldn't live amid the trappings of her childhood any longer; she had moved too far beyond their confines.

Three days later, Eleanor signed a lease for a small apartment on Barrow Street, not far from her office. A four-flight walk-up, it had a front room that faced the street, and a back room that looked out over a tiny garden. She had no access to it and nothing was in bloom, but there were all sorts of shrubs and even what she thought might be a cherry tree; come spring, she would find out. Between the two rooms was a combination kitchen and bathroom, with a hinged-over tub that served as a counter when not in use, a hot plate, and an old-fashioned icebox under which she kept a pan, to catch the drips. The toilet was just outside the apartment, behind a separate door.

She told her mother two days before she was set to move in, over cups of tea and the new issue of *Vogue*. "You're leaving? Why?" Irina said. "Are you so unhappy with me?"

"Not with you, Mother. But it's true that living here isn't making me happy. I need to be on my own."

"Alone? What kind of girl lives alone, without parents or a husband?"

"The kind of girl I am," said Eleanor.

"If your father were here, you wouldn't be doing this. You always loved him better."

Eleanor was stunned. This was in fact true—she had always felt closer to her father than she had to her mother—but it wasn't something that had been discussed in her family. Ever. She had thought that by never actually saying the words, her mother would remain ignorant of her preference. But clearly she'd been mistaken. How to reply to this without hurting Irina? Or telling yet another lie? "It's not that I loved him better. It was easier with him, that's all. He didn't worry so much."

"That's because he left all the worrying to me," Irina said bitterly.

"You sound . . . angry about that," Eleanor ventured. Had her mother been angry at her father? Of course her parents had squabbled, but as a child, Eleanor had thought that was just what grown-ups did.

"What difference does it make now anyway?" Irina said. "Your father is dead. And you're abandoning me."

"Not abandoning you," said Eleanor. "Finding me. I want to live on my own, and I think I would want that even if Papa were here."

"I don't understand you," her mother said. "I left your grandmother to marry your father. That's what girls did. Nice girls anyway."

"That was a long time ago," said Eleanor. "Things are different now. And you helped make me different. You sent me to college."

"I did even though it broke my heart to let you go. But I knew you were a smart girl. I wanted you to make something of yourself. To have chances that I didn't have."

"You see? You understand better than you think. You expected something else from me. And I expect something from myself too."

"What is that thing?" Irina no longer sounded angry. She sounded like she truly wanted to know.

"I can't say exactly," Eleanor said. "But living on my own is the only way I'm going to find out."

Irina stood and began clearing the table. "Maybe you're right," she said finally. "And I have to accept it." There were tears on her face and Eleanor crossed the room to hug her. "I love you," she said. "And I'll come back to see you. I'm only going to be a subway ride away."

"As often as you like." Irina wiped her eyes. "I'll be here."

TWENTY-FIVE

Patricia walked quickly past the wrought iron gate, the row of painted ornamental jockeys, and through the doors of Jack & Charlie's 21 Club. During Prohibition, 21 had been a speakeasy—definitely not the sort of place she would have frequented. But she'd heard all about the police raids and the clever way the owners had outwitted discovery. As soon as the raid started, a system of levers tipped the bar shelves, sweeping all the liquor bottles through a chute and into the city's sewers. Knowing this gave the place an added cachet in Patricia's eyes—there was something daring and illicit in its history. Tom was less enchanted by it, but he'd still suggested that they meet here. Why?

"Good afternoon, Mrs. Bellamy," said Clyde, the maître d'. "Your table is in the Remington Room. Right this way."

With its collection of horse-themed paintings and bronzes, the Remington Room was one of Patricia's favorites. "Thank you so much, Clyde." When she got to the table, she saw Tom was already seated and waiting for her. Tom on time? That never happened.

"Tricia," he said, rising from the table to kiss her on both cheeks,

a little trick he'd picked up in Paris. "You're looking especially rav-
ishing today."

Patricia knew her new, celadon-colored suit was flattering, but
he was going overboard. Yet she'd take the compliment anyway.
"Glad you approve." She sat down and Tom ordered martinis while
she perused the menu, settling on the Swedish herring and then the
guinea hen.

"So why did you suggest meeting here?" she asked as soon as the
drinks arrived.

"What do you mean? You love this place."

"But you don't, which makes me think you're up to something."

"You think I'm so devious?"

She swatted him with her napkin. "Come on, out with it."

"Out with what?"

"Don't be coy. You suggested this place for a reason. Is there
something you want to tell me?"

"Tell you about what?"

"Oh, I don't know." She pretended to study the place setting on
the table. "Maybe something about Eleanor?"

"I'm seeing her now. What else do you need to know?"

"The last time we talked about her, you said you were worried you
might be falling in love."

Their appetizers were placed on the table and Tom took a forkful
of caviar. "I'm not worried about that anymore."

"Why not?" A stir at the other end of the restaurant distracted
her; a celebrity must have walked in. Patricia had once spotted FDR
in this very room. Also Humphrey Bogart, William Holden, and
Bette Davis. She craned her neck but couldn't see who it was today.

"Now I know I'm in love with her. In fact, I'm going to ask her to
marry me."

"Marry you!" Patricia turned back to her brother, no longer caring who might have come in. "My God, Tom, are you out of your mind?"

"Not at all. Besides, she doesn't even work for you anymore so I don't see why you have anything to say about it. I love her and—"

"That's not what I'm talking about and you know it. This isn't about love. This is about the rest of your life. Even you have to admit . . . she's . . . just not from our set. I understand that's part of her appeal for you. But once the novelty wears off, then what?"

"And what defines our set, Tricia? Are we really that bigoted, narrow-minded, incapable of seeing beyond a bunch of petty and meaningless distinctions—"

"They're not so meaningless. Have you thought about what your future would be like with Eleanor as your wife? The opportunities that would dry up? The doors that would close, politely but firmly, in your face?"

"Maybe they're doors I don't give a damn about going through," he said a little too loudly.

"Shh," she said. "Would you please lower your voice?"

"Anyway, this is all theoretical at the moment. She hasn't said yes. Or at least not yet."

"Oh, she will," Patricia said darkly. "She's been working that angle from the very beginning."

"Is that really what you think of her? The heaven-sent girl who single-handedly saved Margaux?"

"Well, maybe not from the start but—"

"But nothing. You've been listening to Wynn for too long—you're even starting to sound like him. Because that kind of talk isn't you, Petunia. It never was."

Chastened, Patricia said nothing. The use of that old childhood name sent her straight back into the past, when Tom was her everything. He could have that effect on her, acting as her conscience and guide, pushing her toward her better self.

". . . I know she's young," he was saying.

The main courses arrived, and the dirtied plates were whisked away.

"Very." Patricia tried to remember herself at that age. She was already a mother then, but her life had seemed so much easier, less fraught. Wynn was still her prince, and Margaux their perfect blond baby. She'd been blessed, and she had known it too.

"So when will you pop the question?"

"As soon as the moment's right."

"I can just imagine how Wynn's going to take it . . ." Patricia hadn't intended to say this aloud; the words just slipped out.

Tom looked up from his pheasant. "It's none of his business either. Far from it. She told me all about that pitiful farce with the earrings."

"He was being ridiculous and I said so."

"Ridiculous? I think it was a bit more than that, don't you? I mean, what he did cost Eleanor her job."

"I didn't fire her. She was the one who chose to leave."

"Can you blame her? Wynn was out to get her."

"Maybe it was time for her to go."

"Meaning . . . ?"

"Margaux needed to get out of the house and start socializing again. With people her own age. Eleanor even said so."

"Oh, did she?"

Why did he sound so argumentative? "Yes, as a matter of fact she did. She's the one who told me about Oakwood, and she even telephoned the headmaster about Margaux."

"That sounds like her," he said. And smiled in a besotted way that Patricia found especially irritating.

"How's your pheasant?" All at once she was sick of this conversation.

"A little dry actually." He continued sawing away at the bird. "Doesn't Henryka do pheasant? I remember having it at your place, maybe New Year's Eve. It was delicious. Ask her to make it again when I'm over."

"You haven't heard? Henryka's left too. She's working for a family on East Seventy-Second Street." Patricia could not meet his eyes as she disclosed this still painful bit of news.

"Henryka? Gone? But she's been with you forever. And with Mother before that. Why in the world did you let her go?"

"I didn't." And then, to her distress, she began to cry, right there in the middle of the 21 Club.

"Tricia." Tom stopped eating and reached out to take her hand. "What is it?"

The whole story, which she had not planned on sharing with him, came tumbling out. "She wouldn't say what Wynn had done to Eleanor. But whatever it was, it required a trip to Dr. Parker in the middle of the night."

"I know. Eleanor told me everything."

"She did? When?"

"Just recently. Made me furious. If he wasn't your husband and Margaux's father, I'd have gone after him myself . . ." He pushed his plate away. "I don't know about you, but I'm ready for dessert."

It felt better to have unburdened herself, really it did, and over the plate of profiteroles *au chocolat* that they shared, she also told him all about the separate rooms and her growing disgust for Wynn.

"Why stay?" Tom asked. "Look at the kind of man he is. He went after Eleanor. And Henryka, for God's sake."

"Because I don't want to be divorced," she said. "Divorced women are outcasts. Social lepers . . . I'm not sure I could bear it."

"What about Audrey?"

"It ended up all right. But at first, people shunned her. There were invitations that dried up, phone calls that went unanswered. She had to endure all of it."

"And so you'd live with a man who, in your words, disgusts you, a man who bullies and takes advantage of the women in his employ, because you're worried about a few invitations?"

"You make it sound so trivial. Think of what it would do to Margaux."

"What exactly? It would let her see that her mother had some principles and was more committed to living honestly, and with a chance at happiness instead of—"

"You may be my older brother, but in some ways, you're so young. The world isn't like you make it out to be."

"That's where you're wrong," he said, licking the last bit of chocolate from the spoon. "*You* make the world you want to live in. Not the other way around."

She looked at him fondly, remembering how firmly wedded he'd been to his convictions, even as a boy. The Christmas he was twelve and she nine, he'd earnestly lectured their father about the need to treat the servants "like human beings" and insisted that in addition to the cash tucked discreetly into an envelope, each of them receive something of a more personal nature. But Tom had always made his own rules and paid a price for doing so; it was a price she'd never wanted to pay.

Tom reached for the check when it came, one of his inbred gallant gestures, and he hugged her tightly on the sidewalk as they were about to part. "I do assume that you're sleeping with her," she said.

"I don't kiss and tell, sister dear." He put his arm out to hail a taxi.

"Since when?"

But he only smiled and waved as she got in and the cabbie took off. Patricia waved back and settled into the seat. They had invited Audrey, Harold, and another couple for dinner this evening and she wanted to get home as soon as possible. Although it had been a relief to talk to Tom, their conversation had also stirred up disquieting feelings about Wynn. And about Eleanor. It was bad enough that Wynn had behaved so stupidly around the girl. And that her daughter kept pestering her about when Eleanor could come to visit, something Patricia was not keen to have happen.

"Why can't I see her?" Margaux had asked during their last telephone call. "Or at least write to her?"

"I just don't think it's wise," Patricia said.

"But you haven't given me one good reason."

That familiar—and irritating—whine had crept into her voice and the sound of it set Patricia on edge.

"Because I'm your mother and I say so," Patricia snapped. "Now can we please talk about something else?"

"I'm just going to write her myself," said Margaux. "You won't know and you won't be able to stop me."

"If I have to ask the school to monitor your correspondence, I will." Even as Patricia made this threat, it sickened her slightly. Was this the relationship she wished to cultivate with her daughter—adversarial and filled with suspicion?

"If you'd just tell me why you don't want me to see her, maybe I could understand . . ."

Now Margaux had switched from the petulance of a child to the reasonableness of an adult.

"I know she was a wonderful influence on you." Patricia tried to choose her words carefully. "And that she helped bring you out of

280

your shell. But her role in your life ought to diminish now, not increase. Your dependence on her is . . . unhealthy. You need to find other confidantes, like your friends. Or me."

Patricia had surprised herself with that. It made her sound, well, jealous of Eleanor. Which perhaps was true.

"I don't believe you," Margaux said. "I think you don't want her to be my friend because she lives on Second Avenue and her family hasn't got any money. And because she's a Jew. You and Daddy—you don't have any friends who are Jews, do you? So you don't want me to have any either."

Patricia had gone silent. Her daughter was growing more astute and more liable to lay bare motivations that Patricia would rather keep under wraps, even—no, especially—from herself.

"There may be some truth to what you're saying, though I wouldn't put it quite like that. But you need to trust that your father and I know what's best for you. You're not an adult yet, and you need to listen to us."

After that, she found her feelings toward Eleanor had calcified and hardened: her name became a reminder of complexities Patricia didn't want to engage with or face. And just today, barely an hour ago, she'd learned that Eleanor might actually become her sister-in-law. The news bothered her—it bothered her a great deal. And it would bother Wynn too—there was no doubt about that. She could just imagine the quarrels that would ensue if Tom went ahead with his crazy plan.

Patricia shifted irritably in the seat. Was she really bigoted and narrow-minded, as Tom had suggested? No—it wasn't that Eleanor was Jewish, though that might have been the start. It was that Eleanor was part of a larger problem. Before her, their lives had a certain predictable flow. But she disrupted it, just because of who she was

281

and what she represented. Patricia didn't like the disruption, and felt she wasn't equipped to handle it.

The cabbie came to a sudden halt and she was pitched forward, putting her hands out to brace herself against the impact. "Can you please drive a little more carefully?"

"Sorry, lady," the cabbie said. "But that guy was jaywalking and I had to stop or I'd have hit him."

Patricia said nothing. The jaywalker, oblivious, continued across the street. The nerve of some people. But no one was hurt. No one had been hurt—or at least not badly hurt—on that June day when Patricia's cab rammed into Eleanor's. Yet she was still feeling the reverberations of that accident, right up to this very minute.

When they arrived at her building, Patricia's watch said it was almost 5:00; her guests weren't due until 7:30. She wondered whether Wynn would be home yet. Despite their separate rooms, they still continued to have dinner together most evenings, especially if she was expecting company. And it was Friday; he often left the office early on Fridays.

When she opened the door, she smelled roasted chicken. She had forgotten about this evening's menu when she'd ordered at lunch; now she would have to eat chicken again. "Evening, Mrs. Bellamy," Bridget's clear voice rang out. Patricia sighed. She did not want to engage with the woman and she went directly into her room to change.

She'd just zipped up her dress—black satin with three-quarter sleeves and a square neckline—when Wynn came into the room.

"For you," he said, handing her a bouquet of small, blush pink rosebuds tied with a black velvet ribbon. "I know you always order flowers for the table, but these are just for you."

"Thank you." She was surprised, and even touched by the gift.

She also felt a little guilty for the harsh way she'd spoken about him at lunch. Patricia went to fill a round, cut-crystal vase with water and when she returned to her room, Wynn had gone. She continued her toilette, but when she was looking through her jewelry box for a pair of earrings, she saw the pearl-and-diamond pair Wynn had so crudely planted in Eleanor's pocket and her moment of tenderness withered instantly. The evening would have to be endured somehow. She didn't know how many more such evenings she could take.

But to her relief, Wynn was on his absolute best behavior. He told jokes, poured cocktails, flattered the men, lavished compliments on the women. Although he outpaced them all in the number of drinks he consumed—Patricia was keeping an eye on that—he seemed perfectly in control, and even charming. She relaxed and began to enjoy herself. She had felt cut off lately, her own doing of course, and it was good to have people in the apartment, laughing, having fun. Bridget's dinner was exclaimed over, as was the Viennese Sacher torte that came from the bakery on Second Avenue Patricia had discovered when she'd visited Irina's hat shop. So when Audrey excused herself to "powder her nose" and Wynn stepped out of the room a moment later, Patricia didn't even think to connect the two departures.

It was only when Audrey returned looking a bit flustered that Patricia's inner alarm began a quiet but insistent bleating.

She took Audrey into the foyer, on the pretext of showing her the new chandelier she'd just had installed. "Are you all right?" she asked.

"Yes, I just need to fix my face."

Patricia saw that her lipstick was smeared. But Audrey had just gone to the bathroom and she was holding her small evening bag. Why hadn't she reapplied her lipstick then?

From her vantage point in the foyer, Patricia could see Wynn, who had come back into the room and was now holding forth about the recently implemented Marshall Plan in Europe. He spoke without hesitation, but she saw that telltale mottling of his cheeks. Audrey had gone into the bedroom and Patricia followed her.

"Audrey, you can tell me. You seem—off."

Audrey wouldn't meet her eyes at first and when she did, her expression was pitying. "It's nothing, really. I mean, we're all used to Wynn's wandering hands, only he used to be more . . . playful about it. Now he's just getting, well, rather boorish."

Patricia was speechless. They were joined by the rotund, bespectacled, and ever jovial Harold. "Who's being boorish, precious?" He hovered close.

"Oh, just Wynn got a little too familiar, that's all. I don't want to make a scene, and I'm sure he didn't really mean anything by it—"

"Didn't mean anything by what?" asked Harold.

Audrey looked from her husband to Patricia, clearly deciding how much to reveal. "Wynn followed me to the bathroom and when I came out, he tried to kiss me."

No wonder her lipstick was smudged.

"Kiss you!" Harold seemed distinctly less jovial.

"Audrey, I'm so very sorry," Patricia managed to choke out. Mortification had swallowed her whole. "He's been drinking, and when he drinks he can get a little—"

"I know how he can get. But he stuck his hand right down my dress too." Audrey gestured to the bodice of her low-cut brocade that exposed a generous swath of cleavage.

"How dare he." Harold's arm went protectively around his wife. "Patricia, you don't have to see us out. And I'm sure you'll understand why we'll never come back here." The look in his eyes was scalding.

Patricia said nothing as Audrey adjusted her shawl and touched her hands to her hair, trying to envision how she could patch together the ruins of the evening. But Wynn came over and intercepted them at the door, "Leaving so soon?" He let his hand rest lightly on Audrey's shoulder and the disdain with which she shook him off could not have been lost on Joan and Cameron Barlow, whose seats in the dining room gave them a full view of the foyer.

"Please keep your hands off my wife," Harold said coldly.

"Excuse me, old man." Wynn retreated. "No offense meant at all. I just thought we were among friends here."

"We thought so too. But you haven't behaved like a friend. Or a gentleman. You're just lucky I'm not a violent sort or else I'd punch you."

Wynn's expression looked bemused, but his face was now a riot of splotchy red patches.

Harold gave Patricia a quick peck on the cheek before taking Audrey's elbow and ushering her out. Patricia stood at the door for a moment with her back to Cameron and Joan. She couldn't face them, she just couldn't—

"Whose drink can I freshen?" Wynn said loudly. No one said anything. When Patricia finally turned around, she caught the look that passed between the Barlows and within minutes, they were saying how it was late, and that they needed to be going.

After the Barlows had left, Wynn refilled his own glass and offered to refill hers. Patricia just shook her head. She'd sent Bridget home, and asked her to come in early to do the cleaning up tomorrow. For the last fifteen or so minutes, she'd been trembling with anger, and the effort of containment caused a pain that was almost physical. But now that she and Wynn were alone, her anger evaporated and she was left hollow and spent. "Why?" she asked.

"Oh, come on," he said. "If a woman walks around half naked like that, what can she expect?"

"That her host will have the manners and self-control not to go sticking his hand down her dress or his tongue in her mouth."

"Maybe if her host's own wife had a shred of passion or even affection for him, he might not have to resort to the charms of strangers."

"Oh, so this is my fault."

"In a way—yes." He downed the drink quickly and poured another.

"You've had enough," she said. How many had he had? She'd lost count.

"Since when did you become Carrie Nation? I notice you never criticize your brother when he ties one on—"

"Because my brother doesn't ambush the dinner guests outside the bathroom."

"No. Just the tutor."

"That again? She hasn't worked for us in months." He didn't answer. "You embarrassed me tonight. I'll never be able to invite them here again. And don't think they won't tell everyone we know. You'll be banned, and I'll be banned right along with you. I should file for divorce."

"You'd never do that." His voice was quiet but mocking. "Never."

"That's what you think. But I may surprise you yet."

He shook his head. "Oh no. We're done with surprising each other. All done." He finished his drink and walked out of the room.

Once he was gone, Patricia poured herself a drink and sipped it slowly, so that the ice in the glass began to melt and the scotch turned from deep amber to a pale and watery yellow. It must have been very late—two or three o'clock in the morning—when she finally went into her bedroom. The cluster of pink rosebuds had opened and she could smell their sweetness as she approached her dressing table. She opened the window—it faced the back of the building—and picked up the crystal vase. There were a few seconds of silence, and then a flooding of satisfaction when the vase crashed to the pavement below.

TWENTY-SIX

Living alone was everything Eleanor had thought it would be. Every time she turned the key and walked in, she thought, *Mine, mine, mine.* How good that felt. How right. This place was both sanctuary and oasis. She invited her college friends over to show it off. They oohed and aahed as they drank the martinis she'd made and looked around at her secondhand Louis XIV reproduction armchair, the diminutive marble-topped table she had lugged home from the curbside, the cloudscape by Ansel Adams that had been a gift from Tom. Two of these girls were still living at home, and one of them was engaged. Another was living at the Barbizon Hotel for Women on East Sixty-Third Street and she too was engaged. Not one of them was on her own in the way Eleanor was—not transitional, not finite, but open-ended—and Eleanor could tell her solitary living arrangement, an arrangement that challenged the norm, was puzzling to them. Somehow, that pleased her too.

Even Ruth, another visitor, acted like Eleanor's decision to live alone was a temporary aberration, and that Eleanor would soon assume her designated roles in the familiar female pageant: fiancée, bride, wife, mother. "Maybe you'll be next," Ruth said. "That Tom sounds like a dreamboat."

"He hasn't asked me to marry him," Eleanor said. "And even if he did, I'm not sure I'd say yes."

"But you've slept with him." Ruth looked down at her hands, where the infinitesimal diamond sparkled on her finger.

"Haven't you slept with Marty?"

"Yes, but that was after he'd proposed."

"So my sleeping with Tom means I have to marry him?" Last summer, Eleanor would have said yes to that question.

"Well, no, but, if you . . ." Ruth looked very uncomfortable.

"Sleep with a man you're not going to marry then you're a tramp?" Eleanor knew that was what Wynn Bellamy thought. And that his assumption, incorrect at the time, that she was sleeping with Tom meant that she automatically would be available to him too.

"I never said *that*, I only meant that your reputation—" Ruth vainly tried to retrieve the situation.

"It's all right," Eleanor said. "Really it is. Now tell me again about the dress."

Happy to leave the topic behind, Ruth launched into the relative merits of floor versus tea length, taffeta versus moiré.

That evening, she had a date with Tom. They had dinner at his place and then strolled east, to Fourth Avenue, which was lined with secondhand bookstores. A few were still open, and they wove in and out of the shops. Tom drifted toward the art books and Eleanor toward the poetry, where she found, on a bottom shelf, a small, clothbound first edition of *A Few Figs from Thistles*—poems by Edna St. Vincent Millay. She blew the layer of dust off the top and opened it up.

We were very tired, we were very merry—
We had gone back and forth all night on the ferry.

Tom came up behind her and read over her shoulder. "Is she one of your favorites?"

Eleanor nodded. "She was a Vassar girl, you know. And she came up to do a reading while I was at school. It was—enthralling."

"We should do it," Tom said.

"Do what?"

"Ride the Staten Island Ferry together. That's what inspired the poem."

"Actually I've never been on the Staten Island Ferry."

"And you call yourself a New Yorker?"

"Born and bred." She smiled.

"We have to fix that. Immediately."

"You want to ride the ferry? Now?"

"Why not?" he asked. "It's Friday. They leave every thirty minutes."

"All right," she said, caught up in his sense of adventure. "Let's do it."

Tom bought the book—"We'll read stanzas of the poem to each other on the boat," he said—and then they took the subway down to the terminal, where they were able to board almost immediately.

"It's such a nice night," said Tom. "Let's go stand outside."

Eleanor followed him up the wide metal stairs that led to the deck. The Manhattan skyline unfurled as the ferry slowly pulled away from the dock, tall buildings lambent against the darkened sky. There were three sharp bleats and a colony of seagulls fluttered and then settled on the worn wooden pilings that lined the waterfront. Tom put his arm around Eleanor and she could feel the edges of the book, which he had tucked in his pocket. Up above, the moon shone bright as a dime.

"I have some good news for you," Tom said. "I rented a gallery space. It's not on East Tenth Street though. It's on Hudson Street."

"A gallery!"

"I've been thinking about, talking about it for years. But you were the gadfly, Eleanor. You pushed me to do it."

"You'll organize shows? Invite people to see them?"

"When I've gotten the place together, yes." He drew her closer. "Happy?"

"Very. You?"

"Happier than I ever thought I could be."

Eleanor pressed her face against his chest; even through the light jacket and shirt, she could feel the steady pulse of his heart.

"Marry me," he said.

"What?"

"You heard me."

She moved out of his embrace and suddenly the night, which had felt so temperate, went cold. "I don't know what to say." Last summer, she had wished to hear exactly those words. But things had changed. No—she was the one who had changed.

"Say yes."

"Can I think it over?"

"Are you serious? I thought you loved me." Angrily, he turned away; the ferry approached the terminal in Staten Island. Then he turned back to her. "I'm sorry. But that wasn't the answer I was expecting."

"I do love you." She reached out to touch his face and he clasped her hand in both of his. "But I've only lived alone for such a little while. And I like it so much. I'm just not ready to give that up and become a wife."

"So you're not saying *no*, you're saying, *not now?*"

"Exactly." Relief washed over her. She didn't want to hurt him. Or alienate him. But as the ferry docked with a small jolt, she realized just how much she didn't want to marry him either.

They were mostly silent on the ride back to Manhattan, and when he dropped her off at her apartment, he didn't kiss her good night. Inside, she went straight to her bed, slipped off her shoes, and lay down in the dark. Tom had just asked her to marry him. She ought to have been over the moon. Wasn't this what every girl wanted, what she'd wanted and believed she'd never have? Yet she'd turned him down and she might have been even more surprised than he was. She wasn't the same girl she'd been last summer. That girl was on a straight path: marriage, husband, children. Now she'd changed direction and didn't know where she was going. Marriage might not have been the goal any longer. And even if she did want to get married, she didn't know how she could marry Tom. How would it feel to be living in his world—the clubs, the hotels, the apartment buildings, the entire towns that said no to Jews? No to *her*. He'd say he didn't care. But she cared. And so would her mother. Would Irina ever accept him? Accept them?

Hours later, the ringing of the telephone roused her from her light, restless sleep. Maybe it was Tom. Oh, if only it was. She hadn't wanted to hurt him, she just—

"Eleanor, Eleanor, is that you?"

It wasn't Tom. The voice was unfamiliar. Also drunk. "Who is this please?"

"Who is this? Why, it's Wynn Bellamy of course!" He chortled.

"Mr. Bellamy!" Eleanor switched on the lamp and looked at the clock: 3:30. "Is everything all right? Has something happened to Margaux? Or to Patricia?"

"Margaux, no, nothing's happened to her. Unless you've been poisoning her against me, just like you poisoned my wife." The chortling turned to a snarl.

"I didn't *poison* Patricia. I just told her what happened, that's all——"

"And what happened anyway? Just what? Was it so terrible that I asked for a dance? Or a kiss, one lousy little kiss? Was that a reason to make such a fuss——"

"Mr. Bellamy, I don't think this conversation is going anywhere and I——"

"Such a fuss and over nothing! You'd think I ravished you, for Christ's sake! Now my wife despises me and God only knows what you've told my daughter——"

"I haven't told your daughter anything. But if I ever hear from you again, in any way, shape, or form, I'll tell her. I really will. Maybe she ought to know just what kind of man her father is."

There was a short silence. "Oh no, you wouldn't, you couldn't . . . not my baby girl, no not that . . ."

He trailed off, and Eleanor realized he was crying. She listened and then put the receiver down. After a moment, she lifted it again, and when she heard the dial tone, she placed it next to the clock, off the hook, until morning.

TWENTY-SEVEN

The morning after the ruined dinner party, Bridget was already in the kitchen when Patricia came in. Wynn was sleeping it off in the guest room—thank God for small favors. The coffee didn't taste nearly as good as Henryka's, but at least Bridget had made oatmeal. Oatmeal was good for a hangover, and Patricia definitely had one. She sipped the coffee and took tentative spoonfuls of the hot cereal.

Then she went into the library and dialed Audrey's number. She wasn't calling to talk about the night before. She was calling to get the name of the lawyer who had handled her divorce.

"So it's finally gotten to you?" Audrey asked. "I'll confess I've wondered why you haven't left him before this. But then again, I know it's not easy to go. Look at how long it took me."

"It was hard, wasn't it? Especially in the beginning?"

"Awful. All those people you thought were your friends—pitying you, judging you, ostracizing you."

"And yet you did it."

"Because staying was worse than all that. Much worse."

"That's how I feel. Or I think I do. And it will help to talk it over with a lawyer."

"His name is Theo Prescott and he's experienced, discreet, and a gentleman—utterly unlike my ex-husband. Tell him I told you to call."

Patricia took down the name and number. "You won't mention this to anyone, Audrey? Please?"

"Not a word," Audrey said. "You can trust me."

As they were saying good-bye, Patricia heard a subtle but still audible click—someone had picked up the extension in the other room.

"Hello? I'm on the phone."

There was another click. Whoever it was had put the receiver down. Had it been Bridget? Or more likely, Wynn? She went in search of her husband and found him.

"You were listening," she said.

"And why shouldn't I? You were talking about me."

"All right then. I don't care if you know. In fact, I want you to know."

"Know what?"

"That I'm serious," said Patricia. When he didn't answer, she said, "Did you hear me? I'm divorcing you, Wynn. You said I wouldn't do it, but you were wrong."

"Go ahead, call the lawyer. Spin your little tale of woe for him, and then brace yourself for the bill. A telephone call? Easy. Divorcing me, not so much. I'll fight you, Tricia. I'll fight you with everything that's in me. And it won't be pretty."

"Are you threatening me?"

"No. I'm just telling you what to expect. Giving you fair warning, as it were. You really don't want to do this. Think of Margaux, for God's sake."

"I think of her all the time. And I've decided that maybe it's time she understood what kind of man her father truly is."

Wynn visibly paled. "She's behind all this. It's her fault. She's turned you against me and she'll do it to Margaux too."

"What are you talking about?"

"Eleanor Moskowitz. That's exactly what she said—that she'd tell Margaux what kind of man I was."

"She said that? When?"

He turned away abruptly. "Last night, not that it matters . . ."

"Last night! You went to see her?"

"No. I telephoned." His back remained to her.

"You did? What were you thinking?" She stared at his back and when he wouldn't turn, she walked around to face him.

"What was I thinking? That I wanted to get my life back from the she-wolf who devoured it." There were tears in his eyes. "I want things to be the way they were before she came here."

"Can't you see it's too late for that?" But a tiny part of her wished it too.

They stood staring at each other for several seconds, seconds during which Patricia tried to absorb the enormity of what was happening. She could remember so vividly how Wynn had looked at her from across that room, the dawning happiness she'd felt when he'd walked over and asked her to dance, and the exhilaration when he spun her around. He wouldn't let anyone cut in and she didn't care if it was rude—she'd wanted to be with him, and only him. Later, they'd gone outside and when the cool night air made her shiver, he'd taken off his white coat and slipped it around her shoulders. She'd thought him so gallant, so charming, so dear. He hadn't even kissed her that night—later he told her how much he wanted to, but he knew she was going to be someone special in his life and he'd wanted to wait.

Patricia turned and left the room. She didn't know what he planned to do with himself and she couldn't let herself care. Instead she dressed quickly and left the apartment. She'd go to the Colony Club; the spring day was so lovely that she would walk down Park Avenue to Sixty-Second Street. Once there, she was able to telephone Theo Prescott with privacy, and then she stayed on for lunch. She walked home on Fifth Avenue and on impulse, stopped into the Frick Collection on East Seventieth Street. There she spent a long time in front of Ingres's *Comtesse d'Haussonville*, whose smooth, rounded arms were crossed over her body and delicate hand propped up her chin. The shimmer of her ice blue satin dress seemed palpable, and Patricia suddenly wished that she, like Maddy, could write about why such a thing moved her, almost to tears—the magical illusion that turned two dimensions into three.

When she returned home, Bridget was waiting. "Mr. Bellamy, he asked me to give you this," she boomed and handed Patricia a sealed envelope.

Patricia opened it. *I'm going to Argyle to sail*, he'd written. *Back Sunday night.* Finding him gone was like an unexpected gift. She gave Bridget the night off and went to 21 by herself, to see how she felt dining alone; she found the experience unfamiliar but not intolerable. Sunday dawned clear and bright so she skipped church and took a taxi to the Claremont Riding Academy on West Eighty-Ninth Street instead. She hadn't ridden in Central Park in years, but Jester, the dark brown gelding she'd selected, was sure-footed and even-tempered, and he seemed unfazed by the stream of parkgoers strolling, pushing prams, lugging picnic hampers, or flying kites. The day clouded over and the wind picked up but Patricia was loath to leave the park. It was nearly seven o'clock when she took the horse back; she watched him being walked into his stall and she wanted to say *Not yet, please, just a little longer.* But she hailed a taxi and rode uptown, pleasantly tired from her exertion.

"There's roses in your cheeks, Mrs. Bellamy," Bridget said when Patricia came through the door. "They become you, yes they do." Then she drew herself a bath and afterward had dinner alone, in her robe, which felt both a bit decadent and thoroughly delightful. She wasn't at all lonely, and she dreaded Wynn's return. But the evening wore on and Wynn didn't appear.

"Are you sure there weren't any messages today, Bridget?" Patricia asked.

"No, ma'am," said Bridget. "The apartment was as quiet as a tomb."

So Patricia said good night. She wasn't unduly worried. There had been a couple of times when he'd stayed at the Yale Club after a quarrel. He'd come back. He always did. Fortunately, her day on horseback had worn her out, and despite her apprehension about seeing him, she slept soundly.

She was still in bed on Monday morning when the telephone rang, the sound shrill and vaguely ominous. It was Wynn's secretary, Miss Blodget.

"It's after nine thirty and Mr. Bellamy hasn't come in yet, so I was wondering if he might be home sick," she said.

"No, but maybe he has a meeting with a client outside the office."

There was a pause. "I keep his calendar," Miss Blodget said. "There's no outside meeting today."

"He was away for the weekend," Patricia said. "He might have been delayed. I'll be sure to have him call you as soon as I hear from him."

"Thank you, Mrs. Bellamy," said Miss Blodget.

She was an older woman, and she'd been with Wynn for several years. Wynn never seemed to keep the young ones around for very long, and suddenly, the reason for that seemed obvious. Why hadn't she seen it before? Patricia got dressed, and decided to call Dottie. Perhaps she'd been in Argyle over the weekend. If she had, she might have seen Wynn. But no, Dottie hadn't gone to Argyle. And Patricia ought to have remembered that the substance of Dottie's conversation was almost always gossip, often of the wounding variety. Today was no different.

"I heard your dinner party got a little out of hand."

"Where did you hear that?"

"Joan Barlow. She couldn't tell me what happened, only that Audrey and Harold left in a big hurry, and that Harold threatened to punch Wynn."

"He didn't threaten him, for God's sake. He was just upset because Wynn was being . . . uncouth."

"There is that side of him . . ."

Something in the way she said this alerted Patricia to a possibility she hadn't considered previously. "Dottie, was Wynn ever . . . I mean, when we were in the country did he . . . ?"

"I'd rather not say . . ."

"Please tell me," Patricia said.

"Well, he wasn't quite so bold, but yes, there were a couple of times when his hands were a little too . . . familiar—if you know what I mean."

"You never told me."

"Did you really want to know?"

Patricia didn't have to answer aloud. They chatted for a little while longer before hanging up and then she chided herself for staying on as long as she had. By tying up the line, she might have prevented Theo Prescott from reaching her—his office said he would call on Monday. Or Wynn's office—they could have been trying her as well. But when Patricia called Miss Blodget, the secretary said no, they had not heard from him, and that one of his clients had waited for him for over an hour before finally leaving. Patricia hung up and then called the Yale Club. No, Wynn had not checked in there either.

Where could he be? Patricia vacillated between concern and irritation. Maybe talking about divorce had hurt him more than she knew. Or maybe he was once again behaving selfishly and irresponsibly. Then it occurred to her that he'd probably gotten drunk and was sleeping it off. Of course that was it—why hadn't she thought of it before? Quickly, she dialed the number of the house in Argyle but the phone just rang and rang.

At twelve thirty, Bridget asked if Patricia wanted lunch, but Patricia told her she'd eat later. She was upset, angry, and though she'd slept well the night before, she felt utterly drained. If she could close her eyes for a little while, she might feel better. Sleep came easily and the loud knocking on the door had insinuated itself into her dream for several seconds before she finally woke up. "What is it?" she said crossly.

"Telephone, Mrs. Bellamy," Bridget called through the closed door.

"Is it my husband?" Patricia's mouth was dry and her head hurt. So much for a nap improving things. "Or his office?"

"No ma'am."

"Then take a message and say I'll call back."

"It's a gentleman calling from Connecticut," said Bridget. "He says it's urgent."

It must have been one of their friends calling about Wynn—finally. Patricia got up, smoothed her hair, and hurried to the phone.

"Mrs. Bellamy? This is Norville Ledbetter. I'm the chief of police here in Argyle and I'm calling to—"

"Have you found him?" she interrupted. "I do hope he hasn't caused any trouble."

"Trouble, Mrs. Bellamy? No, I wouldn't say that he's caused trouble—" Ledbetter sounded surprised.

"He's not . . . drunk, is he?" She ardently hoped the answer was no.

The man was silent and Patricia felt her irritation simmering, about to boil over—

"No ma'am. Not drunk. You see . . . well, I'm sorry to say the truth of it is that Mr. Bellamy—he's dead."

TWENTY-EIGHT

The morning after she'd gotten the call from Wynn Bellamy, Eleanor was afraid to replace the telephone receiver. That conversation had so disturbed her that she didn't want to risk hearing his voice again. But she knew she wasn't being practical. She'd have to put the phone back on the hook sooner or later. And she did want Tom to be able to reach her, so with some hesitation, she gently set it back in the cradle.

Tom didn't call though. Not Saturday, and not Sunday either. She debated whether to call him and got as far as dialing the first few digits before she decided against it. Finally, she picked up the phone again, but not to call Tom; instead she called her mother and invited her to dinner.

Eleanor set her tiny round table with the pale blue damask cloth and napkins she'd found at a secondhand shop. The tablecloth had a blurred, red-brown stain in the middle but she was able to cover it with the dishes, also secondhand. She prepared fresh fettuccine from Raffetto's on Houston Street, and served it with the bottled tomato sauce they sold. With a salad and a loaf of Italian bread, it made a satisfying meal.

Irina seemed to enjoy it, though she declined the grated Parmesan cheese Eleanor offered with a dismissive wave of her hand.

After dinner there was tea and the lace cookies Irina brought from Kramer's. "So you've made a home for yourself," Irina said, looking around. "I still don't understand *why*, but at least you've done it well."

"Thank you, Mother." Eleanor helped herself to a cookie.

"You like the new job?"

"Very much."

"And what about teaching? You have a gift, you know."

"Maybe I'll get back to it. But for now, Zephyr is where I want to be." Eleanor didn't say that although she did miss working with students, she was also excited by the people she met through her work—writers, editors, literary agents—who were very different from the sort of people she met in the staid world of Brandon-Wythe.

"It might work out," Irina mused. "You could become an editor. That's a good job."

"That's what I think," Eleanor said. "My boss says I have a real flair for the work."

"That doesn't surprise me," Irina said. "You were always with your nose in a book. Now you're getting paid for it." She sounded proud.

"It's a different kind of reading though."

"Different?"

"Reading was always like letting a wave wash over me. But when I read for work, it's a more active process. I'm on the alert. Or even on the prowl—like a mountain lion, stalking my prey."

"So the job is good. The apartment is good. Now, what about a young man?"

"What do you mean?"

"Don't pretend with me. You'll be twenty-six soon enough. You don't want to wait too long."

"To get married? Have children?"

"Exactly," said Irina, setting her cup carefully back in its saucer. "By the time I was your age, I was already a mother. I want to be a grandmother too."

"I'll try not to disappoint you." Eleanor began to clear the plates.

"You didn't answer my question. About a young man."

Eleanor was hesitant to tell her mother about Tom. *I can't explain him to her*, she thought. But this was followed by a more surprising thought: *Why not?* Her mother had accepted so much about her new life; who was to say she couldn't accept this?

Irina was quiet as Eleanor spoke and remained quiet for several seconds after she was through. Finally she said, "Not Jewish. More than ten years older than you are. That's why you had to have this apartment. So you could see him. Sleep with him. Now it all makes sense."

"That wasn't the reason I wanted to move out—"

"Do you love him?"

"Yes, I do."

"Will he marry you?"

"He asked me. But I'm not sure I want to marry him."

Irina stared at her. "Why not?"

"Because he and I come from such different worlds. I'm not sure I'd ever fit in his. Or even want to."

"Then why are you carrying on with him?"

"I wouldn't call it carrying on—"

"Then what would you call it? Don't you want to start a family?"

"I thought I did," Eleanor said. "But now I don't know."

"Well, you need to make up your mind. And in the meantime I just hope you're being . . . careful."

"Of course I'm being careful," Eleanor said testily. Did her mother think she was an idiot?

"I meant with your heart, *tochter*," said Irina gently.

When it was time for her to leave, Irina hugged Eleanor for longer than usual before releasing her. "So do I get to meet him?" she asked.

"Do you want to?"

"Well, if he's important to you, yes. I can't say it won't be hard for me. But what you said when you told me you were moving out? You were right. Papa and I did send you to that fancy school. You met different kinds of people, were exposed to different ideas and values. So I suppose I shouldn't be surprised that you've absorbed some of them."

"Surprised is not the same as unhappy. Are you unhappy?"

Irina seemed to consider it. "I've been unhappy before," she said finally. "It's not fatal."

Monday was a hectic day at the office. Adriana was out with the flu, the author whose manuscript was already two weeks overdue called to say that it still wasn't ready, and there was a delay with a shipment of the linen stock used for many of the covers. Eleanor barely had time to go to the ladies' room, much less out to get lunch. And there was certainly no time to think about Tom.

On the way home, she stopped to buy eggs, coffee, cream, and butter and allowed herself to imagine she was married to Tom and doing the marketing for the two of them. From the breakfasts they had shared, she knew he took his coffee very light with three sugars, that he liked his eggs any way but poached, and that he thought the meal wasn't complete without bacon, sausage, or ham. Although her family had not kept kosher, Eleanor never bought and rarely ate pork; she had never developed a taste for it. But that was the least of it. How would she feel being married to a man for whom every day was Saturday, who spent over an hour with the newspaper every morning, who could pick up and travel on a whim?

It was past six when she reached her building, arms laden with packages, as well as a bunch of red tulips—an indulgence, but the vivid color had called out to her. Eleanor set her bundles down, fished for her key, and went upstairs. When everything was put away, she heated up a slice of meat loaf that she had left over from the weekend and while she ate, she read a manuscript she'd brought home from the office. Every now and then she glanced over at the tulips.

A loud buzz interrupted her reading. Maybe it was Tom. But somehow she didn't really think so; he would have phoned first. More likely it was someone ringing the wrong apartment. But the buzzer kept ringing and finally she went down the stairs to see who it might be. To her utter surprise, Margaux was standing there, looking wild-eyed and distraught.

"What's the matter? Are you all right?" Eleanor ushered her in and then glanced at the narrow stairwell, which was going to be hard to navigate with the walking stick.

Following her gaze, Margaux said, "Don't worry, I can make it up. I'll just go slowly."

Eleanor went first and when they were upstairs and in her apartment asked, "How did you find me?"

"I called directory assistance."

"And your mother—does she know you're here?"

"No, I snuck out."

"She's not going to like that."

"I don't care!" And then she pressed her face to her hands and began to weep.

"Margaux, what's wrong?"

"Don't you know?" Margaux lifted her tear-glazed face.

"Know what?"

"Daddy—my father . . . he's dead. Dead!"

"What are you talking about?" Eleanor's first thought was that the girl might be delusional; she had been overwrought when she got here.

"Just what I said. He went sailing by himself. His boat capsized and he drowned. Mother said he was drunk."

"She told you that?"

"No. But I overheard her on the telephone. She drove up to school to tell me and brought me back down here. The funeral is tomorrow—it's at the Church of Heavenly Rest."

"I can't believe it." Eleanor sat back in her chair. Wynn Bellamy had drowned. She knew he drank heavily. But the idea that his drinking could result in his death was somehow incomprehensible to her. He'd seemed too powerful, too protected by his wealth and his status for such a thing to have happened. But when he telephoned her in the middle of the night, he hadn't sounded powerful at all. He'd sounded panicked at the thought that she would expose him to his beloved daughter. Because she was beloved by him; Eleanor had to concede that.

"I couldn't either. Mother is acting so strangely, too. She's barely cried at all." Margaux gave her a probing look. "I know he wasn't nice to you, Eleanor. So maybe you're not sorry about what happened. But even with his faults, I loved him. And he loved me." She began to cry again.

"Of course he did," Eleanor said. And he hadn't wanted to lose his daughter's love. If Eleanor had been kinder during that last conversation, if she hadn't made that threat, would he be alive now? The thought was highly upsetting. She despised the man—she couldn't pretend otherwise. But to feel implicated, in any way at all, in his death, was terrible. Margaux continued to cry and eventually allowed herself to be led to the sink to wash her face.

"Are you hungry?" Eleanor asked.

Margaux nodded.

The meat loaf was gone, so Eleanor set out an apple, a banana, and the remaining lace cookies from Sunday and poured a glass of milk. As Margaux devoured the food, Eleanor noticed a new, angular grace to her cheekbones and a clarity to the line of her jaw. She looked more like Patricia than ever.

"Thank you," Margaux said. "I feel better. Or a little better anyway."

"I should call your mother," Eleanor said. "She must be worried."

"No!" Margaux sounded desperate. "Not yet."

Eleanor relented, and Margaux began to talk about her father, one memory unspooling and leading to others: Wynn taking her to the zoo in Central Park, and ice skating in Rockefeller Center. There had been a father-daughter dance at her school, visits to his office where he let her sit at his desk, and of course, sailing. "Last summer I was nervous about getting back on the boat. But Daddy encouraged me. We had the most wonderful day. There was just enough wind and the sky was so blue. The water too. I was so happy it didn't even matter that I was a cripple."

"I wish you wouldn't use that word about yourself," Eleanor said.

"I don't know why it bothers you. It's just what I am."

"Not to me," Eleanor said. "Never to me."

"To my father though. He couldn't get used to what had happened to me. I know he always compared *now* and *then*. I think it did something to him."

"Really?"

"Oh yes. Before I got sick, he was much nicer—to everyone. I think he would have been nicer to you too."

"Perhaps." But what Eleanor didn't say was that had Margaux not contracted polio, they never would have become close—or even met—at all.

"Would you come tomorrow? To the funeral?"

"Why, I don't think, I mean—" Why would she attend Wynn Bellamy's funeral? To spit on his grave? The grave she may have helped him into?

Margaux studied her. "You hated him that much?"

"It's not hatred," she said carefully. "It's more like—"

The telephone rang so she was spared having to answer.

"Eleanor, it's Tom. I'm with Patricia and something terrible has happened. Wynn drowned in a boating accident and Margaux's disappeared and—"

"I know about the accident," said Eleanor.

"But how—"

"Margaux told me. She's here now. Tell Patricia she's safe."

"With you!" He turned away from the receiver and she heard him speaking rapidly to Patricia. Then he said, "Can you put Margaux on?" Eleanor handed the phone over.

"I'm sorry, Mother. I didn't mean to scare you." She paused. "Yes, I'll stay right here. I'll wait for Uncle Tom, I promise." She handed the receiver back to Eleanor.

"I'll be there as soon as I can," Tom said.

"Is Patricia all right?"

"I don't know."

Eleanor hung up. Margaux's question was still unanswered. "The funeral . . . ," she said. "Your mother wouldn't want me there."

"Why not? She likes you."

Eleanor said nothing.

"Doesn't she?"

"Yes," Eleanor said. "But I've been asking to see you. And every time she says no." There, it was out.

"I've asked her if I could see you too," Margaux said. "Over and over. Maybe it will be different now."

She didn't have to say, *because my father's not here anymore*, because that was something they both understood.

Eleanor switched on the radio while they waited for Tom to arrive, and sometime later, when the buzzer rang, Eleanor got up to let him in. He hugged Margaux and then Eleanor. The last time she'd seen him was the night she'd turned down his proposal. That seemed so long ago though. Right now, he looked shaken by Wynn's death. "What was he thinking, going out alone like that? He should have known better," Tom said.

"He wasn't thinking," Margaux said. "He and Mother had quarreled, and he was still angry."

Tom looked at Eleanor but said nothing. Clearly Margaux had been attuned to the ebb and flow of her parents' marriage.

After they had left, Eleanor crushed the empty cookie box, wiped the table, and did the few dishes in the sink. She knew the church, on East Ninetieth Street, where the funeral was being held. It was right across from Central Park and within walking distance both from the Bellamy apartment and the hat shop. She'd passed it many times though she had never once gone in.

For Margaux's sake, she wanted to attend. She could sit way in the back, call no attention to herself. But she was uncertain about Patricia's reaction. Or her own. She couldn't mourn him, and so didn't belong with those who could. If what Margaux said was true, he'd brought his death upon himself. It seemed fitting—a thought that made her feel ashamed. His was a sad, ignominious end, alone in the water, no one to hear him thrashing or extend a hand. Even in fantasy, she had not wished that on him. No, she'd wanted to see him exposed and humiliated—as she had been.

The question shadowed her as she tried to return to the manuscript, gave up, and readied herself for bed. And it was with her as she lay alone in the dark, waiting for sleep. The more she thought about it, the more importance it gained, so that it seemed whatever decision she made would mark a crossroads, a point at which she would turn in one direction or another. She'd always felt this conflict with the Bellamys, right from the start, her attraction for them tempered by her misgivings. She hadn't even wanted to take the job as Margaux's tutor. But Margaux herself had tugged at something in her, and she'd yielded, overcoming her own resistance. And as Eleanor finally surrendered to sleep, she realized that the pull of the Bellamys—and this meant Tom too—was once more going to draw her in.

TWENTY-NINE

Head bowed, Patricia sat in the first pew of the church listening to Reverend Everett Sprinchorn eulogize her dead husband. She had been coming to this church since she was a child, and it had hosted several significant events in her life: her marriage, the funerals of her parents, Margaux's christening. She remembered sitting here as a little girl, transfixed by the large, looming cross on the altar screen, the sober image of the risen Christ. Today, the area in front of the screen was filled with pots of the white lilies she'd ordered, and the sun that streamed through the oversize stained-glass windows created vivid spots of color on the marble floor.

Reverend Sprinchorn had a sonorous voice, and Patricia was soothed by its sound as he extolled Wynn's virtues—devoted husband and father, his support of various charities, his life as an attorney. The image he painted with his words had nothing to do with the man Patricia had shared a life with in recent years, or the pale and bloated body she'd been asked to identify at the morgue in Greenwich.

"Yes, that's my husband," she said as the sheet was pulled up. She was already turning away. She'd spent the rest of the day arranging to have the body sent to New York; she then drove up to Oakwood to tell her daughter.

After the reverend had finished, a few other people spoke—John Talbot, a cousin, a colleague from the law firm, the Yale friend Wynn had reconnected with at Audrey's wedding last year. The final speaker was Margaux, who'd insisted that she be given a turn. Patricia watched as her daughter used her stick to ascend the two wooden stairs to the pulpit, taking the hand the reverend extended. She was wearing all black for the first time, and the add-a-pearl necklace Wynn had started when she was born.

"Wynn Bellamy was different things to different people," she began. "But I was his only daughter and so I knew him in a way no one else did." She looked drawn but she did not cry. "He was a good father and he used to say that I was the best part of him. So maybe there's a part of him that will live on in me. I hope so. I'll miss him for the rest of my life."

There was a murmur from the crowd as Margaux carefully descended the stairs and walked over to join her mother in the pew.

"You did that beautifully." Patricia covered Margaux's hand with her own.

But Margaux withdrew her hand. "Don't pretend you care, Mother." Every word was like a tack pressing into Patricia's skin. "I know you and Daddy argued about something and that's why he went off on the boat alone. You're probably not even sorry about what happened to him."

Patricia stared straight ahead, unable to meet her daughter's eyes. How could Margaux say that? From the altar, the painted Christ stared down as if he concurred with Margaux's assessment. Music was playing now, though Patricia was not familiar with it.

She'd asked the reverend to select something he thought was appropriate. The pallbearers lifted the casket and took it down the aisle to the hearse waiting outside. Patricia stood up, ready to walk down that same aisle and stand near the doors, so that the mourners could offer their condolences as they filed out of the church. Margaux and Tom were supposed to accompany her. "Are you coming?" she said.

"Of course." Tom stood too, and took her by the elbow.

"I meant Margaux," said Patricia.

Margaux looked up at her and waited for several long and excruciating seconds. Finally she used her stick to hoist herself up. "I'm coming," she said. "But I'm doing it for Daddy. Not for you."

The three of them moved slowly, accompanied by different music this time. Something from Brahms, Patricia thought, and suitably lugubrious. Margaux was wrong. She did care, but not in the way her daughter thought. She grieved over the young Wynn with whom she'd fallen in love, and their early, happy days. And she grieved at how suddenly and randomly all their lives—her dead husband's, her own—could be undone.

They reached the end of the aisle and Patricia turned to face the people who had begun to walk in her direction. They clasped her hands or embraced her, and in muted voices offered their consoling words. She thanked them, returned the pressure of hands or the embrace. Then repeated it with the next person. This went on for a while; Wynn's funeral was well attended and most of their friends were there, even Audrey and Harold.

When everyone had gone, Tom and Margaux would get into the car that was waiting outside, and follow the hearse to the cemetery in Queens. She was ready for all the talking to be over and was looking forward to a reprieve on the ride. But there was still one more person waiting to speak to her. It was Henryka. "How did you even know?" Patricia asked.

"I hear," Henryka said. "And I so sorry, missus."

"Thank you," Patricia said softly. "Thank you for coming." They hugged, somewhat awkwardly, and Patricia breathed in the faint lily-of-the-valley scent Henryka always wore. Then she noticed that there was someone else standing there—Eleanor Moskowitz.

She stepped back. "You," was the only word she could summon. But it represented the fury, outrage, grief that rose in her throat and choked off all the other words she could have said. All her life, Patricia had done what was expected of her, toed the line she'd been shown since earliest childhood. Hiring Eleanor had been one of her very few acts of rebellion, a risk she'd taken for her daughter's sake. But where had it gotten her? To this bitter moment, filled with sorrow, reeking with disgrace. "What are you doing here?" she practically hissed.

"I invited her," Margaux said quickly.

"I'm not asking you. I'm asking her. Eleanor."

"It's true," Eleanor said. "Margaux did want me to come and I thought I should. For her."

"For her," Patricia mocked. "That's so like you, Eleanor. So saintly. So good—good at ruining everything. Because that's what you did— you ruined my life." She had the satisfaction of seeing Eleanor's stricken face.

"Missus, you upset and don't mean what you say," said Henryka.

"That's right." Tom turned to her. "You've had a shock."

"Oh yes I do. I mean every word of it." She turned to Henryka. "It's because of Eleanor that you left, and because of her that my daughter can't abide me. Eleanor came between Wynn and me too. We argued about her constantly. It was after our last fight that he left and ended up going out on the boat and drowning." Had she ever in her life spoken so loudly in public? She was sure she hadn't, but once she started, she didn't want to stop.

"Mother, you have to get hold of yourself."

In Margaux's horrified tone, Patricia heard the echo of her own voice. How many times had she tried to rein her daughter in, and in so doing, sounded exactly like that? But what Margaux must have known—and Patricia was just discovering—was the savage joy that spewing such words, thick and hot as lava, could elicit.

She ignored her daughter and brother, and spoke to Eleanor alone. "He told me he called you that night. He said you threatened to expose him to Margaux."

"No." Eleanor shook her head. "You're taking what I said out of context."

"What are you talking about?" Margaux looked from Eleanor to her mother. "Expose what?"

"Your father called me in the middle of the night shortly before he died. He'd been drinking and he was feeling sorry for himself. He accused me of ruining his life. I told him if he ever called me again, I wasn't going to keep his secret anymore, and that I would tell you about what he'd done." Eleanor seemed in control of herself, yet the tears running down her face suggested otherwise. "And your mother is right—I shouldn't have said that. But he frightened me, calling to accuse me. As if he was the injured party."

"Did my father . . . hurt you in some way?"

"Don't," Patricia broke in. "Don't you dare tell her."

Eleanor turned to Margaux. "Something did happen between your father and me last summer. But your mother is right. This isn't the time or place to discuss it."

"Stop treating me like a baby," said Margaux. "I deserve to know."

"You do," Eleanor said. "And you will. Only not now."

"I suppose I should thank you for that," Patricia said. "But I won't. You're not welcome here and I'd like you to go."

"Trish, you need to calm down—" Tom tried to take her arm.

"Leave me alone." Patricia shook him off. "I've been calm my entire life, and where has it gotten me?"

"I know you're upset," said Tom. "But this isn't helping."

"It's helping me," she said.

"Eleanor doesn't deserve this and I want you to stop it right now."

"Or else what?"

Tom sighed. "Or else nothing. I'm not delivering an ultimatum, Trish. I just want to spare you because I think you'll regret all of this later."

"That's for me to decide," said Patricia. "Anyway, the car is waiting. Are you coming with me? Or are you going with her?" She threw her arm in Eleanor's direction.

Tom hesitated. "I'm going with you," he said finally. "But not before I apologize to Eleanor for your behavior." He looked at Eleanor, who was looking down. "Even if she won't say she's sorry, I'll say it for her. For all of us really."

Patricia was infuriated—he was patronizing her, as if she couldn't be held accountable for her words. "If you're coming, you'd better come now. You too, Margaux." She turned abruptly away but not before she was stabbed by the tender, even maternal way Henryka's arm encircled Eleanor's shoulders and led her from the church.

The ride to the cemetery seemed fueled not by gasoline, but by Patricia's pure and unadulterated rage. Neither Tom nor Margaux spoke a word to her on the ride, and at the gravesite, they stood together on one side of the gaping hole in the ground while Patricia stood on the other. The mahogany casket was lowered carefully into the earth and Reverend Sprinchorn delivered a final blessing. Then the gravediggers began their work. It was over.

The next day, Tom drove Margaux back to Oakwood, which worked well for Patricia, because Margaux wasn't speaking to her. Left alone, she began the tedious task of packing up all Wynn's things to give to charity. There was precious little she kept, and what she did—an engraved money clip, a silver shoehorn, cuff links in the shape of tiny sailboats—she left in Margaux's room, an offering. Patricia herself wanted nothing. When it was all done, it was almost as if he'd never lived in the apartment. With the exception of the study, he'd left no imprint on these rooms. But when she finished taping up the last of the boxes, she slid to the floor beside them and wept.

In the weeks that followed, she did not become the social pariah she had expected to be. Wynn's indiscretions may have offended their friends, but his death had wiped the slate clean. Invitations still filled her mailbox, perhaps even more plentifully than before. There were bridge games, luncheons, and dinners. She went to some, and declined others. Those she attended were laced with a new and unctuous solicitude. *How are you holding up?* was a frequent question. And *You're so strong, Patricia. I don't know how you manage it.* That last was tainted not just with phony concern, but also with schadenfreude, and she hated it. What she did not hate, however, was the dawning realization that Wynn might actually have done her a favor. Divorce could have been long, drawn out, and messy, especially if Wynn had fought her. Instead, his death had cut cleanly through that morass.

In late May, before Margaux's term at school finished, Patricia decided to drive up to Argyle. She hadn't been up to the house since last year, and the thought of spending another summer there, even alone, was unbearable. She would take what she wanted or arrange to have it sent to New York, and then she would sell the place without looking back.

The drive was traffic-snarled, slow, and hot. She put away the few groceries that she'd bought on the way, fell into bed, and did not wake until the sun was streaming through the curtains she'd neglected to close. She went into the kitchen and made herself a cup of coffee. It tasted like poison; she poured it down the drain. The wicker furniture, the hooked rugs, the watercolors of lighthouses, fields of poppies, carousels—she cared about none of them. Even her clothes did not inspire any sense of ownership. There was nothing here—or anywhere, for that matter—that she truly wanted. But what about the books? There weren't many—a few novels Dottie had loaned her, a quaint old volume on Argyle's history written by some local dowager, a biography of Vincent van Gogh she'd long meant to read. And the illustrated volume of Shakespeare's sonnets she'd bought for Eleanor and never gotten around to giving her—Henryka must have put it here.

She smoked cigarette after cigarette, lighting the fresh one from the embers of the old. The room stank of tobacco smoke; it would probably waft into the other rooms and settle in the drapes and the rugs. So what? The new owners would have to deal with it. She looked down—the hand that held the cigarette shook slightly, so she stubbed it out. There had to be something she could do to calm herself, and she knew just what it was. Although it was still morning, she poured a glass of orange juice and added a generous splash of vodka. When the first cooling sip spread through her, the horrible tension in her chest finally relented, just a little.

She went onto the back porch and stared out at the yard, which was weedy and overgrown. Glow had liked to stalk her prey—

small birds, the occasional chipmunk or baby rabbit—out there. But Glow was gone; she'd succumbed to some feline malady over the winter and Patricia had not had the heart to get another cat. When her glass was empty—all too soon it seemed—she filled another, promising herself to drink it more slowly. Then she returned to the porch.

Looking out past the weeds, her gaze was drawn to the cottage. Wildflowers had sprung up around the door and it had an enchanted look, like a dwelling in a fairy tale. But that was where all the trouble in her life had started. Right there. A little unsteadily, she went outside and crossed the matted grass.

Tiny white butterflies flitted around the Queen Anne's lace and bumblebees lazily hummed around the clover. There was always a key under a flowerpot; Patricia found it and let herself in. The cottage was warm and stuffy, the bedroom door closed. She opened the windows in the main room and sat down on the love seat, the one she'd had redone before Eleanor had moved in last summer, and ran her hand over the floral pattern, a medley of pink, pale yellow, and white. Had Wynn sat here with Eleanor? She knew Tom had.

Unsure of what she was seeking, Patricia went into the bedroom. The curtains were closed here too and the room felt oppressive. She pulled the curtains apart and opened the window. The light that poured in revealed the coating of dust on the furniture, and, under the bed, the smallest glimpse of something red. She got down on her hands and knees to investigate. It was the corner of a leather case or envelope of some kind. She wiped the layer of dust that covered it with her hand and opened it. It was filled with papers—letters, it seemed—in various stages of completion. It belonged to Eleanor; she must have left it behind.

Patricia sat down on the bed. These letters weren't meant for her eyes. She ought to leave them alone—didn't she want Eleanor out of her life and out of her thoughts? But the temptation was too great; she just had to read them.

Margaux Bellamy is such a proud, angry girl. I love her for that, the anger as much as the pride. What happened to her is such a blow; she needs her anger to burn her clean so she can move beyond it. Only that way will she have a chance at the rich, fulfilled life she deserves. I'm not sure her parents understand this—certainly not that father of hers— but I do, and I'm glad I can be here for her.

Then, another page that was about—her.

I admire Patricia, I really do. First of all, she is the most truly elegant woman I have ever met, and I mean that in terms of character as well as looks. She is measured, refined, and she thinks before she speaks. I want to be more like her. And I wish we could be close—friends rather than just employer and employee. Maybe if we'd met under different circumstances that would have been possible. Instead, there are too many things that divide us and I don't think either of us can get beyond those obstacles. She will always look down on me a bit—daughter of an immigrant hatmaker, and a Jew besides. And I will always resent her sense of entitlement. Yet we are bound by our mutual love for Margaux, and that counts for something. Quite a lot in fact.

Eleanor could have been right—in other circumstances, they might have been friends. But they had no other circumstances, only these, the ones that shaped and defined them. Some of the sheets were blank. Then she found one addressed to someone named Ruth and dated almost a year ago. It was about her late husband.

Wynn Bellamy was here last night. I was sleeping when he showed up, and I was too afraid to ask him to leave. He'd been drinking—no surprise there—and he wanted to dance with me. Even though I didn't want to, I said yes again because really, how could I say no? He was my employer. Margaux may love me and Patricia may like me, but in the end, Mr. Bellamy is the boss. So I agreed to the dance and then he wanted a kiss—and who knows what else. He was holding me so tightly and I tried to get away. We struggled, and when we fell, he landed right on top of me. He grabbed my face with one hand to kiss me and then he tore the buttons off of my pajamas—I was frightened, Ruth. Terrified. For a moment it seemed that he might—rape me. But I scratched his arms, and threatened him with a pitcher, and he finally left. I would never have told anyone what had happened but I was seeing double and I'd thrown up, so I knew I needed to see a doctor. Henryka—she's the cook I told you about, the one who didn't like me—was actually kind enough to drive me. I didn't tell her what happened, but she guessed. I didn't tell that Dr. Parker either. What good would it have done? No one would believe me. Maybe not even you, Ruth.

Patricia felt invaded by a familiar revulsion as she read these words. The account of Wynn's behavior was not a surprise. But the extent of Eleanor's fear and powerlessness—these were a revelation, and one that made her feel ill. It wasn't just what Wynn did, it was the potential embedded in his actions. And there was something else too—this letter was never sent. Eleanor said that she had not shared the events of that night with anyone and Patricia believed her. Yet Eleanor had needed to unburden herself and here was the proof.

Maybe it was the warmth of the room, the vodka, or both, but Patricia felt robbed of energy, and after putting the letters back in their case, she stretched out on the bed and closed her eyes. When she awoke, over two hours later, she was at first unsure where she was. Then she remembered. She had violated Eleanor's privacy, but that violation was a portal to a new way of viewing what had happened, and it loosened the stubborn knot of her anger. Eleanor had loved her daughter and Margaux loved her; she had expressed admiration for Patricia and a wish to be her friend.

Patricia left the cottage and returned to the house. The vodka bottle was on the counter in the kitchen and on impulse, she poured what remained in it down the sink. Then she went into the bedroom she had shared with Wynn to do a more careful appraisal. She would leave most of the furnishings but began to methodically pack her summer wardrobe—sundresses, straw hats, bathing suits, riding clothes, sandals—as well as her toiletries and a sterling silver dresser set with her mother's monogram engraved on the hand mirror. To these things, she added the book of sonnets and the biography of van Gogh.

It started to rain as she worked, a soft, misty rain that made the air smell fresh and sweet. She kept the windows open, shutting them only right before she left. If she started out now, she could be in New York by evening; the traffic would be lighter on the way into the city. But she decided to drive up to Oakwood instead, and surprise Margaux with an impromptu visit. She was on a new footing with her daughter. Margaux's anger—stubborn, implacable—had turned her into an adult almost overnight, and Patricia was almost afraid of her. But she missed her too, especially now that she was alone, and she was going to risk the visit no matter what the outcome.

With everything packed and ready, Patricia put the key in the ignition and started the car. On the seat beside her sat the batch of letters and the two books. She was finally going to read that biography, and to go see the painting again too. Might it help in reclaiming that part of herself, the part that was so drawn to the self-contained, slightly aloof Comtesse and the mystical fury of those blazing stars? Tom had been talking about starting a gallery—what if there could be a place for her there? She would talk to him about it. The windshield wipers began to move, tracing a graceful arc as she began her journey north.

THIRTY

It was warm for early June, a slightly muggy afternoon. Eleanor walked swiftly along Hudson Street until she came to the bottle green door. She put down the bags filled with groceries and pressed the bell. There was a short pause and then Tom appeared. "I got everything but the wine," she said. "It was too heavy to carry."

"I didn't expect you to bring that," said Tom. "The liquor store said they would deliver it later. Three cases of white, already chilled."

"Three cases!" she said. "You're expecting a big crowd."

"A mob." He smiled, and picked up the packages. "I've invited everyone I know."

"Including your sister?" asked Eleanor. She hadn't spoken to Patricia since the day of the funeral, and although she and Margaux had been writing to each other, she knew Margaux had not told her mother about their correspondence.

"Well, yes, but you don't have to talk to her if you don't want."

"I don't," Eleanor said and then asked, "Will Margaux be coming too?"

"She's got exams and couldn't get away. About Tricia though—do you think you two will ever make it up?"

"Don't ask me that," she flared. "Ask her."

Tom looked hurt and Eleanor went to lay a white cloth over the long table at one end of the gallery. Eleanor tried to calm herself as she began setting out the food. Of course Tom would invite Patricia. Had she thought otherwise? She would just be sure to steer clear of her. Right now, she would focus on the prospect of Tom's success, which made her very happy. It wasn't about the money. He had more than enough to cover his own needs, especially since he didn't want to live the life—posh apartment, expensive car—for which his upbringing had prepared him. No, she saw this gallery endeavor as a step toward maturity and adulthood that Tom was just now taking.

She arranged the thin, almost translucent slices of the prosciutto—*treyfe*, she couldn't help but think—and the cheese on gold-rimmed oval platters Tom had bought expressly for this purpose at an antiques shop on East Twelfth Street. "I may not be an artist," he said, "but I have an artist's eye. I want everything in here to reflect that."

Ever since he'd rented the space, he'd thrown himself into its transformation and had succeeded in creating an inviting environment, illuminated by an elaborate blown-glass chandelier from Venice. He painted the walls a glossy vermillion and on them he hung the work he'd been steadily collecting for the last decade: nineteenth-century American landscapes, a brilliantly colored predella panel he'd bought in Florence right after the war, meticulous French architectural drawings, and hazy pastels. His prized possession was a cutout by Henri Matisse that showed Icarus falling from the sky, body pierced by bloody red patches. It was not for sale.

Eleanor put the olives, black and glistening, into a cut-glass bowl, and arranged the coin-shaped slices of sausage, still more *treyfe*, on the thick cutting board where she'd placed a loaf of Italian peasant bread. She looked up to see that Tom had been watching her. "I like your dress," he said. The black crepe with its georgette pleats was new, purchased just this week. "Very chic."

"Thank you." Then she noticed he had changed, and was now wearing the summer-weight wool suit he'd had made in London. "You're looking pretty swanky yourself."

"You like it?" He looked down at himself. "I could wear it more often," he said. "In fact, there's one special occasion I'd like to wear it for very soon."

Now why had he gone and raised another sore point between them? The arrival of the wine offered a welcome distraction and she stepped out from behind the table to direct the deliverymen. By the time she'd returned, Tom was off, attention directed elsewhere. Soon, the guests started arriving, and as Tom had predicted, there was quite a crowd. Most of the faces were unfamiliar to Eleanor but she did recognize a few people. So, apparently, did Tom. At one point, he pulled her over to indicate a woman in a hat with a cluster of cherries pinned to one side.

"That's Liesel Schalk. She's an art critic. She's new in town, but she's written a few things for the *Times*."

"Do you think she'll write about the gallery?"

"I'm going to chat her up in the hope she'll do just that."

Eleanor watched Tom for a moment before she began to circulate. And then, across the room, she saw Patricia Bellamy and she froze. Eleanor thought she looked thinner and older, yet the wistful, slightly haunted look on her face gave her beauty a depth it had not had before. It pained Eleanor to see it, but she turned away before Patricia noticed her, and found herself face-to-face with Adriana Giacchino.

"Oh, here you are!" said Adriana. "I've been looking for you. I want you to meet Drake." She turned to the man—gray shaggy hair, gray shaggy beard, loose artist-style smock—and made the introduction.

"Adri talks about you all the time," Drake said. "She calls you her little protégée even though I tell her she's not old enough to have a protégée."

"Just because I haven't reached your advanced age doesn't mean I'm not old enough for a protégée," said Adriana. "It's hardly fair. You have them by the dozens. Don't I deserve one too?"

"I'm delighted to be your protégée," Eleanor said. "Honored in fact." She knew that Drake was quite a bit older than Adriana, divorced, and the father of two grown sons. Adriana was thirty-three; she claimed to have no interest in getting married. "Do you want children?" Eleanor had asked her a few weeks before. They had become close enough for the question not to seem rude.

"Some days I do, some days I don't." Adriana lit a cigarette, one of the many she smoked throughout the day. "I'm waiting until I want them all the time."

What if it's too late and you get too old? Eleanor did not say. Yes, they had grown close. But not that close.

"So nice to finally meet you," said Drake. "And to put the name to a face. A very pretty face, I might add." He kissed her hand.

Oh, he was quite the ladies' man. Eleanor could see just what Adriana liked about him; what woman didn't want to be charmed?

The gallery had grown even more crowded, and people had started to spill out into the street, the warmth of the evening an invitation, the pink-tinged sky an enticement. The wine ran out, and so did the food. Liesel Schalk promised a brief write-up for the next day. Tom sold three paintings, including the Jackson Pollock. Pollock's work—erratic drips and splotches of paint flung all over the canvas—did not impress Eleanor at all. Yet Tom was convinced that he was poised to become a very important and influential artist.

The last guest didn't leave until almost nine, sent off into the June evening with waves and airily blown kisses. Tom was jubilant and broke into a spontaneous dance, twirling Eleanor around the gallery. "*Now* will you marry me?" he asked. "Finally? We can go to city hall tomorrow. Or if you want the white dress, the veil, and the orange blossoms, we can do that. Only say that you will, Eleanor." His face was close to hers and his lips parted. In another second he'd be kissing her, and if she kissed him back that would signal she was saying yes—

Eleanor stopped dancing but remained in his embrace. "No," she said, looking into his impossibly dear face. "No, Tom, I won't." It had been such a lovely evening but now he'd gone and spoiled it.

He dropped his arms from her waist. "Damn it, why not?"

"There are so many reasons. Your sister for one. My mother for another."

"We'll talk to them. They'll come around."

"Maybe," said Eleanor. "Maybe not. My mother said she would meet you, so that's a start. But Patricia—she'll never accept me. And there's something else too." She fell silent.

"Aren't you going to tell me?" he demanded.

"I don't know if you'll understand. But—it's you."

"What are you talking about?"

"I don't know if I can count on you."

"Of course you can—I love you. You know I do."

"You may love me. But can I trust you? You disappear when you're scared or uncomfortable. That's not a good trait in a husband."

"If you marry me, I'll never leave you."

"You say that now," she said. "What happens when we have a fight or there's trouble?"

"You won't believe whatever I say, so why should I even try?" said Tom, his voice ragged. "If you don't trust me, loving me is useless." He dug into his pocket and fished out a set of keys, which he handed to her. "I'm leaving. Stay as long as you like. Just lock up before you go. Tomorrow morning you can drop the keys through the mail slot, on your way to work."

"Where are you going?" she asked.

"I don't think that's any of your business."

"Tom, I—"

But he reached the door quickly and then was gone. Eleanor surveyed the empty gallery. The crumb-littered table was covered with partially filled glasses in which soggy cigarette butts floated. Crumpled napkins, olive pits, and waxy rinds of cheese completed the tableau. Listlessly, she began gathering the bottles, taking the glasses to the sink in the back room.

Back at Vassar, she had sensed herself on the periphery of new and unfamiliar territory, unsure if she could—or even wanted—to enter. Now Tom was offering her a passport. But even if she became Mrs. Thomas Harrison, it would change nothing. The name would be a cloak, not her true skin. She would never be one of them; she'd be dressing up, pretending. And that might end up feeling worse than simple exclusion.

The job of cleaning was too daunting; she gave up and switched off the lights before locking the door behind her. Then she began to walk, making her way along streets that were by now familiar. Last year at this time she never would have dreamed that the Village would have become her neighborhood. Her decision to leave her teaching job had led to the Bellamys, and the Bellamys led her to where she was now—unmarried, unfettered, a free agent in the world.

Even though there were many people out, Eleanor felt lonely. Alone. Soon she found herself in front of Tom's building and she looked up at his window. Dark. The thought of losing him was shattering. She could fix it though. Make it right. Tomorrow she'd tell him that she was being silly, of course she'd marry him—but something in her kept resisting because she didn't want her acceptance of his proposal to feel like a capitulation, as if they'd struggled and he'd won. No, that wasn't how she wanted it to happen, or how she wanted to feel.

Finally she turned down her own street. Marriage came with a particular template, one that seemed less desirable the more she examined it. Maybe there was a different way to be married, one that didn't rely so heavily on the conventions she saw around her. But if there was, she suspected she'd have to invent it.

As she approached her building, Eleanor could see a tiny, red pulse in the distance—someone holding a lit cigarette. Maybe it was Tom. She felt relieved—she hadn't wanted to leave it like that. She quickened her pace and when she grew closer, the figure revealed itself to be not Tom at all, but Patricia.

"What are you doing here?" Eleanor said, not caring if she sounded rude.

"I was looking for you." Patricia put the cigarette out under the heel of her shoe.

"I thought you never wanted to talk to me again." She still felt the wounds Patricia had inflicted on the day of Wynn's funeral.

"I didn't." Patricia fingered a fold in her dress. "But I'm here now, aren't I? Here to tell you I'm sorry and I hope you can forgive me."

"Sorry? You?"

"You don't believe me."

"Is there a reason I should?"

"No," Patricia said. "No reason at all. I'd just hoped . . . But maybe I shouldn't have come."

Eleanor surprised herself by saying: "You're already here. We might as well talk."

"I'd like that."

"Why don't you come upstairs? We'll be more comfortable." Eleanor immediately regretted the offer. But she wouldn't take it back now.

"Tom tells me your apartment is very nice."

"He did?" What else had he told her?

"Yes. And he also told me that you turned him down—again," Patricia said. "I saw him right before I came here. He seemed— crushed."

"Oh." Eleanor didn't like him discussing their relationship with his sister.

"He gave me something to give you." She reached into her purse and handed Eleanor a small white box and a sealed envelope. "But maybe you want to open it upstairs."

Eleanor unlocked the front door, wishing again she had not extended the invitation. The stairs were steep and worn, but Patricia followed her up without comment. Once they were inside, Eleanor tried to see the place she loved through the other woman's eyes. A white voile curtain hung at the open window. Three pink peonies nodded in a cobalt vase on the table, and when she turned on the floor lamp near the armchair, the light radiated softly.

"It's lovely in here." Patricia surveyed the Ansel Adams photograph, the flowers, a needlepoint pillow Irina had made and given Eleanor as a housewarming gift.

"Thank you," said Eleanor. She hadn't realized that she wanted Patricia's approval until it had been bestowed. "Can I make you a gin and tonic?"

"That would be nice." Patricia sat down.

Eleanor got the glasses and poured, spilling a little tonic on the table. She took a sip of her drink and then another. "So why did you come?"

"I already told you: I wanted to apologize," Patricia said. "I blamed you for things that weren't your fault—they only seemed that way at the time."

"And now?" Eleanor held on to the apology. She knew it wasn't easy for Patricia to offer, and like Patricia's praise, it mattered to her to have it.

Patricia gave her a cool, appraising look. "Sometimes I still do. Other times—not so much. Or not at all."

Eleanor took another long swallow; she needed the fortification. "I understand." Why had she even said that? But she pushed past her regret to consider Patricia's new circumstances. They couldn't have been—comfortable. "How are you managing?" she asked.

"It's been difficult. But maybe not in the way you might think."

"How then?"

"I was so angry at him at first. Wynn. But I felt so guilty too."

"Guilty?"

"That last morning—we'd had a terrible quarrel and I told him I was filing for divorce."

"You did?"

"Yes. No one knows that. Not Tom, not Margaux. Especially not Margaux, though she suspects something of the sort. I'm not sure if he believed me, but then he went off to Argyle and got on that boat with a bottle or a flask. The coroner told me he was . . . inebriated . . . when he died."

"I feel guilty too," Eleanor admitted. "In that last phone call, when I said I would tell Margaux about him . . . that really upset him."

"I'm sure it did. He really loved her you know."

"And she loved him. She always will." Eleanor couldn't really stretch herself to understand, but it was true whether she understood it or not. "I don't know if I even meant it. But that call . . . I wanted to make sure he never contacted me again. And now he never will."

"I hope, I mean, I can't stop you I suppose, but I do wish—"

"That I won't tell Margaux?" Eleanor finished the sentence. "No, I won't. Even though she's asked."

"So you've been in touch with her?"

"Yes. She's been writing me and she's going to keep on writing me. And I write back—I'm not going to ignore her. You brought me into her life and you can't control what happens from there. Not anymore."

"No, I can't." Patricia studied the gin and tonic remaining in her glass.

"Does that bother you?" asked Eleanor.

"I suppose it does. But not as much as it might. Things are different between us now. Sometimes I feel that she's the mother, and I'm the child."

"She's grown up a lot lately. She's had to."

"Did she tell you we're going to be moving soon?"

"No," Eleanor said. "Where?"

"I've found a place on Fifth Avenue and Ninth Street. I want to be downtown. It's closer to Tom."

That was so close; they would almost be neighbors. Though they had lived only blocks apart uptown, Eleanor reflected. Eleanor saw that Patricia's glass was empty and she refilled it as well as her own, no spilling this time.

"I have something else for you." Patricia reached into her bag to pull out a red leather case that she nudged across the table.

"Where did you get this?" Eleanor was a little shaken to see the case again—she'd missed it some time ago but had no idea what had become of it.

"In the cottage. You must have left it behind."

"Did you read what was in it?"

"I know I shouldn't have. But yes. Enough anyway."

"Enough for what?"

"To know that you and I—we have a bond. It began with Margaux, but it's more than that now."

"Is that what you think?"

"I do," said Patricia. "Do you?"

"I'd like to think that too . . . But I'm not sure." Eleanor wasn't going to lie to her—not here, not now.

"You know, I was wrong to ask you to hide what Wynn did to you that night. That's when it all changed. And I realize now that whatever happened, it happened to both of us."

"I'm not following you," said Eleanor.

"What he did was an attack on me too—my trust, and my faith. I had to regard him differently after that."

"I've never thought of it that way," Eleanor said.

Patricia reached into her bag again, this time for a cigarette. "When I first found out what he'd done, I tried to put it in a category of behavior that I knew and understood. To believe that he wasn't really so—reprehensible. So I had to lay the blame somewhere else and I laid it on you. Reading your letters made me see it differently though. You must have been *afraid* of him. Along with disgusted, really and truly afraid. But you stayed anyway. For Margaux."

"For Margaux," Eleanor repeated.

"So tell me about you," Patricia said. "I hear there's a new job, and of course this apartment—" She gestured with her left hand, now ringless.

"I'm doing well," Eleanor said. "Things are falling into place." She glanced down at the box and note that were still on the table. Alongside those things was a flat object covered in lavender paper; was it also from Tom?

Patricia's gaze had followed hers. "That's from me," she said. "You can open it first if you like."

Eleanor loosened the paper and found inside a volume of Shakespeare's sonnets—a gift both thoughtful and beautiful—but why? "It's lovely," she said. Then she turned to what Tom had sent. Inside the box was a small silver pin in the shape of a deer. The deer was running, its front legs extended in one direction, its hind legs in the other, its neck straining forward, toward an unseen destination. No more than an inch long, it was a precious little thing. Eleanor put it back in the box and set it aside while she opened the note. Written on a torn-off sheet of paper and in a hasty scrawl, it read:

I'm sorry I stormed off but a fellow does take a beating, asking again and again and hearing no every damn time. As for the pin, I bought it a while ago and planned to give it to you tonight, after the opening. It's not a ring, and it's not made of diamonds, so I figured you wouldn't read too much into it. You're the deer, Eleanor. The deer in flight. And me? I'm the guy who's hoping to coax you back. To make you mine. I guess now is not the right time though. Will it ever be? I'm willing to wait. But not forever.

Leaving my heart in your hands,
Tom

She put the note down and lifted her eyes to the woman seated across from her. One man had put a wedge between them. The other a bridge. But the choice about which path to choose—that was theirs alone.

"Do you love him?" Patricia asked. Irina had asked the same thing.

"I do. The problem's not Tom. Or not entirely. The problem is his world. Your world really. He says it won't matter to him. Maybe he's right. Maybe not. But I know it *will* matter—to me."

"I understand," said Patricia. "Or I think I do. Can you tell me more?"

"Yes." Eleanor placed her elbows on the table and inclined her body slightly forward. "Yes, I can. I'd like to tell you—everything."

ACKNOWLEDGMENTS

I would like to thank Lisa Friel, Patricia Grossman, Jennie Mason, Sally Schloss, Alexandra Shelley, Kenneth Silver, and Sonia Taitz—cherished friends who read the manuscript and were so generous with their responses. I would also like to thank Judith Ehrlich for the time and thought she devoted to this novel.

Judy Greenspan, for her kind help with the research on the mikvah associated with the synagogue on Eldridge Street.

Susanna Einstein, literary agent extraordinaire, and gifted writer Holly Robinson, who brought us together.

Emily Griffin, incisive and brilliant editor who shaped this book in ways I would have never imagined, and unfailingly cheerful and efficient Amber Oliver, who made sure its course always ran smoothly. There could be no better publicist than Heather Drucker, and I'm so grateful to her as well as to Stephanie Cooper and Katie O'Callaghan, who taught me just what makes social media tick. . . .

ABOUT THE AUTHOR

KITTY ZELDIS is the nom de plume of a Brooklyn-based novelist and children's book author.

About the author

About the book

Insights,
Interviews
& More . . .

Read on

Meet Kitty Zeldis

KITTY ZELDIS IS THE PSEUDONYM OF A
novelist and nonfiction writer of books
for adults and children. She lives with
her family in Brooklyn, New York. ∾

Questions for Further Discussion

1. DESCRIBE THE TWO CENTRAL characters, Eleanor and Patricia. Are they more similar than they are different? What are the biggest differences between the two?

2. HOW DOES THE AUTHOR USE THE characters' clothing to convey details about their social standing or interior lives? Why do hats play such a major role in the novel, in your opinion?

3. WHAT DOES ELEANOR'S AGREEMENT to change her last name versus Irina's reaction to it reveal about their generational differences? If you were in Eleanor's place, would you consider altering your last name for financial or other kinds of opportunities?

4. MARGAUX OPPOSES THE THOUGHT OF attending a school for polio survivors but is immediately drawn to Larry when she meets him. Why do you think that is?

5. WHAT DOES WYNN'S BEHAVIOR toward the adult women in the novel say about the power that men held at the time? What do you think has changed since then, especially in light of the #MeToo movement? And how might his transgressions affect the way Margaux views her father after his death if she were to find out?

6. DISCUSS ELEANOR'S VISIT TO THE mikveh. What purpose does the water in the ritual serve for her?

7. BOTH PATRICIA AND ELEANOR SHARE guilt over Wynn's fate, though for different reasons. How do they each react to the trauma, and how do you see it affecting each of them in the future?

8. HENRYKA HAS KNOWN PATRICIA ALL her life, yet she sides with Eleanor at the end of the novel. What does Henryka and Eleanor's evolving relationship say about their roles in the novel—both in each other's lives and the lives of the Bellamys?

9. THE NOVEL TAKES THE READER TO exclusive settings, including the ▶

club in Argyle, Vassar College, the Bellamys' building, and Brandon-Wythe. Which of these settings have official restrictions on membership, and which only have informal ones? What do you perceive as the differences between the two kinds of restrictions?

10. WHAT DO YOU MAKE OF TOM'S relationship with Eleanor? Are you rooting for them to marry or otherwise spend their lives together?

11. WHAT DO YOU THINK ELEANOR AND Patricia talk about in the book's final scene? What do you think comes next for each of them? And for Margaux?

12. TV SHOWS LIKE *MAD MEN* AND *THE Marvelous Mrs. Maisel* and books like *Not Our Kind* offer new insight into midcentury issues, but do you think they also give us a window into twenty-first-century American culture and who we are today? ∽

A Conversation with Kitty Zeldis, Author of *Not Our Kind*

What was the inspiration for Not Our Kind?

The inspiration for each book seems to form in its own inimitable way—no two have been alike for me. The idea to write *Not Our Kind* came from a conversation with my agent at the time. She said she thought I could be writing a novel with a broader canvas than I had previously attempted and felt that a novel juxtaposing two worlds—one Jewish, one Gentile—would be a good way to accomplish that. Her suggestion led me to think about my experience as a Jewish girl at Vassar, a decidedly un-Jewish kind of institution. Once I had that notion, the characters and their situation seemed to flow very naturally.

What kind of research did you do to create these characters and settings?

In some sense, I felt I'd been researching it for decades—I've loved the films and fashions of the 1940s for years. So I had a clear image—drawn from period ▶

A Conversation with Kitty Zeldis *(continued)*

movies, photographs, and magazines—of how things would have looked. I added to that by buying a shelf's worth of photographic books so I could immerse myself more completely in that world. I also researched hat-making, and looked up some small but telling details, like the date when the first bikini showed up in the pages of a fashion magazine, and when Dior introduced the New Look. I also did quite a bit of research about polio, both the effect it had and the treatments then available.

Why did you decide to publish this book under a pseudonym, and how did you choose the name?

Not Our Kind was sufficiently divergent from my previous work to warrant a pseudonym. Kitty is actually a college nickname, and I still have many friends who use it. Zeldis is my maiden name so that too was familiar. Seeing the full name on the cover of this book feels somehow fitting and natural.

Which of the characters came the most easily to you? Who was the hardest one to write?

Eleanor came easily as hers was the voice closest to my own. But even though Patricia was quite different from me, her voice came to me clearly; I felt as if I knew her well. Hardest, I think, was Wynn, because he was so hateful it would have been easy to flatten him into a two-dimensional, cartoonlike villain. The villain should be fully rounded, idiosyncratic, and interesting in at least *some* ways. Shakespeare's villains are often given the most memorable speeches and the most searing lines of poetry—there's something even a novelist can learn from that. I had to work to make Wynn human (if not appealing) and give him likable qualities; in so doing, I hoped to bring him more fully to life.

What are you working on now?

Now that I've had a taste of writing a novel steeped in another time, I want to continue. I've started a novel that takes place in New Orleans in the years 1916–1917; it concerns a successful madame who runs a brothel in the city's notorious red-light district. ∾

Kitty Zeldis's Six Favorite New York Novels

THE HOUSE OF MIRTH, EDITH WHARTON

How was Wharton, a woman of great wealth and privilege, so exquisitely attuned to the situation facing Lily Bart, a well-born but impoverished young woman desperate to make the marriage that she ardently believes will save her? Wharton's sharp understanding of the ways in which women's lives were constrained and defined by money is as relevant today as it was when the novel was first published. Reading it made me understand how much has changed— and how much hasn't.

A TREE GROWS IN BROOKLYN, BETTY SMITH

A classic coming-of-age story, set in the Brooklyn of another century. I was—and still am!—a Brooklyn girl too, and so I was perfectly poised to fall in love with Francie Nolan, whose story I read over and over again when I was a girl. Francie moves from the world of childhood, with its keen disappointments but keener joys, to the world of adulthood, where she finds that the equation has been cruelly flipped. She emerges bruised but hopeful, a brave pilgrim intent on putting one foot in front of the other.

INCOGNITO, GREGORY MURPHY

Murphy's elegant and eloquent novel unfolds in the New York City of 1911. It's a mystery of sorts, and it builds slowly but majestically, revealing its secrets in its own time, and with consummate poise. William Dysart begins as a man of his time, tightly bound by its conventions, and by a marriage that holds no joy for him. It's enormously satisfying to watch him evolve into a different sort of man, one who has the strength of character to claim the woman he loves and to forge his own happiness with her.

THE BIRD CATCHER, LAURA JACOBS

While Jacobs is brilliant at capturing New York's dazzle and glitter—windows at Saks, posh parties, and gallery openings—she is even more adept at conjuring a more elemental and wilder incarnation of the city. Margaret Snow ▶

and her husband, Charles, are devoted birders, and when Charles is suddenly killed in a plane crash, Margaret returns to Central Park in search of the birds she and Charles loved. Only now it's not the living birds she seeks, it's the dead ones, and what she does with them offers her an unexpected and extraordinary form of comfort—and salvation.

BRIAN IN THREE SEASONS, PATRICIA GROSSMAN

Brian Moss is one of those marginal figures that hover at the edges of the city. Neither young nor old, he's just getting by, unhappy with his stalled career and the random, anonymous couplings that fill his nights, but unable—or unwilling—to do anything about it. Yet during the several months that this novel spans, his world is shaken, first by his father's stroke and then by his reckoning with a man who overturns all his ideas about love and challenges him to take possession of the life he's always wanted—and deserves. Grossman is a measured, controlled writer yet the tale she tells pulsates with feeling, and her view of the city—by turns tender and harsh—creates the perfect setting for Brian's story.

FIRST LOVE, ADRIENNE SHARP

The backdrop of Sharp's novel is the exalted but sometimes torturous hothouse that is the New York City Ballet. As a former dancer, Sharp has an insider's perspective on the profession, and her characters are utterly convincing. Even more astonishing though is the way she stitches together fact and fiction—one of the characters is none other than legendary choreographer George Balanchine, shown here nearing the end of his life and desperate to work his magic on just one more young ballerina, one last time. Sharp's portrait of this great man is one of her most memorable creations and one of this novel's enduring joys. ᴄ〜